RULES OF THEIR PARISIAN FLING

ELLIE DARKINS

BAHAMAS ESCAPE WITH THE BEST MAN

CARA COLTER

KT-164-718

MILLS & BOON

First Published in Great Britain 2022
by Mills & Boon, an imprint of HarperCollins*Publishers* Ltd,
1 London Bridge Street, London, SE1 9GF

www.harpercollins.co.uk

HarperCollins*Publishers*
1st Floor, Watermarque Building,
Ringsend Road, Dublin 4, Ireland

Rules of Their Parisian Fling © 2022 Ellie Darkins

Bahamas Escape with the Best Man © 2022 Cara Colter

ISBN: 978-0-263-30219-6

06/22

MIX
Paper from
responsible sources
FSC
www.fsc.org
FSC™ C007454

RULES OF THEIR PARISIAN FLING

ELLIE DARKINS

MILLS & BOON

CHAPTER ONE

'AH, HERE SHE IS. Livia, I'd like you to meet Adam Jackson.'

Livia frowned, her brother's introduction and the man's name not giving her any clue who this stranger in her office was or what he was doing there. She turned to look at him, her eyebrows raised, waiting for the pair of them to fill her in. He was hardly an unwelcome addition to the décor, she had to concede. Tall, dark-haired and handsome, he was a walking cliche, and she offered him her hand, wishing that she wasn't meeting him at work, and wondering whether she was going to have the chance to get to know him better. His thoughts had clearly gone somewhere similar. She watched the widening of his eyes and the slight pinking of his lightly tanned white skin and knew that her interest was very much mutual.

'Adam is a management consultant specialising in the luxury beauty industry,' her brother said. 'I've hired him to work with you on the fragrance project.'

Livia's brows raised further as she fought the urge to snap. What on earth was her brother playing at? But that wouldn't exactly be professional, and she didn't want to spoil the mutual ogle that she had going on with this guy she was about to eject from the building. So she turned to her brother and smiled, trying to keep her voice smooth. 'Is there a reason you think that I can't handle it myself?'

Jonathan shook his head. 'I think you're perfectly competent,' he said, his voice as carefully controlled as hers. 'But this is an ambitious project and I don't want you to be overstretched. Don't think I haven't noticed how many hours you've been putting in recently.'

She turned to the man standing beside her brother, cursing the universe for providing such a crushable item, and then immediately snatching it away from her. 'Adam, I'm so sorry you've had a wasted journey but there is no position available on my team.' She headed for the door to show them out, with just a touch of regret, but her brother was taller than her and beat her to it, with Adam not far behind. She crossed her arms, waiting for the pair of them to move.

'I tried to tell you last week,' Jonathan said. 'I requested a meeting and you said you had no time, if you remember?'

'I prioritised a meeting with Claude Gaspard. If I'd known that you were going to go over my head to do this, I would have made the time,' she explained.

'Liv, it's not like that,' Jonathan said gently, which pushed her blood pressure just that little bit higher. 'We all want this to be a success, but not at any cost. You're working yourself too hard and you need someone who can share the load.'

'Oh, and you just assume that I'm not capable—?'

She was interrupted then by a very unsubtle clearing of a throat to her left. She glanced across at him, remembered how pretty he was and fixed her eyes back on Jonathan, cursing the universe once again.

'I'm sorry, Adam,' Jonathan said, seeming to remember that they weren't alone. 'Liv, we'll talk about this more later. For now, find a way to work with Adam because he's staying. Adam, come see me before you leave for the day and we'll talk about that other thing.'

And with that, her brother left them alone. She knew that her anger shouldn't be directed at Adam. It should be directed at her overbearing older brother who had been a stand-in dad since their parents had abandoned them when she was a teenager. But she couldn't be mad at him, because he was only doing it because he loved her. He was marrying her best friend, and he'd just walked out of the room anyway. Or she could be mad at the universe for showing her something that she wanted, but she couldn't have. So she turned all that on Adam.

She'd betrayed herself a dozen times over in her mind—her imagination was a quick worker, and his tight T-shirt and muscled arms provided plenty of fantasy material—but she forced the thoughts out of her mind as she turned to face him.

'Adam. I'm sorry that my brother has got ahead of himself—'

But Adam folded his arms, emphasising the muscles in them, and looking irritatingly unconcerned by the fact that she was trying to fire him.

'Your brother is the CEO,' he said, without a hint of doubt in his voice. 'This is his call.'

'That's a technicality,' Liv replied. 'This is a family business and—'

'Everyone reports to him, don't they?' Adam interrupted. 'Including you. That "technicality" means he signed my contract this morning and there's nothing that you can do about it.' He thought for a moment, his lips pursing slightly in a way that did nothing for her fickle libido. 'Well, you can sue me out of it, I suppose,' he conceded eventually with every appearance of generosity, and a smile that made her want to do bad things. 'If you wanted to, that is. But it would be a waste of your time and money and it sounds like you haven't got a lot of either to spare.'

He was right, she knew. She didn't have time to be distracted by trying to get rid of him. Since she'd finally talked her brother into their family's fashion house launching its own fragrance and cosmetics line, she'd devoted what felt like every waking hour to the project. That was the reason she'd not been able to find time for a meeting with Jonathan when he'd tried to find half an hour in her schedule at the last minute without telling her what it was about.

At the time, she'd been playing phone tag with a master parfumier in Paris who she was trying to convince *did* have space in his schedule this year to recreate the scent that her great-grandmother had developed but never launched in the nineteen-thirties. Her best friend, Rowan, had found the old paperwork in the family's Cotswold manor house in the summer of the previous year. And if Rowan hadn't somehow come out of that weekend having mostly pulled the stick out of Jonathan's backside and making him somewhat human, and then fallen in love and got engaged to him, the project probably would have gone nowhere.

But a lovestruck Jonathan who was marrying her best friend had been more willing to listen to her than he ever had been before. She realised now that she'd been relying on those changes being permanent, rather than a honeymoon period, and it had made her complacent.

'So we'll pay you,' she told Adam, trying to think through the quickest way to get this obstacle out of her path and to keep her project on track. Hoping he wasn't aware that the company didn't have the money to spare for spurious legal cases. 'But I don't need your help. I've been working on this for months and I'm perfectly capable of launching it myself.'

Adam shook his head, not moving from where he appeared to have grown roots right in front of her desk. 'I'm not being paid for a job I didn't do.'

'Then return the money,' she said, trying to make it sound flippant, as if she really didn't care what he did. She flicked through some papers on her desk, trying to look as if she were perfectly collected.

Adam laughed and the sound caught her by surprise, making her look up and stare at him for a long couple of seconds. His face was transformed by it, and for a moment she wondered what it would be like to make him laugh like that without it carrying such a heavy dose of contempt for him. But she fought the thought down. She had no interest in making him laugh—or do anything else, for that matter, other than leave her office.

She saw heat in his expression too, and something more dangerous. Something that told her she couldn't let this desire of hers off the leash for even a second if she didn't want something to happen between them.

'I'm sorry. I don't have time for this. I'm expecting a phone call,' she told him, her eyes anywhere but on him.

'If it's a call about the fragrance project, then I

should be on it,' Adam replied, which was not the answer that she had been looking for.

There was no way she was letting that happen. The only slight hitch with that determination was that the call would be coming into her office any minute now, and she wasn't sure how to get a six-foot beefcake out of a room in that sort of timeframe. Right on cue, the phone on her desk rang, and, without breaking eye contact with her, Adam leaned forward and pressed the button that answered the call on speakerphone. She glared at him but there was nothing she could do about it as the line connected to Paris.

'*Bonjour,*' she trilled, trying to keep her irritation out of her voice. She listened to the rapid-fire French at the other end of the line—which would have been a thousand per cent easier if she hadn't been trying to force the fact that Adam was in the room out of her mind at the same moment she 'uh-huh'-and-'*oui*'-ed her way through the call, making none of the carefully considered constructive feedback notes she'd been working on the night before. Which was perfect because now Adam thought that she was incompetent and he and Jonathan could have a good laugh about how useless she was. And then Jonathan would probably work out that she wasn't worth the trouble, push her out of the business and have Adam take over completely.

She got the call over with as quickly as she could, deciding that she should probably quit while she was ahead. Or, at least, before she fell any further behind.

'Are all your calls as pointless as that?' Adam asked, that beautiful mouth turned up in a sneer that made her want to smash a cream pie into it, just to see whether he was capable of any other expression.

'I work better without a guard dog watching over me,' she told him, wondering how long he was planning on standing idly at her desk while she pretended that she was able to get her work done. 'Were you planning on getting out of my office at any point?' she asked in return.

'I don't know. Depends whether you're planning on sharing your diary with me so I can join your meetings.'

She forced out a fake laugh. 'You're going to have to try harder than that if you want to read my diary, Adam.'

He crossed his arms again and stared her down. *Secret Confessions of a Little Princess*? Thanks, but I think I'll pass.'

'You don't know anything about me.'

'I've seen enough,' he said with a smirk that she assumed was meant to imply that he had met plenty of women just like her—rich and pretty and working for a family business.

Oh, he thought that he knew her. Most likely thought that she only had a job here through nepotism. That she'd been given a position at the family business because that was what families like hers did with girls like her. But he didn't know her. Didn't know how hard she had resisted drawing on her family name or joining the company. How she had spent months preparing business plans, digging through archives and researching her market. Adam might think that he was about to walk in and take the reins from some spoiled little princess who didn't know what she was doing, but he was wrong, and he would have to prise those reins from her cold, dead hands. This project was her passion, and she did not mess about when it came to her passions.

True, she hadn't been at her best on that call just now, but that was entirely Adam's fault. She would have handled it just fine if he hadn't been there looming over her desk in a childish attempt to intimidate her.

'Fine. I'll have my assistant share my schedule with you if it will get you out of my sight. We're done here, Adam.'

Conceding to Adam's demands was really not a precedent that she wanted to set, but she had to come up with a plan for what she was going to do to deal with this completely unwelcome development. She just needed some time to think.

He smirked. Again. And there were a dozen things that she could do to wipe that expression off his face. At least fifty per cent of them would lead to prison time and the rest involved more nudity than was typically wise in one's place of work.

'This conversation isn't over,' he said. But didn't turn for the door. She rolled her eyes and turned back to her desktop monitor, hoping that eventually he'd get tired of trying to stare her down, do her a favour and leave. Eventually she heard his shoes on the carpet, moving towards the door of the office, and as his footsteps faded down the corridor she finally let herself breathe normally.

'Liv, I need you in my office!'

She suppressed a groan at the sound of her brother's voice. It was gone eight o'clock and she was starving. What was more, there would be no escape from him when she got home. Since he'd revealed the money troubles the business was having, they'd all clubbed together to work out the best way to use their assets to provide a cash injection. And right now, that meant that she and her two brothers had all given up their individual homes to live in the house that she had inherited from her grandmother the year before. She'd probably sell it, once they had a minute to think about how to do that, given the amount of paperwork selling a listed building that had been in her family for a hundred years would produce.

'Jonathan, couldn't this wait until we're home?' she said, pushing files into her bag as she walked through the door to her brother's office.

When she looked up, she was half a step from colliding with the broad chest and black T-shirt of Adam Jackson.

'Oh, of course you're here,' she groaned, earning her a smirk from Adam and a tired sigh from Jonathan. At least she would be home soon, where—with Rowan or alone—she could lock herself in her room and pretend that her brother didn't exist. 'Jonathan, can't we do this at home? It's late, and I'm sure you want to get back to Rowan.' It was a cheap shot, but she wasn't above taking advantage of her brother's one soft spot. Not after the day that she'd just had. Jonathan's face melted, until he caught himself and scowled, realising what she'd just done.

'We need to do it now,' he told her. 'Because it's *about* home. Adam's moved down from Scotland to take up this position, and the hotel he booked has just called to cancel his reservation. I've invited him to stay at the house.'

Livia gaped at her brother. He couldn't seriously

be dropping this on her now, with no warning. 'At *the* house? At *my* house, you mean.' She knew that she sounded childish. And spoiled. And everything that she had wanted to prove to Adam that she was not.

'I thought we were all okay with inviting people to stay in our homes,' Jonathan said, with a show of wide-eyed innocence. Which would have been fair, if she'd been in a mood to acknowledge it, given that she'd been the one to invite Rowan on their trip to his house the year before, not able to face the thought of spending the week with her brothers without the backup of her best friend.

She shouldn't have been surprised, really, how spectacularly that had backfired. Now she couldn't even depend on her best friend to always take her side. They tried their hardest to never mention the elephant in the room, because she couldn't bear the thought that if it came down to it, Rowan would choose Jonathan over her.

She didn't need a therapist to tell her that her parents' flight to South America to avoid tax evasion charges made her paranoid that people were going to leave her—though several therapists had told her exactly that, of course. None of The Work that she'd done in her very expensive therapy had managed to stop her believing that they wouldn't have gone if they'd loved her a little more, if she had been a little more loveable. It had seemed easier since she'd decided that she would simply not make herself available for getting hurt. It was too late to not love Rowan. She had been her best friend for years and would be her sister soon too. But that was it. She was officially bolting the stable door. No more people in her life. No one who could leave her. No one she could lose. So their domestic situation was already loaded with enough emotion without this irritating man crashing.

'No, Jonathan, absolutely not,' she told him.

'I wasn't asking your permission. You set the precedent last year,' he said, taking the high-handed headmaster tone that she hated so much. God, it was so annoying when he used her own behaviour against her.

'This is not the same,' she said with forced politeness. 'I invited *Rowan*,' she reminded him. 'Who we had both known for years. Who you were already half in love with. Not some strange man who might murder me in my sleep!'

She thought she heard Adam suppress a laugh and didn't trust herself to look at him.

'If it helps,' Adam offered, with a hint of amusement in his voice that made her see red, and also clench her thighs just a little, 'I really don't have any interest in murdering you. In your sleep or otherwise.'

If only that feeling were mutual. She took a deep breath, reminded herself that she was at work, and was a professional, and losing her temper at Adam would only be handing Jonathan a stick to beat her with.

'It doesn't help, and this is actually a private conversation, so why don't you just wait outside, Adam?'

CHAPTER TWO

ADAM WAITED OUTSIDE the office, though he wasn't sure why they'd bothered to chuck him out when they were first going to raise their voices so half the building could have heard them if they hadn't been the only people still in the office long after everyone else had left to have a social life, or a personal life, or any sort of a life that didn't revolve around their job.

He didn't envy them. He'd made his work his whole life and had never regretted it. It had started from necessity—when you started with nothing you worked every hour of the day or risked spending the rest of your life with nothing. Somewhere along the line it had stopped being something he did and just became who he was. If he stopped, if he risked his life taking a backwards slide... He knew what abject poverty felt like—the constant aching grind of going to bed, night after night, cold and hungry. And then the years when even a bed wasn't a given and he and his mother had surfed from sofa to sofa, until he'd left school and got his first job and between them they'd finally scraped enough money together for a deposit on a tiny flat. From then on, his only focus had been keeping that roof over their heads. And the day that he'd bought a house had felt like the first day of his life he'd taken a truly deep breath. And the next day? He'd been back in the office at six.

While the little princess currently yelling at her brother on the other side of this insufficiently sound-proofed door might have been the most adorably pint-sized piece of perfection he'd seen in a really long time, he had no patience for her. Having her little tantrum because there was going to be one less spare room in the mansion she got to live in rent-free. He'd already booked a hotel for this week while he tried to find a place to buy now that he was back in London. But when they'd called to say that they'd cocked it up and Jona-than had offered him a room, he had agreed. Old hab-its died hard, after all, and the hotel hadn't been cheap.

The shouting from the office had stopped, and he leaned against the assistant's desk directly in front of the door. The tense silence in the air was every bit as voluble as the shouting had been.

Livia exited the office first, stalking out of the room with her face thunderous and her arms folded. The tense line of her jaw had done something that made her cheekbones pop, and her lips were pursed into a lush pout. Her eyeliner hadn't quite lasted the day and the smudge under her lower lashes gave her a hard-edged look. The overall effect was... Well, it was devastat-ing, wasn't it? And there was no point trying to deny what he wanted, because seeing it for what it was would help him to focus on all the reasons why he didn't want her. She was spoiled. And entitled. And had hated him almost on sight, which helped. Only, that 'almost' was doing a lot of work. Because he couldn't quite make his brain forget those seconds before Jonathan had introduced him properly when her eyes had raked over him as if she'd wanted to follow them with her nails. They'd started on his face—eyes, jaw, chin. Across his shoulders and down his chest. Slowing down over his belly, until her eyes had flared and she'd shaken her gaze loose somewhere around his thighs. He'd had the ridiculous urge to flex for her, even though she represented everything he hated.

'You finished?' he asked as the yelling seemed to have been replaced by a stony silence.

'There's no need to look so smug about it,' she replied.

Her privileged life made a mockery of the years, decades, of work that he'd put in to become her social and business equal. She'd been planning on helping herself to him too, he was sure, until she'd discovered he'd been brought in to do the actual work on her little pet project.

And if he'd had any doubts about how much his help was needed, listening in on her phone call had been enough to dispel them. She'd been flustered and unfocussed and he'd had no qualms about pointing that out to her. The sooner she accepted that she needed his help and let him do his job, the better.

She pushed past him, her shoulder giving him a little shove even though there was plenty of space between the desks, and he suppressed a little smile at her show of defiance. A tiny, tiny part of him—which he absolutely wasn't going to indulge—got off on the fact that she couldn't hide her reaction to him, even the urge to give him a shove like a kid in a playground. Fine. Good. He wanted her hostile to him, angry.

And if she wanted to find excuses for her body to knock into his, he wasn't going to complain.

'Careful there,' he said, and smiled at the glare she sent in his direction. Her being angry with him was safer anyway, so he wouldn't be tempted by that body and those big sad eyes.

He waited for Jonathan, and they walked down to the parking garage beneath the office building, where Livia was leaning against the hood of a black saloon car.

'I'm driving, she said, holding her hands out to Jonathan for the keys.

'Sure. I'll sit in the back,' Jonathan said. 'Give you two a chance to get to know each other.'

Adam did his best to hide a smile at the absolutely murderous look Livia sent in Jonathan's direction. He shouldn't be enjoying Livia getting riled. He shouldn't be thinking about Livia at all, apart from in a purely professional way.

'What's your next step with Gaspard?' he asked her, wanting to get things back onto a safer professional footing, but she turned that murderous look on him. It was decidedly less enjoyable when he was the victim rather than a bystander.

'I was trying to decide between doing nothing and doing something catastrophically incompetent. Which would you recommend?' she asked sweetly.

Adam decided that grin was getting harder and harder to resist. 'Well, you tried incompetence on the phone today. Perhaps doing nothing would be for the best. Just let me know if you want me to step in.'

She turned a full-watt smile on him, glancing away from the road for a second, and he was momentarily stunned at the sight of it, wondering if she was going to turn sweet, grateful. His imagination was way ahead of him, imagining all the ways that he could enjoy a grateful, pliable Liv.

'You can step in if it's over my rotting, bloated corpse,' she said, her voice still sweet, and with a flirtatious bat of her eyelashes. 'If you're trying to force me out,' she added, 'you're going to have to do a lot more than just ask me nicely.'

He held up his hands. 'I'm not trying to force you anywhere. I just want to see a job done well.'

'And what makes you think that I can't do that? You don't even know me.'

He wondered whether Jonathan was listening from the back seat and wondered about the dynamics in their relationship. He'd read about what had happened with their parents, leaving the country—that was bound to mess a person up. Didn't siblings bond over shared trauma?

He'd always assumed that would have been the case if he'd had any. But then he'd never been able to get his head round companionship versus another mouth to feed. Another bed to find every night. So in the end he'd been glad it was just him and his mum against the world. He tried to picture what their relationship would have looked like if they'd lived the sort of life where houses like this one just dropped into your lap, and he simply…couldn't. Their relationship, for so long, had been about surviving; he didn't know who else they were to one another. Didn't know another way to love.

And when it came to women, sex, relationships— he didn't want to be responsible for anyone else's happiness. It was too much—hurt too much—when you failed someone. He thought about the nights when he hadn't been able to find somewhere for them to stay. When dinner had been a shared Pot Noodle after his mother had finished a twelve-hour shift. How utterly useless he had felt, and how much worse it had been than letting himself down. He had no idea why anyone would willingly seek out more people to be responsible for, to love. Couldn't get his head round there being entire industries built on it. He'd figured out a long time ago that the minute he thought he might have feelings for someone, it was time to walk away. And as long as he found like-minded partners and everyone was upfront about what they wanted, everyone came out of it feeling…fine.

He slid a look sideways at Livia, wondering if she was a like-minded person, or whether she was the 'hearts and flowers and diamond rings' type.

He gave himself a mental slap. Because he didn't care what sort of relationships Liv liked. It did not matter what Livia was into. He wasn't going there. Even without all his usual relationship rules, this would be too complicated. She was too complicated. So he probably shouldn't let his eyes drop to her soft thighs.

The twenty-minute drive dragged, and by the time they pulled up outside the white stucco-fronted town house that could only be described as a mansion Adam could barely suppress his eye roll. Of course their house looked like this. No doubt theirs was still a single residence. He remembered the weeks he had spent in a bedsit, one of six that had been carved out of a building that must have looked just like this one once. He'd lost count of how many people had lived in those six tiny flats, and felt a wave of resentment towards the siblings who were having this whole house land in their laps and didn't even seem to realise how lucky they were.

How did they live with themselves, owning a place like this, when he knew without a doubt there must be people within streets of here experiencing hunger, homelessness and the sort of bone-deep insecurity that he still carried with him years after he'd considered himself successful and financially stable?

'We're here,' Liv said, unbuckling her seat belt and sliding out of the car, evidently not expecting a response. Good, because he doubted that she'd like what he had to say. He followed Jonathan and Livia up the stairs to the glossy black front door, flanked by classical pillars, with his hands clenched into fists and his jaw so tight that he thought he might crack a molar.

'Honey, I'm home,' Liv called out in the grand, checked-floor hallway, and it was enough to distract him momentarily from his anger. He'd just assumed that she was single, but that was ridiculous really, because just look at her. He rapidly readjusted his assumptions when a tall, striking woman appeared on the stairs. But when she kissed Liv on the cheek and Jonathan on the mouth he guessed that this must be the Rowan he'd heard so much about.

After introductions were made, Rowan and Jonathan disappeared down the stairs to the lower-ground floor—where he guessed the kitchen was located—and left him alone with Liv, who had been given vague instructions to 'get him settled'.

She looked fairly annoyed about it, but didn't say anything, which he guessed was a result of Rowan's influence.

'Come on, then,' Livia said, walking up the grand

staircase. He followed her along a long hallway as she pointed out the bedrooms.

'Rowan and Jonathan's room, Caleb's room…' He heard the sound of typing within, and guessed Caleb had locked himself away. He couldn't blame the guy.

'My room,' Livia went on as they reached the end of the corridor. 'This is the only spare room on this floor. It, er, has an interconnecting bathroom with mine. The other bedrooms are in the attic and are usually used for storage, so…'

'This will be fine,' he said, mainly to annoy her, because he suspected that she'd like nothing more than to send him up to what must have been servants' quarters so he could be neither seen nor heard. Which meant that, as much as he'd prefer to be as far as possible from the ostentatious glamour, and shared bathroom, of the family rooms, he would put up with it if it meant annoying Livia.

CHAPTER THREE

LIVIA SAT AT the kitchen worktop, nursing a sweating glass of Sauvignon Blanc. This was so typical of Jonathan. Inviting someone she was inclined to hate to stay in their house, and then stealing Rowan away with the least subtle, 'We're just going to…ahem… something…ahem…upstairs…ahem…something…' she'd ever heard in her life. And Caleb was showing no signs of suddenly wanting to leave his room and actually spend time with his family. She really would rather be anywhere but here, but her best friend was upstairs being *unsubtle* with Jonathan and there wasn't anyone else she could drag out at a moment's notice as she could with Rowan.

She heard footsteps on the stairs, and, as it was only one set rather than the four-footed Rowan-Jonathan, she assumed that hunger had tempted Caleb down from his cave.

'Oh. It's you,' she said, surprise forcing the words out of her as Adam appeared in the doorway.

'Do you make all your guests feel so welcome?' he asked with a smirk that irritated her to the tips of her fingers.

'You're Jonathan's guest,' she said with a swig of her wine. 'Nothing to do with me.'

'What is it with you two?' Adam asked, leaning on the marble countertop opposite her and fixing her with a look that on a less detestable man might have done things to her insides. She rolled her eyes.

'Just sibling stuff.' Like trying to be your dad when you really wanted a brother, and stealing your best friend away and making her love him more. But she didn't feel quite like sharing that with a guy that she'd decided she detested on sight.

'And Rowan?'

So he'd picked up on that? He was so irritating.

'Rowan was—is—my best friend. Got engaged to Jonathan last year.'

'Can't have been easy for you.' She narrowed her eyes at him, trying to work out what his angle was. Because that sounded suspiciously like empathy, and she knew he wasn't down here empathising with her out of the goodness of his heart. He had to have an angle.

'We're all used to it. It's fine.' She finished her wine and headed to the fridge for the bottle. 'Want anything?' she asked, thinking that it wasn't giving too much away to do the absolute minimum of hostessing.

'A beer, if you have one.'

She snorted. Did he think she'd been born with a glass of Sauv in her hand? 'Yes, we have beer.'

She took the cap off a bottle and handed it over to him. 'So do you people eat?' he said, and if it had been said with any less hostility she might have confused his insult for the suggestion that they have dinner together.

She shrugged, tracing patterns in the condensation on her glass. 'I was waiting for Rowan to re-emerge.'

'So you all work and live and eat together. Nothing weirdly co-dependent about that at all...'

She rolled her eyes. 'It's temporary. Jonathan explained this, right? That we don't normally all live together like this. It's not exactly what any of us would choose.'

'God. It's bad enough that people get to own places like this. Then you whine about it?'

Liv raised her eyebrows, her glass raised halfway to her mouth,

'Judgemental much?' she asked, slightly surprised by his hostility. 'That's my family you're talking about. Just because I bitch about them doesn't mean you're allowed to.'

Adam took a stool across the breakfast bar from her and took a sip of his beer before answering. 'I'm just telling it how I see it. As far as I'm concerned it's immoral for one family to have so much wealth. Even if you do all live here together.'

Liv narrowed her eyes at him, not sure whether she was more impressed or annoyed with his bald honesty. 'Well, I apologise on behalf of late-stage capitalism,' she said. 'But you do know that I couldn't actually do anything about my family's accumulated wealth until I actually inherited it, and now I appear to be using it to house my entire family and whatever waifs and strays that they happen to encounter in the office.'

'Oh, right, this is a veritable homeless shelter,' he said with a humourless laugh. 'You're certainly doing everything you can for the poor.'

She stared at him a moment.

'Did anyone ever tell you you're a very rude house guest?'

'Yes, actually.' He leaned back against the countertop with his hands in his pockets and she momentarily didn't know whether to scratch his eyes out or drag her nails down his back. 'I get that a lot from the beneficiaries of inherited wealth.'

Her laugh took her so much by surprise that she snorted her wine.

'Why, Adam, anyone would think that you're trying to offend me.'

He smiled at that and it couldn't have been more different from the smirks that he'd sent in her direction earlier. His real smile was smaller, warmer. A twitch of the corner of his mouth, a crinkle at the corner of his eyes and a warmth that somehow projected from somewhere between the two. For a second, she forgot that that smile was entirely at her expense, and just enjoyed soaking it in. Until she remembered that he hated her and her family and apparently everything that they'd worked for over the decades. She shut down her face and made sure she wasn't smiling back. Because she still hated him and resented the fact that she was being forced to share her kitchen with him.

'Anyway, to answer your question, yes, we eat. I think there are leftovers in the fridge. But feel free to order takeout and eat in your room if it offends your sensibilities.'

'Me and Jonathan have work to do,' he replied. 'Might as well make it a working dinner.'

Liv fixed him with a stare. 'If it's regarding the fragrance project, then you need to be talking to me,' she reminded him, because she had no intention of being pushed out of her own project. But Adam shook his head, looking slightly indulgently at her in a way that made her certain she would go for the eyes first.

'Look,' he said, tilting his head as he spoke. 'I know you enjoy having this pet project, but if you're going to meet your ludicrously optimistic launch date, you really need me to take the lead on this. I'm sure you've been allowed a lot of leeway, but it's time to take this seriously.'

She folded her arms and glared at him. 'You think I'm not taking this seriously? Of course, because I'm a spoiled little princess who has feelings about things but can't actually do the work?'

Adam leaned back a little, regarding her carefully. 'Now you're just putting words—sexist words—in my mouth,' he argued. 'I'm just saying that the documentation I've seen so far speaks for itself.'

She strode over to him—well, a stride for her was probably a teeny-tiny fairy step for him, and she realised how close she had already been when she found herself having to tip her head back to look him in the eye. 'And I'm telling you,' she said, 'that if you want to see the documentation for *my* project, you should have come to the person working on the project full time—me—not the nearest available man.'

He shook his head, looking right down his nose at her. 'Oh, my God, would you stop making this about the fact that you're a woman?'

'You literally called me Princess,' she all but hissed. 'You get that that makes you a textbook misogynist, don't you?'

'No,' he said slowly, drawing out the syllable, and she guessed that meant he thought he was about to get a good shot in. 'It means I hate spoiled little rich kids.'

She raised her eyebrows at him, arms still crossed over her chest. 'Glad we've cleared this up. Funny, though, how you don't seem to have a problem with Jonathan.'

'He comes with a reputation for how hard he works.'

That earned him a raise of her eyebrows. 'Ah, so you're judging us by reputation. That always ends well for young women. What do people say about me?'

He paused, considering, and she was surprised that he was pulling his punches. 'What would I need to hear other than that you're a Kinley? It doesn't take a genius to work out how you got the job.'

'Great,' she said, nodding and going back to her bar stool, taking another sip of her wine. 'Good to know exactly what you think of me.' He actually looked a little shamefaced, which took her by surprise, as if he only realised how judgemental he was being as the words left his mouth. She hated that she had to make concessions to get her work recognised but, if Jonathan had hired him and the contracts were signed, she had no hope of getting rid of him. Better work in the system she was faced with than waste her time raging against the machine.

'So do you want to see my research or not?' she asked, refusing to rise to the provocation of his words.

He simply nodded, and she pulled up her files on her iPad and slid it over to him. She didn't bother with nerves as he looked them over. She knew her work was good, regardless of what the gossip mill in the industry said about how she got her job. She'd studied management and marketing at university. Had worked in-house for several management consultancies on product launches before setting up her own consultancy. Jonathan had asked her to come in-house at Kinley more than once, but she'd always resisted before now, for all the reasons that Adam was making so clear to her.

If the family business hadn't been in so much trouble, she might still have said no. She couldn't think of anything worse than working with her brother, constantly having to prove her worth to him professionally, as well as personally. The aching dread of being pushed away gnawing at her. That feeling had been a constant companion since their parents had left them all, proof that unconditional love didn't, in fact, exist, and that the presence in her life of the people she loved the most was not something that she could rely on.

When Jonathan had told her that Kinley was in financial trouble and desperately needed a new line of income, and they had come up with the idea of developing the fragrance that her great-grandmother had once intended to launch, she had finally agreed to give it a try. The plans had been scrapped eighty years ago, and under normal circumstances her risk-averse brother would never have taken a gamble on something new. But after they'd all agreed to work together to save the business, she'd thought that he'd finally trusted her to do this. But it turned out she was wrong.

Jonathan had taken his responsibilities as head of the business and head of the family seriously—too seriously—and had committed himself to wrapping her in cotton wool and generally treating her like a child. If she'd thought that being engaged to a woman exactly her age would make him treat her like a grown-up, she'd been sadly mistaken. And she couldn't even complain to Rowan about it as she once would have done. She and Rowan were still working out how they made their friendship work now that Rowan was dating not only Livia's brother but her boss as well.

For a moment, the loneliness hit her like a flood. Rowan hadn't left her, she reminded herself, as she'd had to do several times in the past months when the gnawing ache had spiralled to a panic. Her best friend didn't love her any less than she had before she'd decided she loved Jonathan too. But regardless of how she tried to reason with herself, she couldn't help feeling that her best friend had slipped a little further away, and she was a little closer to being completely alone.

Talking about Jonathan with Rowan had to be off-limits, if their friendship was to survive, but the distance that forced into their relationship sometimes felt like a chasm between them. Livia had nowhere to go with her complaints about her brother, with the underlying fear that one day he would simply not be there.

She forced the feeling away. She didn't wallow. She hadn't when her parents had moved half a planet away. When they had boarded a plane without a backward glance and left her and her brothers to fend for themselves, and to deal with the hefty tax bill that they'd been running from.

At first she had thought that Rowan marrying into her family would bring them closer, and yet the easy intimacy that they'd once had was just out of reach. For a moment she yearned for simpler days when they could spend the their time lazing through study sessions with regular breaks for cheap coffee and cheaper wine.

She shook her head, trying to throw off her melancholy, realising too late that Adam was still there, watching her carefully now.

'What's wrong?' he asked her, and she fought down

a shiver, hating that he, of all people, had seen something that she kept hidden from everyone.

'Nothing. Why would it be?' she lied. She heard two sets of footsteps on the stairs down to the kitchen and allowed herself a long breath of relief. She didn't like how much Adam seemed to see.

Rowan was rosy-faced and disgustingly cheerful when she appeared at the bottom of the stairs a minute later. 'Everyone ready for dinner?' she asked, going to the fridge and pulling out a foil-covered dish. Liv grunted a reply, not wanting either Rowan's or Jonathan's attention right now, so she grabbed cutlery from the drawer and set five places at the table. She shouted up the stairs for Caleb to get himself down here, half hoping that he had his noise-cancelling headphones on so that she would have to go and find him. But the universe was not her friend today, and she heard heavy footfalls above her. She went through the motions until they were all seated. Making small talk about the food while Jonathan topped up their glasses, making his self-appointed position as patriarch clear.

Caleb shovelled down his food, getting his obligatory family time out of the way so he could get back to his laptop. She wondered if she should ask him more probing questions about what he was doing up there. He was no stranger to working long hours, but, from the look on his face, he didn't look as if he'd just been dragged away from an eight-hour coding session. Jonathan and Rowan were doing their communicating-without-words thing, Rowan breaking off occasionally to remember that there were other people at the table and to ask Liv about her day.

She was hit by another wave of loneliness—not for

what Rowan and Jonathan had. She didn't want someone to fall in love with her, she couldn't see that leading
to anywhere other than disappointment, abandonment
and pain. But until a few months ago, Liv thought, she'd
at least had a *person*. At least after a break-up, you got
to be angry with your ex, but she couldn't be angry at
Rowan—especially not when she saw how happy she
was, and how much easier her life was when Jonathan
was happy as well.

Liv suppressed the sigh she could feel brewing and
looked up from her wine glass, only to be struck hard
in the face by the heavy weight of Adam's gaze, fixed
firmly on her. She creased her forehead. Frowned at
him. *What?*

'You okay?' he mouthed back. She rolled her eyes at
him. She could do without his false concern. She just
didn't have the energy to work out what he was up to.
She took another sip of her wine and flicked her eyes
back to Adam. Still watching her. Well, she wasn't
going to let him psych her out. She stared back. If he
wanted to make this a contest, then she'd give him one.

He quirked an eyebrow with what looked like
amusement when he realised what she was doing. And
then, without looking away, he forked a huge spoon-
ful of pasta into his mouth. She refused to smile. She
wouldn't look at his mouth, though she was sure from
glimpses in her peripheral vision that there was a
smudge of sauce on his lower lip that would make her
warm if she were to look at it directly. She stared until
her eyes were dry and stinging, her food had gone
cold and her wine warm. Finally, with one of those
micro smiles and a shake of his head, he looked away.
It took every ounce of her self-control not to pump a

fist in the air at her victory. Instead, she finally dug into her pasta, emitting what she knew was a glow of smug self-satisfaction. Fine. It was childish, she knew it was childish. But she so rarely felt like a success. Especially in this company, so she was going to take her petty little win and cherish it.

Adam was shaking his head again as she realised that Jonathan was trying to get her attention. 'I was asking Adam about market research and he said I should talk to you.'

'What?' she said, trying to catch up and remind herself that this was a working dinner, kicking herself for falling for Adam's mind games, no doubt to distract her. No need to tell Jonathan that she was incompetent—why would he when he could simply scramble her brains and let her embarrass herself?

'Right. Market research,' she prompted herself. 'I have the reports from the latest focus groups in my inbox. We could all go through them together?' She ground the words out because the last thing she wanted was to give up her tight hold on her project. There was a reason why Adam hadn't got the full picture from Jonathan. She didn't trust him not to be disappointed at her work and decide that the company was better off without her after all. So she'd got into the habit of not sharing with her brother until the last possible moment, delaying the inevitable anxiety. But doing that had no doubt contributed to him deciding that she was so incompetent that he had to hire Adam to do her job for her.

She talked both Adam and Jonathan through the results of the latest research into packaging and branding. She was holding her own, even under Jonathan's questions and Adam's no-doubt critical silences. But she was happy with the report and it had thrown up a few interesting ideas she would come back to later.

'Right, enough shop talk,' Rowan said after an hour and a half, wrapping an arm around Jonathan's shoulder, kissing him on the cheek and smiling at Liv. They all owed Rowan one for saving them from themselves.

Out of the corner of her eye, she saw Rowan whisper in Jonathan's ear and colour rise in his cheeks. She fought down the urge to spew on the table. 'I'm, erm, going out,' Livia said without thinking the words through. When she'd already established that she had no one to party with. Fine. She was a grown-up. She could sip a drink at a table for one for a couple of hours while her brother and her friend…ugh, she was not going to think about that.

Caleb had already disappeared back to his lair, leaving the four of them at the increasingly uncomfortable table. 'You should take Adam,' Jonathan said, eyes still on Rowan, as if that were a perfectly reasonable thing to say, rather than completely deranged.

'I'm… I…' She was so shocked that she couldn't think of something to say.

'Sounds great,' Adam said, and she turned her glare on him. What the hell?

But he rose from the table and grabbed a leather jacket from where he'd thrown it over the back of a chair. Liv looked beseechingly at Rowan, but she clearly had other things on her mind. So she cleared their plates from the table and grabbed her bag. Was she seriously doing this? She just had to get out of the house and then she could ditch him. No way was she spending the evening with him.

He'd already invaded her work life and her home life. He didn't get to crash her social life too. She snorted to herself as she tucked her phone into her back pocket. *What* social life? She knew that drinking alone didn't count—she really shouldn't let it count. Didn't want Adam to find out that she didn't even have someone to go for a drink with any more. But if playing along was the fastest way out of here, then she'd pretend to go for a drink with Adam.

'Fine. Good. Let's go,' she said, getting away from Rowan and Jonathan before she saw something she couldn't unsee. She pulled on boots and a denim jacket at the front door and turned to see Adam watching her.

'What?'

'Nothing,' he said with a smirk that she wanted nothing more than to wipe off his face. She pulled the door open and shot him a frustrated look.

'Come on, then,' she said. 'Let's go.'

CHAPTER FOUR

SHE JOGGED DOWN the steps from the front door to the pavement, eyes fixed firmly ahead. She shoved her hands in her pockets and didn't look back to see if Adam was following. With any luck he'd walk the other way and leave her to her bottle of wine for one. But she heard his irritatingly long strides behind her until he was walking alongside and showing no sign of leaving her to be lonely in peace.

They walked in silence to the corner and she realised she had no idea where she was going. Her great-grandparents' choice of where to buy the town house that had been passed down through the generations didn't exactly chime with her idea of a good time. There was a champagne and toffs wine bar on the corner. Not her kind of place at all. A single glass would probably cost her a week's salary. But the most important thing was that it looked like the last place on earth that Adam would follow, so she pushed open the glass door. She'd order a tap water if she had to.

When Adam followed her inside, she didn't bother hiding her groan.

'Worried I'm going to embarrass you in front of your friends?' Adam asked with an expression that told her that he'd like nothing more than to make her uncomfortable. But the second he'd spoken she'd realised the problem. He was expecting her to be meeting people here. He'd tagged along to mess with her and now he was going to see the truth. That she'd left the only people in her life back at the house because she couldn't bear to be around them.

'So? Where are they?' he asked as she hesitated and glanced around the room, wondering what the odds were of there being a friend or a colleague or even a vague acquaintance. But she didn't recognise anyone.

As silent seconds ticked by, she felt him come to realisation by degrees. She waited for the gloating that she was sure had to come. But as she stared him down, braced for his barbs, she saw his face soften.

'Should we get a table?' he asked, and she was taken aback by his words and the soft look in his eyes and the kindness in his voice. She let herself be led to a table in a way that she would never have allowed if he hadn't been so weirdly...nice?

'So,' he said, once they'd taken a seat and ordered drinks. 'You didn't really have plans?'

'Wow, they did hire you for your huge analytical brain after all,' she said, her voice drier than the wine she'd ordered.

He ignored her deliberate taunt. 'Why lie?'

She shrugged. 'I wanted to get out of there.'

'Why not call a friend?'

She shifted in her seat, embarrassed. She hadn't realised until too late that she'd spent so much time at work that she'd lost pretty much all her friends but Rowan. There was that...*kind* look again, the one that she couldn't stand. She shrugged, covering.

'Last-minute decision. And I don't mind my own company.'

He nodded understandingly, which made her want to strangle him. 'Those are both very valid positions to take. But they don't explain the look on your face when we got in here. Why did you freeze?'

She thought for a moment. Wondering which reply would get him off this line of questioning. 'Just surprised that you followed me. I was wondering how I was going to get rid of you.'

That snort again.

'If that were true, we wouldn't be sitting here right now.'

She didn't have anything to say to that. 'You don't have plans either?' she asked, diverting attention from herself.

'I've been in Scotland for a few years. My speed dial down here isn't what it used to be.'

She had a sip of her drink, because she wasn't really sure what to make of that.

'I still don't get why you're here with me.' Dammit, she hadn't meant for that to come out sounding so... truthful. But now she was really curious. Why was he here, if not to mess with her?

'Why wouldn't I want to spend time with you?' he asked.

It was her turn to snort. 'Seriously? Like we haven't been arguing every second since we met?'

'Not every second,' he said, with a look so heated that it didn't take a genius to work out what he'd been thinking about the moments that they weren't actively sniping at one another. She was worried—deeply worried—if he'd thought anything remotely along the lines of when she'd first met him, and had been far more interested in his forearms than the fact that he was completely irritating.

There was nothing wrong with a little one-sided fantasy, she knew. He never had to know the things that she'd imagined in her weaker, lonelier moments. But fantasies that ran both ways… Fantasies that might spill into real life… Absolutely not—far too dangerous. Even if she didn't detest this man. Even if he weren't effectively stealing her job from under her, she wouldn't get involved. He was just too…under her skin. Already. On day one. And she didn't like that sensation. Didn't like anyone closer than a comfortable arm's length away. If you let people closer than that, it hurt when they left. You could feel the space where they'd been. She'd healed around too many empty spaces already. She was so riddled with hollows that sometimes she didn't feel quite real, any more.

'Not every second,' she agreed with Adam, because apparently her brain resembled Swiss cheese too.

'So, is this your local?' Adam asked, glancing around the bar as if a member of staff might emerge from one of the booths and force him to drink something other than a beer. 'It's really not,' she told him. 'It was just the closest.'

He smiled. One of those tiny, secret, genuine ones that did bad things to her. 'You were that desperate to get rid of me?'

She groaned.

'Has anyone told you how irritating you are?'

'People generally find me quite charming.'

She full on belly-laughed at that, snorting wine

through her nose and having to hold her sides until she could breathe normally again. She took a few shuddering inhales to make sure she had herself under control, and took the cocktail napkin that Adam held out to her. She wiped her eyes and, mortifyingly, her nose, and when she looked up at Adam, something had shifted. She couldn't detest him as she had an hour ago, and the knowledge made her nervous. But there wasn't really anything she could do. That was the other thing. People were like barbed arrows. Once they got you, you couldn't get them out easily.

'I can't believe the idea of me being charming is so hilarious.'

'I can't believe that you think that you're charming. You must know that you're not. You've been glowering at me all day.'

'I don't want to be all "Yes, but…"'

'Yes, but?'

'You started yelling approximately three seconds after we met.'

'Because you were trying to steal my job!'

'I turned up for a meeting and accepted a consulting position without even knowing you were on the project. I don't think your fight is with me, babe.' She was so taken aback by that 'babe' that she didn't manage to put words in order and get them out of her mouth before he started to speak again. 'Your fight is with Jonathan— though I'm not sure I can blame him if you weren't sharing your work with him. But you can't have it out with Jonathan because he's marrying your best friend so you're taking it out on an innocent bystander. Me.'

She narrowed her eyes, hating how many hits he'd

got in there. 'It's so impossible that I just disliked you on sight?' she asked, feigning innocence.

He took a sip of his beer, and she tried not to watch. Honestly tried. But his long, thick fingers wrapped around his glass caught her eye. And when she forced herself to look away from that, there was his throat, long, tanned, his Adam's apple moving as he drank. He put down the glass and she tried not to let her little lust diversion show.

'Come on. We can quit pretending. I don't think either of us is stupid enough to act on the fact that we're attracted to one another,' he said, as if he were commenting on nothing more controversial than the drinks menu. 'We might as well acknowledge it,' he went on. 'Clear the air. We'll get a lot more work done if we're not constantly at each other's throats because that's easier than admitting that we want each other.'

She stared at him for half a second, weighing up how much it would cost her to just agree with him. 'Oh, my God, your ego really knows no bounds, does it?' she said, refusing to let her voice waver.

He shrugged, leaning back in his seat and drinking. 'So which part isn't true?' he asked as he set his beer back on the table.

'The part where I'm attracted to you, for a start,' Liv said, her voice just a touch sharper than she wanted it to be. Adam smirked, and stretched an arm across the back of the booth. It pulled his T-shirt tight across pecs that belonged on a men's magazine cover, and pulled the fabric up to reveal a trail of hair under the waistband of his jeans. When she finally tore her gaze away and looked at his face, she realised he'd done it on purpose.

'I hate you,' she told him.

'So you've been thinking about me,' he said, looking as if he was deep in thought. 'And you say that you're not interested.'

The scale of his ego was enough to snap her out of the dark spell that Adam had somehow cast over her by stretching in a tight T-shirt.

'Fine. So what if I'd probably bang this out of my system if you had an entirely different personality?' Liv declared. 'Like you said: we're both too smart for that—and your personality is completely objectionable and I'm not a masochist.'

'So we just ignore it?' Adam nodded, leaning forwards and resting his elbows on the table. 'How would you feel about calling a truce?' he asked.

Liv frowned, trying to see if there was anything in his expression to tell her if he was being disingenuous. 'That definitely sounds like a trap,' she said carefully. 'I agree to a truce and all of a sudden your name is on my research reports, and my project, that I've been responsible for from day one, disappears from under my nose? No way. I'm not... I'm not going to start any trouble. But I'm not going to agree to not fight for something that's so important to me.'

'I wasn't planning on starting a fight,' Adam said.

Liv shook her head. 'Of course you're not. But you're planning on doing your job. And when what I think is right for the project comes into conflict with what you think is right, you're not going to try and pull rank and insist we do things your way? Because you know that's throwing the first punch.'

'I'm not in the habit of punching people at work. Believe it or not, I have other conflict resolution techniques up my sleeve. I'm a professional. Not just some bloke your brother pulled in off the street.'

'Fine, then. It's a truce, unless you throw a punch at my work.'

He finished the last of his beer and Liv glanced at the door. Would it be safe back at the house yet? If she and Adam had reached an uneasy truce, she didn't want to push that peace too far by dragging this evening out. She couldn't help but feel that staying for more than a single drink with Adam would end in a fight or, worse, some light groping.

'Shall we go somewhere else?' Adam asked, and she examined his face for ulterior motives. But, she told herself, talking about the fact that they were attracted to one another had robbed some of the power out of it. Now that he'd asked, it all seemed a little less dangerous. So she followed him out of the bar and they walked along shoulder to shoulder. Well, more like shoulder to elbow, given that he towered over her more than a foot.

They walked until they found a pub, noise and smokers spilling out onto the pavement. They went inside and it couldn't have been more different from their first venue. The building had to be hundreds of years old, and the walls and bar were panelled in rich, burnished oak. The real ale pumps were highly polished brass, and she ordered a pint of ale, because it would be wrong to drink anything else in these surroundings.

A real fire burned in the fireplace against the early-autumn chill, and beside it was the only free table, small and circular with two stools tucked underneath. Livia ducked through the crowds to get the seats while Adam followed in her wake, carrying the drinks. The tiny space pressed them together with an intimacy that hadn't been there at the last bar. The warm buzz of chatter created a comfortable background noise, taking the pressure off the need to force conversation, and the minutes passed as quickly as the beer slipped down.

With the serious conversation out of the way, there was room for something more friendly. Smaller things, movies that they'd liked and comfort food they turned to and, when that started their stomachs rumbling, the bar snack and flavour of crisps they preferred when they were in a proper pub, rather than somewhere with wasabi nuts served in a miniature tea chest. They picked through a packet of cheese and onion, and then prawn cocktail, neither of them commenting on how those particular choices of flavour would help with their stated determination to not kiss each other.

They were eventually hustled out of the door half an hour after closing time with questions about whether they had homes to go to. She shivered when she walked outside—she'd been sitting by the fire for so long that her denim jacket didn't quite cut it. Adam shrugged out of his jacket and she watched him, confused, until he tried to drape it over her shoulders and she skipped out of his reach.

'What the hell are you doing?' she asked, with a tone of barely suppressed mortification.

'You looked cold,' Adam said, frowning and plainly confused.

Liv snorted. 'Of course I'm cold, I should have worn another layer. But how does you freezing to death because you're wearing nothing but a muscle tee help?'

Adam stopped dead on the pavement, hands on his hips as he looked down at her. 'This is a normal T-shirt,' he said, while his pose pulled it skintight across his shoulders, arms and chest, which rather proved her point.

'Then how come I can count your abs?' she asked, attempting an air of innocence, but ruining the effect entirely by licking her lips.

'Maybe because you can't help looking,' Adam asked.

Her breathing faltered, because he was right and she absolutely hated that. Almost as much as she hated that he'd noticed. He was a looming presence in front of her, the lamp post behind him casting him in shadow. Maybe it should have intimidated her. She shivered again, and it was nothing to do with fear, or the cold.

It was all to do with him. The fact that she had been looking at his muscled torso all night, even though she'd tried not to. The deep charcoal of the fabric creasing into perfectly symmetrical contours. Six, no, eight well-defined ridges below his broad chest.

'So, you don't want my jacket,' Adam said, thoughtfully. 'And I don't want you to be cold. Any ideas how we can warm you up?'

She was so panicked at the million different ways that she wanted to answer that question but knew that she couldn't if she wanted to retain any sense of sanity. Finally the words that left her mouth, quite without her meaning them to, were, 'Race you!'

You would think that being best friends with an ultrarunner, that acting as support crew for someone who frequently ran a hundred miles *for fun*, she might have picked up a few tips. Like, not marathon-running skills, but perhaps the ability to reach the end of the street without feeling like she might die. Unfortunately, it turned out that cardio health wasn't something you absorbed by osmosis, and she had to lean over at the end of the street, resting her hands on her knees, trying to catch her breath.

Adam strolled up with that long easy stride, not an eyebrow out of place, while she was there with her hands on her knees, gasping for breath, wondering whether she'd left a lung in the gutter somewhere. 'Hot,' Adam commented as he reached her while she was still struggling for air. 'Really hot.'

'Stop making fun of me while I'm dying,' she managed to gasp.

Adam only crossed his arms and leaned against the lamp post. 'Stop making it look so funny, then. How did you get to be such a gifted athlete? Please, tell me your secret.'

'Stop it,' she said again. 'Rowan does my share of physical exercise. I carry her sandwiches.'

He laughed again, the utter pig. 'Well, then, I'm glad I didn't try and beat you. I would have embarrassed myself.'

She stood up straight and narrowed her eyes at him. She took a step forward, somehow forgetting that that would only bring her eyeline to his nipples, rather than his face. And she didn't exactly feel the boost of confidence she'd hoped to get from being eye to eye. Especially as she didn't even seem to be able to lift her eyes to meet his for several long seconds. She'd never minded being short before. Other than her brothers teasing her when they were kids.

Her best friend was nearly a whole foot taller than her. But this, standing with her chin by Adam's chest, the sheer size of him unavoidable, was the absolute tiniest and most helpless she had ever felt. She tipped her chin up, thinking that somehow that would help, but she realised immediately that she'd made a gross miscalculation, because this was far more intimate than she'd been prepared for. And that was before Adam's hands came to each side of her face. His palms skimmed her cheeks, his thumbs skittering along the ridges of her cheekbones. They stopped just in front of her ears, the tips of his fingers hitting every sensitive spot along her hairline before pressing just hard enough to the nape of her neck to force a half-gasp, half-groan from her lips.

'How's the breathing going?' he asked with a self-satisfied smirk that suggested that he'd forgotten the very sensible conversation they'd had earlier about acknowledging their attraction taking the power out of it.

'Uh huh,' she breathed, knowing that it didn't answer his question at all. Aware too late that it gave away far too much about how she felt about him.

He laughed at her, gently. But it wasn't unkind. Didn't make her bristle the way so many of his comments had. Instead it made her melt and she had to look down and make sure she wasn't a puddle at his feet.

But she'd somehow forgotten his hands on either side of her face. He turned her face back up to look at him, and she could see the indecision in his eyes. That he wanted this—her—but wouldn't let himself take it. And somehow his reluctance set off a self-preservation instinct that her own doubts hadn't. She took a step back and he dropped his hands but didn't take his eyes off her.

'Talking about it was meant to stop stuff like this happening,' she observed, and Adam nodded but didn't look away.

'Feels like *stuff like this* is going to be hard to ignore.'

'We should probably be more careful,' Livia said. But she didn't move, and neither did he, and they were just standing there under a lamp post on the corner of a London street, waiting for something to rescue them from their own worst impulses. It was a police van that did it in the end, blazing past with sirens and flashing lights and so close to the kerb that she took a step backwards to be sure she wasn't in its path.

They continued to stare at each other in the fading red and blue flashes, and then turned, in sync, to walk back towards the house.

'So, any bright ideas how we stop something like that happening again?' she asked.

'You could stop literally running away from situations that make you uncomfortable,' Adam suggested.

'You were the one being suggestive. Running away was supposed to help.'

He snorted. 'Please, for God's sake, don't *help* by doing anything else that will require mouth-to-mouth resuscitation. And no more drinking together. It was a stupid idea to even come out like this. Tomorrow I'm going to give you the cold shoulder and you're going to thank me for it.'

Liv nodded.

She should really hate him talking to her like that. She hated being told what to do. So she absolutely shouldn't be feeling her nipples go hard at the thought of it. It was a cold night, she told herself. That was a much more reasonable explanation for her reaction than Adam going all alpha on her.

'It'll be like you don't even exist,' she promised him.

CHAPTER FIVE

HE DIDN'T EVEN exist for Liv—and that was exactly as it should be, Adam thought as he got ready for work. He'd barely caught sight of her for a week, and at last the tight-chested feeling he got when he thought about that moment on the street when they'd so nearly done something stupid had started to loosen. They'd been idiots, straying far too close to things that would have messed up his job and his life and—well, everything, really.

He'd never been particularly interested in a relationship before, but he'd never been terrorised by the thought of one either, not the way that Livia terrified him. She moved so…easily through the world. Tripping up the front steps of the grand regency house as if that was just what people did. As if it were a perfectly ordinary place for someone to live. She didn't stop in front of the grand facade and gaze up at it, which he was sure must be a normal reaction to such polished grandeur. Her obliviousness to it felt like fingernails across freshly grazed skin. Raw and sharp. He resisted hissing out a breath at another of those waves of resentment he'd felt ever since he'd met this family.

The house was big enough that they'd managed to

stay out of each other's way for days, but even so he should probably never have agreed to stay here. He should have known how such blatant unearned privilege would grate on him. But old habits died hard. He could have booked a different hotel—the cost had already been budgeted and accounted for, after all—but Jonathan had offered him a place to stay free of charge and the compulsion to save whenever he could was as ingrained in him as his name.

Would he have made the same decision if he'd known it would cost him his peace of mind? He laughed, grimly, to himself. Probably. Some things were worth more than peace of mind. Things like a roof over his head and breakfast in the morning. Three meals a day, every day. But it wasn't the offer of a spare room or the streets, he reminded his rapidly beating heart.

It didn't matter how many times he told himself that things were different now. His body had learned its fears and responses when he was still in primary school. It wasn't just going to unlearn them now. He didn't want to unlearn it anyway. Never knew when you might need those instincts again. No one planned on becoming homeless. He knew his mother hadn't. She had worked every hour in the day to pay the rent on their flat and put food on the table morning and night. Extra hours in the school holidays when he didn't get free school lunches and there were babysitters to pay for. It had been a finely balanced system that had worked…until it hadn't.

A fender bender in a supermarket car park had made her car undrivable, which had meant that she hadn't been able to reach half of her cleaning jobs. Their income had only been just enough to pay the rent and they'd fallen short first one month then another. He hadn't been supposed to know any of this, of course. But he'd overheard his mum on the phone. Seen the way she looked at the letters that landed on the doormat almost every morning.

And there had been no missing packing a single holdall of his things and staying on a procession of sofas. Occasionally, if they were lucky, a spare room for a while. When he'd reached his teens, he'd started working part-time but his mother wouldn't let him drop out of school. The day after he sat his final A-level exam he started a job in the city. Had talked his way onto a training scheme that usually only took graduates. Had saved every penny until he'd had a deposit and first month's rent on a flat. And then every penny after that until they could afford one with a second bedroom— he'd insisted his mum take the one bedroom in their first place. Another six months of sleeping on a sofa bed wasn't going to do him any harm.

The first night he'd had his own bedroom since his age had been in single figures, he'd shut the door and let the relief wash over him in waves. It was only the next day when it was all still there—the panic, the fear, the checking and rechecking the door, the post, their bank balance—that he'd realised having a door to close wouldn't be enough to keep all those away. That he'd realised for the first time that he'd thought that those were things that could be left behind, rather than something that was so much a part of him that it was baked into his bones.

Most of the time it was just there, quiet, under the surface. Buried so deep inside that he didn't even notice it any more. And then he'd see something, smell something, bump into someone he went to school with, and he was a child again, waiting for a long, hungry afternoon to pass.

And sometimes he'd dream. When he'd slept last night, he'd been back in the damp-smelling room they'd lived in for a few months round the corner from Livia's house. He could still feel the moisture in the walls under his fingertips, the peeling paint on the flimsy door to their single room. The broken lock on the shared bathroom door.

He'd woken from the dream with a start, stumbled, still not really awake, towards the bathroom he shared with Liv, and when he'd flicked the light switch, he'd been paralysed with confusion, staring at the marble basins and gold taps where he'd been expecting paint-flecked avocado and chipped Formica.

And then he'd caught some sort of movement across the room and realised two things at once: one, he had frozen in the doorway to the bathroom—the shared bathroom. And two, he'd been wearing only his boxers. He'd looked up as the second door to the bathroom had opened, revealing Livia in the doorway, wearing little more than he was. She'd clutched her robe a little tighter around her when she'd realised she wasn't alone.

'Adam! What the…?'

He'd opened his mouth to speak but realised he didn't know how to explain this.

How opening the bathroom door had unleashed waves of memories and anger and half-forgotten resentments. And how much, right then, that had all been turned on her and her family. Instead, all he'd been able to do was scowl at her, slam the door, and stop himself saying something that would have made a bad situation even worse.

Some damage had already been done—that was undeniable, even though Livia hadn't said a word since he'd slammed the door in her face. But he'd heard it in the way that she'd been crashing around in the cabinets. The aggressive slam of the door on her side of the room, an angry bookend to his own.

Oh, he knew that the Kinleys had had their share of tribulations. Who hadn't read about their parents' attempts to not pay the taxes that, in theory, stopped the least well off from starving in the streets? But they'd had grandparents who'd inherited a property portfolio from *their* parents, and who in turn left it to the Kinley siblings, meaning that they could raise the capital needed to appease the authorities, and still have this house and a couple of others left over.

They could cry all they wanted about how badly that had affected them, but they didn't have a clue about how hard life could really be.

How hard some people worked just to keep a roof over their heads, never mind to live in this sort of luxury.

He'd barely got back to sleep before his alarm had woken him at five. His steps were reluctant as he went down to the kitchen, hoping for a cup of coffee to kick-start his brain before he made his way into the office. Perhaps if Jonathan was already up he could give him a lift. He and Liv had managed not to see each other before work all week and he didn't want to break that run now. But to his annoyance, taking him off-guard again, it was Liv who was sitting at the kitchen island, coffee in hand as she swiped through something on her iPad.

She greeted him with a scowl.

He tapped on his phone while he was eating and pulled up an app to order a car. 'Don't bother,' Livia said, glancing up and seeing what he was doing. 'I'll drive, but I'm leaving in five minutes so you'd better get a move on.'

A monosyllabic communication style had held strong for a week now so he just said, 'Fine,' and avoided eye contact. They had been different people that night in the pub. Somehow he'd managed to ignore that she came from everything that he hated. He'd fallen victim to his libido, had seen everything that he liked about her and had somehow managed to ignore everything that he hated. Until he'd dreamed about his old life and found himself so out of place in her home that he had frozen solid.

He'd been distracted by a pretty face, he realised. Distracted from everything that was important to him. His values. The ones that his mother had instilled in him. He tried to imagine what his mother would make of her—a woman whose job and home and whole secure, prosperous future had been handed to her at birth.

Why was he even thinking like that? His mother was never going to meet Livia. He would be working with her for six months and then he'd never see her again. But he'd been irritated by colleagues before, and had never found himself worrying about what his mother would think about them. And many of them had been richer and stupider and more privileged than Livia. But he'd never cradled any of their faces between his hands either.

The conflict he felt between how utterly right it had felt to have her standing in front of him, below him, looking up at him with her lip between her teeth and so clearly holding herself back, waiting to see if he would make the first move. It had been a gift to her, that control, as if she knew exactly how much he liked having her at his mercy. There was a reason he hadn't let himself think about it. It would be utterly dangerous for her to know how perfect she felt for him, sometimes.

'I'm leaving—are you ready?' she said, and he looked up. The expression on real Liv's face so different from the tightly wound lust that he'd seen there the night they'd gone to the pub.

Liv parked the car in a reserved space outside the great steel and glass facade of Kinley Head Office.

Her great-grandparents' had bought this building in the nineteen twenties, and it had somehow survived the financial cuts that had been made to pay the tax bill her parents had run from. Apparently they could generate more income by leasing out some floors than by selling the whole thing outright.

Sometimes she wished that they'd just got rid of it. Another link to her family gone. She didn't need a building to remind her of how her parents had cut her out of their lives. She had been able to understand, sort of, that they had had to leave when the money had run out and everything had hit the fan. She could have understood anyone doing that. But it didn't explain why they had left her behind.

It was okay because she was eighteen, they'd said. In her first year at university. There was no need to turn her life upside down to leave the country with them. Especially as Jonathan was there to keep an eye on her in the holidays. It would be difficult to keep in contact regularly at the start—she'd expected that while they found somewhere to stay and got settled. But as months and then years had passed with barely more than an email a few times a year, she'd had to draw the conclusion that they simply didn't care enough to make the effort to see her. They had abandoned her. Left her behind and not looked back, even for a second.

That was part of why she had resisted Jonathan's attempt to give her a job. Because being here always reminded her of her parents, and she really had no desire to be constantly thinking about the people who were meant to love her unconditionally but had been able to walk away from her with barely a backward glance.

But something about dragging Kinley into the twenty-first century while harking back to its heritage appealed to her. She'd been working in marketing luxury goods—she'd never intentionally leveraged it, but her surname was Kinley, and her brother was the CEO of one of the oldest British luxury brands. She wasn't naive enough not to believe that had opened doors. She'd made a point of working harder than was always called for, to stave off accusations of nepotism—for her own ego as much as anything. And she liked to think that she'd earned a reputation for hard work and impactful campaigns. But apparently that reputation hadn't reached Adam, who had made no secret about turning his nose up at her being given this job by her big brother.

'About last night,' Adam said, just when she'd started to wonder whether they were going to make this awkward silence permanent.

She raised her eyebrows, waiting for him to continue.

'I wasn't staring at you.'

She frowned.

'It felt quite a lot like staring, when you were just standing there looking at me,' she said, glancing at him from the corner of her eye as she slid from the car and locked it behind her.

'I wasn't, I promise,' Adam said. He walked around to her side of the car and fixed her with a serious look that stopped her, made her look up at him, remember how much she'd liked the way he had loomed over her when they'd walked home from the pub the week before.

'Then what were you doing?' she asked, wishing that she'd managed to make her voice a little steadier. But she still had the upper hand, she promised herself, because she couldn't see a way for him to talk himself out of this one, however silver-tongued he could be when he tried.

'I was thinking.'

'About my bathroom?' Liv asked.

'Sort of, I suppose,' Adam said with a shrug that looked slightly stiff. 'About your house, in general. I kind of zoned out, and I know I should have turned away as soon as I realised that you were there and I'm sorry that I didn't. That was inappropriate of me.'

Liv narrowed her eyes. 'We're colleagues who share a bathroom. I think we passed inappropriate a while ago.'

'It won't happen again. That's all I'm trying to say.'

'Why did my bathroom make you zone out?' Liv asked, knowing that she was missing something vital, and for some reason finding that irritating. It shouldn't, she knew. It shouldn't bother her that she couldn't figure this man out. He shouldn't be anything to her, but she couldn't shake his expression when he'd stood in the doorway of her bathroom, and she wanted to know what had put that look on his face.

His lips disappeared in a thin, flat line, and she knew that he was holding back. For some reason that irked her. 'No, tell me,' she prompted him. 'I really want to know.'

'It's just so…over the top,' he told her, shaking his head.

She laughed. 'I know, it's not exactly my taste either…' but her voice died off when she saw the expression on his face. 'This isn't about my great-grandmother's taste in interior design, is it?'

He had no reason to tell her this stuff. Had no idea why all these ghosts of feelings he'd thought that he'd long dealt with were coming up now. Perhaps it was being back in London after so long. Seeing first-hand the sort of lives that were being lived literally around the corner from where he and his mother had eked out a living while sleeping on other people's sofas. He found himself completely unable to hide that from Liv. She'd seen him half naked, all his fears on show, and it was harder than he could have expected to pile those protective layers back on again.

'It's just very different from what I knew growing up. I still find it hard to believe sometimes that all this was just around the corner the whole time. Literally and metaphorically. The metaphorical part I've been getting to grips with over the years. The literal parts only started hitting me since I've been back. It's weird being somewhere so familiar and so alien at the same time.'

'You lived near here?'

He had to laugh. He couldn't have been further from this if he'd actively tired.

'For a while anyway. My mum and I stayed with a friend on Gosford Street.'

He saw her flinch and couldn't even blame her. He'd flinched when they'd walked up the street the first time, the high-rise apartment building looming at the end of the road.

'Did you stay there long?'

'A few months. Even good friends lose patience with you living on their sofa eventually.'

There was no way that she could understand what it would have been like for him. And maybe that was the beauty of it. She would no more be able to grasp the precariousness of his childhood than if he'd explained the ocean to a pampered goldfish kept in a marble-lined kitchen.

'So you moved around a lot as a child?' she asked as they walked through the lobby of the Kinley building.

'Something like that, I guess.'

'You guess? I'm trying to make small talk here and you're being less forthcoming than your average murder suspect. I didn't realise the details of your life were going to be classified information.'

'Not classified. But not everyone's childhood lends itself to sharing. Your privilege is showing again, Princess. It's not much fun explaining to strangers that you basically didn't live anywhere in particular for large parts of your childhood.'

She stood staring at him and he could see the cogs turning as she processed what he had just said. Dammit. It wasn't as if his experiencing homelessness was a secret. Objectively he knew that it was nothing to be ashamed of. But he found it hard to talk about, which meant he did so rarely, which in turn meant that most people simply didn't know that it had happened. They had reached her office, which was where they should have parted ways and got on with their day, avoiding each other as much as possible. But he couldn't just walk away after saying something like that. So when she opened the door to her office he followed her in, standing in front of her as she propped her hip against her desk and crossed her arms, waiting for him to speak.

'You were homeless?' she asked, her voice wavering slightly, presumably because she knew that she was on fragile ground.

'I periodically experienced homelessness,' Adam corrected her. 'We didn't sleep in an underpass. But we didn't have a permanent home either,' he said on a sigh. For some reason, he knew that keeping the truth from her was only delaying the inevitable.

'We?' Liv asked, and he was pleased for the reprieve of her asking about the 'who' of the situation, rather than focussing on the fact that he'd had nowhere to live. He would always be happy to talk about his mum.

'My mum and me,' he said, and something of how he felt about her must have shown on his face because Liv smiled back at him.

'You two are close?' she asked, and he saw something yearning in her expression. He softened his voice, remembering what he knew about the Kinley parents, and how they'd fled the country on the back of their tax scandal.

'Yeah,' Adam said. 'We both lived in London until she got married a few years ago and moved up to Scotland, and I decided to go too. I travelled a bit after that. It felt strange being here without her.'

'And your dad?'

Adam shrugged, because there wasn't anything to tell there. 'He's never been on the scene. Never missed him.'

'Well, there's something we have in common. Terrible dads.' Liv's wry smile didn't hide the obvious hurt in her voice when she spoke about that. 'I'm not sure that's something we should drink to,' she added, her voice slightly flat.

He let one corner of his lip turn up. 'I'm not sure we should be drinking to anything at seven-thirty in the morning.'

'Or together at all. I thought that was what we decided.'

Of course it was, because it was far too dangerous for them to have conversations that were anything other than strictly professional. They had come far too close to doing something stupid the week before, and they would have to take care not to find themselves in that sort of position again.

He had an idea for how to put some space between them. For a couple of days at least. He just needed Jonathan's buy-in before he told Liv.

'Can you meet me in my office in an hour?' he asked. 'There's something I need to talk to you about.'

Liv looked surprised, but agreed. 'Of course. I'll see you then.'

CHAPTER SIX

'SO WHAT'S THIS ABOUT?' Liv asked, walking into Adam's office, her arms crossed across her chest to remind herself as much as him that she was to concentrate on maintaining distance between them. But she drew up short when she walked into the room and found Jonathan already there. Were they going to spring more surprises on her?

'So,' Adam said as she took a seat at the table, looking directly at Jonathan. 'I've been looking over all the emails and meeting notes with the parfumier and I don't think there's anything more that we can do without visiting in person. Liv's gone back and forth on the phone and by email and we're not any further—'

'I've been doing every—' Liv tried to cut in, but Adam just spoke over her.

'I don't doubt it,' he said. 'And you've pushed him as far as I think you're able. I know you have a trip planned next month but I don't think it can wait that long. I want to go before the end of the week, which means we need all the briefing documents finished before I go.'

'Before *you* go?' Liv asked, trying to keep a lid on her temper. There was absolutely no way that he was going to take this from her. She'd put in too much work to turn this over to someone who had only been working with them for a little over a week.

'You've said yourself how busy you are, and we don't seem to be getting anywhere with this one. I thought a change of tack might help, and it would take something off your plate as well,' Adam tried to explain.

'Oh, no,' Liv said, her anger making her laugh. 'Getting Gaspard to agree to our schedule is the most crucial part of the project. This is my baby and I'm not going to let you—'

'Liv, stop,' Jonathan said, and she turned to glare at her brother. After all the effort he had put into their relationship since he had started seeing Rowan, and now he was going to take Adam's side…

'I agree with Liv,' Jonathan said, turning to Adam, and her jaw dropped with disbelief. 'This was her idea, and she knows the background better than anyone. She already has the relationship with Gaspard. It doesn't make sense not to use that.'

'Jonathan.' Adam squared up to the other man, and she saw her brother note it and his hackles rise. 'I appreciate you wanting to defend your sister, but—'

Liv watched as Jonathan pinched the bridge of his nose and winced.

'I am not in the mood to referee this right now,' Jonathan said, his jaw tightly clenched. 'Both of you go to Paris, and if you could find a way to work together without giving me the stomach ulcer I'm so desperately trying to avoid I think we would all be grateful.'

With that last rebuke, Jonathan walked out of the office, leaving her alone with Adam.

'We can't both go. That's a terrible idea,' Liv said as soon as Jonathan was gone. The very last thing she needed in her life right now was a weekend in Paris with this man who she knew it was so important that she resist.

'I agree, but I want to be in on this, so the only solution is that we both go,' Adam said, mirroring her body language and giving her a challenging look. 'Like your brother said.'

Liv shook her head, because that was madness, and he had to know it. 'You know that's not a good idea, we said—we *both agreed*—that we need to be more careful around one another. We don't want to start something that can only end badly. A trip to Paris together is a terrible idea.'

He raised an eyebrow, not backing down. Then he took a step towards her, arms still crossed, a dangerous look on his face. 'You're going to find it that hard to resist me?'

'You think it's *my* self-control we need to worry about?' Liv asked, wishing her voice hadn't chosen that moment to wobble. Ugh, he was so, so right. When he looked at her like that it was all too easy to forget herself. 'You're not as pretty as you think you are,' she told him, doing her best not to show that she was affected by him at all. 'And Paris is just a city. If I can resist jumping your bones here, I'm not going to struggle just because we're the other side of the Channel.'

'Great. I'll get Maria to make the arrangements.'

She gave him a strong look. 'If we get there and it turns out there's only one bed, you're sleeping in an alleyway, so don't even think about it.'

'We're never going to get through all of this tonight.' Liv groaned long after she would normally have headed out for dinner. Her assistant had managed to book last-minute flights, but she'd taken *as soon as possible* as literally as she could, which meant that they were flying out at seven the next morning, when she'd normally be having her breakfast, and that meant pulling an all-nighter to get the briefing documents ready to present the next day.

She had been collating market research for more than three hours in the quiet of her office, keeping herself blissfully distracted from the knowledge that first thing tomorrow morning she would be flying to the most romantic city in the world with a man whose body she desperately wanted. Probably enough to ignore his entirely objectionable personality if she didn't have her guard up at all times. But she had put together all of her own research and she'd taken these briefing documents as far as she could without consulting with Adam on his parts of it. She had been waiting for him to come to her, not wanting to show the weakness of needing him, even in a professional capacity. But they didn't have time to mess around playing games, so she pushed her chair back and walked confidently from her office, and rapped on Adam's door.

He looked up as she pushed open the door, and she saw the start of a smile on his lips before he caught himself and stopped it in its tracks.

'Everything going okay?' he asked, with his face and voice professionally neutral.

'I've finished with the research section. We need to put it together with your financials and go over the whole thing together.'

Adam nodded. Clearly he agreed that they had delayed being in the same room for as long as possible. It would be good practice for the two straight days they were about to spend in one another's company.

She sat in the chair the other side of the desk from Adam, at once hating the power dynamics it created but grateful for the solid piece of furniture between their bodies. An entirely immovable barrier between them if their self-control alone wasn't enough.

'This is good,' Adam said, looking through the pages that she had slammed onto the desk between them.

'No need to sound so surprised. Did you think I was here for my winning personality? Or did you simply think it was the Kinley name that got me through the door?'

'Are you denying that your name helped you?'

'What would you like me to do about it? I can't change who my parents are. God knows, if that had been an option I would have taken it a long time ago. Did you miss the part where they walked out and abandoned me?'

It was only as she took a couple of deep, slow breaths that she realised at some point she had got to her feet and raised her voice. Adam leaned back in his chair and held up his hands as a peace gesture.

'I'm sorry. I clearly hit a nerve.'

'Don't make out I'm being oversensitive. If you're going to imply that I'm somehow lucky in my parentage, you can deal with me being annoyed at you. This is cause and effect. Don't annoy me if you don't want me to be annoyed.'

'I just think that this would go easier if you accept your name has given you a leg-up in this business.'

'And *we* would get along a lot better if you would accept that the deeply traumatic effects of being abandoned by the parents who treated you as a princess for the first eighteen years of your life—while simultaneously dragging your family name into disgrace—might balance out some of that privilege. If you could just for a minute stop obsessing over the things I had that you didn't, you might be able to see that I've not had things as easy as you seem to think. That you have things that I'd gladly give up everything for.'

He let out a long breath, his eyes soft as he looked at her. 'Liv, I'm sorry, I didn't think.'

She shook her head, because no, he hadn't thought. 'You didn't think that spoilt rich kids have things tough sometimes too? That we can hurt? Maybe just occasionally you should count your blessings before you go on about how easy I've had it, and how tough it's been for you.'

She slumped back in her chair, feeling suddenly exhausted. She'd had no idea that emotional outpourings were so tiring. No wonder she didn't make them a regular event. No, she had to wait until she was stuck on a deadline in an office with a man she badly wanted to dislike and just as badly wanted to kiss. Because that was clearly the ideal time to lose your chill.

'You need a break,' Adam said, and she took his ignoring her outburst as a peace offering. It was a gift, really, not to have to think any more about the things that she had said.

'We both need one. And something to eat.' And with that he walked out of his office, pulling on his leather jacket and leaving her watching his behind as he headed for the bank of lifts.

Liv looked through his parts of the briefing documents while he was gone, dovetailing their work together and highlighting any areas that would need more work before they could say that they were done for the night. She glanced at her watch. They were going to be here until two, three o'clock at this rate. She wasn't even going to make it home to pack a suitcase. She sent off an urgent message to Rowan, asking her to throw a few things in a bag and send it over with Jonathan first thing in the morning. Her best friend shacking up with her brother had to have some advantages at least.

She looked up from Rowan's message telling her not to work too hard to the sound of the lift arriving back at their floor. Adam stepped out of the elevator enveloped by the smell of excellent Thai food from the place on the corner, and she honestly could have kissed him if they hadn't already agreed that that would be a very bad idea.

'I take everything back. You're my hero,' she told him, pushing their work to one side to make room for the food on his desk. Adam emptied out the carrier bags and lifted the lids on fragrant curries, fluffy white rice and a *pad thai* topped with toasted peanuts.

'We can't work with empty bellies,' Adam said, handing over bamboo cutlery and chopsticks.

Or fight, Liv silently added, because they hadn't exactly been working before he'd headed out. She talked through some of the gaps in their work that she'd found as they ate, which would have been a lot easier if she hadn't kept getting distracted by the way his fingers held his chopsticks. How her gaze was drawn to follow up to his lips. The amusement in his eyes when he caught her looking and his whole expression lit up.

'That was part one,' Adam said when the food was gone and the containers cleaned away.

'Part one of what? And of how many?' Liv asked, suspicion heavy in her voice.

'Of "we have a lot to do tonight and we're going to burn out if we don't take breaks".'

He stood up and came round to her side of the desk, holding out one hand to help her up and brandishing a set of keys in the other.

She hesitated for a moment. 'Where did you get those, where are you taking me and should I share my location with a friend?'

Adam tsked at her. 'Such little faith in me. I got chatting to the security guard. Turns out we went to the same school, I mentioned we needed a break and he let me in on a secret.'

She followed Adam up a flight of stairs, down a corridor where the floorboards were coated in a thick layer of dust, with just a few footprints on one side.

'I'm still getting quite strong serial-killer vibes, just so you know,' she told him.

'I am devastated that you have so little trust in me.' As he spoke, Adam searched through the keys until he found a long, old-fashioned type in heavy brass. The lock didn't seem to want to cooperate at first, but then gave way with a heavy clunk, and the doorway opened onto the sky.

Well, technically, it gave way onto a flat roof and a fire escape five stories up. But it was a flat roof and a fire escape with an unimpeded view all the way out across the city of London.

'This is incredible,' she breathed. 'From now on

you're always in charge of making friends with the security guard.'

There was a mossy old set of patio furniture with a rather newer looking lighter and ashtray at the centre, which at least answered the question of what the security guard used this place for.

'Let's work out here for a bit,' Adam suggested, and Liv nodded her agreement. She'd lived in London her whole life and had been a part of the Kinley family just as long. But occasionally something came along—a new view of the world—which made her entirely re-evaluate what she thought she knew about it.

She needed to write, now, while she could feel the city pulsing around her. While she was at once in the heart of it and high above, able to see it as it truly was in a way that was lost at ground level. She could see the dark shell of Grenfell tower just a mile away, and Canary Wharf blinking at her in the distance. When she looked down there were headlights and phone lights and streetlights, and when she looked up she could just make out the stars.

Sitting atop the headquarters of the family business, she could feel the Kinley blood in her veins, feel all the ways that she was connected to this company, this brand, that went back more than a hundred years. And at the same time, she was something new. She was the incomer who was going to show this brand and this business what it could be again, if it were to take a risk some time.

'I don't know that look,' Adam said when he returned with their laptops, looking at her with an air of slight concern. 'Should I be worried?'

'This is my inspired face,' she said, opening her

laptop, 'and you should only be concerned if you're intimidated by my brilliance.' He smirked and opened his own laptop, calling up the shared document they had both been working on.

'Would you stop deleting that paragraph?' Liv snapped half an hour later when he'd done it for the third time. 'I'm tired of pasting it back in.'

'Then take the hint and stop doing it,' Adam replied, not breaking the rhythm of his typing. 'We don't need it. You've made all the same points elsewhere.'

'But I make them best there.' She backspaced through a particularly verbose section on their ideal consumer that Adam kept trying to get past her.

'Kill your darlings, babe,' he said, in a sardonic tone that made her want to gouge his eyes out.

'But it's so much more fun killing yours.'

She looked up and made eye contact before very deliberately highlighting and hitting delete on the page he was working on. He didn't back down from the challenge of her stare, but instead stood up, very slowly, planting his palms on the table and letting them take his weight. Was this meant to be threatening? Liv wondered, crossing her arms and looking him in the eye before he dipped his head and leaned in closer, closer, and—oh, my God, was he going to kiss her? Liv watched him move towards her, knowing that she should be putting a stop to this, but instead licking her lips, and wishing to God that she'd brushed her teeth after their Thai food.

If this was a test, she was going to fail it miserably, she thought as Adam continued to move so slowly towards her that her mouth was watering, her bottom lip caught between her teeth in anticipation, and then finally leaned all the way across the table and—

Shut. Her. Laptop.

'What the hell?' she asked, standing up so abruptly that her chair clattered to the floor behind her. Adam stood across the table from her, hands nonchalantly in his pockets, his expression unbearably smug. He shrugged.

'Seemed like I should stop you before you deleted everything we've written tonight.'

'Before *I* did?' she asked, realising that her voice sounded strangled as Adam closed his own laptop too, casually picked up his things and gestured towards the door that led back inside. 'I think I'm done here. Going to head back to my office.'

She was absolutely not letting him have the last word and walk away from her. 'Well, you might be done here, but I'm not,' she said, following him to the door. 'You were the one telling me to make cuts,' she pointed out.

'Yes—to the parts that you had written,' he said, striding down the corridor so that she had to keep doing little trotting half-steps to keep up. She was certain that he was doing it on purpose.

'You know that I hate you, don't you?' she asked, her voice deadly serious as they reached the stairs. 'The best part of launching this perfume isn't going to be that it will inject money into the business and be a professional triumph and create family unity. It's the fact that I'm never going to have to see that smug grin of yours again.'

Adam stopped suddenly on the stairs and turned around, a step below her so she was almost at eye level for once. 'You didn't seem to mind it a moment ago, when you thought I was going to kiss you,' he said, with a deadly accuracy that pierced her right in the gut.

'I was thinking of ways to let you down gently,' she lied. 'Or, failing that, to push you off the roof.'

He snorted. 'No, you weren't. You were thinking about how good it was going to be. That you know as well as I do that we have chemistry so strong that it's making it impossible to get any work done together. That you are terrified of going to Paris with me tomorrow because you don't know how you're going to resist me.'

She crossed her arms, determined that she wouldn't show him how many accurate statements he'd managed to pack into that one little speech.

'Tell me you don't really believe all of that,' she demanded.

'I know it because I feel it,' he said, leaning closer, right into her personal space. 'Because you've been the only distraction in my entire career that I can't seem to ignore. Because I'm thinking about how close I'm going to be sitting to you on the flight tomorrow and wondering how I'm going to stop myself touching you. Because just as I was telling myself that I was pretending to kiss you to mess with you, the whole thing was playing out in my head and I've never wanted anything as badly as I wanted that kiss.'

She stared at him, unable to believe that he'd just offered all those secrets up. Made himself as vulnerable as he was asking her to be. More, because he'd gone first and she could turn around now and lie and tell him this was completely in his head and she could walk away from him without a second thought.

But she'd hesitated too long for that. Stared at him too long. Let her eyes sweep down his body, and back up to his face, and she was certain that every filthy thought she had about him on the way was written all over her face. What was the point of denying it when he already knew everything?

'So what do we do about it?' she asked, her voice so low it was nearly breaking.

'We've tried ignoring it,' he said.

She nodded. 'Didn't work.'

'Not for me.'

'Then I think the only thing we can do is go with it. We get this out of our system, now, before it gets in the way of our work any more than it already has.'

'And, just to be clear,' he said, and she took the strangled note in his voice as a win, 'when you say that we get this out of our systems…'

'I mean we do this the old-fashioned way. We bang it out so that I can stop thinking about you every second of the day and get the hell back to work.'

He stared at her for a full minute before he found his words. 'Fine. If that's what it's going to take. My office or yours?'

Instead of answering, Liv grabbed him by the shirt and shoved him against the wall, taking full advantage of the way the staircase evened out the difference in their height. She crushed his lips with hers, determined to win at least once tonight. He'd driven her to absolute distraction. Forced her to face the truth of how she felt about him, what she wanted, and now she was going to make him pay.

Except, he didn't seem to understand that this was a punishment. Because he groaned with pleasure and tightened his arms around her waist, pinning her tight against him. Then he was sliding his hands down her thighs, catching her behind her knees, lifting and turning at the same time so that she was the one against the wall now.

And he simply refused to meet her punishing pace, responding to her bruising kisses with tenderness, gentleness. Until he was going so slowly that she pulled her mouth away from his in frustration, pushing at his shoulder to get his attention.

'What the hell is this?' she asked.

'I thought we'd already talked about what this is.

'We never talked about being *nice*.'

He had the absolute balls to laugh at her. She was going to kill him, just as soon as she'd got what she wanted from him.

'I hate you,' she said again, which only made him laugh at her again. She tried not to react when he started trailing the lightest of kisses along her jaw. When his hands stroked along her thighs where they were locked around his waist. But she couldn't stifle the sound that escaped her when his fingers found the buttons at the front of her shirt and pinged them open, one by one. When she reached for his belt buckle, desperate to get what she wanted, to get this over with, he grasped her wrists and pinned them to the wall, then leaned back when she tried to kiss him again.

'You just want to torture me,' she accused, knowing that her expression was petulant.

'If you've got a problem, feel free to make a complaint to HR. Personally, I see no point in rushing,' Adam said. 'If we're going to do this, we're going to do it properly. I want you well and truly out of my system and that means being thorough. The torture's just a bonus.'

She groaned and let her head fall back against the wall, realising for the first time that the harder she pushed, the more he would resist her attempts to get this over with quickly.

'This is meant to be hate sex,' she reminded him as he walked them both towards his office, then cleared the papers from his desk with one sweep and dumped her unceremoniously on the edge of the table, so that she had to look up at him, feeling dishevelled and out of sorts, while he looked…

He looked so hot she didn't know what to do with herself. She knew that if she reached for his belt again, he'd only slow down further. So she leaned back on her hands, letting her shirt fall apart and reveal the silk and lace of her bra. He wanted torture? Fine. Two could play at that game. She glanced down at herself, teasing the edge of the lace with a fingertip, and then looked back up at his face, to make sure it was having the desired effect.

His jaw was so tense that she worried they'd be calling an emergency dentist before they left for Paris. Well, good. She had him exactly where she wanted him. She pushed her shirt off one shoulder and then the other, and, oh, would you look at that, one bra strap just happened to fall too, so that the top of her breast was offered up to him, and it would take the tiniest of nudges from him to reveal her hard nipple, just peeking from under the lace.

This time when she reached for his belt, he didn't try and stop her. In fact he held himself so deadly still that she knew that he was clinging onto self-control by the tiniest, most fragile of threads. She smirked to herself. She was going to break him, and afterwards she'd make him thank her for it.

'You look pretty pleased with yourself,' he observed from somewhere above her head, his voice strained.

She licked her lips, because she absolutely was pleased with herself, she thought as she tugged down his trousers and boxers and gasped an inbreath when Adam caught her wrists and leaned over her, so that she had no choice but to lean back, let him pin her hands to the wooden tabletop, feel his weight pressing her down. 'But you should know that I'm going to make you pay for that,' he said, before he crushed her mouth with a kiss.

He refused to break her gaze as he hooked an arm behind her knee, pulling her close. And all of her urgency fell away. Because she didn't want this to be rushed. She didn't want this to be over. If this was all they were going to have, she wanted it to last. Maybe for ever. This was so much better than fighting. This was so much better than winning. One of Adam's hands came to the side of her face and she turned her cheek into it, biting the inside of her mouth to cut through the intense wave of tenderness she felt for him at that moment.

'Okay?' he murmured, close to her ear, and she pressed her lips against his skin, savouring the taste of him, the closest to a 'yes' that she could manage while her mind was reeling and her body falling apart.

CHAPTER SEVEN

LIV'S THOUGHTS CAME back to her slowly as she tried to catch her breath, lying on the floor of Adam's office, looking up at the underside of his desk, not entirely sure how they had got here. Or, if that was meant to be a fight, whether she had won.

She sat up and looked around her, wondering what had happened to her bra. Eventually she spotted it hooked over the corner of the computer monitor, and her panties on the office chair, so she slid those on first and gradually started putting herself back together.

'Mmm...' Adam said, still lying on the floor, propping himself up on his elbow so that he could watch her. 'I guess we should get back to work.'

'If we don't, that was a complete waste of time,' she pointed out, trying to locate her usual bluster, but unable to resist a smile when he laughed at her. It was so much more difficult to be angry with him after they'd had sex. It wasn't the ideal working relationship, she had to admit. But from where she was sitting, it didn't seem so bad right now.

Probably, it would be simpler if that had been a little less good. If she had stuck to her guns and made him take her quickly against the wall in a stairwell rather than letting herself be lulled into…feelings and gentleness and what felt suspiciously like an emotional connection between them.

But that was just hormones messing with her head. Right now, she was bathed in endorphins, but she knew better than to mistake them for something real.

She sat in his office chair once she was dressed, as Adam was pulling on his trousers, and opened her laptop. There were only five hours before their flight, and this had to be finished. Adam took the seat opposite her without a word, which she refrained from mentioning because just because they'd had sex didn't mean they had to be all polite with one another. And she got back to work on their shared document.

They worked without speaking, their rapid-fire typing the only sound breaking the growing quiet of the night, glancing occasionally away from their screens to make eye contact over a snarky comment or deleted paragraph. But somehow, it worked. Their combined business experience, their completely polar-opposite life experiences. They complemented one another and challenged one another and created something that surpassed anything either of them had done alone.

Jonathan knocked on the door at six, and she glanced up at him, realising they had barely moved except for the odd bathroom or coffee break. He frowned, and then looked a little too knowing at the sight of her in Adam's seat.

'Everything okay here last night?' he asked. She made absolutely sure not to make eye contact with Adam, knowing that the briefest of glances would give them away.

'Fine, we're all done,' she said, shutting her laptop and faking a smile in her brother's direction. She glanced at her watch. 'With five minutes to spare before the car to the airport gets here.'

'Rowan asked me to give you this.' He handed over her holdall, with everything that she would need for her night in Paris.

'Thanks,' she said, taking it from him. 'Was there something else?' she asked, as Jonathan hesitated in front of her.

'Just… I believe in you. You'll be great over there,' he said, somewhat awkwardly, and this time when she smiled at him, it was for real.

'Oh, Jonathan,' she said, swatting affectionately at his arm. 'Did you just have a feeling? Rowan's such a good influence on you.'

He looked heavenward and pinched his nose. 'Just go and don't make me regret it.'

She walked out of the office without looking at Adam but heard him exchanging a few words with Jonathan behind her. She stepped into the lift and turned to watch the two men. When Adam started to walk towards her, she planted her hands on her hips and let herself smile at him. As the doors started to close, she finally locked eyes with Adam's and grinned just as the doors closed with him on the other side of them.

'Well, that was childish,' Adam said when he caught up with her in the lobby after seemingly jogging down the stairs.

Liv flashed him an innocent smile. 'Just didn't want you thinking that I'd be a pushover now—'

'I've got my leg over.'

'You're so classy, Adam. That's what I like about you.'

'Get in the car.'

She glared at him as he opened the door for her and she slid into the back seat, conscious of not causing an argument in front of the staff who were starting to make their way into the building. Once the car door closed behind Adam, they fell into uncomfortable silence.

The silence held for an impressively long time. Through the car journey, into the airport, through the long security queues and right up until they were shown to business-class seats on the plane.

'I think there's been some sort of mistake,' Liv told the flight attendant.

'No, no mistake,' Adam said behind her, waving off the cabin crew with a smile. 'I upgraded us,' he said to Liv in a quiet voice, putting his carry-on into the overhead locker and holding out his hand for her case.

She stubbornly held on to it. She wasn't handing over anything without answers. 'Kinley is in the middle of a cost-saving exercise, and you organise an upgrade without even speaking to me about it?'

'I paid for the tickets,'

Liv snorted, amused. 'I'm the spoiled princess but you're the one who can't face a flight to Paris in economy? It's only an hour, Adam.'

He took a step towards her, so his voice barely had to be more than a whisper for her to hear him.

'And do you want your thigh pressed against mine for an hour without being able to touch? You'd have dragged me into the bathroom before we were even over the channel.'

Liv looked up at him, considering. Then lifted a

hand to his cheek and pulled his head down so she could whisper into his ear.

'As if you'd make it to the bathroom.'

He pulled Liv's bag from her hand, shoved it roughly into the overhead locker, then steered Liv into her seat with a hand on each of her hips. He pinned her there with a stare while he fastened her seat belt and then crossed his arms and leaned back to look at her.

'It really scares you that much?' Liv asked. 'What you feel for me?'

Adam wasn't sure what it was that hit him in the gut—Liv's words, or his own realisation that they were true. She did scare him. The chemistry between them scared him. The fact that sleeping together had made things a thousand times worse scared him.

Because they couldn't take that back. He had thought that it was hard being near to her when the sexual chemistry was all about the unknown. When he had been permanently distracted, wondering what it would be like if she let down those barriers for a minute. Wondering what she tasted like. How she would sound.

Having the answer to those questions was meant to stop him wondering. Stop him being distracted. He was meant to be concentrating right now on the meeting they were flying to. Not indulging himself in a frame-by-frame replay of what had happened in his office that morning. How was he ever going to get any work done on that desk again? But Jonathan had seen them in there. It would be way too obvious to start switching out furniture, or suddenly deciding that he'd rather hot desk.

He returned from the bathroom to find Liv still in her seat, though she had undone her lap belt.

'Are you feeling better after your caveman act?' she asked with her brows raised as he sat down beside her. He gritted his teeth and resisted the urge to snap at her. That was exactly what she wanted, so he had to refuse to give it to her.

He had to find a way to undo the damage that they had done the night before. Had to forget all the things that they had learnt about one another. It was only as the adrenaline buzz of their all-nighter was wearing off that he was realising how stupid he had been to think that this was something that he could get out of his system and then move on from.

He wondered whether she felt the same. Or if she'd forgotten it already. Perhaps she'd got him out of her system, just as they had planned. He had to know. He glanced across at her. She was staring out of the window, looking for all the world as if she were relaxed and carefree. But he wasn't all the world. He knew her more intimately than that. He only had to close his eyes and he could kiss her. Smell her. Taste her. And when he looked at her staring out of the window, he also saw the way that she tangled her fingers together. The tension in her shoulders that kept her turned away from him. She was anything but unaffected. Well, that could only make things worse.

This trip would be a challenge. There was no doubt about it. It would be stupid to think that he didn't have to be on his guard if they weren't going to end up back exactly where they were the night before. He knew that he would be tempted. He knew that he could talk himself into it again. That it was *logical* and *sensible* and that he was doing it for *reasons* rather than because he wanted her so desperately that he couldn't resist her for a moment longer.

He couldn't allow himself to get any more involved with her than he already was. He knew that relationships only worked if you were prepared to be vulnerable, and he had learned early on that being tough was how he'd survived. How he and his mother had dragged themselves out of poverty and homelessness. He had finally found stability. Security. And he wasn't prepared to jeopardise that by introducing an element as disruptive as Livia Kinley.

The business-class seats did their job, and he was able to get through the whole flight without touching Liv—accidentally or otherwise—and thank God Liv seemed as determined to stay away from him as he was from her.

By the time that they were checking into their hotel, he had been lulled into a false sense of security. So when they reached the reception desk, and the receptionist's brows knitted together, he was instantly back on his guard.

'Is there a problem?' he asked as the receptionist clicked through different pages.

'Are you certain you booked two rooms?' she asked in lightly accented English.

'Yes!' they both said with such force that she looked up at them in surprise.

'I have both your names assigned to a double room at present, but—'

'No. That is unacceptable,' Adam said.

At the same time as Liv declared, 'Absolutely not. Find us another room. I don't care how you do it.' Liv didn't want to know what their expressions were show-ing to make the receptionist have to try hard, as she clearly was, to hide her smile.

'Well, I have no regular rooms, but I would be happy to upgrade you to a suite at our expense. Would that be acceptable?'

'Separate bedrooms?' Liv and Adam both asked together, making the receptionist smile at them prop-erly this time.

'Separate bedrooms,' she confirmed. 'And a shared living and dining space.'

'That's fine,' Liv said. 'Thank you.'

'My apologies for the confusion with the booking. I hope it won't affect the rest of your stay.'

Adam nodded, his jaw tight. 'I'm sure it won't.'

They followed her directions up to the suite, and when they felt the door close behind them, she felt the ten-sion ramp up.

'Was the universe trying to interfere?' Liv asked as she set down her bag.

'Just an administrative error,' Adam said, rubbing his hand over his jaw. 'It doesn't mean anything. And it's fixed now anyway.'

'Right,' Liv said, crossing to one of the doors, and finding behind it a bedroom with a view of the Eiffel Tower.

'Shotgun this room,' she called over her shoulder. She walked to the huge windows and looked across the city to the tower.

'Whatever you want, Princess,' Adam called back to her.

She smiled to herself because his jibes didn't sting

any more. Instead, they did something much more dangerous. They warmed her, sparked memories of the night before, which couldn't be anything other than a mistake. They'd dodged one attempt by the universe—or the hotel's booking system—to try and throw them back into the same bed. Now they just had to get through the rest of this trip without doing something as stupid as they had done the night before. Because it didn't matter how they tried to justify it, last night had been a stupid idea. Had either of them genuinely believed that sex would make their chemistry better, rather than worse? Or, as she was realising now, had he simply used that excuse to take something that he'd wanted, regardless of the fact that it was dangerous?

Well, at least they wouldn't be able to fool themselves with that logic again. Because they could be in no doubt this morning that they absolutely had not got it out of their systems. If the way Adam had turned away from her on the plane was anything to go by, his body was as up for round two as hers was. They were relying on their better judgement now to keep that from happening.

She pulled her laptop from her bag and got it set up at the dressing table in her bedroom. There was nothing like work to keep her mind occupied.

The master parfumier they were meeting with later today worked with only a select few clients each year, and had told Livia on the phone that he absolutely did not have room in his schedule to create a signature fragrance for the house of Kinley.

But he was the great-grandson of the parfumier who had created the original Kinley fragrance for her great-grandmother, and there was no chance that Liv would be leaving Paris until she'd convinced him to update his great-grandfather's vision for the twenty-first century. They had a shared history. A shared story, and Liv wasn't going to be shy about leaning on that family connection if it meant that this meeting was going to go the way she wanted it.

'Are you ready to go?' Adam asked, knocking on her door an hour later—she'd showered, changed into a smart black shift dress and given her briefing document one last read-through. If she wasn't ready now, she wasn't sure when she would be.

Which was when she made the mistake of looking up at Adam, waiting for her in the doorway of her room. Ever since she'd met him, he'd lived in a uniform of jeans, black T-shirt. That leather jacket she wanted to steal. They were on their way to a meeting. She'd got changed. It shouldn't have surprised her that he'd swapped his casual clothes for a suit. But then, the effect shouldn't have been so devastating. It was only a suit, but it was such an unexpected look on him that she couldn't help staring. Not too long ago he would have liked that, she knew. Would have liked having that power over her. But not now that he knew what they were like together.

'It's just a suit,' he said with a scowl, and she looked deliberately away from him, angry at herself for being so transparent.

But as she slid her feet into her patent black stilettos, she could feel his eyes on her, and he didn't look away until she shrugged on her cream wool coat and grabbed her bags and her papers.

It was a short walk to the parfumier's, and it was a relief to finally reach his office and allow the presence of other people to pierce the tension between her and Adam.

They were shown into a stylish room adjoining Monsieur Gaspard's office and she crossed her ankles neatly to stop herself from fidgeting. When the door to his office opened and Claude Gaspard stepped out, she couldn't help her eyes widening. What was it with beautiful men in suits in this city? He was as tall as Adam, with warm brown skin, close-cropped hair and wide, dark eyes.

But she wasn't here to look at either of the men in the room, she was here to work. She shook Gaspard's hand and then kissed him on both cheeks for good measure. 'Thanks so much for seeing us at late notice, Monsieur Gaspard,' she said. 'This is Adam Jackson. He's working with us on the launch.'

'A pleasure,' Gaspard replied. 'Please call me Claude. My great-grandfather would never have forgiven me if I'd not made time to speak with Madame Kinley's great-granddaughter.'

Liv smiled. 'Liv, please. I found their letters, you know. It seemed as if they were great friends. I think she would have been so pleased to know that their vision would finally become reality.'

'Ah, well,' Gaspard said with a laugh. 'I knew you were here to try and convince me to change our entire schedule for the next year. I suppose I should hear your pitch before I have to give you disappointing news.'

Gaspard smiled at Livia and gestured with a sweeping arm for her to precede him into the office. Adam followed them in and tamped down the urge to glower. Gaspard hadn't been flirting, he had been friendly, he told himself. Not that there would be anything wrong with him flirting with Livia. Adam had absolutely no justification for the surge of jealousy he felt in his chest at the idea.

He wasn't here being all jealous of some guy Liv had only just met. Who she was charming because she wanted to work with, not because she wanted to date. Anyway, he wasn't the jealous type, and he had no claim over Liv. They'd wanted to get each other out of their systems. That was why last night had happened. If she wanted to do the same with the wealthy, cultured, good-looking Frenchman who was smiling at her from across the desk, that was none of his business. So why did the thought of it make his fists clench until his finger muscles were stiff?

It had been his intention to take charge and lead this meeting. He hadn't even wanted Liv to be there. But she was on a roll, talking through their plans with such enthusiasm that Gaspard was hanging on her every word. He could have interrupted and steered attention in his own direction, but he couldn't think of a good reason to interrupt when she was doing just as good a job as he would have been.

She was talking schedules now, which had always been the sticking point with Gaspard. This had been the whole reason he had flown out for this meeting. But sitting watching Liv talk him round, he realised that she had this. In the end, he just sat back and enjoyed watching her work. She went heavy on heritage, the shared history of their two companies, something he would never have been able to pull off. The experience that he'd built up over the last decade counted for nothing alongside people whose great-grandparents had done business together.

Eventually Gaspard held up his hands with a smile and a laugh. 'Okay, okay, you have convinced me what a wonderful partnership this would be, and I have committed to trying—' at this point Liv gave him a hard stare '—to *trying* to find a way to make your schedule work. Now, it is my duty, as you are a visitor to my city, that I ask if you would like to have dinner with me tonight.'

Adam froze, wondering how Liv would react. Because, no matter how professionally his invitation was worded, it was painfully obvious that he was asking her on a date. Liv's shoulders stiffened slightly and he knew that she was aware of it too. He held himself utterly still beside her, wondering what she was going to say. In the end, when she smiled, he recognised that it was slightly strained. 'That's a very kind offer but I have a lot of work to do this evening. I'm excited to visit the laboratory tomorrow and I want to think over everything we've talked about today.'

Gaspard smiled at Liv magnanimously, accepting her gentle brush-off at face value. 'Of course,' he said. 'Perhaps next time you are in the city.'

'Perhaps,' Liv agreed, standing and offering her hand across the desk. Adam noted the lack of cheek-kisses this time, and then berated himself for noticing. There was absolutely no reason for him to notice or care whether Liv observed English or French social conventions at the end of their meeting.

He avoided making eye contact as he shook hands with Gaspard and they were shown out of the building. Light flooded the avenue as they exited onto the street, and Liv turned to look up at him with a beaming smile. 'I think he's going to do it,' she said.

'I think there was a point in that meeting when he would have given you anything that you asked for.'

'What's that supposed to mean?'

She stopped and glared at him, stepping in front of him with a hand on his chest so that he couldn't ignore her.

'Nothing. I'm sorry, I shouldn't have said anything,' Adam said, trying to sidestep around her. But she stepped in front of him again.

'No. Tell me what you meant.'

He hesitated, but then the words burst out of him, uninvited. 'He asked you out.'

'He was just being polite,' she countered. 'I'm sure the invitation included you too.'

He had to laugh. 'I'm absolutely certain that it didn't, and I think you know that too.' She shrugged his comment off, turned around and carried on walking back to their hotel.

'I'm not going to apologise for him asking me out.'

'I never asked you to. Why would I even expect that? It's nothing to me if you go out with him.'

Liv snorted, which really irritated him. 'Really, it's nothing to you if the girl you had sex with last night agrees to a date with a gorgeous French guy right in front of you? Sure, you're a very cool customer.'

Adam forced himself to shrug, though he was sure that it looked stiff and unnatural. 'We both agreed that it didn't mean anything. If you wanted to go to dinner with him, you could have said yes.'

'I know that I *could have* said yes. I didn't need your permission, but I didn't want to! Why would I want to go out with him when last ni—?' Liv stopped, cutting herself off. 'We've got completely off track,' she said after a long deep breath. 'I didn't want or expect him to ask me out. I didn't want to go so I said no.'

Adam put a hand to her shoulder, and she stopped as soon as he touched her. 'I'm sorry,' he said, really meaning it. 'I was just being…'

'Jealous and annoying?'

His instinct was to deny it, but he couldn't. He *was* jealous, and Liv knew it, and it was pointless to deny it.

'You're right. I was jealous. I know it doesn't make any sense.' It was surely just some lizard-brain, cave-man response to sleeping together. That was all this feeling was. Right now he'd ignore the fact that he'd had sex plenty of times without getting attached before. Without ever feeling jealous.

It didn't mean anything because he wouldn't let it mean anything. All he had to do—*all* he had to do—was not have sex with Livia again. That really shouldn't feel like as difficult a prospect as it currently did.

'So you wouldn't really have been okay if I had gone to dinner with him?'

Somehow honesty seemed to work between them. Burying their feelings only made them more potent. So he told the truth. 'I would have been gutted if you'd gone out with him,' he said.

'Good, because if the roles had been reversed, I would have scratched their eyes out.'

He tried not to let his smile show, but could feel his mouth twitch at the corner. 'Well, I'm not going out to dinner with Gaspard,' she said, 'and it would be too tragic to get a table for one in Paris, so are we going to eat together tonight?'

'Working dinner with room service?'

She shook her head. 'We barely stopped for dinner last night. We've earned a couple of hours off.'

'You told Gaspard—'

'I know what I told him. Anyway, I'm not sure that dinner in our room is a good idea.'

Adam smirked at her. 'Afraid you won't be able to resist me?' Liv didn't smile back.

She looked at him seriously, enough of a change of tone to make him break his stride. 'What?' he asked.

'Do you think it worked?' she said, and he couldn't be sure what she meant. Couldn't answer her if he couldn't be sure what she was asking. 'Do you think we got each other out of our systems?' she asked, catching her bottom lip between her teeth, showing her discomfort.

Selfishly, he wanted her to go first. Not to have to be the one to expose their vulnerabilities. But she had asked the question, and they had been intimate enough that he felt he owed her honesty, if nothing else.

'I don't think it did. Not for me at least,' he confessed. 'I want you just as much as I did before. More, probably.'

She listened to him in silence, leaving him desperate to know what she was thinking. Was she going to come out and tell him that this was completely one-sided now? He drew in his emotional armour, getting ready to front this out if it turned out that he'd just made a huge mistake.

'It didn't for me either,' she admitted with a groan. 'And I hate how much I liked you being jealous.'

'That's bad,' Adam acknowledged.

'You don't have to tell me that,' she said as they reached the hotel, stopped briefly at reception to ask for coffee to be sent up, and then took the old cage elevator up to their suite.

'So what do we do about this?' Liv asked, as she kicked off her heels and dropped onto a couch. 'Ignoring our attraction to one another didn't work, and we've tried getting it out of our systems but that didn't work either. I don't know what else we can try.'

'Well,' Adam said, sitting beside her and leaning forwards, his elbows resting on his knees. 'Really there are only two options…'

She looked up at him, her expression urging him to go on.

'We either have sex again or we don't,' he said, and Liv laughed at his bluntness.

'I guess that's what it comes down to,' she agreed.

'We've tested both options already,' Adam went on, 'so the question isn't what does each achieve—because we already know that they both lead to the same place: to wanting one another. So that leaves us with the risks to evaluate.'

'I can't believe you're subjecting our…' She paused, and he waited for her to finish her sentence and define whatever this was that they were doing here. 'Whatever,' she finished, wimping out of giving this any kind of name. 'I can't believe you're doing a SWOT analysis to decide if we should have sex again.'

'Do you have a better idea?' Adam asked, and she shook her head.

'I'm so embarrassed that I don't. Business school nerds are the worst.'

'So if we don't have another idea, let's do the analysis. Having sex. What are the threats? Go.'

Liv thought for a moment. 'You fall madly in love

with me, get too attached and make things awkward when I break your heart.'

Adam snorted. 'Somehow, I think I'll survive. But you make a good point. Once wasn't enough. What's to say twice would be? Or three times? Four?'

'So the biggest threat involved with having more sex is…wanting more sex?'

'Honestly you're not making it sound that threatening.'

'So come up with something else. There have to be other good reasons not to do this.'

'It could distract us from our work. Ruin things with Gaspard.'

'I'm a professional. I'm not that easily distracted. You have a very high opinion of how good you are at sex.'

'You think I couldn't distract you from your work?' Adam asked, with a dangerous smirk. 'We're doing a SWOT analysis on our affair right now rather than something more productive and you haven't even seen me naked yet.'

Liv groaned. 'Don't talk about being naked when we're trying to make good decisions. Think of another reason not to do this.'

'Your brother might kill me?' he suggested, which made Liv roll her eyes.

'I don't care about that.'

'Babe. You're really not helping,' Adam pointed out.

'Nor is calling me babe. I don't like it.'

That got one of his proper smiles. 'Why do you think I keep doing it?'

'I hate you,' Liv declared with a melodramatic sigh, leaning back on the couch with a hand over her face.

'That seems like it would be a good enough reason not to have sex with me,' Adam pointed out. She pulled her hand away and narrowed her eyes at him.

'You'd think so, wouldn't you?'

'So we've got…nothing?' he asked, his elbows on his thighs.

'The worst we've got is that it'll make us want more sex—not an effective deterrent—or that we'll end up liking each other, which is just not realistic.'

'So, we should just go with it?' he asked.

She shrugged. 'As long as we don't bring feelings into it, I can't see what harm it could do.'

'You really need to work on your sweet-talking game.'

'If you don't like it, feel free to walk away. You'd be doing us both a favour.'

He stood from the couch, and for a moment she wondered whether he was going to take her up on her suggestion and walk away. Instead, he came to stand directly in front of her, nudging her knees apart until he was between her thighs. She let out a shaky breath as she looked up and met his gaze, which was more intense than she had ever seen it.

Adam held out his hand to her, and her palm was in his before she had even decided to do it. When he pulled her to stand he was close, too close, and she had no choice but to let him help take her weight if she didn't want to topple backwards. Adam wrapped his arms around her waist, and hers came up around his neck. She knew what came next; she could feel Adam's breath on her lips. She wasn't quite sure why they weren't kissing already. Why she wasn't kissing him. All she knew was that brushing her lips on his was putting everything on the line. She caught her lip between her teeth instead, wondering if it was too late to back out now. Oh, she had no worries about Adam pressing her to do something she didn't want to. It was her own judgement, her own self-control that she couldn't trust.

Kissing Adam when they'd both agreed it was a one-off was one thing. But this had suddenly become frighteningly open-ended, and the stakes were maybe too high.

But this was just stalling because as intimidating as this was, it was also inevitable. She'd spent the last twelve hours not kissing Adam and she knew that her resolve was running on fumes. This was going to happen. The only questions were how, and how much it was going to cost her.

Not getting emotionally involved had never been a problem before. Once she'd been abandoned by her parents—the very definition of having your heart broken—it had become second nature to keep her feelings out of her relationships. What was the point of putting your heart on the line when you had unequivocal proof of how easy you were to leave? She would have to be a masochist to start something knowing how bad it hurt when the person you loved didn't love you back.

Rowan had been the exception. Whatever benevolent higher power had engineered them sharing a flat at university had been her saviour. She hadn't *let* herself love Rowan, it had just happened, slowly, over time. It had snuck up on her without her realising it was something that she should have been guarding against. It had never occurred to her that Rowan could break her heart. Until she had fallen in love with Jonathan. Oh, Liv was pleased that they were happy, of course.

But Rowan had been *hers*. She'd been the person she'd relied on most since her parents had left. And now? Rowan had promised Liv that nothing would change. But how could that be true? She would put Jonathan first now. Liv knew how selfish it made her to even think that. But she couldn't help it.

Adam tucked a strand of hair behind her ear and gifted her with a smile.

'I don't think your heart's in this,' he said, his hand cupping her cheek. 'Please tell me you're thinking better of this and you're going to save us from ourselves.'

She gave herself a mental slap on the forehead. This was Adam she was talking about. He'd made himself absolutely clear that he didn't want anything more than sex. There couldn't be a safer man to have a series of one-nighters with and then leave. It was the most honest she had ever been going into a relationship. So, finally, she pulled him down, pressed her lips on his, and gave herself permission to stop thinking. Let Adam do the thinking. He was never going to give her any reason to think that this was more than it was. And that would keep her safe too. All they had to do was keep this about the sex, and not let feelings creep in at the edges.

CHAPTER EIGHT

LIV DROPPED BACK on her pillow, trying to catch her breath, trying not to think how embarrassing it would be to die in a foreign hotel room of too much sex. She glanced across at Adam, who had hit the pillow next to her, his skin shiny from sweat, chest heaving as he tried to catch his breath.

'I need some air,' Liv said, pulling the sheet off her bed and wrapping it around her as she crossed to the curtains and the balcony beyond. She drew back the drapes and gasped. She'd somehow forgotten that she'd selected this room for its view. The light show from the Eiffel Tower spilt into the room and she followed its path to her bed, where Adam was stretched out, entirely unabashed by the fact that her theft of the sheet had left him naked. He'd stretched one arm up behind his head, and, despite the hours they had just spent in her bed, there was still heat in his eyes.

'I'm starving,' she said, and Adam smirked. She rolled her eyes. 'For food,' she clarified, whacking him on the chest. 'Don't be so predictable. I need to eat something.'

'Room service?' Adam asked as she stepped back towards the bed.

'I don't trust you not to get distracted,' she replied, finding a robe on the back of the bathroom door and throwing it at him. 'Put some clothes on,' she told him, and then stepped back in the bathroom to turn on the shower. 'I'm taking you out for dinner.'

Adam let the shower wash the scent of Livia from him, his skin stinging from the water pressure.

There was no point in second-guessing their decision to go to bed together. An altogether different experience from his desk, or the floor of his office. It had been inevitable. Had felt that way since the minute that he'd met her. She was less distracting when they weren't trying to pretend not to see something that was right in front of them.

And he didn't need to worry about getting too involved. She had made it perfectly clear that she was no more interested in that than he himself was. And dinner? It wasn't as if it were a date. She was right: they both needed to refuel, and that was unlikely to happen if they didn't leave their suite.

He was still pulling his T-shirt over his head when he walked into their living area. She was in jeans, trainers, a white T-shirt knotted and revealing a strip of skin at her waist. He hadn't realised how much he'd needed to see that she wasn't treating this like a date. Her still-damp hair was scraped back into a high ponytail, her face free of make-up, and his gaze caught on the freckles across her cheekbones, the bridge of her nose. The sight made him want to drag her back to bed, pin her to the mattress until he'd made a thorough survey and kissed every one of them.

'Ready to go?' she asked, an inquisitive expression

on her face. His brain stumbled a moment, realising how distracted he'd let himself get.

'Yeah, ready,' he replied, pulling on his shoes and grabbing keys and his phone from the table. They both turned to the stairs rather than the lift, keeping moving, avoiding the forced intimacy of that enclosed space. They shouldn't need to take such measures now that they'd decided to stop fighting their attraction. But sex wasn't the same thing as intimacy. It was good that they were being cautious right now. These post-coital, endorphin-flooded moments were the most dangerous. It would be too easy to let their hands brush together, to twine their fingers. To set a pattern that would blur the lines between what this thing was, and what it wasn't.

They paused outside the hotel restaurant downstairs, and Adam raised his eyebrows. It was atmospherically lit, and from the lobby he could see crisp white tablecloths and candles glinting on crystal. It was the very picture of Parisian romance. He risked a look at Liv, who was looking slightly green beside him. 'Walk and find somewhere else?' she suggested.

'God, yes,' he said, letting out a breath.

'What's with you?' she asked. 'How can you be so tense?' They walked out onto the street, a wide, elegant boulevard, and turned towards the river. 'I feel like I'm made of noodles.'

Adam smiled. His smug feeling of self-satisfaction was entirely involuntary. Liv was right, though. He was tense. He could feel his shoulders up somewhere around his ears. They reached the river and stopped, leaning on the balustrade, watching the water. He took a couple of deep breaths and let his shoulders fall.

'There's a lot riding on this trip,' he said. Liv nodded, and he thought he might just get away with that obfuscation.

'So you're not freaking out about the fact that we had sex and then were immediately faced with one of the most romantic cities in the world? And now you're not wondering if I meant it when I said I wanted this to be casual and you're spiralling and wondering how you're going to get out of this without breaking my tender female heart?'

Adam laughed, turning away from the water and leaning back, looking across at her.

'I think at the moment I'm mostly worrying about how you can read me like a book.'

'Well, stop worrying. And stop with the brooding expression. It's making me want to kiss it off you, and my tender female heart is still absolutely starving.'

'Fine, fine,' he said, pushing away from the wall and grabbing her hand to pull her with him. They were halfway to the bar on the corner before he realised what he'd done. It was nothing. Just a casual gesture to ensure that they were walking in the same direction. He fought down the urge to flex his fingers, knowing it would only draw her attention, make her think that he thought it was a big deal. Something other than a completely unremarkable gesture.

When they reached the bar—loud, lively, not in the least romantic—he dropped her hand and reached for the door. He reached past her and pushed the door open in front of her. They pulled up stools at the bar, and Liv looked through the wine list before ordering herself a glass. Adam ordered himself a beer and they both ordered food. They could eat right here at the bar, the furthest thing from a romantic dinner for two that he could imagine.

He should be sated, he thought. He'd had more sex than he'd had in a year. A rare steak and a cold beer. They'd had a good meeting that morning, with the promise of another tomorrow. There was really no reason he could think of for this mild sense of dissatisfaction in his chest. It was because they hadn't slept the night before. He was tired. That was all.

'Ready to call it a night?' Liv asked, as the music slowed. Their plates had been cleared, their glasses refilled. The atmosphere was edging closer to intimate, and Adam was looking as if he needed to bolt.

It was adorable, she thought, how utterly terrified he seemed. As if, if he wasn't careful, feelings were somehow going to sneak up on him and bite him. If he wasn't constantly vigilant.

'Time to go,' Liv suggested, and Adam practically sprang from his seat.

'Yeah, if you want,' he said, as if the thought had only just occurred to him and he hadn't been glancing at the door every thirty seconds for the past ten minutes.

'You're twitchy,' she commented as they walked back towards the hotel. 'It's giving me a complex.'

'It's not you, it's me,' Adam said, forcing an eyebrow raise from Liv. 'I'm generally not great at the whole talking thing. *"I had a difficult childhood, blah-blah-blah..."* This just feels...unsettling. I wasn't expecting it. And in my life, unexpected and unsettling has never led anywhere good. Feeling like I don't know what is round the corner—I don't know. I guess it's tapped into something.'

She bumped her side against his. 'You don't need to feel unsettled. You can just ask me what's going on if you feel like you don't know.'

He gave her a weak smile. 'I know. And you've already told me what you want. It's not about that.'

'Then what is it about?'

'I don't know. I'm not used to feeling like this. Like I've had too much of you and like I can't get enough. Like I need you.'

She frowned as they walked along, doing her best to understand. 'And needing someone is a bad thing?' she asked. 'Set aside the fact that it's me, for a moment. Let's just talk hypothetically.'

Adam nodded. 'Needing *anything* is a problem when you can't be certain you're going to be able to get it,' he explained. 'We, I, *people* already have enough needs: something to eat, somewhere to sleep, some way of keeping warm. Hope—a way out and a plan to get all of those things.'

Liv was starting to understand, and it made her ache for all he had suffered. Not that she could ever tell him that, of course. 'And what about someone to care about?' she asked. 'To care about you?'

Adam shook his head. 'I have that. I have my mum. She's been the one constant whatever was going on in my life. I have unconditional love from her, because she's been through it. Seen it all. I can't expect that from anyone else. I can't let myself want something when it's out of my control.'

Which made sense of why he was so jumpy at even the thought of an emotional connection with her. It was lucky for him, for both of them, that they were both as messed up as each other. That simple fact—the fact that they had both been irreparably damaged—was what was going to make this work.

'And here I am avoiding intimacy because the people who were meant to love me unconditionally didn't. We're a pair.' She forced a smile, because what else could you do?

'Mutually hopeless,' Adam agreed.

'Well, maybe that's a good thing,' Liv mused. 'Surely two such messed-up people can manage a short affair without it turning into something more serious.'

Adam nodded, and she felt something unclench inside her, some part of her she hadn't realised had been terrified that he was going to end this. 'I promise if I see you getting even remotely attached, I'll get rid of you.'

She laughed, but it sounded a little forced. 'Do you want to go straight back, or go for a walk?' Adam asked, changing the subject. 'We've seen barely anything of the city. It'd be a shame to go back to London having seen nothing but the inside of the hotel.'

'Oh, I don't know, I think I'm going to have fond memories of that particular hotel.' Adam grinned, and she couldn't help smiling back. 'Do you ever think we might be in trouble if a moonlit walk in Paris is the safer option?' Liv asked as they reached the Eiffel Tower.

She walked close to the tower, looked up so the gridded ironwork was a dark silhouette against the sky. Around her, she was aware that everyone else was hand in hand—or taking loved-up selfies—and she begged the universe not to let anyone drop to one knee and propose, drawing further attention to the fact that this was one of the most romantic spots on the planet. But the universe held, and the other couples drifted away leaving her and Adam alone.

'You're a nice guy,' she felt compelled to say, in an awkward moment of silence. Then she turned to look at him, mortified at what she'd just said. His gaze was fixed ahead and only the ticcing muscle in his jaw gave away that he'd heard her at all. She could see how nervous he was about what she was going to say, as if she were going to force him to have some feelings. She hid her smile.

'I'm just saying. You're an okay guy and if you met a girl less messed up than I am, you would probably make someone an okay, you know, guy.'

He glanced sideways, clearly still perturbed.

'God, that's it,' Liv said. 'Would you stop looking at me like I'm trying to trap you or something? Shall we just go back to the hotel and have sex now?'

He grinned, the relief coming off him in waves.

'God, yes. Let's go.'

They walked away from the tower side by side, and when his arm looped around her shoulders it felt friendly, not anything scarier. And it was friendly when they came through the door to their suite and he reached past her waist to lock the door. It was very friendly when she found herself caged by his arms with his hands resting on the door either side of her head, one thigh pressed between her legs, nudging her knees apart, and she knew he was teasing her, waiting for her to snap and turn this from something sweet into something fiery and fast and hard. But they'd done that. Several times, and she hated to repeat herself.

So she waited, wondering what else they could come up with, but the drawn-out tension of the moment curled in her chest as her ankle curled gently around Adam's calf, and she let her head fall to one side. If Adam wanted to go slow, then she was going to see what it felt like to be okay with that. What would she learn about him, about herself, if she didn't follow her usual playbook and allowed this to go somewhere different? It was still just sex. Just a different tempo than she was used to.

Adam lifted her and moved them through to her bedroom, and neither of them broke away to pull the drapes. And so when his mouth moved against hers in time with his body, he had reflected lights from passing cars across his bare shoulders. When she turned her head towards the window, unable to take the sweetness she saw in his expression, she could follow the lights on the tower where they had been standing a couple of hours before, when she had told him he was a nice guy, and not realised how dangerous that made him. Now she knew that she had been wrong, he wasn't just nice. He was achingly sweet. Gentle, now that she wasn't making him fight her for every concession.

It was too late to protect herself now, when he had drawn out everything she had to give and had made her beg him to take even more. His eyes met hers, and she felt the echo of her own feelings in his body as something passed between them, something intangible that twisted in her chest and tied her to him.

This was why she'd resisted, before. Why she always took control, took what she wanted. Because when she was calling the shots she could always be sure that she wouldn't be asked for more than she could give.

That was why she'd pushed him against the wall and kissed him so hard that she couldn't think. Because that was safer than this. Safer than feeling something shift in your chest and knowing what you were doing couldn't be undone. Knowing that you wanted more and wouldn't be able to stop yourself taking it.

With anyone else, she would have squeezed her eyes shut. She would have made a joke and flipped the guy on his back and have taken control again. But when Adam's wide brown eyes met hers, looking every bit as surprised and scared as she did, she couldn't do that to him. Couldn't leave him alone with whatever it was he was feeling. So she pressed her cheek more deeply into the palm that cupped it, and clutched Adam tighter to her with a hand in his hair, and the other at the small of his back, so that there wasn't even a breath of air between their bodies.

She held on for countless minutes afterwards, when Adam gasped heavily into her neck, and she could only guess that he was as shell-shocked as she was, and breaking away, talking, looking him in the eye would make that real. And if it was real, she would have to run.

CHAPTER NINE

THEY'D FORGOTTEN TO draw the curtains, Adam thought with a slow smile, as morning sunlight turned his eyelids pink. If it weren't for the daylight that had woken him, they could pretend that last night wasn't over.

He reached an arm out across the bed and felt a stab of panic when he realised that Livia was gone. He sat abruptly, pulling back the sheets, as if somehow she could be under there. He forced himself to take a couple of breaths to calm his heartbeat. It was fine. There was nothing wrong, this was never going to be the sort of thing that involved long, lazy mornings in bed. There was no reason to have felt anything other than a mild 'huh' when he'd realised that he was alone. Which was why his reaction scared him so much. Because somehow between arriving back at the hotel last night and waking up this morning, something had shifted inside him, and now his body no longer just liked being close to Livia, it expected it. Needed it.

He should be grateful that she wasn't here—that he'd had this opportunity to see what was happening and put a stop to it. If he even needed to. Because Liv wasn't here—did that mean that she'd already had the same freak-out that he was currently experiencing and had done the right thing for both of them and scarpered?

He should be grateful, but instead he was mildly irritated, sorry for the loss of this morning before he had to face reality and put some distance between them. Where was Liv anyway? The suite was nice, but not so large that you could lose a person in it. Even one as neatly packaged as Liv. And he was in her room. Had she left right after he'd fallen asleep—unable to bear the thought of sharing a bed with him? If she had, he couldn't decide if he was more annoyed or pleased that she'd stolen the signature move from his playbook.

He pulled the sheet around him and looked around for his clothes. He found his boxers kicked over by the dressing table and pulled them on. A quick glance in the bathroom confirmed that Livia wasn't in the shower, so he took a deep breath and opened the door into their shared living space. Livia was sitting at their dining table, croissant in hand, papers and her laptop scattered around her. 'Good morning, sleeping beauty,' she said, with a smile that seemed as if she was genuinely pleased to see him until she tamped it down to make it something more careful and polite.

'How long have you been up?' Adam asked, taking note of the empty coffee pot in front of her, and the bouncing of her toe. She was ready for their meeting in another smart dress, with her hair shiny and dried in neat waves that made him want to run his hands through it until she looked like his again. No, not his. He didn't *do* possessive. He didn't do jealous. He definitely didn't do being crestfallen at waking up alone and feeling as if he wanted to demand an explanation.

To draw her close to his body until the unquiet, insistent part of his chest settled at having her near.

He should just stick with his tried and tested morning-after routine, grab a quick shower to wash away the memories and any residual feelings and carry on with his day as if nothing had happened.

'I was starving,' Livia said, not looking up at him, her eyes on her laptop, and he fought down the urge to turn her face up to his and make her meet his eye. He didn't know what had got into him that morning. Only that he was grateful that she was more together than he was. Maybe it was because she'd already started on the caffeine. He'd feel himself again once he'd had a coffee.

'There's food,' she said, gesturing at the plates under silver cloches. 'But I finished the coffee. Go for a shower and I'll order some more.'

Adam crossed towards his own bedroom, with only a grunt as an answer—safer than words—and realised belatedly that he was still only wearing boxers. But it didn't matter, he supposed, if she wasn't going to look up from her work and acknowledge his existence. The fact that she wouldn't stung somewhere that hadn't existed before last night.

Livia rubbed the heels of her hands into her eye sockets before she looked up at the door that Adam had just closed slightly more firmly than was necessary. Perhaps the wind had caught it. Though she hadn't got around to opening any of the windows, or the door out onto the balcony.

So she had to assume that he was annoyed at her about something. Had he guessed the thoughts she'd been incapable of fighting off last night? He couldn't know, could he? She was certain that he didn't know how she'd stared at him in the half-light that morning, her eyes catching on each of the hairs in his eyebrows, following the lines that bracketed his mouth. The shadow of stubble on his jaw. She had watched him as the sun had crept over the horizon behind him, until he'd taken a deep breath, stretched and turned towards the window, and she'd slipped out of bed with her heart racing, terrified that she was going to be caught looking at him as if…as if she cared.

That he was going to know how she had felt about him, even if it had been only for a moment, before she had tamped down those dangerously tempting feelings.

She was simply going to concentrate on her work. She had an important meeting with Claude Gaspard, and she was not going to allow herself to be distracted by a boy just because she'd decided to let someone kiss her gently, for a change.

A change. That was the only reason why she felt a little different this morning than she had after previous sleepovers. Just because something felt different didn't mean that it was something to be afraid of. So why did she feel so unsettled? So tempted to push her work to one side and follow Adam into his bedroom, into the shower she could hear running in his bathroom.

No. This meeting had to go well. It would go well. She would return to London with a space for her fragrance in Claude Gaspard's schedule for that year and she would be triumphant, having done what she knew that Adam could not, that no one in her family could, and be the one who would rescue Kinley from its state of chronic cash-flow problems. That was what she wanted for her life. To make her career a success.

To show her family that she did have value. That she was worth sticking around for.

Her parents wouldn't care. If they did, they wouldn't be on the other side of the world now. They didn't care about Kinley and they didn't care about her, and they would feel the same way whether she was a success or not. It was utterly pathetic that she cared about proving herself. She had spent most of her adult life trying to protect herself from other people's opinions but still found herself vulnerable to them. It was why she still had to take a deep breath and pull on all her armour every time Jonathan called her into his office, sure before he started speaking that he was about to tell her how disappointed he was in her. Each time it didn't happen—each time he thanked her for her work, praised her for a suggestion—she felt her guards weaken slightly, a chink of belief shining through them that perhaps she had judged him too quickly. That not everyone would treat her as carelessly as her parents had. That perhaps she'd been unfair to her brother all this time.

She glanced at the clock in the corner of her screen and started to gather up her papers. Tucking them into a folder and into her bag. She knew it all. There wasn't anything else she could do now other than hope that Gaspard shared her views on how completely well suited their two companies were and agreed to work together.

Adam walked out of his bedroom in a suit, his hair parted and slicked into neatness. She let her gaze glance off him, because he was too beautiful to look at directly. She felt something lurch in her chest.

When had he upgraded to beautiful? That word

just felt so…meaningful. As if there were feelings behind it or something. As soon as they were done with this meeting, she was downgrading him back to 'hot'. Maybe that way she could look directly at him again.

'I just need to throw my things in my case,' she said, 'and then I'm ready to go.'

'Great,' Adam replied. 'If, er, you find my clothes. I…'

'Right, yeah.' She felt her cheeks heat. 'I'll go and grab them.'

'Thanks. Do we, um, need to talk…about anything?'

Something lurched. 'Why would we need to talk?' she asked with feigned ignorance. 'This was nothing, right?'

At her words, he looked equal parts relieved, and as if he had been punched in the stomach. It was comforting to see him unsettled, as she felt similarly.

'Right. Nothing. And when we get back to London?'

She tried to think about what she wanted. What it was safe to have. She shrugged, as if the answer didn't mean much to her. 'We can carry on like this, if you want,' she said carefully. 'No strings.' He nodded. Apparently considering it. 'As long as no one knows about it. I'm already combining work and family.'

'Sex and work and people knowing is too much,'

'Precisely. If no one else knows about it, I can pretend it's not happening and that makes everyone's lives simpler.'

'It doesn't exist outside the bedroom. Got it.' And suddenly, he was looking at her with heat in his eyes. 'Does a hotel suite count as a bedroom?' he asked.

She shook her head, slowly. 'No. This is definitely a living room.' She glanced at the table. 'A dining room at a push.' She allowed herself a moment of smug enjoyment at his disappointment. 'But if you followed me to retrieve your clothes, we would find ourselves in a bedroom.'

Livia collapsed into the airline seat with an exhausted sigh. She'd done it. Despite Claude's adamant conviction that he could not accommodate them, she'd shown him how good her plan was. The prestige—and cold, hard cash—that it would bring them both if he could meet her deadlines. And he'd agreed. He'd agreed.

She listened, her eyes still closed, as Adam lifted his bag into the overhead locker and then sat beside her. Bless him for upgrading their tickets. She had no intention of living up to 'poor little rich girl' stereotypes. She would have flown economy without complaint if he'd not done it. But now she was here, with space to think and bask in her victory, she couldn't be mad at him for arranging it.

'We should have champagne, to celebrate,' Adam said beside her, and she smiled and turned to look at him.

'We'll make a toff of you yet.'

'Well, even us plebs know the theory. I'm serious, though. We should. Celebrate, I mean.'

She smirked at him. 'I know how I want to celebrate, and it's not with champagne.' She grinned, and looked around them.

'Here? It's not a little…public for you?'

She blushed. 'I think I can make it back to London. You're not that irresistible.'

'In London you live with your family. Who we're hiding this from. How's that going to work?'

Liv frowned and turned to him.

'I hadn't thought about that. I think you need to find a place to stay. Quickly.'

'I'm not arguing with that. But won't your brother be suspicious if I decide I suddenly need to leave?'

'I'll be really mean to you. Make it realistic that you don't want to be there any more?'

He laughed and twisted in his seat to face her, his body language mirroring hers. 'I think I like it more now you're being nice to me.'

'Pfft, I've not been nice to you.'

He frowned, though it was distinctly mocking. 'Last night felt pretty nice. This morning too. If that was you being mean, then I think we definitely can't do that in front of your brothers.'

'It was nice,' Liv conceded. 'But I wasn't being nice to you. That was all for my own benefit.'

'Oh, really?' Adam asked, raising his eyebrows. 'Even when you—?'

Liv slapped her hand over his mouth and glanced around to check that no one was listening. When she met Adam's gaze, it was full of mischief, and he nipped at one of her fingers as she drew her hand away. Adam caught her wrist and pressed a kiss there. Then to the base of her thumb, and the tips of her fingers.

'We'll find a way,' he promised. 'We can be sneaky. It'll be fun.'

She smiled back. 'Okay. We'll find a way.' She turned to face forwards, but let her head fall to the side, resting on Adam's shoulder as the plane taxied down the runway. Once they were back in London, they would have to hide this. It was the right thing to do—the sensible thing.

It would stop these hook-ups slipping into something like a relationship. But while they were thirty thousand feet in the air, she could afford to be a little soft. To soak this up. So she smiled to herself. Nothing that happened over international waters could possibly count. So she allowed herself an indulgence that she'd usually cringe away from. She slipped her hand into his, let their fingers tangle, and leaned into his side while she caught up on some sleep. For some reason—it couldn't possibly be the hours-long marathon they'd indulged in the night before, could it?—she was absolutely shattered. She didn't even complain when Adam rested his cheek on the top of her head and pressed a gentle kiss to her hair.

But when she woke from her nap, her body still warm and comfortable tucked in against Adam's side, she knew that their time out had to come to an end. She sat up and stretched as the plane touched down onto the runway. Adam blinked awake beside her. So she'd worn him out too. She suppressed a smug smile.

Liv used her key to let them both into the town house, and they shared a conspiratorial look before she opened the door. Game faces on. She absolutely did not want her brother knowing what was going on with her and Adam. Other people seeing it would mean that she might have to look at it head-on, and if she did that, she wasn't sure that she would be comfortable with what she would see.

'You okay?' Adam asked, and she faked a smile and opened the door.

"Course I am. Why wouldn't I be?' She'd thought that she'd nailed a breezy tone, but a glance at Adam's face made her wonder. She walked into the hallway, noting the quiet, other than the clip of their shoes on the check-patterned marble of the entrance hall. 'Anyone home?' she called out, only to be met with silence.

'Empty house,' Adam observed in a neutral voice.

'Don't get any ideas,' Liv said, and he held up his hands, all innocence. 'I need to get to the office and tell Jonathan that we've got the go-ahead from Claude, and then brief the team that we're now working to our tightest projected deadline.'

Adam nodded, his posture just a little more upright than it had been a moment before. 'I'll drop the bags upstairs, then you bring the car round and we'll go in together.'

Two hours later, Liv had brought Jonathan up to date, taken a meeting with her team to prepare them for the fact that their schedule had just got incredibly tight, and then she'd started on her to-do list—which soon ran to several pages—of everything that they would have to do in order to launch their fragrance in the ideal window. She stared at the project-management software on her screen, moving different tasks, different teams, different deliverables, until she had every last task assigned and jigsawed together.

She was starting to wonder if she'd made a huge mistake pulling their whole schedule forward by a year, when there was a knock on her door. She looked up to find Adam standing there, silhouetted slightly by the florescent lights behind him. When had it got so dark in here?

He leaned into the room and flicked on the lights. 'It's late,' he said. 'Are you going home tonight?'

She stretched up, cringed at the crunching sounds that came from her spine and sighed. 'I've got so much to do.'

'More than you can finish tonight,' he pointed out. 'It'll still be there in the morning. You've barely slept in days.'

'And whose fault is that?' Liv mumbled under her breath.

'Sorry, what was that?' Adam asked, and she glared at him, because he had heard her perfectly well.

'Okay, fine. I'll go home and work there if it'll stop you nagging me. Is Jonathan going back with us?'

'He left an hour ago.'

Liv huffed. 'Part-timer. Honestly, since he and Rowan got together he's actually developed a work-life balance. I don't know what's got into him.'

'You sound jealous,' Adam mused.

'I love Rowan, but not in that way,' Liv said, deflecting the question. She unplugged her laptop and shoved it into her bag along with her phone and a travel mug.

'You know what I mean.'

She shook her head. 'I could have a work-life balance if I wanted one. I prefer a work-work balance.'

Adam took a couple of steps closer, and fixed her with an uncomfortably knowing look. 'You've said yourself Jonathan is happier,' he observed. 'Are you sure you don't want something like that for yourself?'

Liv shuddered. It wasn't as if it were really up to her anyway. Even if she decided she did want what Jonathan and Rowan had, she couldn't have it. She'd been abandoned once in her life, and she really wasn't on board with giving someone the chance to do it again.

'I like my life how it is,' she told him sharply. 'I don't appreciate being told that I'm not capable of knowing what I want. If you've decided you want something else, I'm afraid you'll have to—'

Adam stopped her with a hand on her jaw, turning her face up to his.

'Hey, stop spiralling,' he said gently. 'I want *this*. What we agreed on. That's all.'

'Good,' she said, glancing at the door and pressing a kiss against his mouth. 'This doesn't give you a say in my life, okay? I'm not being a bitch. I'm just making sure you know what my boundaries are.'

'I've got it. Now, are we going home?'

He shouldn't have used the word home, Adam told himself. Liv's house wasn't his home. He could never live somewhere like this. Somewhere so…extravagant. It was just a figure of speech. He'd lived in a hundred different places in his life, and the only place remotely like this had been divided into one-or two-room flats decades ago. He didn't belong here. He needed to remember that. Liv was right, he needed to find somewhere else to live. The thought fired up a long-suppressed fear, and he took a few deep breaths to steady himself, remind himself that he had a roof over his head tonight and enough money in the bank that he would never, ever have to sleep rough.

He glanced at the bathroom door, remembering that it connected with Liv's. If he wanted to shut out bad memories, there were worse ways to do that than to make new ones. They'd sworn to keep this a secret, that her family and her friend wouldn't find out that they were sleeping together. But they could be careful. They could be quiet. The house had been silent when they arrived home. Everyone was either out or already in bed. He didn't need to overthink this. They were casually hooking up, that was all. He opened the door before his brain demanded that he reconsider.

He scratched quietly at Liv's door, which opened in front of him before he had a chance to change his mind. Liv was wearing a nightdress that reached the top of her thighs and had fallen off one shoulder. He clenched his fist to stop himself reaching out and fixing it.

'Hey,' she whispered, but didn't move aside to let him through.

'Hey.' He stuck his hands into his pockets, leaned against the doorframe.

'Do you want to come in?' she asked, which was everything Adam wanted to hear. But there was something not right, and he didn't know what it was.

'Is that what you want?' he asked.

Liv shrugged. 'It is. I want you. I want to have sex with you. But it feels different here. Weird.' Liv leaned on the doorframe too, and he figured they were having this conversation here, half in and half out of a shared bathroom.

'You don't bring guys home?' he asked.

She shrugged again. 'Of course I do. I don't know why I'm freaking out.'

He smiled, a little indulgent, before he caught himself. He pushed himself off the doorframe and framed her face in his hands. Because he could see exactly why she felt weird. 'You're exhausted, babe,' he said, tucking her hair behind her ears and then turning her around with a hand on her shoulders and steering her over towards the bed. He pulled back the duvet and Liv climbed in with a contented groan. He bent to kiss her on the cheek, and she caught him with a hand on the back of his neck before he pulled away.

'Where are you going?'

'To bed. My own bed. You need to sleep.'

'Mmm…' she agreed, unable to stifle a yawn. 'But stay anyway. I just need a power nap.'

He laughed. 'You've got such a one-track mind,' he told her. Liv muttered her agreement, pulled him down on the bed by the waistband of his boxers, then rolled over and went to sleep. Adam hesitated. He hadn't planned on sleeping in her room. It seemed like asking to get caught. But Liv had pulled him into her bed. Wanted him to be here when she woke so that they could… He slid under the duvet before he changed his mind.

When he woke, it was to fingers gently stroking his belly, sliding along the lines where his abs would be if he weren't all soft with sleep. He smiled to himself as Liv hugged him from behind and pressed a kiss to the back of his shoulder. 'I slept,' she whispered into his skin, into the dark. 'I'm feeling much better now. Not weird at all.'

He chuckled under his breath.

'I can feel that.'

'Are you awake?' she asked. He laughed, turned over and pulled Liv into him.

'I am now. You know that you're not subtle, don't you?' he whispered into her ear.

'Good. Being subtle doesn't get me what I want.'

He rolled above her, and she squealed in surprise. He shushed her with his fingertips against her mouth. They both watched the door, breath held in suspense, waiting to see if they had given themselves away. But when nothing broke the silence other than their own breaths, Adam let himself relax.

'Can you be quiet?' he asked Liv, who was little more than shadows and warmth beneath him in the half-light. He felt more than saw her nod. He skimmed a hand down her side, found the hem of her nightgown, thoughts of which had kept him awake long after Liv's body had gone heavy and her breathing slow. She gasped but didn't make a sound when he skimmed his fingers over the hem, ghosting over soft skin underneath, retreating when he saw Liv bite down on her lip. She arched up towards him in protest, so he lifted his weight off her, resting on his elbows. When she dropped back to the mattress, he lowered his weight back onto her.

He knew what she wanted. She wanted this hard and fast, so she didn't have to think about what she was doing. She wanted to be swept away by something greater than herself.

He wanted her present.

He wanted to feel as every kiss landed on her skin, not glancing off as they turned or tumbled. He'd seen what she was doing. Had felt the difference in Paris when he'd had her, really had her, and now he wouldn't accept anything less than her being fully present.

She let him touch her gently, and her own fingers went exploring. The lines of his stomach, each of his vertebrae, from his neck down, slowly, slowly... When she reached the small of his back, she pressed him close again, but an invitation, rather than a demand. He bit down on the inside of his cheek as he rolled his hips against her, a reward for her honesty. A reward for Liv that had sparks following the path of her fingers down his spine. He rested his forehead against hers. Fighting for control.

'Are you okay?' Liv asked, her hand cupping gently around his backside, not demanding anything, just anchoring them together. He kissed the corner of her mouth, and then full on the lips, their tongues sliding together—familiar now. Knowing how to tease a gasp or moan.

Her eyes stayed open the whole time, locked on his, and he gasped at the intimacy of it. He had demanded this of her, not realising how much it would expose him.

Could she see how much he needed this? he wondered afterwards, as they both caught their breath, breaking their gaze. Could she see how much he craved her touch, as if it was only by being pressed against her that he felt truly himself? His mind snagged on the thought. He didn't really believe that, did he?

Liv had talked about boundaries earlier. That was what he needed now, he realised. He flinched away from Liv, eased himself out of her arms, one eye on the door. 'I should be…' he said, glancing at their interconnecting door.

'Um, yeah, of course,' Liv said, finding her nightgown by the bed and pulling it over her head, suddenly awkward.

'If I fell back asleep…' Adam began, knowing that it sounded as if he was making excuses. 'I don't want to get caught in here.'

'No, yeah, of course,' Liv said, covering herself with the duvet, tucking it right up to her armpits. Adam felt a black hole somewhere in his chest. It had no right to be there. This was casual. It was what they both wanted—it was what they had agreed.

He kissed her cheek, perfunctory now. 'I'll see you at breakfast. Catch up on your sleep, yeah? Goodnight, babe.'

CHAPTER TEN

LIV SLAMMED THE lid of the coffee pot closed and suppressed a yawn. This bad mood had absolutely no reason to have hung around for three straight days. She'd had plenty of time to catch up on her sleep and get over being irritated with Adam because he hadn't spent the night or knocked on their interconnecting door any of the nights since. Not that there was anything wrong with that. He was absolutely right not to risk them being caught.

She'd done the same thing to him in Paris. Worse, really, sneaking out before he even woke up. So why was she throwing her teaspoon into the sink, and slamming closed the lid of the bin? She spun on the spot at the sound of footsteps in the doorway. 'Adam,' she said, in what was meant to be a friendly, neutral tone, but came out somewhere between a gasp and an accusation. He glanced behind him to make sure they wouldn't be overheard.

'Good morning,' he said, with a smile that threatened to melt away her bad mood. If only he would come over and fold her into his arms, into his body, she knew that this mood would disappear. But that would be a distinctly boyfriendy move, and she didn't want to want or need that from him.

'Coffee?' she asked him, but he shook his head.

'I think I'll make tea. Do you want one?'

She raised her coffee cup and her eyebrow.

'Right, no, of course. Have you, er…got plans for today?' he asked.

Right, because it was Saturday, and weekend plans were something that most people had. Why was he asking, anyway? Were they doing small talk? As if she hadn't breathed in his moans, taking them down into her chest, where they'd mixed with her own. But this was the deal. This was what she had to do to protect herself. 'Need to go into the office' she said. 'Lots to do. You?'

He shrugged. 'I'll work this afternoon. This morning I need to find a gym to join. I've not been since I got back to London.'

'Oh, you're really going to seed,' she said, rolling her eyes, and then catching herself. That was exactly the kind of intimacy that she couldn't allow herself where they might be seen or overheard. Adam just smiled.

'There's one in the basement of the Kinley building,' she said. 'Adam should have mentioned it. If you don't want to have to spend time looking around.'

'Yeah, that'd be good,' he said. 'Do you want to go in together or—?'

'No,' Liv interrupted. 'I'm ready to go now and I don't want to rush you, so…' A weak excuse, and they both knew it. But that was fine. She didn't owe him Saturday mornings. If that was what he wanted from her, he could have stayed the other night. Locked her bedroom door and wrapped his arms around her and tucked his chin into the notch of her shoulder from behind.

She had been there for the taking, sleepy and satisfied, and he'd chosen his cold, empty bed instead. Even a casual hook-up had a right to be offended at that, didn't they?

'Okay, well, I'll see you later, then?' Adam asked.

'Uh, yeah, I suppose so.'

She poured the remaining coffee from the pot into a travel mug for later and grabbed her backpack. She'd walk in. It wasn't much more than a mile away, and she could do with the space and the air.

She skipped down the front steps, glad to be away from the house and Adam, and all the confused feelings she was carrying that morning. She walked quickly, trying to outrun her thoughts. She had no reason to be angry at Adam. All he had done was abide by the boundaries that she herself had set down. No, the only person she could possibly direct this anger towards was herself. This feeling, as if she had been abandoned. As if she hadn't been enough. That wasn't about Adam's failings, it was about her own. She knew well enough where she was weak, what small slights could feel like deep, penetrating wounds.

She was usually more careful than this. She could usually calculate just how close she could get without risking aggravating those old wounds. She would recalibrate; if she gave herself some space, it would be easier to see where she had got too close. And the next time she was with him, she'd keep herself safe.

Thank God she had so much work to distract her. She'd lose herself here for a few hours. Refuse to think about the other night. Or their night in Paris, or how warm and utterly peaceful it had been to sleep tucked into his side on the plane. That was what her body had craved, she realised. That sensation had crept into her unconscious, making itself comfortable there, so that her brain was bypassed completely. Her body just felt unsatisfied now, when his wasn't pressed against her.

She forced herself to concentrate again on the spreadsheet in front of her, trying to make the figures cooperate. Even with the cash injection that she and Caleb had given the business, using their inheritances, things were tight, and she had to keep a firm hand on the budget. If she'd had more money at her disposal she could have simply offered to pay Claude over the odds for space in his schedule. But instead she'd had to fly out there to put on the charm offensive. And that was only one item on her very long to-do list. She had to decide on production, packaging, and then actually sending it out into the world. A publicity campaign. Advertising, print and social media and…

She allowed her head to fall into her hands and rubbed at her temples. It was a big job, but not too big. She'd managed product launches before, a dozen times. But they had never been so personal before. All the different areas of her life had converged in the last months. Living and working with her family, her best friend becoming something more like a sister. And now Adam. She was sleeping and working and living with him, which in the cold light of an English Saturday morning seemed like an utterly terrible idea. All the different areas of her life were tangled together and she had nowhere to hide from her mistakes.

She needed more coffee. She grabbed her mug and walked towards the staff break room, where she'd brew a large pot, enough to keep her going for the rest of the afternoon. And then she'd think of something to do this evening, so she didn't have to go back to the house, didn't have to go back to—

'What the hell?' She crashed into a hard, sweaty body, and had to put out a hand to steady herself. 'Adam?' she asked, not finding herself able to take her hand off his biceps, which flexed subtly beneath her fingers. It was smooth and slick with sweat, upper arms and muscled shoulders defined by a gym vest. She kept her eyes fixed safely at arm height as she traced a finger around the outline of that muscle. A shame it didn't come with a simpler package, she thought as Adam tipped her face up with his knuckles under her chin. 'Is this what passes for work wear now?' she asked, trying to keep things light.

'Anyone would think you like it,' he said with a barely suppressed smirk.

She finally looked up and met his eye. 'It's very unprofessional.'

'Are you suggesting I take it off?' he asked.

Liv smiled. This was just banter. Smutty banter, yes, but nothing more meaningful than that. She breathed a sigh of relief. She'd been freaking out for no reason. She knew how to do this. How to keep it safe.

She sniffed theatrically. 'I'm suggesting that you go for a shower,' she said, taking a step back from him. 'You smell terrible.'

Adam chuckled and stepped even closer than he had been before. 'Am I right in thinking that it would be unprofessional to ask you to join me?'

She took a sip of coffee, looking at him over the rim of the cup. 'Very unprofessional,' Liv confirmed. 'And I think we've probably pushed our luck as far as it will go on that front.'

Adam nodded. 'Later, then? At the house?' When she didn't reply straight away, she saw the doubt creep into his expression, and then the tension in his body as he realised that she wasn't jumping on his proposition. 'Or not, that's fine too, of course.'

'Let's just play it by ear. See how we feel later,' she said.

That was better. Casual hook-ups should come with no expectations. If they happened to find one another later that night, then great. She'd like that. But making plans gave people the opportunity to let her down. Spontaneous fun was better. Except…it didn't really matter what she told Adam, when she knew full well that she would be sneaking into his bed that night, if he would have her.

'All right, then,' Adam said, his hand at the back of his neck, revealing darkly haired underarms, and flexing his muscles in a very distracting manner. 'I'll see you later, then. Maybe.'

Liv dug her nails into her palm to stop herself reaching out for him, undoing all her good work.

'Yeah, maybe.'

She watched him walk down the corridor, nursing her coffee cup in hand. And then she shook her head and walked back to her desk. She had work to do. She wasn't a teenager, and if she'd wanted to spend her afternoon mooning after a boy, she could have done that at home. In bed. But she'd come into the office to work and she wasn't going to let things slide because of Adam.

She worked solidly until she was hungry, and she guessed that it must be past dinner time. She couldn't risk Adam coming to her and suggesting dinner again. Instead she texted Rowan as she gathered her things and left the building. She needed a drink and some time ignoring how complicated her life had suddenly become.

Several cocktails and not enough carbs later, her tongue bitten so many times to prevent herself spilling something about her and Adam, she was home, more than a little bit squiffy, a smile on her face from spending so much time uninterrupted with her best friend. If Rowan had noticed black holes in their conversation that she'd stepped carefully around, she trusted that Rowan would assume that they were Jonathan-shaped, rather than relating to their new house guest.

When Rowan and Jonathan had started dating, they had mutually agreed that discussing him was a no-go for either of them, so it wasn't unusual for one or the other of them to hide their opinion on something relating to her brother. They'd mostly talked about Liv's other brother, Caleb, who had bailed the family business out of trouble the year before with some cryptocurrency investments none of them had known about. He'd always been happy with his own company, or that of a keyboard, to which his hands were semi-permanently attached. And yet, it seemed he was spending even more time than usual at his computer.

Rowan had already tackled the workaholic habits of one Kinley brother, and wanted Liv's opinion on staging an intervention with Caleb, forcing him to leave his computer for more than food and bathroom breaks.

Liv had promised to think about it. When was the last time she had seen Caleb leave the house? Maybe Rowan was right. Seemed her friend had a better idea of what this family needed than she did. She felt a tipsy rush of affection for her friend as she poured herself a glass of water, congratulating herself for excellent hangover preparation, knowing how grateful she'd be in the morning.

Next, Adam, she thought to herself with a grin. She'd turned him down earlier, not wanting to be distracted from her afternoon's work. Not wanting to commit herself to plans even for casual sex. But there was absolutely no reason not to show up at his door for a booty call. Neither of them could possibly get the wrong idea about that. She got to her bedroom, bumping her hip on the doorframe on her way. Ouch. She'd have a bruise there in the morning. She dug around in her dresser for something sexy to wear, and pulled something skimpy and lacy over her head, giggling to herself and wondering what Adam was going to say when she snuck into his room.

She tiptoed across the bathroom, the marble floor freezing on her bare feet. Then breathed a sigh of relief when the door to Adam's room opened under her hand. She hadn't realised until it opened that she'd been worried that he might have locked it.

Adam was asleep, snoring gently, moonlight coming through the blinds showing his bare back and arms, one hand under his pillow. 'Adam,' she whispered from the door, trying to arrange herself into an inviting pose. 'Adam!' she hissed a bit louder when he didn't stir.

She crept over to him, trying to be stealthy, but nearly crying out when she stubbed her toe on the corner of the bed. 'Adam,' she whispered again. She was right beside him now, could see the soft curve of his lips, gentle in sleep, when he had no cause to smirk at her. She crouched, slightly wobbly, by the side of the bed, and touched her fingers softly to his mouth, until she slipped, and whacked her forehead against his. His eyes flew open, and she planted a hand over his mouth before he could cry out in alarm. 'It's me,' she whispered, a giggle escaping her.

'Liv?' Adam asked sleepily, pushing himself up and pulling her hand from his mouth. 'What the hell are you doing?' he asked.

'Don't you recognise a booty call when you see one?' she asked, gesturing down at her scraps of black lace.

He groaned, falling back on his pillow, which was not exactly the reaction that she had been hoping for. 'It felt more like a headbutt,' he said, rubbing at his forehead, and she planted a kiss there, climbing onto the bed and into his lap.

'Liv,' he asked as she kissed his neck, settling on top of him and making herself at home. 'Babe?' he added, when she didn't answer him.

'Yes?' Her lips curled around a smile, because she didn't hate hearing him call her that.

'Are you drunk?' he asked.

Liv sat back on her heels and thought about the question. 'Yep. Definitely tipsy.' She leaned back into him but he stopped her with hands on her hips.

'I think you should go back to bed,' he said, very seriously. She pouted.

'I haven't been to bed yet.'

'Then you should.'

Heat rushed into Liv's face, as cold took the rest of her body, and she crossed her arms over her stomach, embarrassment setting in.

'Is this because I turned you down earlier? Payback?' she asked, grabbing a pillow now and holding it to her front.

Adam pushed himself up on his hands and frowned at her. 'No,' he said slowly, watching her face. 'It's because you weren't sure if you wanted to earlier, and if you've only changed your mind because you've had too much to drink, that's not exactly an enthusiastic yes.'

Liv's face flushed with heat as she climbed off the bed. Off him.

'I'm sorry. I shouldn't have woken you. I shouldn't have come,' Liv said, pillow still clutched to her front as she walked backwards towards the door.

'Liv, wait, don't run off, it's not that,' he said, half rising from bed to follow her. But she shut the door, mortified, crossed the bathroom in a hurry and back into her own room. She locked the door, and then stood staring at it. This was bad.

Not so much that he'd turned down her slightly wobbly booty call. She could live with that. She'd had brush-offs before and taken them in her stride. What was different this time was that it had hurt. It hadn't felt as if he was turning down a quick fumble. He was saying no to *her*. Pushing her away, and that had cut through her. She pulled off her lingerie and found a simple cotton T-shirt and shorts. And then she climbed into her bed and hugged the pillow to her, tight. He'd made her care, the absolute pig. He'd made her want him enough that he could hurt her and she couldn't forgive him for it.

CHAPTER ELEVEN

ADAM WOKE SLOWLY the next morning, with a twisting feeling in his gut telling him all was not well. He didn't regret turning Liv down last night; it had been the right—the only—thing he could have done in the circumstances. But he regretted the hurt that he had seen on Liv's face. It was more than just disappointment about a rejected booty call. He was sure that she had seen more in his no than he had intended, and that was even before he'd had a chance to tell her how he had spent his evening.

She'd probably have a sore head this morning, so he went downstairs and brewed a pot of strong coffee. She appeared at the kitchen door ten minutes later. Her hair was mussed, her face pale, with dark circles under her eyes. She looked as if she was in a terrible mood, in a cute sort of way, and it took a great deal of self-restraint not to pull her into his arms and kiss the top of her head. To tell her to go back to bed and he would bring her coffee and bacon sandwiches and paracetamol. But, given how they had left things last night, he couldn't assume that she'd want him acting so...friendly. No, that was not just friendly. That was *boy*-friendly.

So he kept his mouth shut and poured her a cup of coffee, and resisted the urge to run a hand over her hair when she rested her head on the table. 'That bad?' he asked, sitting at the table, resisting the urge to laugh softly.

'Worse,' she groaned. 'I'm never drinking again.'

'Yeah, right.'

She looked up at him and winced when she met his eye. 'I'm so embarrassed,' she admitted, looking quickly away.

'Don't be,' he said, knowing it wasn't enough to fix what had gone wrong between them last night. 'Honestly, Liv,' he went on, 'you've got nothing to be embarrassed about.'

She grunted, still not looking at him. So he gave in to the urge, and smoothed his hand over her hair. 'I like that you wanted me. You looked incredibly sexy, and if you hadn't been so far gone that you literally fell over and headbutted me, I wouldn't have let you out of my sight, never mind out of my bed. Okay?'

She lifted her head and rubbed a spot just above her brow, which he could see was darkening with a bruise. 'So that's what this is. I'd forgotten that part,' she mused. 'So what did you get up to last night?' she asked. 'It's not fair that you look all…not hideous.'

Adam hesitated. They had talked about this; he had no reason to be worried. This was just a casual thing. But he had seen how hurt she had been when he had pushed her away, and he didn't want to do anything else that hurt her, however good his reasons. However much she agreed with his reasons for putting space between them. And he was more sure than ever that living together was a bad idea. He was growing far too used to this. Enjoying a grouchy, hungover breakfast far more than he should do. It wouldn't take many more mornings for this to feel as if it was his real life. As if he wanted to rely on it—on Liv—being there. Not just for casual nights or snatched moments at work, but every day, stretching out ahead of him. A future together.

But he couldn't allow himself to want something that could so easily be taken away. He couldn't bear *needing* something. To risk more months, more years of wondering how to get through the day, through his work, when all he could think about was how to get the thing he wanted. Needed. Couldn't live without. He had only known Liv for a couple of weeks, and already she had him so unsettled. He had to act now, to stop this becoming something that couldn't be undone.

'Adam?' she prompted.

'I, er… I saw a couple of apartments.' This time her head snapped up. 'Staying here was only meant to be temporary,' he said, not sure which of them he was reminding.

'I know that,' Liv replied, as if he'd accused her of something. She took a deep breath, and he watched her choose her words carefully.

'Did you find somewhere you like?' she asked. He shook his head.

'Not yet.' None of them had felt like home. He wasn't sure what it was that he was looking for. Only that he hadn't found it quite yet.

'I've got a few more to see this morning,' he added, hoping that he wasn't making a mistake. 'Do you want to come with me?'

'Doesn't that defeat the object of getting some space?'

He could hardly argue with her logic. But, he told

himself, there was a difference between not sleeping together and not spending any time together at all. He shrugged, trying to convince her, as he had himself, that it wouldn't mean anything. 'It's viewing a flat, not a quicky in your office,' he said baldly. 'But it's fine if you don't want to.'

'I don't have anything better to do today. And I don't love the idea of playing third wheel to Rowan and Jonathan doing the whole Sunday domestic bliss thing. Why not? What time's the first viewing?'

He glanced at his watch. 'An hour. Can you be ready?'

She groaned and nodded at the same time.

'Need me to prop you up in the shower?' he asked. It had been meant as a joke. Not a serious invitation. Yesterday, it would have been okay. Yesterday it would have been a playful remark to be taken up or ignored. That was when he realised that something had changed. If anything like that happened again, it would not be casual. He could see that in the way that she had reacted when he had rejected her. The way he had felt about her when he'd first seen her that morning. Tired and sore and vulnerable. Nothing between them was casual any more.

'I think I'll manage,' Liv said with a forced smile as she headed out of the room. She was back downstairs in an hour, looking human again, if still tired. His heart did a weird little flip again at the sight of her, and he took a couple of breaths until it stopped. This suddenly seemed like a stupid idea, and he wondered if there was a way to get out of it. But then he remembered the look on her face when he had pushed her away last night and he couldn't bring himself to hurt her again.

When had her feelings become more important than his own? It was clear that he had crossed a line somewhere along the way, and he didn't know how to get back to the other side. The best solution he could think of was to ignore it. To pretend that he didn't feel this way. Or that he hadn't noticed them. Hadn't seen them for what they were. Something that scared him. So he smiled at her, as simply as he could, and pulled his car keys from his pocket.

'Ready to go?' he asked, his voice full of false cheer that made Liv wince.

'Ready,' she said, pouring coffee into a travel mug and shoving it into her bag—truly, her capacity for caffeine was equal parts frightening and impressive.

They walked out to the car in silence, and Adam wondered if things were always going to be this awkward now. He wanted to go back. Back to before she had climbed into his bed last night. Back to before he had felt anything for her. For anyone. When he'd finally reached a time of his life when he had everything that he needed. When both he and his mother were settled and safe. And happy.

He wasn't happy this morning. He was…unsettled. And every time he looked at Liv, he knew why. Suspected what it would take to shift this pressure in his chest. And he couldn't do it. Couldn't face the idea that this change in him was permanent.

'Oh, God, looks like this is the place,' he said, as the satnav directed them into the underground parking of a sleek new tower of luxury apartments. His estate agent, a tall, sandy-haired man in chinos and a V-neck sweater, was waiting for them by a parked car, and he reached out to shake his hand as he walked up to him.

'Hi, I'm Matt,' he said, introducing himself to Liv. Adam panicked momentarily.

'This is Liv,' Adam said, knowing full well that it looked as if she were his girlfriend. 'My colleague,' he added, though that was the least she was to him. He glanced across at her, wanting to know what she had made of that description. Her slightly raised eyebrow didn't tell him much—and his glances across at her as they travelled up in the lift didn't give anything away either.

When the private elevator doors opened, he groaned. It was perfectly clear from the moment he stepped out of the lift that this place must cost ten times what he'd told Matt his budget was. How could he justify spending multiple millions on an apartment when he knew for a fact that there was a homeless shelter within half a mile of here? He was their largest donor, as well as a trustee on their board. But it seemed as if every estate agent in London had done some research, decided his budget for themselves, and had taken it upon themselves to show him every luxury bachelor penthouse inside the M25.

Liv raised her brows at him as she stepped out of the lift and spun around to face him. 'Fancy,' she observed, walking backwards into the flat a few paces, before turning round and walking across to the kitchen area of the open-plan space, running a finger along the chrome, top-of-the-range appliances. 'This'll be perfect for all the baking you do,' she said, flicking the switch on a KitchenAid.

'I could learn,' Adam said with a smile. Liv smiled back, and he felt it low down in his belly. She walked away from the kitchen and over to the window wall that looked out over the city. He followed her over, and it was only the presence of Matt in the room that stopped him wrapping his arms around her from behind. Instead, he stood as close as he was able while keeping up their pretence of being nothing more than colleagues.

'It's almost the same view as the roof at Kinley,' she murmured, and his mouth turned up in a smile.

'Well, then, that's the one thing it has going for it,' he replied with a smile, remembering the night when he had stopped fighting what he felt for her. When they'd managed to convince themselves that this was something that they could get out of their systems and then go on as normal. How stupid that seemed now, he thought. As if having Liv, being close to her, was something that could ever make him want her less, rather than more. As if, once he knew the taste of her, he could go through the rest of his life without her. Sweat prickled at his hairline and his face flushed hot as he realised how deeply in trouble he was.

'You don't like it?' she asked over her shoulder.

'I hate it,' he told her. 'Do you know how many people you could house for the price of a place like this?'

'I didn't think it was your style,' she said with a smile, turning away from the window. 'So what are we still doing here?'

She had a point, so he followed her to the door, where Matt was standing, looking hopeful.

'What do you think?' he asked.

'I think that if you add a zero to my budget again, I'll find a new agent.' The estate agent laughed. 'Well, it was worth a shot. I promise you're going to love the next place.'

They typed the postcode that Matt gave them into the car's satnav and when they pulled up in front of a house so similar to Liv's that it could have doubled for it in the movie of her life, Adam gripped the steering wheel a little harder.

'Well,' Liv said, 'this feels…familiar.'

Matt got out of his car and held his hands up to pre-empt Adam's objections. 'I know what you're going to say but it's within budget, I promise. A garden flat.'

'Okay,' Adam said, losing a little of the tension in his shoulders. 'We'll take a look, at least.'

They walked up the steps to the front door, the line of buzzers to one side the only difference from the entrance to Liv's home. The hallway was smartly kept, and a second door led into the ground-floor apartment. Most of the internal walls had been removed, to create a light, airy, open space, but Liv noticed that the fireplaces and decorative ceiling plasterwork were so similar to her own that they must have been original. The old floorboards had been stripped and sanded and polished, and the rich golden colour bounced warm light around the room. At the back of the apartment, French windows opened onto a terrace and a garden, where sunlight played on the leaves of the tall trees that screened the space from view.

Liv watched Adam, standing unmoving in the centre of the room, hands planted in his pockets.

'What do you think?' she asked, when Matt excused himself and left them alone together. 'Better than the last place, right?'

Adam nodded, but didn't lose his preoccupied expression.

'What's wrong?' she asked.

'It's a lot like your place,' he said, and, although he didn't expand on that, it was clear he didn't mean that it was a good thing.

'Well, I'm sorry I've ruined an entire style of architecture for you,' Liv said, crossing her arms.

He turned to look at her, his expression calling her out on her childish tone without him having to say a word.

'I like it,' he said, looking pained. 'And I like that it reminds me of your place, that that makes it feel like it could become home really quickly. And at the same time—'

'That scares you,' Liv finished for him. 'It would really be that bad? Falling for me?' She asked the question knowing that it wasn't fair. Knowing that if the tables were turned, the answer would be yes, it was that bad.

Adam sighed and looked at the ceiling. 'I don't know if it's too late now anyway.'

And Liv was just about to launch a tirade of questions, first and foremost being *What the hell?*, when Matt reappeared.

'I think you like it,' he said with a smile. 'Do you want to see the bedroom?'

At which point, Adam seemed to choke on fresh air and Liv felt the room swim in an entirely unhelpful way. 'I'm just going to…' she said, and bolted for the door.

Once she was outside she dropped to sit on the top step and tried to sort through her racing thoughts. What had that meant? Too late for what—to not fall for her? She scrabbled around for any other possible meaning she could ascribe to his words but came up with nothing. He was falling for her? The only saving grace from the whole thing was that he seemed as mortified to say it as she had been to hear it. Surely this had to be the end of their... Of whatever this was. If he was falling for her then it could only be a matter of time before things went sour.

But the thought of it turned her stomach. That it would be pulled away from her without warning. Without knowing that their last time would be their last time. Maybe she was jumping to conclusions, maybe he had meant something else completely. Maybe this didn't have to be over yet. They still had time. And the fact that she was hanging on so desperately to that told her everything she needed to know about how she felt about him. If Adam was in too deep, so was she. They should both be putting an end to this. It would just be a case of which of them had the guts to do it first.

She turned and looked over her shoulder as the front door opened, and Adam appeared behind her. Matt jogged down the steps with a quick goodbye, leaving them alone with their awkward atmosphere.

Adam came to sit beside her on the step.

'So?' she asked, forcing a smile in his direction.

'I've bought it,' Adam said, and her eyes widened.

'Even though it reminds you of me?'

He smiled back at her, but it was hollow. A little sad.

'Did you mean what you said?' she asked when he didn't say anything.

He leaned forward, with his elbows on his knees, then looking straight ahead, avoiding eye contact.

'Yeah,' he sighed. 'I think I did. This has turned into something I wasn't prepared for.'

Liv nodded. Took a deep breath. 'For me too.' They sat in silence for a few moments more. If they had a different sort of story, this would be the moment when their shoulders bumped, and they leaned into each other. When she might have reached for his hand, pulled it into her lap and laced their fingers together. But that was the sort of happy ending she had never expected for herself. Being open to that meant being open to being hurt, and being with Adam these past weeks had only shown her how ill-equipped she was to handle that.

She hugged her knees to her chest and wrapped her arms around them.

'This is over, isn't it.' Not a question. She couldn't feel Adam's warmth beside her. Could feel the millimetres of space between them as a chasm.

'It's probably for the best,' Adam replied. Which wasn't the same as saying he wanted it to end, but made clear that he didn't want him to fight for her either. Was that what she wanted? she had to ask herself. Or was it just her ego that made her want to persuade him to change his mind, that painted a picture of the next few days, weeks, without him in it and how quickly that had become something so difficult to countenance? She glanced across at Adam.

'I feel like at least one of us should put up a fight for this,' Liv mused.

'Is that what you want?' he asked. 'To fight? To try and make it work?'

She fixed her eyes ahead of her. 'No,' she said, taking a deep breath and deciding on brutal honesty. 'But I wish you would.'

'I don't want this to end,' Adam confessed, and it was clear from the tone of his voice that it *was* a confession. She waited, because there had to be more to that sentence. 'But I don't want to be the one who fights for it either,' he went on. 'Because I know that if we keep doing this, it's going to go wrong. You'll panic and bolt, and I'll be left needing you and not able to have you, and that will be torture. Which is why I need you to do this. I'm begging you to end this now, before either of us get hurt.'

She reached for his hand, but stopped herself before she could grasp it, to keep a hold of just part of him. 'I think I'm already going to get hurt,' she confessed. 'Breaking this off with you hurts. But it's better now than it will be later.'

Adam nodded. 'I can move in here today,' he offered, and Liv's eyes widened.

'How is that possible? What about solicitors, and surveys, and…?'

'I'm going to rent it while we take care of all that,' Adam explained, which didn't make the hard knot in her chest go away.

'So you're really that desperate to get away,' Liv mused, resting her chin on her knees, her whole body curled in on itself.

'You said for yourself it's for the best.'

Liv nodded, because of course it was for the best, but she'd thought that she would have a little time to get used to the idea. Not that it would be happening now, this minute. She'd thought that they'd have another night at least.

'Does it have to be now?' she asked, and she tried to make sure that there wasn't a hint of desperation in her voice. Tried not to glance back at the door to his new flat, thinking about the bedroom she hadn't trusted herself to see earlier. But her eyes darted behind her, and Adam's followed, and she guessed that he knew exactly what she was thinking. He took her hand, squeezed, and she threaded her fingers through his as he pulled her up to standing and they walked together through the front door.

CHAPTER TWELVE

ADAM SMOOTHED A hand over Liv's hair as she slept on his chest, telling himself with each glide of his hand that they were doing the right thing. This had been their last hurrah. A goodbye. Except neither of them wanted this to end. They'd both recognised that, even so, there was no way for it to continue. They'd drunk each other in. He'd run his hands, his mouth, over every inch of her. Knowing it would be their last time. That he was going to cling to this memory, and he needed all the details, knew that he would want to revisit it again and again, and he wanted to be sure he had it all exactly, the taste of the skin on the inside of her elbow, the smell of the nape of her neck, where wispy hairs swirled. The curve of the base of her spine under his hands, the sound of her gasps when she fought to keep control of herself, and the deep groan when she realised it was a losing battle and she gave herself over to him.

She stirred against him, and his arms tightened around her involuntarily. He held his breath and his entire body still, hoping against hope that she'd sleep a little longer, just to delay the moment that they would have to say goodbye. She relaxed again in sleep, and he allowed himself to breathe again. Maybe he'd have another half an hour like this. An hour if they were lucky, before they had to drag themselves into wakefulness. Into real life. The light behind the blinds grew brighter, and he held Liv a little tighter, protecting her as much as he could from what was to come. There was practical stuff to work out first. Clothes, showers, coffee. None of them a simple prospect in a house furnished for estate agent showings rather than for comfort.

Then the short drive back to Liv's house. Both of them sneaking in without being caught. Because this had to be the worst time for that to happen. Having to explain themselves just at the point when there was nothing to explain any more.

He kissed the top of her head, and the next time she moved, he pulled himself out of her arms and found yesterday's jeans on the floor. A defensive measure. If he woke up naked with her one more time, that would be it. Game over. He might as well cut open his chest and pull his heart out now.

Once he was dressed, he woke Liv with a kiss to her cheek.

'Hey,' he said as she stretched. 'Probably time we were going home.' And at that moment he saw her snap awake and remember what was happening. That this was the end. He watched her wrap something invisible around herself, something that meant that he could no longer reach her.

'What time is it?' she asked, sitting up and gathering bedding around her.

'Just after seven. Enough time to get home before work'

Liv nodded, considering. She opened her mouth to

say something, but then seemed to change her mind, her mouth closing with everything still unsaid.

'Can I have some privacy?' she asked. 'I need to get dressed.' Adam nodded, stepping backwards from the bed. So this was over, then, he thought, feeling as if his centre of gravity had up and disappeared completely. He waited for her on the doorstep, and when she joined him he locked the door behind them. It had been stupid to do this here. Would he ever walk into this house and not think about this night with Liv? Had he ruined his new home the first night that he owned it?

Liv turned her key in the door and prayed for a silent, empty house beyond. Her prayers were answered, and the house was mercifully quiet as she pulled her shoes off and padded through the hall in socked feet. She didn't say a word to Adam, couldn't think of what they could say to end this. In the end, neither of them said anything. Adam took the stairs up, to his bedroom presumably, and Liv the stairs down to the basement kitchen. Where Rowan was sitting at the kitchen table, two cups of coffee in front of her, a very amused expression on her face.

'And what sort of time do you call this?' her best friend asked over the rim of her mug as she pushed the other towards Liv. 'I brought you a cup of coffee since you were sleeping in so much later than usual. And what did I find? An empty bed.'

'Rowan,' Liv said, feeling her heart start to race, her hand start to shake in panic. 'I can explain.'

But Rowan went on as if she hadn't heard her. 'And when I glanced in the bathroom,' she said, 'I just happened to notice that Adam's door was open and he wasn't home either. Fancy that for a coincidence.'

Liv dropped to a chair at the table and grasped the coffee that Rowan slid right in front of her.

'Want to talk about it?' Rowan asked at the same time as she heard the front door slam above them. Which was when she felt the tears at the back of her eyes, and she rested her forehead in one hand.

'It's nothing. Or it *was* nothing. Whatever it was, it's over now anyway,' Liv said, her hands still shaking as she held tight to her coffee cup.

Rowan frowned. 'And is that what you want, love?' she asked gently.

Liv shook her head. 'I don't know if it's what either of us want. But it's the right thing to do.' The words reminded her that she had chosen this. She straightened her shoulders, telling herself that this was what she wanted. This pain wasn't something being done *to* her. That was meant to make it better. This was meant to be what she was protecting herself from. She turned to Rowan.

'What am I going to do?'

Rowan wrapped an arm around her and pulled her into a hug. 'Why don't you start from the beginning and tell me everything?'

Liv groaned, turning to bury her face in her friend's shoulder.

'I think you're going to tell me that I've been an idiot,' Liv mumbled into her dressing gown.

Rowan laughed.

'If I do, I promise it'll be in a really lovely way. I'm going to be your sister, remember. You can't get rid of me, no matter how stupid you are with extremely pretty men in leather jackets.'

The laugh that burst from Liv brought tears with it, and she was a snotty mess within seconds. It was the word 'sister' that had done it. Because she'd spent months thinking that Rowan falling in love meant that she was losing her best friend. But she had been stupid not to see before now that she was gaining so much more than she was losing. Which brought on a final wave of tears so intense that they couldn't last for more than a few minutes. She scrubbed her face clean and dry on the tea towel that Rowan handed her and finally took a sip of her coffee.

'Rowan, I think I really like him,' she said. 'And if this is what it feels like to not be with him, I don't want to do it. I don't want to choose to feel this just because I'm scared of what might be somewhere down the road.'

Rowan gave her a considering look. 'It sounds to me like you do know what you want.'

'Yeah, but what about what Adam wants, or doesn't want?'

'It sounds like he wants you to fight. I think him specifically telling you that was the giveaway.'

'Then why doesn't *he* fight?' Liv asked, though she knew his reasons perfectly well.

Rowan forced out a breath from between her teeth. 'I know talking about me and Jonathan is a bit of a no-go, but I'm speaking from experience when I say don't underestimate how much simply being stubborn and stupid can get in the way of something really good.'

Liv tilted her head and fixed Rowan with a stare. 'Are you trying to tell me that I'm as stupid and stubborn as my brother?'

Rowan smiled, a little wistfully, and Liv reminded

herself not to barf. 'I'm saying that Jonathan and I came very close to not being as happy as we are, and I hate to see you unhappy. But whatever you decide to do, I'll support you.'

Liv gave a sob as the tears made a reappearance.

'What?' Rowan asked. 'What did I say?'

Liv thought about it. If she couldn't talk about her feelings with her best friend, what hope did she have of overcoming these fears she'd been carrying around for years? So she told Rowan how insecure she'd been feeling about their friendship and how scared she was of being left behind. And the tightness of the hug she received held her heart together and gave her enough confidence to go and have this talk with Adam, because whatever she'd thought she'd wanted, it couldn't be this.

Everything in her stomach and her heart and her head told her that what they'd decided was wrong. Her whole body felt as if it were fighting against her decision. The only slight hitch in her plan was evident when she went upstairs to shower, and the door to Adam's room was open, showing that he'd cleared his stuff out already. He must have thrown it all in his bag and taken it to the office with him. She sighed, pulling out her laptop and powering it up. She was running too late this morning to go into work, so she might as well work from home. It was merely a bonus that she wouldn't have to run into Adam on the day that they had broken up and he'd moved out without even shouting goodbye down the stairs as he went.

Adam stared at the clock on the wall of his office. It was only eight a.m. No reason to think that Liv wasn't coming into the office at all. But he'd thought that yesterday, and the days before that, and had started at every footstep outside his office until he'd received her emails to say that she was working from home. He wasn't sure that he could take another day of watching, waiting for just a glimpse of her. And being disappointed.

This was ridiculous. He could just call her. Email her, even, in a professional way. She'd see through it in a second. It was one of the things that scared him the most. One of the things that he loved the most. He'd been so close to asking her for... He wasn't even sure what he wanted to ask for. For her not to let him ruin this. To force him to do the thing that scared him the most. And then she hadn't come into the office. He'd been left wanting something he couldn't have, with a sore heart, and no idea what to do about it.

He heard high heels outside his office, but reminded himself that it probably wasn't her. But then he looked up, and there Liv was, framed in the doorway, her expression inscrutable.

'Hi,' he said, shaking his head at the inanity of that one syllable. She half smiled, and it was without question the most beautiful thing he had seen since they'd left the apartment that he could hardly bear to be in now. He had been so stupid to spend the night with her there; it reminded him more of Liv than of a fresh start as he'd planned.

'Have you got a minute to talk?' she asked him, and his heart leaped.

'Yeah, of course. Here?'

'I was thinking the roof. Five minutes?'

He nodded, struck silent, hardly allowing himself to hope. Because not only was there something to say, she wanted to say it somewhere that was meaningful to them. That had to be a good sign, didn't it? He ran a hand over his hair, smoothing it down, and then stared at the clock, each of the three hundred seconds he had to wait feeling like the one where his heart might finally give out on him.

Exactly five minutes after Liv had walked out of his office, he started after her. It occurred to him as he reached for the handle of the door out onto the roof that he probably should have spent some of those five minutes thinking about what the hell he was going to say to her. But he had been so focussed on just getting here that he hadn't thought about what he would say when he did. All he knew, all he could tell Liv was that the last five minutes—the last few days—had been torture, and if she was up for anything other than being apart, whatever that looked like, then he wanted to try it. He took a final breath and opened the door.

Liv was standing at the edge of the roof, leaning up against the wall looking out over the city. The wind had caught her hair, was playing it around her shoulders. He took a deep breath because if he was going to do this, he had to be sure. He couldn't mess Liv around. Couldn't do that to her, or to himself.

'Liv,' he said, and she turned to look at him, obviously so lost in thought that she hadn't heard the door. She smiled at him, before catching it, neutralising it.

'Adam, hi,' she said. He didn't know how it could hurt so much just to hear his name on her lips. It was the lack of feeling that really punched him in the gut. He'd heard her say his name so many times since he'd met her, and never with such lack of feeling. Was that real? He wondered, had she really been able to stop feeling anything so quickly? Or was it a front to hide how affected she had been by their break-up?

'Thank you for meeting me,' she said. He couldn't believe how awkward that sounded. Was it really only a few days ago that they had been so close? When he had been inside her body, in her life, in a way that felt impossibly distant now?

But somehow they both found themselves at the little table where they'd worked that first night. Liv sat, so he copied her, but then that felt like a mistake. This lump of filigreed iron furniture between them when what he really wanted was to pull her close. It was probably better like this, he reasoned. They needed to talk, and he wasn't sure that they could do that if they had the constant distraction of sitting too close.

'I've missed you,' he blurted. It wasn't exactly what he'd meant to say, but it was true, and, from the quirk at the corner of Liv's mouth, she was happy to hear it. That emboldened him, and he spoke again. 'I've missed you, my new bed smells of you, and I think maybe we made a mistake calling quits on this.'

Liv raised an eyebrow and he had no choice but to keep talking. 'I know I…you…we, always said that this was going to be casual, and that it was the right time to put an end to things. But if the way that I've felt since we left the flat is anything to go by, I think we've made a mistake. I should have fought for this then, but I was scared. And…' He trailed off, looking at her. Because he was spilling his guts and Liv hadn't said a word. For all Liv was saying, he could be on completely the wrong track, and she'd not given him a thought since a few nights before.

Just as he was about to lose his nerve, she reached

for his hand across the table. He looked up and met her eye, and that spurred him on to finish. 'So I know you had your own reasons for being afraid of this, and maybe I'm making an idiot of myself. But if you want to try being afraid together, then I'd really like that.'

For the most nerve-racking minute of his life, she didn't say a word.

'I think I'm falling for you,' Liv said, and Adam felt his eyebrows head for his hairline. He felt a jolt of adrenaline, and he wasn't sure whether it was the fear and anxiety he would have had a week ago at those words, or excitement that she might have had the same second thoughts that he had over the end of their relationship.

'Is that…something you're happy about?' Adam asked, because it was impossible to guess from the expression on her face.

Liv shrugged, which wasn't exactly a passionate declaration. 'I wish I knew,' she said, leaning forwards, forearms on the table, her hands playing distractedly with his. 'I like you. You know how much. And these last few days have been…really awful. I don't want to give up on us. But I have all this baggage, and so do you, and what if it all goes wrong anyway and it's even worse?'

He trapped her hands with both of his. Deprived of her distraction, she looked up and met his eyes. 'That's the risk,' he said, because she'd summed up what he was feeling exactly. 'That's the risk, isn't it?' he said again, squeezing her hands and pulling them closer to him. What he really wanted was to pull her into his lap, but for now, this would have to do. 'Whether we think it's worth it to fight for this. We both have to want it, and I do. I'm terrified, but I'm not ready to give up. I've never tried to make anything like this work before, but I want to. With you. And when you get scared, I'll be there for you, or give you space, whatever you need. And when I freak out, you'll be there for me. I think that's how this usually works. Whatever scares us, we face it together.'

He saw Liv visibly shudder and her expression turned to a glare. 'But what if we don't? What if you change your mind and run off and leave me, and I'm left with all this—' she gestured up and down her body '—all these *feelings* alone? You can't promise me that you won't leave.' Her words shocked him into silence, because he realised she was completely right. He couldn't make promises like that. And even if he did, he wouldn't be able to make her believe him.

'You're right,' Adam acknowledged. 'I can't make promises like that. I'm not sure anyone could promise that. I suppose that's where trust comes in. Can you trust me?' he asked.

Liv inspected his face, as if the answer to her question would come from his face, rather than within. 'Do you trust *me*?' she asked, batting his question back at him. He thought about it seriously, because this wasn't the time to think without speaking. But the truth didn't come from careful consideration. It came from his gut.

'Yes,' he said. 'I trust you. I trust you to be honest with me about what you want and how you're feeling. I've never even tried to make a relationship work before, so I've got no more idea how to do that than you have, but that seems like a good place to start. If we tell each other what we want and what scares us and agree to deal with it together, I'm pretty sure that's how people build a relationship.'

Liv pulled her hands away, and a yawning chasm of panic threatened to open in his chest, so he took a deep breath to try and appease it. He was just wondering if having to prompt Liv to talk about what she was afraid of meant that they were beyond saving, when she groaned, shook her head and then spoke.

'If you abandon me like my parents did, it will break me completely and I'm not sure how I could survive that.'

He nodded, because he could see how deep those wounds cut. He could only cling to the fact that she was telling him about it, rather than holding her fears close, too scared to share them with him.

'I can promise you that I'll never ghost you,' he said. 'But it's up to you whether you can take a risk on me.'

She looked thoughtful.

'I want to trust you,' she said at last. 'And I don't want another day like these last few. But I'm going to need patience. I'm going to have to practise, and you'll be my guinea pig.'

He finally shoved his chair away and came around to Liv's side of the table.

'Is that a yes?' Adam asked, hearing the hope in his own voice.

'You heard the bit where you're going to be a guinea pig and I'm probably going to mess up? A lot,' Liv checked, as if she couldn't quite believe that he'd agreed to her terms.

Adam pulled her up, bent his head so that he could look her properly in the eye. 'I heard the bit where you want to try. Where you're as mad about me as I am about you.' Because that was the important part.

Liv rolled her eyes, but he knew she didn't mean it. Knew that what he'd said was right. 'You're not too bad. I'm prepared to admit that now,' she admitted, as he turned her face up to his with a finger under her chin.

'I'm glad about that,' Adam said, feeling a rush of courage. 'Because I'm falling for you so fast that I can hardly keep up.'

Liv tightened her arms around his neck and pulled herself up to lay a hard kiss on his mouth, only pulling away when they were both breathless and inappropriately aroused for the workplace. 'What do we do about—' she waved her arms around '—all this?'

'Work?' he asked.

'Yeah, like, are we still a secret?'

Adam shrugged. 'If that's what you want,' he said carefully.

'What do you want?'

'To shout it from the rooftops,' he said honestly, after taking a deep breath. And then glanced around them, realising where they were. 'Metaphorically speaking, that is. Unless you really want me to do it.'

'God, no,' Liv said, smiling. 'Saying it just to me is good enough. And not having to keep secrets sounds good too. Better. We could start small, with telling people.'

'Your family?'

'Yes,' she said carefully. 'Though Rowan noticed we didn't come home the other night, so...'

'So maybe we could hang out at your house sometimes. That'd be good,' he said. 'I like that we have somewhere a bit more private as well though.'

Livia gave him a self-satisfied smirk. 'Did I really ruin your flat for you? In one night?'

He gave her a stern look, tightening his arms around her waist in admonishment. 'That was meant to be a bad thing.'

She kissed him gently, and then let her teeth scrape his bottom lip, less gently. 'If it got us here, then I can't be sorry about it.'

Adam grinned. 'You know, Livia, that sounded almost…romantic.' She shoved at him, but he had hold of her too tightly for it to have much effect.

'Next you'll be okay with being called my girlfriend.' Adam held his breath, not sure how Liv would react to the word. Not sure how he wanted her to react. But she merely rolled her eyes.

'Fine, whatever, I'm your girlfriend,' she said. 'But only at home, not at the office. We need to keep things professional in the workplace.'

Adam laughed, and couldn't help pointing out that the first time that they'd slept together had, in fact, been in the office.

'Yes, but that doesn't count, because I didn't like you then,' Liv reasoned.

'And now?'

Liv rolled her eyes and groaned. 'Do you really need to hear me say it?'

Adam thought about it. About what he needed. What they both needed for this to work.

'I do,' he admitted. 'I need to know you like me. I need to know that you're as deep in this as I am.'

'Ugh. Okay, I like you,' she said, her expression

deadly serious, playfulness falling away. 'I more than like you. I've never felt like this about anyone before. This is really special to me. Are you happy now?'

He kissed her gently at the corner of her mouth. She was shaking slightly, and he knew what it had taken for her to trust him with that. He kissed her mouth, pulling her in tight as her lips came alive against his, opening to him, sealing the words that they had spoken. And he held her tight because he knew Liv needed it. Because it anchored him to be there for her.

'We should probably get back to work at some point,' Liv said, and Adam sighed, nodding.

'Before Jonathan comes up here looking for us?'

Liv winced. 'Yeah, that, but also—you know—biggest product launch of my career.'

'Oh, I know you've got that completely under control. I have every faith in you. But I would like to know in advance if Jonathan's going to come after me with a shotgun.'

Liv shrugged. 'I don't know. He's kind of overprotective. But he's also pretty convinced we can't do this launch without you, so I think your life is probably safe for now.'

'So I only have to worry about my manhood? That's very reassuring.'

Liv slid her arms around his neck and smiled. 'Let me worry about your manhood for now.' He laughed, pressed his forehead against hers.

'Okay, I trust you.'

CHAPTER THIRTEEN

LIV CLEARED PLATES from the table and glanced over at Rowan, Jonathan and Adam at the dinner table, chatting as if they did this sort of thing all the time. Her brother's arm was stretched out over the back of Rowan's chair, twirling the end of her ponytail around his fingers. They made this look easy, she thought, though she knew that it hadn't been. That they'd pined after each other for years before they'd taken the plunge and tried to make it work. Blissfully happy that they now were, they'd lost years by just being afraid of opening themselves up to the idea of a relationship.

She didn't want to lose years, or even months. Days, for that matter. As much as she was terrified of what it might lead to, she didn't want to look back on her life and regret the things that she hadn't done because of being afraid.

Especially not as a result of what her parents had done. She wasn't going to let them take this from her along with all the harm they had already done. She jumped slightly as Adam's arms slid around her waist from behind, still not quite used to the fact that they weren't sneaking around. 'Okay over here?' he asked, resting his chin against the side of her head. She twisted in his arms and leaned back against the sink.

She tried not to let her smile stretch too wide, because there was no reason to let him know just how head over heels she was for him. It would only go to his head and, really, the boy didn't need to be any more sure of himself.

'I was just thinking that this is nice,' she admitted, because Adam's lips on her neck tended to have that effect on her.

'I'm glad you're happy,' he said, close to her ear. 'Because I am. But not as happy as I will be when I get you back to my place later.'

Liv grinned. 'What, you don't want to sleep in a house with my whole family?'

'Oh, I wouldn't mind *sleeping*,' he said, still quiet so that no one else could hear. 'But I wasn't planning on letting you get much rest.' She laughed and swatted at him with a tea towel and from the corner of her eye noticed Caleb getting up from the table.

'Where are you off to?' she asked her little brother, turning away from Adam. 'Have another glass of wine.'

Caleb rolled his eyes. 'And watch you four play double footsies under the table? Thanks, but no, thanks.'

She pushed Adam away a fraction, fixing Caleb with a look.

'I'm sorry. Stay, we'll behave. All of us.' From the corner of her eye, she saw Jonathan pull his arm away from the back of Rowan's chair and lean his elbows on the table.

'Come on, Cal. One more.'

He hesitated, but then shook his head. 'Sorry, guys, there's someone I need to speak to.'

Liv narrowed her eyes as they all listened to his footsteps on the stairs.

'"Someone I need to speak to"?' Liv said. 'Do you think he's holding out on us?'

'I don't know. He barely leaves the house. If he's got someone…'

'Hmmm,' Liv said.

'Maybe let's give him some privacy if that's what the man wants,' Jonathan suggested.

Jonathan's hand had found the nape of Rowan's neck again, and Liv averted her eyes, and then turned away from the table completely.

'Ready to head off?' Adam asked, and Liv smiled, wondering whether the mind-reading was a sex thing, a spending-all-their-time-together thing, or a love thing. She stopped herself in her tracks with the word. *Love?* She looked at it in her head for a long time, waiting for the fear, or panic, or need to scarper to set in. But it just…didn't. The word sat there, comfortably, securely, and waited for her to wrap her head around it.

'Ready,' she said, looking up at him, wondering whether it was too soon to say it out loud.

'I don't know why you even bother with separate places,' Jonathan said idly, his eyes fixed on Rowan. 'You've not spent a night apart in weeks.' He looked up abruptly then, and Liv suspected that he'd first received a quick kick under the table. 'Oh, not that it's any of my business, of course,' he added hastily.

Rowan and Liv rolled their eyes in unison.

'Right, let's go,' Liv said, grabbing Adam's hand and heading for the stairs before her brother could make things any worse.

'He's right, you know,' Adam said as they reached the street. 'You've been at my place every night for—what—two weeks? Three?'

Liv stiffened. Was this where the other shoe dropped? Had it all been so good between them that she'd missed that it had been *too* good?

'Stop panicking,' Adam said, wrapping an arm around her shoulders, pulling her in tight and kissing the top of her head. 'I mean it. I know what you're thinking. I like having you here, but Jonathan's got a point. We don't need two places if we're going to spend every night together.'

Liv stalled.

'And maybe you should warn a girl before you spring something like that on her.'

Adam laughed nervously. 'Is that a no?'

'I'm sorry, did you ask a question?'

Adam sighed, but she'd not made this easy for him before, so why should she start now?

'You're really going to make me ask?'

She crossed her arms, not budging.

'Fine,' he said, his face as implacable as hers. 'Liv, will you move in with me?'

'Not if you're not even going to ask me nicely.'

He pulled her to him, wrapping his arms around her. 'Darling.' She laughed at the ridiculous endearment that he'd never used before. 'Liv, babe—'

'Better...'

'Babe. My flat only feels like home when you're in it, and I hate the thought of sleeping in my bed without you there, and I want to make you your first cup of coffee every morning. Will you please move in with me? Satisfied, now?'

He let go of her and crossed his arms, mirroring her body language. But she knew that he wasn't really cross. That he was just giving her the space to think this through without her having the pressure of knowing how much he wanted it.

'Fine,' she said at last, making sure it sounded as if she would be doing him a favour. 'I'll move in with you. I might as well now I've fallen in love with you.' She watched her words hit, slightly amused at how his jaw dropped.

'That's not fair,' Adam said, and she raised a questioning eyebrow. 'I was going to say it first,' he went on. 'And now you've stolen my moment.'

'Can't have you getting too comfortable,' Liv said with a smug smile, the knowledge that he loved her spreading from her chest out to the tingling tips of her fingers. She tucked them into the front pocket of his jeans, using them to pull him closer. 'I'm sorry,' she said, not feeling it in the slightest. 'You can say it now, if you want,' she offered.

'Oh, can I?' Adam asked, sarcastic. 'I was thinking maybe I'll wait. Tell you in my own time.'

Liv smiled. Because she didn't need him to say it. She could see it in his expression. Could feel it every time she was with him. He could say the words in his own time if that was what he wanted. She was in no hurry. They had so much time ahead of them, and she could wait, if it was for him.

EPILOGUE

.

'IS THIS EVERYTHING?' Adam asked, as they carried the last two boxes up into the flat and left them piled by the fireplace.

'I think so,' Liv said, wiping sweat from her forehead and looking around at the chaos. 'Rowan'll text me if any of my stuff got mixed with hers.'

After six months of all living together, she'd decided to rent out her house. Rowan and Jonathan had already been looking for somewhere, and she was never there anyway. When she'd asked Caleb about it he'd merely shrugged, and said that he'd find somewhere.

She'd have to decide what she wanted to do with her inheritance. She could invest the cash in the business. But Kinley's cash-flow problems were further and further behind them and she had bigger ideas than that. Like the homeless shelter around the corner from the town house. She just needed the right moment to talk to Adam about it. A meeting with the trustees of the charity to find out whether a cash donation or the property itself would make the biggest difference to their work.

She could face the idea of selling it, because the idea of change no longer seemed so terrifyingly destabilising. The last few months had brought more changes in her life in any period since her parents had left her without a backward glance, and she was happier than she'd ever been.

It wasn't that she had Adam now—though it was certainly no chore to be woken by his kisses on the back of her neck, his hands on her waist. It was that she had chosen to trust him, and herself, and the future.

'You know, I love…this colour on you,' Adam said, pulling at her dusty, sweaty T-shirt, which had once been white, but was now a delightful shade of dishwater grey. It had become a standing joke between them that he hadn't yet said the words. Liv didn't really mind. She knew that he felt them. And it had been enough of an adjustment to hear *herself* saying the words. More than once, since that first time. But for the first time, she felt a little twinge at not hearing them back. They were living together now, after all.

'Hey,' Adam said, catching her face between his palms, turning it up so that she'd have no choice but to look at him. 'I love you,' he said, desperately serious. She felt the smile break across her face.

'Of course you do,' she replied. 'Why wouldn't you?' Adam laughed, and then kissed her so thoroughly that she could be in no doubt about how he felt about her.

'A lot,' Adam added. 'I love you a lot. Making you so mad at me that you wanted to kiss me into being quiet is the best business decision I have ever made.'

She pushed at his chest, knowing his arms were tight enough around her waist. That he wouldn't let her go.

'I love you a lot too,' she said quietly. 'I can't imagine the rest of my life without you in it,' she confessed, pushing her hands into his chest to stop them shaking.

'Good,' he said, wrapping his hands around hers,

pulling them up to press his lips against them. 'Because I'm not planning on going anywhere.'

Liv sniffed, and he rubbed under her eye with a thumb. 'You'll tell me when I'm allowed to ask, won't you?' he said quietly.

Liv gave him a questioning look, confused. 'Allowed to ask what?'

Adam smiled, but didn't answer her question. 'Let me know when you've worked it out, and I'll know it's the right time.'

She nodded, a little dazed, having just worked out what question he meant, and wondering how mad he would get if she asked him to marry her first.

* * * * *

BAHAMAS ESCAPE WITH THE BEST MAN

CARA COLTER

MILLS & BOON

To Bill and Rose Pastorek,
with deepest gratitude for how generously
they have shared their gifts with me.

CHAPTER ONE

"Sir, we'll be landing in a few minutes."

Matteo Keller opened his eyes. He wasn't sure if he'd been sleeping, or just drifting.

Either was unusual. Usually, he found the time on board his company's private jet to be perfect for catching up on work, uninterrupted.

He had a well-honed jet lag strategy where he used the flight time to start resetting his inner clock from the time in Zurich to the time zone he would be arriving in.

Definitely sleeping, he thought, bemused, as he looked at the business papers that had slid from his tabletop desk and now lay around him. So much for his jet lag strategy. The sun was setting out there, and now he was wide-awake.

Right on top of the scattered papers was a brochure, shiny and colorful. Matteo picked it up. It described his destination, one of the two thousand four hundred cays and seven hundred islands that formed the Bahamas.

Coconut Cay, the safest place on earth.

Glancing at the pictures of the boutique hotel, the white sands and the turquoise waters of the island,

Matteo was not sure why safety had been picked as the main selling feature of the tropical paradise. If he was in charge of marketing...

You're not, he told himself firmly.

And maybe there *was* something to be said for the brochure's claim that doors could be left unlocked and your watch would be safe on the bedside table.

Well, maybe not *his* watch.

According to the brochure, the tiny island, which had several resorts and one village, had a zero crime rate, and each guest was carefully vetted.

He did vaguely remember his assistant asking him questions that had seemed, at the time, both mildly intrusive and slightly irritating.

Welcome to Sullivan's Island, he thought, calling it after a very old and very corny American sitcom about an unlikely group of people shipwrecked.

The island, as the jet descended, seemed idyllic, drowsy and gilded in gold. No doubt safe.

And yet he, of all people, knew that danger lurked in life itself. No matter how hard you tried, there would always be events out of your control, waiting to blow your world to smithereens.

Matteo was taken aback at himself.

That was what he got for dozing, instead of working, for not adhering to his rigid schedule to avert jet lag.

Those were unwanted thoughts, slipping outside of his customary discipline, his ability not to think of the world he had once had or lament how quickly it had slipped away.

He sincerely hoped *the safest place on earth* was not going to make a run at his carefully constructed barriers.

The plane touched down.

"It won't," Matteo told himself tersely, rising from his seat, "because I won't let it."

And yet here it was, nighttime, and he was wide-awake. And for some reason, when he disembarked the plane, he left the scattered business papers—his balm—behind.

Marlee Copeland decided she absolutely hated destination weddings. This was her third one in the past two years.

Admittedly, Coconut Cay was the most beautiful of the three. The small tropical island was extraordinary: gorgeous beaches, calm waters, rainbow-hued flowers the size of basketballs, mangoes, coconuts and banana clusters hanging in trees.

The resort was like something out of a dream. The color palette of the structures, inside and out, was creamy whites and soothing beiges, everything subdued and extraordinarily tasteful, in sharp and deliberate contrast to the vibrant backdrop of the island.

"So, what's to hate?" Marlee asked herself, the warm air—so different than the November dreariness she had left behind in Seattle—caressing her.

She was standing in darkness that felt somehow silky on her skin, on the pathway outside the private cabana she had wisely paid extra for instead of sharing accommodations with the other bridesmaids.

Night had fallen with the suddenness of a dark blanket being dropped over the sky, and she watched the stars wink out, one by one, and then a rising moon paint the caps of the gentle waves nearby in silver. She listened to them lap on shore. In the distance, she could hear laughter and voices at the pool.

The bridal side of the wedding party. Fiona, bride-to-be, had suggested they arrive a few days early, though not to unwind, as one might think after all the stress of planning a wedding three thousand miles from home.

No, the early arrival was to get rid of the "pasty" look. For the photos. Which had to be perfect, naturally. Marlee was fairly certain Fiona had cast her a glance when she made the "pasty look" comment.

Or maybe the bride's choice of a dress for her had just made her overly sensitive. Marlee sighed. She knew she should join them, of course. But she didn't want to. The fact she hated it all was just going to be too evident, no matter how hard she tried to hide it.

"What's to hate?" she asked herself again. A night bird chattered as palm fronds swayed in a faint breeze, the air faintly perfumed.

It was all so *romantic.*

And *perfect.*

And *that* was what Marlee hated. All the weddings she had been to lately—and there had been many as her friends were at that age where they were ready for the "next stage" in life—were like this. Romantic and perfect.

Admittedly, her cynicism had set in after her own wedding had fallen through, cancellation notices sent and her elaborate wedding gown boxed up and sent to the thrift store. Before that, at every wedding she'd attended, she had made notes, gleaned ideas and admired dresses.

This was the first wedding since her own matrimonial debacle. Now she felt weddings—including the one she hadn't had—were pure theater, where everyone played their part, especially the beautiful, joyous bride and the handsome, devoted groom, with eyes only for each other. It was pageantry, blind to the statistics that said it probably wasn't going to work out in quite the way the glowing bride and the besotted groom hoped.

Despite how justifiable Marlee's skepticism around weddings might have been, she knew in her heart that she was kidding herself. She still yearned for all that romance to be true.

"You're jealous," Marlee decided.

Was she? Of course! She was supposed to have had all this. Planning *her* day had consumed the better part of her life for over a year.

No destination wedding for her, because of her huge extended family, but instead a gorgeous old church and a posh hotel…and then, the exit by her fiancé, Arthur, just six months ago, embarrassingly close to their spring wedding date.

Even with the help of sympathetic—make that pitying—family members and friends, canceling everything and letting people know there would be no wedding had been nearly as much work as putting it all together.

Add to that the humiliation…

Jilted at the altar.

"I'm *not* jealous," Marlee ordered herself. She was just tired. There was only a three-hour time difference between this tiny island and her home, but the crazy fifteen-hour travel schedule from Seattle to Florida, onward to Nassau, and then finally to Coconut Cay, had left Marlee exhausted and discombobulated. Really, she didn't know if it was time to get up or time to go to bed. Should she have supper now or breakfast?

The other destination weddings she had attended had not required quite so much effort to get there.

Now everything felt like too much. They had barely been whisked to the resort from the tiny airport when Fiona had rounded them all up and herded them into her luxurious suite for the big reveal: the bridesmaid's dresses.

They were Fiona's "surprise" to her girlfriends who were standing up with her, a gift intended to in some way assuage the huge financial and time commitment involved in saying yes to being a part of a destination wedding. She had collected all their measurements and refused to reveal any details of the custom-made dresses. Until now.

Until they were trapped here and couldn't say no, Marlee thought, perhaps unkindly.

There were three bridesmaids and the dresses were all the same color—hideous. Fiona called it sea foam, but Marlee thought it looked like the Spanish moss that hung in creepy fingers from cypress trees in the Southern parts of the United States.

Though the same color, each dress purported to reflect the personality of the person it had been bestowed upon.

So Kathy's had narrow straps and a form-hugging bodice. The short, full skirt flirted around her long legs and accentuated a subtle but undeniable sexiness. Kathy looked like she had been at the tanning booth for at least a month. Nothing pasty about her!

Brenda's dress was a sleek, strapless sheath that, even while hugging her curves, hinted at a woman in control, and indeed, Brenda was CEO of a huge cosmetics company. That company had made their name—and a considerable fortune—on a tanning product called Beach-in-a-Bottle, so Brenda looked sun-kissed and glowing at all times.

And then there was Marlee's. It was, sadly, the dress of the high-school-girl-trying-too-hard variety. In fact, the dress sang *future librarian gets invited to a prom*. Never mind that she *was* a librarian—and had the pasty complexion to prove it! The dress was high-collared and short-sleeved, and abounded with puff and ruffles.

And, as if the dress in and of itself was not like something out of a nightmare, Fiona had gushingly proclaimed, "It's *so* you, Marlee."

And the others had agreed!

After the great reveal, Fiona had ordered them all to their own rooms to change out of the precious garments, and then suggested meeting at the pool for drinks and hors d'oeuvres.

But Marlee was still here outside her cabana—not as luxurious as Fiona's suite, but still beachy and charming—not changed, and despite being starving, was not going to the pool. The highly orchestrated schedule was already giving her a headache.

Not to mention a niggling but growing sense of rebellion.

Her cabana had come with a complimentary travel-size bottle of rum and a cigar. Apparently, the island was famous for both.

Marlee had never smoked a cigar. Ever. And she had certainly never drunk rum straight, but no mix had been provided.

In defiance of how that horrible dress said she was

perceived—by those who supposedly knew her best—
she cracked the rum open and held the cigar between
her fingertips, liking the way that felt—bold and glamourous in an old movie kind of way. If her friends were
to see her now, they would get the message.

You don't know me at all.

She took a tentative sip of the rum. Her eyes wa-
tered. She choked. On her empty stomach, it was like
swallowing fire.

Still, something warm and bold and lovely unfolded
in her. She took another tentative sip of the rum and
even looked at the cigar, considering whether she
should light it.

That was when she became aware she was no longer alone.

The curving pathway that wound around the cabanas on its way to the beach was only faintly lit, solar
lights twinkling in the deep, flower-threaded foliage
on either side of it, but she could see a man was coming toward her.

In Seattle, alone outside on a dark night, she probably would have ducked back inside. But there was a
light on in the cabana next door to hers, and through
its open doors she could hear the faint sounds of people
talking. Plus, she remembered the brochure's promise
that this was the safest place on earth.

The hotel had even sent a pre-arrival questionnaire
to make sure they were not inviting criminals or mis-
creants into their island paradise.

So, chances of the man coming down the walkway
being an ax murderer were largely reduced.

Besides which, she felt holding the cigar and sipping rum straight from the bottle asked her to be a dif-

ferent person, not quite so timid, not quite so willing to play it safe.

So, instead of moving away, Marlee watched the man approach. He was one of *those* men. You could tell by the way he moved. Not quite a swagger, but something smooth, confident and totally self-assured was in every step of that long stride.

The white towel draped around his neck was practically glowing against the darkness of the night.

He didn't have a shirt on, and as he got closer, the magnificence of him was fully revealed to her.

He was like a poster boy for *perfect*. Wide shoulders, a broad chest, faint lines of ribs under taut skin, a flat, hard belly that dipped into boldly colored swim shorts, the bareness of his legs showing off how long and sculpted with muscle they were. He was barefoot.

Really, Marley told herself sternly, there was nothing sexy about that. Barefoot went with the beach. He was obviously on his way for a swim.

In the ocean. Not the pool. In the darkness. By himself.

Okay. There was something a little sexy about that. Or maybe a lot.

Or maybe not. He'd probably heard all that feminine giggling at the pool and made a fast detour toward the ocean.

Some instinct stopped him in his tracks then and he squinted up the walkway in her direction. The moon painted silver tips in his dark hair and gilded his face, which was as perfect as the rest of him.

He seemed unfairly handsome, exactly the kind of man who never paid any kind of attention to a woman like her.

Marlee resisted, again, the impulse to slide back toward her open, French-paned door. Wasn't it exactly that shrinking librarian attitude that had earned her this dress?

CHAPTER TWO

AT THAT EXACT MOMENT, the man spotted her in the shadows. He hesitated, then moved forward cautiously, as if he knew a shrinking librarian when he saw one.

"I'm sorry," he said. "I didn't mean to startle you."

Since Marlee was trying very hard not to look startled, his apology was annoying. Still, if she was going to be startled, eyes like his would do it. In the faint illumination of the pathway lights and the moon, they seemed as turquoise as the sea had been before darkness fell.

"According to the resort map, I think this is the only way to the beach."

Now he was practically apologizing for using a public path. Exactly how buttoned-up did she look? Well, there was the dress, which she had not taken off, despite Fiona's orders. Perhaps she thought a few swigs of rum could improve it.

She was counting on the the cigar and the rum bottle, now to be contradicting the message of the dress!

His voice was rich and deep and reassuring in some way. She heard a faint and intriguing accent. The old Marlee—the one she had been just minutes ago, before being presented with this dress—would have just nodded, smiled politely and watched him move away, resigned to being dismissed.

"It seems like an odd time to indulge in a swim," she said, not quite flirting, but not retiring, either. *Engaging* him. She took a defiant swig of the rum.

Both the rum and engaging him felt deliciously dangerous in how terribly out of character they were for her.

He tilted his head toward her, faint surprise crinkling around his astounding eyes, making her notice they were fringed in lusciously abundant lashes.

"I've been working all day," he said. "There were some unexpected challenges. I need to clear my mind."

So he worked here. At Coconut Cay. She wondered what he did. Management of some sort, no doubt. There was something in the way he carried himself that suggested he dealt with people, and he was good at it. She wondered if those unexpected challenges he'd dealt with today had anything to do with Fiona's arrival, and was practically certain that they did.

"Well, I'm sure a midnight swim is good for that," Marlee said, though she wasn't sure at all. What did she know about midnight swims? She felt a sudden, sharp and somewhat shocking yearning for worlds unexplored.

Now that he was stopped, he was apparently quite happy to *engage*. His eyes trailed to the unlit cigar in her right hand. A smile twitched, drawing her attention to white, straight teeth, the fullness of his bottom lip.

Something happened to the air. It went from soft, and faintly perfumed, to charged, a before-the-storm intensity humming through it.

Marlee found herself entranced by him, and either

emboldened by the rum—or by the persona she had
indulged by holding the cigar as if she knew what to
do with it—she took a long, leisurely look at him. It
felt like a drink of cold water on a hot day.

More perfection.

His hair was a little long, tucked behind his ears, the
feathered tips riding his shoulders. It was very straight,
dark and milk chocolate strands sewn together. He had
high cheekbones, a straight nose and full, sensual lips.

There was a scent coming off him, as if his golden-
toned skin had absorbed sunshine all day and was now
emitting that tantalizing smell.

She was suddenly way too aware that she likely
smelled of a day's travel overlaid with rum, but it didn't
stop her from wondering if his skin would feel as warm
as it smelled. Her fingertips had this funny little itch
in them.

To touch him. A complete stranger. Ridiculous! She
was not that kind of girl.

Though, for the first time in her life, Marlee was
aware of maybe wanting to be.

She noted again that his eyes were—impossibly—
as turquoise as the waters of the bay.

"Speaking of odd indulgences…" he said. "Cigars
and rum at midnight?"

Marlee noticed that thread of humor that totally confident men always had in their tone in his voice.

"Actually, I don't think it is midnight," she said.

The stranger did not seem the least insulted by Marlee's tone, which may have been faintly querulous in
the face of his sheer attraction, his easy confidence,
and a whole different world his mere presence was letting her know she missed.

He lifted a shoulder. "You suggested it first. *Midnight* swim?" he reminded her.

"It's just a turn of phrase."

"Ah," he said, utterly composed. Of course, he no doubt spent his days dealing with cranky, demanding tourists, and soothing them with his deep, accented voice and his lovely eyes. In fact, his smile deepened. "It's midnight somewhere."

He'd know that, too, dealing as he did, with guests from all over the world.

He had a dimple, just on one side.

"Are you going to smoke that?" he asked, nodding to the cigar in her hand.

Apparently she *was* diverting attention from the sheer ugliness of the dress as he appeared not to have noticed it yet.

"I'm thinking of it," she lied, as if she was sophisticated and mysterious and smoked cigars all the time.

Unfortunately, that made her feel as if she had to prove something. She put it to her nose and sniffed it, something she was fairly sure an expert would do before lighting it.

He lifted a wicked slash of a dark eyebrow at her. "First time?"

So much for sophisticated and mysterious. He wasn't fooled. She wasn't sure how he managed to make those two words—first time?—sound quite so naughty.

She could pretend it wasn't her first time, but there seemed no point.

"What gave me away?"

"You're holding it as if you thought you had picked up a friendly neighborhood cat, but you've just realized it was a skunk, instead."

Marlee felt an unusual tickle. It wasn't the cigar. It was a giggle, and it shocked her, because she was not a giggler.

At all.

Could she chock that up to two or three mouthfuls of rum? Doubtful, no matter how strong the island rum was. It was him, teasing something girlish to the surface in her. So he was charming as well as handsome. He should come with a flashing neon sign.

Danger.

Again, though, if he dealt with people all day every day, this would be his skill set. Charming. Setting people at ease.

"I might smoke it," she said.

"Ah. And what would be the occasion for your first cigar?"

Was he just being conversational, or did he find her interesting? The possibility nearly tied knots in her tongue.

"People should try new things."

He cocked his head at her. "Forgive me for being presumptuous, but you don't look like the kind of woman who would voluntarily try anything that comes with a health warning on it."

Well, that either meant she looked healthy. Or like a nerd.

"It's the dress," she admitted reluctantly.

Why had she said that? First cigars were about celebrations: babies, job promotions... Instead, she had directed his attention to the full horror of her attire. The dress practically screamed wedding, and Marlee didn't actually want him to know she was a member of the demanding wedding party that was driving him into the sea in the darkness in hopes of clearing his head.

He regarded her attire solemnly and at length. She experienced the full, mesmerizing enchantment of the amazing color of his eyes and their framing in a decadent abundance of sooty lash.

She refused to squirm under a gaze that might be called stripping.

"That dress inspired the loss of cigar virginity?" he finally asked.

The word *virginity* coming from his mouth felt as if he had said something naughty and personal, especially since his thorough inspection had left her feeling as if something was tingling along her skin.

He didn't seem to recognize it as a bridesmaid's dress.

"It's vugly," she said.

He tilted his head. "I'm sorry. English is my second language. I'm rarely caught out, but I don't know that word."

"My own creation: vugly. A combination of very and ugly."

Her creativity was rewarded with a smile tickling the luscious sensuality of those lips.

"Vugly," he said, and gave a pleased chortle. "I'll have to file that one away for future use."

Yes, Marlee thought, it might be a useful addition to his vocabulary. He could use it to describe a bride having a temper tantrum over some tiny detail not quite right.

"Besides the fact it's vugly," Marlee went on, "it's frilly and fussy and it scratches."

"Where?" he asked, softly.

He managed to make that sound naughty, too, as if he could aid her in some way.

"Everywhere!"

"Ah," he said. He took a step back from her and studied the dress even more carefully. Those dark slashes of brows lowered in a thoughtful frown.

"It doesn't seem *you*, somehow," he decided.

At his proclamation, Marlee was sure she felt the ground shift under her feet, like rock crumbling in warning right before a cliff.

A complete stranger had *seen* her, when her own girlfriends had not. It made him even more compelling than he had been before. And he had already been plenty compelling.

Well, it wasn't as if she hadn't seen the danger sign.

But Marlee decided, right then and there, she was giving up on her lifelong tendency toward caution.

She would *embrace* the cliff. She wouldn't fall. She would jump! Not her, precisely, but the woman drinking rum and contemplating the smoking of a cigar.

"This dress makes me want to get on a horse, pull a bandanna over my face and rob trains," she told him.

The smile that had been tickling the wickedly attractive curve of his mouth formed fully, revealing the full straightness of his teeth, as white as the towel around his neck.

Then he threw back his head and laughed. The column of his throat looked strong and touchable. The sound of his laughter was more intoxicating than the rum.

She, Marlee Copeland, had just made a very attractive man laugh. That felt like a cigar-worthy reason for celebration!

"The cigar matches your start on your career as a criminal. People sometimes lick them before they light them."

"What?"

"They're usually wine-dipped."

She flicked the cigar with her tongue.

"Here," he said, gently. "Let me take that."

And just like that, his hand brushed hers, and a few more rocks crumbled from that cliff.

He took the cigar.

His eyes lingered on her lips.

A fire leaped to life within her.

"I wonder if there's really a wild, train-robbing outlaw under all that green fluffy stuff."

"It's not green." Her voice was hoarse, a choked whisper. "It's sea foam. Chiffon."

He held up the cigar and his tongue slipped out and licked it, exactly where her own tongue had been. His eyes were steady on hers. It was shockingly sensual.

"I need to get out of this scratchy dress," she said. What had made her say *that*? It was totally inappropriate. Did it sound as if she wanted to get out of the dress *with him*? Did it sound like an invitation?

Why did she always have to be so socially inept, blurting things out awkwardly?

Why did men like this always make her feel like a tongue-tied teenager?

Fiona had been right. This dress *did* suit her.

On the other hand, what would a train-robbing, cigar-loving, rum-drinking outlaw do? She could be that. For just a few minutes in time, she could. Maybe just for one night.

She took a deep breath. She felt as if she was on the edge of a cliff, trying to build up her nerve to jump.

"Want some company for your swim?" she asked. This was complete insanity. She was not a very good swimmer.

He tilted his head and regarded her, no doubt as surprised as she herself was.

Marlee's breath stopped in her chest. That was what you got for trying to break out of your mold, she thought, a little nervously.

A one-way trip off a cliff. The cigar, the rum, the remarks had made her feel as if she could be bold.

One thing she should remember about cliff jumps: as exhilarating as the ride down was, the landing was going to be bumpy. Painful.

He was going to think of a way to squirm out of it. *He needed to be alone. He'd had a hard day at work.*

"Of course, I'd love for you to join me," he said.

A man like him—just like a dress like this—made her reconsider the kind of girl she had always been.

She was on a tropical island with a complete stranger. Why not let loose? Why not let down her hair? Did she really want to be the person that was looked at in a dress like this and heard the proclamation, *It's you.*

Marlee was not the kind of girl who went for moonlit swims with strange men. But what had she ever gotten out of life by being the kind of girl she was?

"Are you allowed to?" she blurted, realizing she was scrabbling for an exit.

He raised a questioning eyebrow at her.

"You know. Um, fraternizing with the guests. It's usually against the rules. Of a resort."

Sheesh. As if she was any kind of expert in resorts.

"You're right," he said, after a moment. "It usually is. But there's something about a cigar-holding woman that just brings out the outlaw in me, too."

She shivered. He was so sexy it felt as if she was swan-diving off that cliff, her arms flung open wide to a terrifying and exhilarating adventure where there was absolutely no way of predicting how or where she would fall.

CHAPTER THREE

SHE DIDN'T EVEN know his name and there was something thrilling and electrical leaping in the air between them.

Marlee was aware she was playing with the proverbial fire.

Still, she was on this island for five days for a wedding. Only three whole days if you took out the travel days. It felt as if the clock was ticking.

She could remake herself into anything she wanted to be.

Couldn't she?

She suddenly couldn't wait to rid herself of the dress and any remnant of the person she had always expected herself to be.

"I'll babysit the cigar while you go change." He put it to his lips again and took a leisurely taste of it. Even though it was not lit, the air was filled with sweet, smoky sensuality.

Unfortunately, there weren't many ways that could draw a woman's attention to a man's mouth more than that.

"Almost as good as a kiss," he decided, his voice

sultry and hot like the tropical night. "I can taste you on it."

As if this wasn't dangerous enough without kisses entering the discussion! She felt a deep sense of wanting to taste him.

And not through a shared, unlit cigar, either.

"I don't even know you name."

"Matteo," he offered. "And yours?"

"Marlee."

He bowed slightly. "The pleasure is mine."

Good grief! It was? *Matteo.* What a gorgeous, exotic name.

"I'll just be a sec," she croaked, and slipped through the open door of her cabana. Her heart was beating as hard as if she had just run a hundred-meter dash with a gold medal at stake.

Now what? She hoped good sense—something she was known for, which meant she probably deserved this dress—would return. But it did not.

Her cheeks felt hot. She hoped the darkness had hidden that from him.

Or did he suspect she was a little naive and not very worldly?

Still, here was the truth. She, Marlee Copeland, librarian from Seattle, was going to go for a midnight swim with a gorgeous, exotic man named Matteo. Was it midnight?

Who cared? It was just as he said. It was midnight somewhere. It was dark. It was completely against her nature to be so spontaneous, so throwing-caution-to-the-wind. Maybe that was why it felt so absolutely exhilarating.

Marlee went through the darkened space of her tiny

cabana, not wanting to turn on a light. What was that about? She was afraid the dreamlike quality of this experience could not hold up to having a light shined on it, that's what.

That should have given her pause, but it didn't. Instead, she found her suitcase, open on the bed, and rummaged through it in the dark until her hands found the slippery fabric of her swimsuit.

She ducked into the bathroom. Again, she was reluctant to turn on the light, as if the fairy tale would come to an end if exposed to light. Plus, of course, she'd have to look at herself in her swimsuit.

That would be enough to make her lose her nerve.

Somehow, she got out of the dress and left it in a rumpled pile on the floor. She wriggled into the swimsuit. It was a one piece. It felt as if it was binding. She knew she had gained a bit of weight since her jilted-at-the-altar fiasco. Five pounds. Maybe ten.

That's why she had been earmarked for the hideous dress. To artfully hide a few pounds so she wouldn't wreck the wedding photos.

Okay, so she wasn't sexy in a swimsuit. She did not need any more sexiness than his presence already provided. And despite the cigar and the rum and saying yes to the invitation, she didn't want him to get the wrong idea.

Or did she?

Suddenly wrong and right and who decided these things seemed like terrible constraints to adventure and boldness and living life one hundred percent.

Was she really going to go for a swim with a stranger?

She came to her senses, just like that. She threw on

the light. As she had suspected, the bathing suit did absolutely nothing for her. She looked like she had been stuffed into a sausage casing.

She looked extraordinarily plain, with her mousy, shoulder-length hair still travel-crumpled. Her green eyes had tired smudges under them. The bathing suit revealed way too much skin that had a certain lard-like shade to it. No wonder Fiona had suggested a few extra days in the sun!

In fact, Marlee thought she looked exactly like a person who spent their days in a library, carefully selecting wonderful books for the highlight of her week—story time!

She was the kind of person *that* dress was made for. The kind of person abandoned a week before their wedding because her fiancé had suddenly discovered the painful truth.

It was all too dull and unexciting for him.

Which she translated to mean *she* was too dull and unexciting for him.

For Arthur. Who had not exactly been a ball of fire himself.

She quickly gathered the dress off the floor and hung it over the shower bar. She took a deep breath, mourning the moment that almost had been. Then, Marlee wrapped a towel around herself, marched across the floor and poked her head out the door.

She could see him standing out there, his wide, naked back to the cabana. Matteo. What was that, exactly? Italian? They liked their women more on the voluptuous side, didn't they?

The words she was going to speak—*I've changed*

my mind, I've come to my senses—froze inside her. She took a deep breath. They still didn't come out.

A voice inside her begged her to prove Arthur wrong.

Live.

For once, just live.

Marlee backed away from the door and returned to the suitcase. Tucked into a corner of it was the lingerie she had chosen for her own wedding night.

When she had packed it, she had told herself she was being practical. Why let it go to waste? The underwear—which had promised to be seamless—had been beautiful underneath her wedding gown. Why not use it with her bridesmaid's dress? Wouldn't those same seamless qualities be great for a day where she would be somewhat in the spotlight? Where she would be posing for pictures?

The reveal of the bridesmaid's dress really rendered all those reasons to use the underwear unnecessary. There were so many frills that an extra underwear line or two would hardly be noticeable!

Her hidden self, she thought, as she touched the exquisite lace on the matching white bra and panties.

Of course, when she had purchased them, she had done so in anticipation that someday her hidden self was going to be revealed to her delighted groom.

The saleslady had even shown her a quick release on the bra, saying, "To minimize the, er, awkward moments of your wedding night."

Marlee was so tired of being the good girl. She was so tired of living by the rules.

Yes. She would go for a midnight swim. With a

sexy stranger. In her underwear, instead of her frumpy bathing suit. These days, and in the dark, who could possibly tell the difference?

Matteo waited on the darkened path in front of Marlee's cabana. The night was unbelievably beautiful: stars studding an inky dark sky, the air so soft and moist it felt like a touch, the waves whispering a timeless song. A nearby bird screeched loudly, and he caught sight of bright feathers through the waxy green foliage of palm trees.

He had not been to the tropics before, and standing here, in the utter enchantment of it, he wondered why.

Of course, how much of the enchantment was his chance encounter with her?

Marlee.

He was, he thought, misrepresenting himself just a bit. For some reason the cigar-wielding vision that had materialized on the pathway thought he worked at the resort.

She had been a surprise, tucked in among the foliage, fondling the cigar and drinking rum.

She said it was because of the dress, but it wasn't until she mentioned it that he had even noticed it.

Not when he was entranced by her eyes. They were as green and lustrous as jade. They were so compelling, now that he thought about it, he couldn't recall the color of her hair.

But he could imagine her lips: wide, plump, unglossed, and not in need of any kind of improvement, either.

There was something about her both understated

and overstated, which made her an intriguing contradiction that begged exploring. She had the clear eyes of an angel, but she was debating corrupting those luscious lips by smoking a cigar and dreaming of robbing trains!

He increasingly lived in a highly predictable world. Everything was highly scheduled. Managed. Controlled.

He liked it that way.

But if he liked it so much, why was he so susceptible to the intrigues of a spontaneous encounter?

Maybe, Matteo admitted reluctantly, it was a distraction from that troubling thought he'd had looking at the brochure, which claimed Coconut Cay was the safest place on earth. His painful experience was that danger rarely came from outside sources.

He didn't want to think about that, revisit the pain of his mother's long illness and his brokenhearted father's terrible slide…

He deliberately avoided relationships deepening into the zone where they could cause that kind of cataclysmic destruction of a world.

He was a numbers man, and he had done the cost-benefit analysis. He had seen, firsthand, the terrible cost that could be extracted at the altar of love.

So, given all that, this distraction itself had the potential for danger, didn't it?

Not really. He was here for a few days. Tonight was his only free evening. There was, thankfully, no time for developments of the complicated romantic kind.

He was going for a swim. Period.

Because of the meteoric rise of the family business he had saved from near ruin, Matteo was a public figure now. He could not risk being politically incorrect, letting his guard down, not even for one playful moment.

As was so much these days, this forever being on guard was part of what made living life in the spotlight so tiresome.

He'd told Marlee he'd been working all day. That there had been some unexpected challenges. She had jumped to the conclusion that he'd been working *here*.

The truth was he'd been thirty thousand feet above the earth, in his private jet, working on a business issue so complicated and dull it had put him to sleep.

To be honest, he found it hard to envision what kind of unexpected challenges might arise in a place like Coconut Cay.

Still, he had not rushed to correct her, to assure her he would in no way be fraternizing with her.

The truth was he had *enjoyed* her not having a clue about who he was. Increasingly, and distressingly, in Europe he was recognized as the CEO of Monte Rosa Alpen. He'd recently been stopped, in downtown Zurich, by a French tourist who had wanted his autograph and a photo together!

But success wasn't just making him highly—and uncomfortably—recognizable by strangers.

It was changing the way people around him interacted with him.

Women, in particular, seemed besotted with what his success could mean to *them*.

And for all that the attention was flattering initially, Matteo found he had quickly become quite jaded.

When was the last time he had been liked for himself, instead of being seen as an opportunity, an important connection, someone who could be *used?*

He was grateful for old friendships, the ones he had had since long before he had achieved such success.

Which was how he found himself on Coconut Cay when he really didn't have the time right now to be here, and when this, despite its exotic beauty, wasn't his kind of place.

Or at least he had thought it wasn't. But now that he was here, he wasn't so sure.

He hadn't allowed himself the gift of downtime for as long as he could remember. He sometimes dreamed of the high and rugged places of his youth, far away from the pressures of his electronics and his life, but he did not indulge.

He was driven, absolutely and utterly. He had been consumed by a single mission. Saving the business that had been in his family for four hundred years.

No, there was no time for frivolities in Matteo's life. Even now, there was a sense that he could not let his guard down, that it all could slip away, as it had done for his father.

But when an old university friend—a friend who knew Matteo inside and out, and was unmoved by the fact he had graced the covers of business magazines or that he had been listed as one of the one hundred wealthiest people in the world—asked a favor, the answer was simply yes.

Because you knew that friend would do the same for you. And would do the same for you regardless of whether you were one of the richest men in the world, or down-and-out on a street corner somewhere.

The door whispered open behind him, and he turned.

Marlee appeared, and it seemed as if she might be dressed in only a towel!

CHAPTER FOUR

MATTEO'S MOUTH WENT DRY.

Though, now that he looked more carefully, he could see—thank goodness—narrow white bathing suit straps over her shoulders.

For some reason, the realization she had something on under the towel did not take away the dryness from his mouth.

He was not sure he had ever seen eyes as green as hers. In an environment that shimmered with a thousand enchanting shades of that color, her eyes put all else to shame.

They invited something in him to let go.

It felt as if his barriers dissolved completely. Instead of feeling terrifying, it felt freeing. For this one moment in time, he would accept the reprieve he had been granted from all his responsibilities and obligations.

Marlee's hair—the hair Matteo hadn't remembered because he was so entranced with her eyes—was light brown, and the moonlight played with that, spinning it into shades of gold.

Her feet and shoulders were bare, the skin of her shoulders milky white, but the moon played with that, too, and her skin seemed to be shimmering with silver.

Were those straps over her shoulders bathing suit straps, or was she in her underwear?

Matteo gulped. What, exactly, had he allowed into his well-ordered life? He set down the unsmoked cigar on a rock wall as if it was the problem, the reason he was in this predicament.

He, of all people, should know what a terrible path giving in to these kinds of temptations could take a man down.

They walked, in silence, to the beach. He was aware the scent of her was clean, fresh, unperfumed.

He had seen the beach from the plane earlier, but nothing could have prepared him for the astounding beauty of it at night. It was a crescent of pure white sand, surrounded by gently swaying palms. The foamy waves caressing the shore were, like her skin, spun to silver.

He hesitated. He recognized this as a jumping-off point. A choice to turn away from the organized life he had made for himself.

This encounter was ripe with opportunities for what Matteo liked least: the unexpected. Could he say to her he had made a mistake? Or that he didn't feel like swimming after all? Could he alter the course, right now, of what was about to happen? Did he want to?

He could feel her hesitation, too.

He turned and looked at her.

Her eyes captivated him, again. So many contradictions. How could she seem both bold and shy?

How could she seem both strong and fragile?

If he said, right now, he had changed his mind, he felt, intuitively, he would hurt her in some way and he could not do it.

He took the towel from his shoulders and dropped it to the sand. He was aware that his senses were intensely engaged: he could smell the sea, and Marlee. It felt as if he could feel each individual grain of sand beneath his feet.

And so, when the towel dropped from her, it was but a whisper, and yet, with his senses so heightened, it sounded like thunder in the distance.

He was afraid to look.

And he could not have stopped himself from looking. Not if his entire future and his entire fortune were on the line.

She was not dressed in a bathing suit.

She was dressed in a bra and panties, brilliantly white against the night darkness. They were heart-stoppingly skimpy and appeared to be constructed of mist and cobwebs. Marlee was a goddess of sensuality. Her creamy white skin—perfect—pebbled as the night air touched it.

Matteo thought of all his control, and how, even with all that, he could not have predicted the day ending like this, in a moment that shimmered and sizzled with her pure allure. Her femininity, the sweet curves of her, made him feel masculine. And strong.

And completely powerless at the same time.

As Matteo took her in, Marlee felt the air turn electric around them, as if a power line had broken and was whipping back and forth, snapping and cracking.

Her skin shivered with awareness as she contemplated the fact that she—Marlee Copeland, librarian—was on a beautiful beach, nearly naked in her wedding night lingerie, with a man she did not know.

It had to be a dream.

And if it was, she was making the most of it. The new her—the one that was surprisingly embracing this bold persona—laughed out loud and relished how Matteo's eyes darkened from turquoise to navy blue.

She broke the intensity and dashed by him.

"Race you to the water," she called over her shoulder.

They raced across the creamy, fine sand. Despite her lead, he surged ahead of her, but they reached the edge of the water together, and the shocking chilliness of the ocean would have stopped her dead, except he continued forward. When he realized she had lost momentum, he reached back, grabbed her hand and flung himself into water the color of black ink, drawing her in with him.

The water closed over her head. Choking, she found the sandy bottom with her feet, and she rose out of the water. It occurred to her she wasn't sure how transparent her underwear was when wet, so she ducked back down, squatting in the water, the sea lapping at her chin.

He was not so self-conscious. Well, why would he be? Marlee watched the water sluice off the beautiful lines of Matteo's sculpted chest. He looked just a little too pleased with himself, though, because he was such a fine male specimen, or because he had managed to duck her, she wasn't sure.

"Hey!" she scolded him. "I wanted to get in slowly."

He made chicken sounds. Because she wanted to get in slowly, or because she was up to her chin in water?

"I'm not a very good swimmer," she said.

He looked immediately contrite, and she took advantage and splashed him mightily. He laughed and darted away from her before she could wind up and get him again. And the game was on. Soon, as they chased each other through the dark water, she lost all sense of self-consciousness. They ran and played until they were utterly breathless with laughter and exertion.

The resistance of the sea pulling on their thighs made it feel as if they were slogging through quicksand.

He was way stronger than her. Way faster. He could have easily outstripped her, but he was deliberately slowing down, teasing her, making her think he was within arm's reach, before putting on another burst of speed.

When he slowed again, with a mischievous, you-can't-catch-me glance over his broad shoulder, Marlee threw herself in his direction. She connected! Gleefully, she wrapped her arms around his waist and clung there. His skin was warm and slick, alive somehow, beneath her fingertips.

With a shout, he toppled, and as he splashed into the ocean, she let go of him, not feeling nearly as cautious of the water as she usually did. When Matteo rose out of the water, she was already running away from him.

She was laughing so hard she could not gain traction. She could feel him gaining on her, his breath hot on her neck. She tumbled down under a wave. He sliced in behind her, grabbed her foot and held while she came to the surface, stood on one leg and tried to kick free.

The water didn't feel cold anymore. It was now as warm and sensuous as his touch.

"I'm going to drown," she warned him, bouncing on one leg and splashing him. "From laughing."

"Ah," he said, not releasing her foot. "But what a way to go."

It would be a great way to go, Marlee decided. It felt as if she could drown on laughter. And joy. Freedom. When had she ever felt this free?

And then he took the captive foot and, his eyes locked on her face, he lifted it to his lips.

It still felt, again, as if she was going to drown, but suddenly not from laughing. Her laughter died. His lips touched her big toe, and then, shockingly, his tongue darted between her big toe and the next one.

The sensation was so strong it felt as if it could not be borne by something as inconsequential as a human being. Time stood still. Her every sense rippled and her every nerve tingled. She could see each drop of water as it slid through his hair, down his neck, caressed his bare, wet chest.

He let go of her foot, apparently as stunned with himself as she was.

She stared at his lips. She wanted desperately to taste him.

It occurred to Marlee that she had nearly married a man who had never once made her feel anything like what she was feeling now.

The earth shifting beneath her feet, the stars swirling in the inky night above her.

Earthquake.

Or maybe tsunami.

The playfulness seemed to be gone from the moment, but it had felt so much safer that she tried to restore what they had been seconds ago. She splashed him, hoping to somehow recapture their earlier mood. But the water caught at her legs and she went down. She swallowed water and floundered. She felt panic set in.

Then strong arms caught her, lifted her to her feet. She leaned into him and sputtered as he pounded her back.

Finally, she got her breath and took a step away from him.

"I think I might live," she croaked.

"Uh," he said, "Marlee?"

She nodded, licked her lips. How could her mouth feel so dry with all this water around them?

"You seem to have, um, lost something."

She tilted her head toward him. She was aware she had indeed lost something. Her sanity. And it was the most blissful loss of her life.

"Your bathing suit top," he said, his voice a hoarse whisper.

She dropped her head and felt the absolute shock of it. Obviously her quick-release wedding night bra was not made for strenuous water play. The magic drained from the moment like air from a needle-pricked balloon.

She squealed, folded her arms around herself and sank down in the water to her neck.

"Don't look!" she ordered him.

"Um, okay."

But he was still looking!

"Stop it!"

"Okay," he said. He held up his hands in surrender and turned away from her.

Not trusting him at all, Marlee duckwalked toward shore, and when she was close enough, she rose and sprinted. Utterly mortified, she practically catapulted from the water and up the beach to where her towel was. She grabbed it, wrapped it around herself and raced for the safety of her cabana.

That had been just a little too *free.*

She did not look back. She did not want to see his embarrassed expression. In fact, Marlee hoped with all her heart that she would never see Matteo again.

This was a lesson for her: she was not the carefree kind of girl.

She was not the woman who could let go of control and experience no consequences. She was not the bandanna-wearing-bandit type.

It had been an experiment and it had failed. She should never have let go of who she really was.

And she never would again.

Never.

Considering how humiliating the experience had been, she expected embarrassment might keep her up all night. Instead, she slept deeply and dreamlessly and woke up ravenous. When she looked at herself in the mirror in the morning, she expected to look as if she had a hangover.

But even though her hair was a mess from sleeping on it wet, her eyes had a shocking glow to them. Her appearance really suggested more had happened than chasing each other through the sea and losing her top.

Marlee tossed on a sweat suit and a pair of dark glasses, and pulled a ball cap low over her eyes. Although satisfied that her disguise would keep her from being recognized for the underwear-clad nymph who had played in the water, or for a cigar-holding, rum-swilling bandito, she kept a wary eye out for a certain hotel employee in case she had to duck behind a palm tree to avoid an encounter.

Marlee made her way to the resort restaurant, marveling at how the early-morning sun made the sweat suit seem as if she was overdressed already.

The resort had a different feel in the bright morning light. The thick foliage lining the curving paths rioted with kaleidoscopes of flowers whose scents tickled her nostrils and perfumed the air. Sparkling white villas and cabanas were nearly completely hidden by thick greenery, even if they were only steps from the path.

The path opened to the pool, blue waters mirrorlike. Navy-striped lounge chairs underneath huge, taupe-colored umbrellas were scattered around it. Off to one side of the pool was the main dining center and a cluster of quaint, partially open-air shops that specialized in resort must-haves: everything from books to snorkels to swimsuits. A bright yellow sundress caught the breeze in front of one of them and danced, flirting with her.

Ignoring its temptations, she entered the restaurant. Marlee lifted her sunglasses and let her eyes adjust to the sudden dimness. The dining facility was utterly gorgeous, displaying an eclectic mix of antique cane furniture and amazing portraits of local island people.

Still, she mustn't let her curiosity and her love of such things get her guard down. She took a furtive look around and settled her sunglasses on the brim of her ball cap. She quickly filled a plate at the buffet, intending to take it back to her room. She was starving. She hadn't eaten at all last night.

"Marlee! There you are!" Fiona came through the doors and sailed over to her, a battleship on a mission.

"You didn't come to the pool last night," she said accusingly.

"I'm sorry. I was exhausted. I fell asleep."

Marlee was a little shocked by how easily the lie tripped off her lips. However, the truth—that she had been playing in the sea with a handsome stranger—was more likely to seem like a fib to the woman who had chosen *that* dress for her.

Fiona regarded her with very real concern. "You're not sick, are you?"

"I hope not."

"Because that would throw a real wrench into the wedding."

Marlee looked at her friend and felt as if she was seeing something she had never seen before.

Not about her friend. Fiona was just Fiona.

But about herself. And what she had accepted in life, from a fiancé who would abandon her at the altar, to a friend who was more concerned about appearances than her friend's well-being.

That was the problem with experiencing life the way Marlee had experienced it last night.

Yes, it had been brief.

But she had been so on fire with life. So engaged. So joyous. So uncontrolled. So free.

A person was changed by that.

No matter how badly the unfortunate consequences made them want to leave it behind them.

"Look," Fiona said. "I want to show you something."

She pulled her phone out of her pocket and held it up to Marlee. A woman in a beautiful bridal gown was kissing the nose of a wide-eyed foal.

"Isn't that the best wedding picture ever?" Fiona asked dreamily.

"Um…" Marlee said. She was aware yesterday she would have just demurred. Sure. Best wedding photo ever.

But she could feel a shift in her. "I guess I don't really see the relevance."

Fiona tsked. "*You* wouldn't. Anyway, eat up." She took a sudden interest in Marlee's plate. "Goodness, all those carbs!"

And the carb addict had been cavorting in the sea with the world's most attractive man last night. Perhaps losing her top hadn't even been the most embarrassing part of the evening. Her wedding lingerie! And the extra bulges from mourning her canceled wedding. Madness.

Marlee thought of Matteo's lips on her foot and shivered, felt again some shift inside.

This time she was annoyed with herself. She and Fiona had been friends since the fifth grade. You didn't start looking at your friends with a critical eye because a strange man had kissed your foot!

"Please don't be sick!" Fiona instructed her. "I've made spa appointments for this afternoon. Pedicures. Matching toenails for all of us! Won't that make a great wedding photo? Not as good as the baby horse, of course, but still."

Despite her desire not to be critical of her friend, Marlee bit her tongue to prevent herself from asking if Fiona planned to have Mike, the groom, in any of her wedding photos.

The door to the restaurant swung open.

Oh no! Marlee felt panicked. It was Matteo. He

looked even more gorgeous in the light of day then he had last night. She felt paralyzed.

He wasn't in the tidy gray uniform the hotel staff wore. In fact, he looked exceedingly casual in a patterned button-down shirt, pressed khaki shorts, and sandals.

His hair was wet. He must have just showered.

He looked effortlessly sexy.

Move, she ordered herself while Fiona was distracted by him. Well, what woman wouldn't be?

The man had seen her bare breasts! She certainly didn't want him to see her crumpled, pale pink sweat suit or her plate full of carbs!

She yanked the sunglasses down and pulled the cap low over her eyes. She set down her food on the nearest table, never mind the looks of the astonished people dining there.

Marlee looked desperately for an exit that would not take her anywhere near him. She saw one and slunk toward it.

CHAPTER FIVE

ALMOST THERE. MARLEE just had to squeeze behind that warming tray full of scrambled eggs and then—

"Oh my!" Fiona squealed. "Matt!"

Marlee froze and watched in horror as Fiona raced across the room and enveloped Matteo in a hug as if he were her long-lost friend. Then, the bride-to-be turned and scanned the room.

Marlee's hand was on the door. She hoped it wasn't one of those exits that was for emergency use only.

She pressed down on the lever and allowed relief to sweep her when no alarm went off as the door swung open a crack. The relief was short-lived.

"Marlee," Fiona cried, "come here! You must meet our best man."

What? No! Matteo was *not* their best man. Their best man's name was Matt. It was somebody Mike had gone to college with. They'd been roommates.

Still, she lost that precious opportunity to make good her escape as she grappled with the fact that Fiona knew Matteo.

Fiona was gesturing her over.

Run, Marlee ordered herself.

She let the door close with herself still on the in-

side of it. If they were all in the same wedding party—
and apparently they were—why put off this horrible
reunion?

With one last forlorn look at the exit, Marlee reluctantly shuffled across the room.

"Marlee, this is Matt Keller, our best man," Fiona
gushed. "Marlee is one of my bridesmaids. I've been
telling her all about you, haven't I, Marlee?"

Yes, indeed she had.

Mike's best man, his friend from college, had gone
on to become some kind of international tycoon who
regularly front-covered all the European business magazines. Fiona seemed to regard someone of his reputation and fame being part of the wedding party as a
personal coup.

"We've met," Marlee said awkwardly. She glanced
into those turquoise eyes. She was pretty sure they
were dancing with mirth. She took interest in the buffet. She didn't offer her hand.

"You have?" Fiona stammered. "But how is that—"

"Barely," Matteo said smoothly, and Marlee shot
him a look. A little smile was tickling the gorgeous
line of those lips. Those lips that had touched her toes
ever so briefly.

Marlee could feel a blush rising in her cheeks. Still,
she tilted her chin bravely and gave him a narrow-eyed
look of warning.

"I found the suit you left me," Matteo said to Fiona
without looking at Fiona at all. His eyes, brimming
with laughter, were intense on Marlee's face. "Double-breasted."

Her face felt incredibly hot, like it might catch fire.
She prayed Fiona would not notice.

"What?" Fiona said. "It was not! Double-breasted? That would be a disaster."

"Not at all," Matteo said smoothly. "I quite liked it."

Marlee felt as if she would like to kick his shin to wipe that smug look off his face.

Fiona's voice rose shrilly. "Please tell me they didn't deliver the wrong suit. I'm not sure it could be fixed at this point. I'm finding out it's very hard to get things here."

"Come to think of it, I don't think it was double-breasted," Matteo said, apparently taking pity on the misery he was causing poor Fiona by having a laugh at Marlee's expense. "I'm just preoccupied."

If his eyes dropped to what he was preoccupied with, Marlee thought she would probably die. But they didn't. They remained steadfast on hers.

"Of course you are, Matt," Fiona cooed. "Such a large company! But if you could check the suit as soon as possible. I'm panicking!"

"I will. No need to panic." He still did not take his eyes off Marlee. She tilted her chin a little higher at him.

Fiona shot a look between Matteo and Marlee. She frowned suspiciously. Marlee could see Fiona didn't really like it that Matteo was focused on Marlee and not her. She whipped out her phone.

"I was just showing Marlee this picture. What do you think?"

Marlee caught a glimpse of the bride-with-foal shot before Matteo took the phone and squinted thoughtfully at it.

"Interesting," he said, his attention turned briefly to Fiona's phone.

"It won the bride photo of the year."

Matteo turned his attention back to Marlee. He lifted an eyebrow. He might as well have spoken, their thoughts were so close.

Who knew there was a bride photo of the year?

Fiona drew in a breath. "There must be horses here on Coconut Cay. There must be! I bet if I can find a horse, the photographer could replicate this shot."

Marlee didn't want to lengthen this encounter by pointing out to Fiona that replicated shots probably had little chance of becoming a bride photo of the year.

"Isn't that odd?" Matteo said smoothly. "I know someone else who was looking for a horse. And a bandanna, and a train to rob."

Fiona looked at him, bewildered.

"Well," Marlee said brightly. "I was just leaving—"

"How hard could it be to find a horse?" Fiona asked. "Matteo, could you do it?"

He lifted a shoulder. "I doubt it. I'm not familiar with this place."

Now it was Marlee's turn to feel her mouth quirking upward. "Of course he could find a horse," Marlee said. "How hard could it be?"

He scowled at her. "I barely found the beach last night."

"Mike says you're totally a genius," Fiona said. "That you can do anything."

"Finding a photogenic horse will be child's play for you," Marlee could not resist adding.

His look darkened. He looked exceedingly sexy with that sinister look on his face.

"So that's settled," Fiona said with relief. "Thank you, Matt."

He looked slightly stunned. Marlee smirked.

"This morning? Please?"

Marlee's satisfied grin turned into a snicker, which she tried to suffocate. A mistake, as it drew Fiona's attention to her.

"Marlee, you go with him."

"What? No. I—"

"I mean, he's a businessman. The artistic aspects of it would probably be totally lost on him."

"The artistic aspects of finding a horse?" Matteo muttered.

"Exactly the problem," Fiona said. "It's not *any* horse. It's a baby horse. Not a white one, though, I don't want it to disappear in my dress."

"Now, *that* would make a photo," Matteo said, dead-pan.

Marlee stifled another giggle.

"I meant the horse needs to contrast with my dress," Fiona clarified, annoyed. She looked between them. "That's the part I'm trusting you with, Marlee. You're very artistic. Remember the time you turned the library into a medieval castle for—"

"The library?" Matteo asked, arching one surprised eyebrow upward.

"Marlee's a librarian."

"A librarian," Matteo said, and the eyebrow went up even further.

"Actually, I can't remember why you turned the library into a castle," Fiona said, tapping her lip thoughtfully with one finger.

"King Arthur Days," Marlee said, a bit tightly. There. She was completely unmasked. Though after her quick exit from the water last night, Matteo had probably already figured out she wasn't really any kind of a wild outlaw.

She was a nerdy girl.

"I'm not asking too much, am I?" Fiona asked with a soft flutter of her lashes at Matteo.

Yes, Marlee thought, *she is.*

"Of course not," Matteo said evenly, seeming to have put away his reluctance for the task. He winked at Marlee. "We will make it our sacred mission."

We?

Marlee was not sure it was safe to think about sacred missions with a man like this.

"Won't we?" he prodded her. "Get abreast of this request, immediately?"

"I had something to do this morning," Marlee said.

"Nonsense," Fiona said dismissively. "Matteo, just make sure Marlee's back in time for pedicures."

He looked pointedly at Marlee's sandal-clad feet. She remembered the feel of his mouth on her toes.

This was the problem with giving up your customary inhibitions. Now, when she should have been shaking his hand and saying, *Nice to meet you*, she was thinking of his mouth on her toes.

"Two o'clock, for the pedicures," Fiona said, "And Matt, please check the suit. Can you take a picture of it and send it to me?"

"I will," Matteo promised.

"I'd love to stay and chat," Fiona said, "but I can't. I'm just going to grab a fruit plate—"

Did she send Marlee a look? Had she shoved them together on this sacred mission on purpose? Was Fiona matchmaking?

It seemed unlikely, since she was so preoccupied with her wedding.

"—and go to my meeting with the floral arranger. She doesn't think she can get gardenias!"

And then Fiona was gone and they stood looking at each other.

"A librarian," he said, tilting his head at her, obviously seeing her in a new light. "I suspected, from your reaction to a little wardrobe malfunction, you were not a rum-swigging, cigar-loving outlaw after all."

"I never said I was. I said that dress made me *want* to be."

"A librarian exploring her wilder side," he said softly, "Ooh-la-la. Take off your glasses for me."

She realized he was teasing her and that she was still wearing her sunglasses.

She took them off.

"Oh, my heart," he said, and placed his hands over it and staggered backward.

Did he have to be so effortlessly irresistible?

She leveled him a look.

"You should have also told me who you were last night," she said.

"I did!" He moved past her to the buffet and took a plate. He was, she noted, a protein guy. Lots of eggs and bacon.

"You let me believe you were an Italian hotel employee," she said, picking her plate off the table where she had left it. She followed him as he took a seat. She sank into the one across from him.

"I never said I was a hotel employee."

"I assumed. Since you said you had been working

all day. You could have fessed up when I asked you if it was against the rules for you to fraternize."

"I had been working all day. On my jet."

His jet? She was sitting across the table from a man with a jet. A man with a jet had tasted her toes last night.

"Plus, I never said I was Italian."

"The name sounded Italian to me."

"We do border Italy," he pointed out mildly.

"You had a million opportunities to tell me who you really were, and did not," she said primly.

"Maybe not a million."

She leveled a look at him.

"Uh-oh," he said, "is that the quiet-in-the-library look?"

"No, it's the I-don't-believe-your-dog-ate-your-homework look."

He laughed. She shouldn't have found it nearly as satisfying as she did. Then, he was suddenly solemn.

"I did play along with your misconception," he confessed. "Sometimes it's exhausting being me. You don't have any idea how precious privacy is until people start recognizing you. I was so relieved that you didn't know who I was."

So now she felt ever so slightly sympathetic to one of the richest men in the world.

"Huh," she said, her sympathy feeling like a weakness, "if you want to be liked for who you are, maybe you shouldn't announce you have your own jet so soon after meeting someone."

His lips twitched. She couldn't tell if he was amused or annoyed.

"I can see there will be no winning with you, since

you're equally irritated by me not telling you who I am *and* me telling you who I am. And meanwhile, you harbor a few contradictions of your own. Librarian or outlaw?"

"I'm all done exploring my wild side," she told him firmly. "Look at how that turned out."

CHAPTER SIX

MATTEO SMILED AT HER, a smile that was bone-melt-
ingly sexy. "I thought it turned out rather amazingly,"
he said.

"It was mortifying. And it's particularly insensitive
of you to not see that and to continue making jokes
about it."

There! Exactly what an uptight librarian would say.

"Don't be embarrassed about last night," he said
quietly, suddenly serious. "Please."

"Does that mean you've run out of puns?"

"Oh, no, I could come up with dozens more of
those."

"Please don't! They aren't funny."

"And that's the naked truth."

She wanted to remain uptight. Prim. For the first
time in her life, Marlee wondered if that was a persona
she hid behind.

Hid what? she asked herself, appalled. She thought
of his lips on her toes. She frowned at him to hide the
shiver that went up and down her spine.

"Okay, okay," Matteo said, holding up his hands,
as if in surrender. "I'll try to be sensitive. Why are

Americans so uptight, anyway? Most of the people in the world enjoy beaches without their tops on."

And he would probably know, because he, sophisticated, star businessman that he was, had probably visited all kinds of beaches like that!

"Speaking of which, I have something that belongs to you."

He took a crumpled wisp out of his front pant pocket and dangled it in front of her.

"Is this your idea of sensitive, waving my underwear around in public?" Marlee hissed at him in an undertone.

"I'm not waving it. But I could."

He gave her a mischievous look. She grabbed her bra—still damp—from him and stuffed it in her own pocket.

"I'll work on sensitivity," he promised. "I'll work on it the whole time we go in search of the horse."

Save your dignity, Marlee told herself. *Wriggle out of this.*

But he was being so charming. How could anyone resist that playful expression?

And really, logically, wasn't the damage already done? It was not as if it could get any more embarrassing.

And they were going to run into each other.

They were both members of the same wedding party. They might as well get along, develop some comfort with each other.

It would make for better wedding photos if she wasn't glaring at him.

That was the logical explanation. The illogical part

was that she *wanted* to be with him. Why? It could go nowhere.

They were obviously from different stratospheres.

But there was also an appeal in that. It could go nowhere. She was only going to be on this island for a few days.

She was newly single, and definitely sworn off the complexities of relationships, anyway. There didn't have to be an agenda all the time. She didn't always have to be the uptight librarian, weighing every option, considering the future. It was marvelously freeing, if you thought about it.

Why not enjoy her time here on Coconut Cay, and by extension, Matteo? He was smart and funny, not to mention attractive. She could have fun. She could! People were always talking about being in the moment.

Last night she had experienced that. It was an elixir that made you want more.

Matteo sat outside the resort gate waiting for Marlee and enjoying the warmth of the sun, so different than the Zurich experience at this time of year.

He had come from the airport by limo last night, through a different entrance, and was now surprised to see the pedestrian access to the resort actually opened onto a chaotic main street of the village of Charlee.

The narrow, cobblestoned street was swarming with morning activity. Buildings, plastered in pastel shades and filled with crowded shops, seemed to lean in toward it. The noise, colors and scents were in such sharp contrast to his own villa that it seemed almost as if the resort was tucked behind a cloister wall.

His observations stopped as Marlee came out the gate. His focus narrowed to just her.

She was carrying a large purse and had on a yellow sundress, the antithesis of that dress she'd had on last night and the horrible velour number she'd had on at breakfast.

While the dress wasn't quite as sexy as her bathing attire, it was decidedly daring, with its spaghetti straps and short, swirly skirt.

She looked darned uncomfortable about it, too, and for some reason her discomfort was endearing.

A breeze chose that moment to lift the hem, showing off the long length of her legs. She tried, unsuccessfully, to pin the dress in place with her arms.

She glared at him when she saw him grinning at her. Arms still holding the dress down, she shuffled over to where he was parked at the curb.

"What the heck is this?" Marlee asked.

"It's a scooter," Matteo said, straddling the two-wheeler he'd rented.

"Clearly it's a scooter," she said, annoyed. She looked down at herself.

She wasn't dressed for a scooter.

It was truly refreshing that she had no idea she was the goddess she had revealed to him last night.

"Sorry," he said. "It turns out transportation options are limited on the island. There are two cabs, both taken. I went online and found the name of a stable, but it's not within walking distance."

"Oh."

"Did you want to go change?" he asked sympathetically.

She considered this, and him. She took a deep breath, like someone about to leap off a cliff.

"No, I'll be fine," she said.

"Okay." He patted the seat behind him, and she slid onto it. Amazingly, given how small the seat was, he could have inserted a travel trunk between the two of them. She put her purse in the space.

"What do I hang on to?" she asked. "There doesn't seem to be any handles back here."

His mouth felt quite dry. The exact same way it had felt when her bathing suit had surrendered itself to the sea.

"Scooters don't come with handles. You hang on to me," he said. "You might want to move your purse."

There was a long silence. Her purse was moved over her shoulder and her hands crept to his sides, and rested there lightly, tentatively. How could that possibly feel so sexy? And it was about to get worse.

"Uh, I think you might have to hold on tighter than that."

"Now, that sounds like some kind of Italian playboy scheme," she said suspiciously.

"I am not a playboy."

"You have a jet. I'm not sure you need many qualifications beyond that."

"And I told you I'm not Italian. Anyway, suit yourself."

"I will."

He gave the scooter some gas. It spurted forward, and Marlee squealed and wrapped her arms around him.

"You did that on purpose," she accused him.

"I didn't. That wouldn't be sensitive. It's been years since I was on a motorbike."

"Jets will do that to a man," she said. "Make them give up their cheaper forms of transport. Don't go too fast."

Which, naturally, made him want to go faster. The next little spurt to get them into traffic might have been on purpose, but he was the one who suffered for it. Her arms wrapped tighter around him, snugging her right up against his back. Those long legs formed a warm V around him.

What kind of strange turn in his well-ordered life was this? Sharing a scooter with an unbelievably sexy woman in search of a horse?

This had not been his plan for this morning at all.

In case he ran into the mystery woman from last night he had intended to be cool.

To let her know he wasn't usually the type of man who cavorted in the sea with strangers.

To not let her know that a mere glimpse of her moon-gilded breasts had kept him awake most of the night thinking of how cool he would be next time he saw her!

But he might as well accept it.

Nothing on Coconut Cay was going to go according to his plan.

This morning being a prime example. He hadn't expected to see her, and he hadn't expected to feel so protective of her when she was so clearly embarrassed about what had happened. How could you be cool in the face of that?

How could you express regret when you had no regrets?

So maybe it was her—Marlee, librarian-slash-outlaw—who threw a wrench into a man's carefully planned life.

Because here he was, going in search of a horse, of all things, and sharing a scooter with the goddess from the sea in a way he couldn't ignore how she stirred him physically.

He should have said no to Fiona. He should be working.

There was always work to do and it was always the antidote to any kind of uncomfortable feeling.

He glanced back at Marlee again, felt her physical closeness to him. Something unfolded in his gut.

"Keep your eyes on the road," she snapped. Then a squeal and "Watch out!"

"I saw her," he said, screeching to a halt that threw Marlee, impossibly, even harder against him.

A ruffled hen glared at him, clucked indignantly and guided her brood of chicks across the road in front of them.

Marlee giggled. Her breath was warm in his ear and he realized how glad he was that he wasn't working.

"I'm going to relax now," she told him firmly.

"Would you?"

With lots of stops and starts—and with near collision with a donkey cart—they finally made it out of the twisted, cobbled streets of the colorful town center.

The main road—it wasn't quite a highway—curved in and out of jumbled neighborhoods of humble but cheery houses with bright, painted doors and shutters and overflowing, flower-filled window boxes. Those districts gave way to ritzy residential areas built onto steep, green hills to capitalize on stunning views. The road meandered through dense vegetation, wound up steeply, hugged the edges of cliffs and then plummeted back down toward the sea.

It was all quite hair-raising, and after having to swerve around a pig napping in the middle of the road, Matteo declared it was time for a break. He pulled over at a roadside café that claimed to make the most famous iced coffee on the island.

They ordered coffee and sat at an outdoor table, chickens pecking around their feet as they admired the view that looked out over the Atlantic. Several other islands were visible in the distance. Matteo consulted his phone for a map to the stables.

"I think we should have been there by now," he said. He couldn't get a signal. He didn't want to tell Marlee, but he was pretty sure they were lost. How did you get lost on an island with one main road?

Marlee looked beautiful, her hair tangled, her face glowing from wind and sun. She did, indeed, look relaxed. She lifted a bare shoulder. "We'll find it. How hard can it be?"

He took a sip of the coffee. His eyes crossed. He pushed it away. "I think the famous coffee might be laced with the famous rum," he said.

She tasted hers. "Oh, yum," she said, and took a generous sip.

"I think your shoulders are getting burned," he said.

"That will never do! Think of the wedding photos." And then she snickered. Could the rum work that fast? He didn't think so.

In between sips of coffee—she had finished hers and started on his—she rummaged around in that big bag and found a tube of sunscreen. He glared down at his phone rather than watch her apply sunscreen to her shoulders. Maybe the rum was working that fast, because unless he was mistaken, she was being deliberately tantalizing about it.

"Can you check my back?"

He could hardly refuse, could he? He took the tube from her hand and got up from the table. He went behind her.

She lifted her hair off her neck, and he looked at the slender column of it and wanted to taste it. What was it about her that made him want to taste her?

He thought of how he'd lifted her toes to his mouth last night.

Stop it, Matteo ordered himself. Her skin, so delicate, was already starting to burn. Steeling himself to be a first aid man only, he slathered the cream onto her skin.

The minx closed her eyes, tilted her face to the sun and leaned into his fingertips.

He capped the tube, tossed it back at her and headed for the scooter. "Let's go," he called.

If he had hoped for a distraction from the sensation of her skin beneath his fingertips, he'd hoped in vain. She melted against him and he could feel her cheek on his back.

"Let's pretend," she suggested gleefully. "You're an Italian beach bum, and I'm an outlaw pretending to be a librarian."

He was going to say, *Let's not*, but he glanced over his shoulder. Her face had a light on in it—playful, invigorated, alive—that would take a man much stronger than him to put out.

He had the awful feeling she wasn't drunk on rum, but on life, and it was unbelievably appealing.

"I've never been on a motorbike before," she called.

"Calling it a motorbike is a bit of a stretch," he called back to her. "It's a scooter."

"Whatever it is, it's awesome. Go faster!"

He thought they were probably at about maximum speed already—in every single way—but if he could squeeze a little more power out of the machine, did that mean she would cling harder? He couldn't help himself. He had to find out.

And just like that, it *was* awesome: the wind, the sun, the charms of the island, a beautiful woman clinging to him. Matteo did something he rarely did.

He surrendered to the day.

He was pretty sure he was lost in more ways than one.

CHAPTER SEVEN

MARLEE WAS WELL aware she was flirting with a wilder side. It had started with the impulse buy of the bright yellow sundress this morning.

It was not the type of thing she *ever* bought. Loudly colored. Sexy. Flirty. Way too short.

But then again, she was not the type who swam in the sea with a stranger, either.

Or rode scooters.

Or invited men to apply sunscreen on her.

But something about breaking all these rules—doing what she had never even pictured herself doing, ever—was making her feel as if joy was shimmering inside her.

Okay, maybe the coffee *had* had rum in it, but Marlee felt intoxicated on life. It probably spoke to a life not well lived that this day, so far, felt like one of the highlights of her entire existence.

She was actually sorry when Matteo doubled back and found a worn sign that pointed down a rutted road to the stable.

The "stable" turned out to be a rickety lean-to with a palm frond roof.

And there was not a horse in sight.

Three tiny donkeys were saddled, and their owner introduced himself as Mackay and welcomed them with gregarious hopefulness.

Matteo explained their mission. Mackay's face fell.

"There are no horses on Coconut Cay," he said. "It's all donkeys."

"Not a single horse on the whole island?" Marlee asked.

"They eat too much," Mackay said. "The donkeys are better here."

Marlee considered this in terms of Fiona's request.

"They are cute," she said, moving over to one of the donkeys and rubbing his head. His friend, jealous, brayed loudly. She laughed and went to scratch his head, too.

"Do you think Fiona would be flexible?" she asked Matteo.

"On our short acquaintance I would guess, no, but you know her better than me."

"Hmm, I guess I'd say no."

"On the other hand," Matteo pointed out, "They are equines, aren't they? Same family?"

She felt doubtful. "It's a bit like calling a scooter a motorbike. A stretch."

"Here's to stretching," Matteo said.

She turned to Mackay. "I don't suppose you have a baby one?"

Mackay sadly shook his head no.

"They look like babies, even though they aren't," Matteo said, "And they aren't white, they're gray. And that one has black ears. That's three out of three checked on Fiona's list—equine, kind of a baby, not white."

"I think that's why I was sent along. For a guy, it's

just a checklist. I'm in charge of the esthetics of the thing. But it's true," Marlee said, "the cute factor is off the scale."

"I think we have to make an executive decision. We've been given an assignment. We have a time crunch. Today's Thursday. The wedding is Saturday. Why don't we book one, and then we've got our bases covered? I'll take a picture and if Fiona vetoes it, that's okay. We did our best. Mackay, would one of the donkeys be available for a wedding on the weekend?"

Mackay puffed up as if one of his children had just won first prize at the spelling bee. "It would be my honor."

They worked out delivery details and gave him instructions to arrive shortly after the wedding for the photos.

"Which one would you like?" Mackay asked giving each donkey an affectionate rub on the head as he introduced them. "Henri, Harvey, Calamity."

"Let's eliminate Calamity just for the name," Marlee suggested.

Matteo inspected the two remaining donkeys with such a pretense of seriousness that she could not help laughing. "This one has the best ears," he decided.

"But look how hopeful that one looks!" she said, the laughter still bubbling.

"Okay," Matteo agreed. "This one."

"Henri, a fine choice," Mackay said with approval as if they had picked a great wine.

Matteo looked at his watch. "Our wedding assignment is completed. And before lunch! Which brings me to the topic of lunch. Are you hungry?"

"Starving," she said, and it was true, despite her carb-loaded breakfast.

"Can you recommend a place for lunch?" Matteo asked.

Mackay preened. "I have a lunch special today! I will take you to a secret beach. Very romantic."

"Oh." Marlee could feel herself blushing. She looked everywhere but at Matteo. "We're not, um, romantically involved."

Mackay looked between them, clearly disappointed. "Maybe by after lunch!" he said.

Matteo wagged wicked eyebrows at her, clearly enjoying her discomfort. "Here's to stretching," he said.

"Here's to sensitivity," she said.

He laughed.

"I don't think we have time," Marlee said. There was, thankfully, no time for *stretching*. Certainly not for romance.

Thank God.

"I have an appointment at two," she said.

"Only an hour!" Mackay promised. "Delicious lunch. Island cuisine, made by my mother."

"Made by his mother," Matteo said persuasively.

How could she resist this?

"It's only just gone noon," Matteo told her. "What do you say?"

And so she found herself perched in a sundress on the donkey named Henri, following Matteo, who was mounted on Calamity. Matteo should have looked hilarious, his long legs nearly on the ground, but instead Marlee found herself loving how he had embraced what the moment offered them. Not to mention loving the view of his broad back.

They rode a rutted trail with a lime grove on one side and a cliff on the other. The views out to the sea were spectacular, as was the scent of the limes. The sun kissed her face and a faint breeze lifted her hair.

It was bliss. No other description would do.

Mackay led the way on Harvey, down a steep, cliff-hugging trail. The stones that they knocked off the path seemed to clatter for a very long time before they hit the ground far below.

She would normally be a nervous wreck, but somehow she wasn't. The sense of bliss continued. It must be that rum-laced coffee!

The trail leveled out, and twisted through mangroves, opening up to the most beautiful beach Marlee had ever seen, the fine sand a pink as subtle as a young girl's blush.

Mackay spread a blanket on the sand and unpacked lunch from huge baskets. The cuisine was unbelievably good. It consisted of a jerk chicken, an amazing salad and a selection of island-grown fruits. Mackay produced a bottle of the local wine. Matteo refused because he was driving, but Marlee had some. It was foolish—she'd already had the rum-laced coffee—but what the heck? She'd never really been foolish before. She was quite enjoying it!

"Swim," Mackay insisted as he put lunch away. "The water is beautiful."

"I don't have a—"

"Not required here. I won't look," Mackay promised with a wink. "Henri might, though."

He shot Matteo a look that was loaded with male kinship. Their host was determined to get a romance going.

It was Matteo's turn to look uncomfortable. Considering he was familiar with sophisticated beaches around the world, he had a deer-caught-in-the-headlights look.

"I'd love to have a swim," Marlee decided. When had she ever felt this relaxed, this go-with-the-flow, this spontaneous?

She'd only had two glasses of wine. It wasn't that.

Matteo looked at her, then looked at his watch and yelped. "It's after one. We can't today."

Did she hear just a bit of relief in his voice at the time constraint? Marlee felt the sharpness of regret. On the other hand, if they got back in the water together, who was to say what could unfold between them? She thought of his lips on her toes. The look in his eyes when she had risen out of the water topless.

Maybe they would end up lovers!

That had to be the wine whispering to her, and still the possibility shivered up and down her spine. She was getting into deep water. She needed to remember she barely knew how to swim!

Matteo seemed suddenly extraordinarily eager to go, and helped Mackay pack up the baskets. In moments, the donkeys plodded their sure-footed way back up the cliff and to the stable. They got off and said goodbye to their host.

Matteo paid Mackay and gave him a tip that made him grin from ear to ear. Marlee kissed Henri right on the tip of his soft, beautiful nose.

And then they turned to where they had left the

scooter. Matteo looked in shocked disbelief at the now empty space.

"It appears we've had a theft," he said.

"No, no," Mackay assured him. "Not stolen. Not on Coconut Cay."

"It's missing," Matteo pointed out. "I parked it right here."

"Borrowed, maybe," Mackay conceded.

"Borrowed, certainly," Matteo said. "The result is the same. We are left without a means to get back to the resort."

"I am without a vehicle today," Mackay said, but then brightened. "We can ride the donkeys to the main road, and from there you'll be able to make your way back to the resort."

"Make our way how?" Matteo asked skeptically.

"There's a bus," Mackay told them, "twice a day."

"I don't suppose I'm going to be back at the resort by two, am I?"

"Just stick out your thumb if you don't want to wait for the bus," Mackay said. "Someone will give you a ride."

"Hitchhike?" Marlee asked.

"Very safe here," Mackay promised.

"Uh-huh," Matteo said. "Safest place on earth. That's what I plan to tell the scooter rental place."

Marlee knew it was the wrong thing to do, but she giggled.

Matteo cast her a look and shook his head.

"It's just such a day of firsts," Marlee said. "Scooter ride, donkey train, and now hitchhiking. It feels kind of amazing when you just surrender to what's happening, instead of fighting it. I don't even really care if I make the pedicure or not."

"Surrender," Mackay said brightly. "The place where the adventure begins."

Matteo contemplated that word. *Surrender.* He was riding in the bed of a truck on top of corn husks bundled together. The breeze from the open-air ride made the temperature feel perfect.

The family who owned the truck were crowded into the cab singing, their joy drifting back to him, and Marlee was nestled under his arm, fast asleep, her head on his chest, her breath causing puddles of warmth on his skin, Her scent—lemony—was mingled with the scent of the sun on the corn husks.

He was not sure when, if ever, he had felt so content.

It pressed at the edges of his contentment that to feel this way was dangerous. It made a person open, vulnerable to being hurt.

Matteo had enjoyed the day.

More than enjoyed it, really. He had been exhilarated by it.

By every second of it, even the loss of the scooter. He had not been this spontaneous for a long time.

If ever.

He had enjoyed Marlee.

No, more. Been exhilarated by her.

She was beautiful. And she was interesting and smart. He wasn't sure if she made him laugh, or if being with her opened him, in some way, to the delights of life that he had been closed off from before.

Whichever, she was just the type of woman who

could make a man forget the inherent dangers of caring about someone.

He gave in to the temptation to touch her hair. It would be so easy to care about her.

Deeply.

To take it one step further…

She stirred, and that dress hitched up a few inches further on the shapely length of her leg. He thought of her in the water last night, goddess rising, and snatched his hand away from the sun-warmed silk of her hair.

He needed to get this situation back into control.

His control.

And he needed to do it fast.

The truck lurched to a stop in front of the resort, and Marlee's eyes snapped open. She struggled to sitting, and he noticed the linen pattern of his shirt was traced in the softness of the skin on her cheek.

She took him in, those gorgeous green eyes bewildered. She looked at the bed of corn husks around her. Drowsy confusion gave way to a smile that tickled her lips.

Beautiful lips. Wide and generous.

Lips that begged to be kissed. He remembered the faint taste of them that had lingered on that cigar they had shared a taste of.

She touched his shirt. "Look," she said, her voice husky—and sexy—with sleep. "I drooled on you."

Matteo had a shocking thought of what a life could be like waking up to her.

He leaped up and scrambled off the back of the truck. Unfortunately, chivalry demanded he help her down. He turned back for her.

Marlee had stood and was navigating the corn

husks. Her dress was rumpled. There was a smudge—donkey spit?—across the front of it. There was also a corn husk tangled in her hair.

He was not sure a woman had ever looked so beautiful.

He held out his hand to her, and when hers closed around his, it felt right and good.

And terrible and wrong.

And as if that control he longed for could be taken by such a simple thing as her hand in his.

She let go of his hand and put her arms around his neck, instead, and of their own accord his hands closed around her waist and he lifted her down off the truck bed.

There was something about the small gesture that made him feel strong. Masculine. Possessive. Protective.

The chatter of the happy family they had shared the truck with died. So did the street noises: cars, horns, vendors calling, children laughing, chickens cackling.

His whole world felt as if it was this: her corn-husk-tangled hair, her eyes, the plumpness of her bottom lip, the sweet sensation of her body pressed into the length of his.

Surrender.

CHAPTER EIGHT

SURRENDER. MATTEO HAD not said the word out loud, and yet it was as if Marlee had heard it. Her body relaxed against his, and she tilted her head upward, her gaze sleepy, unconsciously sensual.

And then her gaze drifted to his lips. Hungry. Curious.

He knew, when her tongue flicked out and wetted her own lips, what was coming. He commanded himself to go into full retreat. But something stronger within him commanded something else.

Surrender.

Pressed full against him, she stood on her tiptoes and her lips touched his lips.

Her kiss was a study in contradiction: sweet and sexy, sharp and soft, questing and fulfilled.

She tasted of salt and wine and of a bottomless womanly mystery.

Everything in him cried to go deeper, to tangle yet further, to know her more, to explore her secrets.

Thankfully, before he totally lost his mind—forgot they were on a public street and tangled his hands in her hair to pull her closer and claim her lips more thoroughly—she pulled away.

Her blush rose above the sun-kissed glow the day had given her cheeks. She laughed, self-conscious.

"Thank you for an incredible day," she said so sweetly awkward that he wanted to kiss her again.

Surrender.

Was it really where the adventure began?

Or was it where life as you knew it ended?

Matteo realized he did not want to find out. He needed to get a hold of himself. He needed to do it now.

It would be easy, wouldn't it?

Their mission was completed. He didn't have to see her again until the wedding. No, that wasn't quite right. There was the rehearsal dinner tomorrow night. That would give him a time to reconstruct his battered barriers.

"Yes," Matteo said, "It's been an interesting day."

It was a deliberate understatement. His tone was formal, and he could see the bewildered hurt in her eyes. He moved past her before his resolve was slayed by that. He opened the gate to the resort and held it for her.

They walked in silence along the pathway to her cabana where he had first encountered her.

It seemed impossible that that was less than twenty-four hours ago. He already felt as if he knew her, deeply.

Which was the dangerous part. Wasn't it better to hurt her now, than later?

This was what he knew: the more you cared about someone, the deeper the hurt you could cause them.

There was no sense following the intrigue that beckoned to him from those jade green eyes. There was no sense following that trail of laughter they had been on all day. Thinking of her laughter made him look again at her lips.

No, there was no sense following *that* desire any further.

One of them had to be the sensible one. He felt vaguely resentful that it didn't appear it was going to be her.

If you couldn't count on a librarian to be sensible, what exactly could you count on?

"I'll leave it to you to brief Fiona," he suggested.

"Sure," she said, uncertainly.

"And I'll see you at the rehearsal dinner."

"But—I thought we might... I thought we had—" She stopped herself. The injured look gave way to one of pride. She knew he was brushing her off.

She apparently had no appreciation whatsoever for all the pain he was saving them both.

"Yes," she said, her voice tight and wounded. "That's fine. All right."

"I have to report the stolen scooter," he said, trying a little too late, to soften the blow. "As the only crime that's ever occurred on Coconut Cay, it'll probably be complicated. I don't want to drag you into it. You know, in case it involves jail time."

His attempt to lighten things fell flat, which made him want to try even harder to coax a smile out of her.

"Not that that would bother a hardened outlaw such as yourself."

No smile. Marlee gave him a long, level look that let him know she was not fooled, and then, head high and chin up, she turned away from him.

"Plus," he said weakly, knowing the damage was

done, "according to the schedule, I'm supposed to golf with the guys tomorrow."

"Oh," she said, trying for breeziness and failing, "Of course. The schedule! Golf."

Her tone made him feel like a complete ass.

Which, come to think of it, he was.

Neither of them had noticed Fiona barreling toward them until it was too late and she was standing, hands on hips, right in front of them.

"There you are! You missed the pedicures," Fiona snapped at Marlee, without greeting either of them. "Everything is going wrong. Everything."

Matteo shot Marlee a look and gave her a slight shake of his head letting her know that now didn't seem to be the time to break it to the harried bride she might have to substitute a donkey for the horse in her photos.

"Let me see what color you got," Marlee said soothingly. "I'm sure I can get a pedicure tomorrow, so that we all have matching toes, just like you wanted."

"As a matter of fact, you can't," Fiona said. "She only comes one day a week, so it's a little late to be thinking about what I wanted."

Still, she wiggled a toe at them, and he caught a glimpse of glittery gold.

"I'll figure it out," Marlee promised.

"I hope so," Fiona said petulantly, and then eyed Marlee. "You must have found a horse."

"Um…"

Fiona leaned a little closer to her and sniffed. "You did!" she said, "I can smell horses!"

She brightened. For a moment Matteo could almost see what Mike saw in her. Almost.

"There are a number of good options," Marlee said carefully.

Fiona visibly relaxed, but instead of acting grateful, she shot Marlee a look. "Good grief! Did you get right in the corral with them? You have something in your hair. And on your dress. You look like you lost a fight with a cat."

So much for glimpsing what Mike saw in her! Her tone was so acid that Matteo felt a need to put his body between Marlee and Fiona.

"You don't," he said firmly to Marlee when he saw she was clearly calculating if that was why he had turned cool toward her.

Fiona glared at him as if she was actually thinking of arguing about it, and then with a miffed sigh turned and left.

He stood there feeling the shock of the encounter.

"Good God," he said. "Is she always like this? She was downright vugly."

"She looked like she'd been crying," Marlee said.

"She did?"

"She just wants everything to be perfect."

He made a note to remember Fiona when he was thinking control was the be-all and end-all of life.

"I'm not sure why you would come to her defense," he said.

"Fiona didn't have the best childhood," Marlee confided in him. "We've known each other since fifth grade. That's when she moved in down the street from me. Her house was always so chaotic. I think that's why she's so intent on perfection with the wedding. From the moment she met Mike it was as if she felt she could finally have what she thought everyone else had."

Matteo looked at her and saw yet another side to Marlee—a deep well of kindness and compassion.

"If getting my toes painted gold will help her feel better, even a little bit, I'll do it," she said.

And somehow, after seeing how her friend had treated her, and how she had responded, he couldn't just abandon her because he needed to be in control.

Fiona had just managed to shatter his beliefs about control, anyway.

"Do you want to have dinner together tonight?" he asked her.

He was shocked at himself.

Because ten minutes ago he had promised to pull back from the temptations of Marlee. And now, he seemed to be entangling himself further than ever.

She stood stock-still and searched his face.

It occurred to him she was going to say no.

"No," Marlee said, injecting far more firmness into her tone than she felt. How did anyone say no to spending more time with him?

It had been one of the best days of her life, sun-kissed and sizzling with connection, fun and adventure.

Of course, then she had to go wreck it all by kissing him. No wonder he was trying to run away from her.

She'd had too much to drink. She'd slobbered on his shirt. She looked—and smelled, according to Fiona— as if she'd been mucking out stalls.

While she'd been thinking *best day ever*, who knew what he had been thinking? He came from a different world, no doubt filled with glamorous novelties that made scooter rides and donkeys and traveling in a truck full of corn husks seem, well, corny to him.

Marlee had known from the outset he was way out of her league, and when he'd dismissed her—said he would see her again at the rehearsal dinner—she had realized he was reminding her of that.

Now he was changing his mind.

She hadn't missed how he had inserted himself protectively between her and Fiona. It had felt rather nice, but on the other hand, she wasn't going to spend more time with him because he felt sorry for her.

The heart that had blossomed at his gesture of protectiveness whined that she could take whatever she could get, even if it was motivated by pity!

Her heart wanted her to let him be in charge: he'd decide when he'd have enough, when they were going to spend time together and when they weren't.

Even though she'd been abjectly disappointed when he'd pulled the plug after their wonderful day, Marlee was so aware something was shifting in her.

You could not have a day like today and not be changed by it, not have a stronger sense of yourself and what you wanted.

She realized she had always felt that with her ex—as if she was begging for his time, for little crumbs of his affection. She realized now she had not required nearly enough. Not of Arthur, who was just Arthur, in the same way Fiona was just Fiona. She had not required enough of herself. She had not set her standards high enough.

Maybe it was the story of her life.

And it was never too late to change that story, so even as a part of her said, *Yes, please, let's have dinner together*, another part of her held proudly firm.

"No," she repeated. "I'm not hungry. I'm eager to

wash off the donkey dust. You need to go make your stolen scooter report. Call me if you need bail, otherwise I'll see you at the rehearsal dinner. Enjoy your golf game!"

Matteo looked utterly shocked. Marlee was willing to bet it was the first time he'd ever had a woman call the shots on his charming self. Particularly refusing his invitation in preference to washing off donkey dust!

As she turned away, went into the cabana and shut the door on his stunned face, Marlee found herself smiling.

She was *glad* she had kissed him. Shaken him out of his stuffy world enough to make him take a startled step back from her.

It felt good to take her power back, even if there was a price to pay. And so when the temptation was to retreat from all her discoveries—stay in her room with a book that evening—she didn't. Using the very rudimentary seamstress kit she always traveled with—librarians ferreted out every potential disaster, after all—she took the bra she had worn last night off the shower bar where she had flung it after its return this morning and sewed the breakaway clasp firmly and permanently shut. She wouldn't be needing that feature anytime soon.

Then she stripped, exchanged the bra she was wearing for the repaired one and slipped a swim cover-up on. She then went to the resort store and bought some chicken being kept warm under a burner.

Then, she took the pathway past her cabana. The cigar was still sitting on the wall where he had left it last night and she picked it up.

Because it was litter, not because he had tasted it!

Then she went down to the beach she had shared with Matteo.

She watched the sun go down in a brief but glorious display of color. For one suspended moment, the ocean turned to fire and every grain of sand on the beach glittered gold.

It was, she told herself firmly, the perfect ending to the best day ever. She didn't need a man to make it all lovelier. It couldn't be any lovelier than it already was.

But then, just as she was on the brink of convincing herself that was true, a shiver up and down her spine let her know she was no longer alone on the beach.

She turned her head to see Matteo coming across the sand. She switched her attention quickly back to the orb of the sun, disappearing on the horizon as if it was plunging into the sea. For a woman discovering her own power, the mere sight of him coming toward her in the soft golden light was doing things to her heartbeat. She felt weak instead of strong.

"Hey," he said, quietly. "Beautiful night."

"It is," she agreed. "Probably looks even better after your close brush with jail time."

The question was, what was he doing here after his close brush with her lips?

"I don't think there is a jail. I reported the missing scooter at the rental place. Same response as Mackay. *No, no, not stolen. Borrowed.* They seemed to have every confidence it will just show up."

"So what brings you here? Extra time now that you've been freed of potential legal wrangling?"

I couldn't get your ravishing kiss out of my mind. Ha ha.

"Fiona saw me. She told me to find you and give you

this." He dropped a tiny brown bag on her lap. "When you weren't at your place, I thought you might be here."

So he hadn't sought her out of his own accord. It was an *errand*. He was here because he had been *instructed*.

He was probably thinking, *Pathetic thing. Reliving memories of last night and very ordinary, workaday kisses that she thought were ravishing.*

Reminder: girls like her were not even on the radar of men like him.

Marlee told herself sternly that she was rethinking the kind of girl she was. Her hand found the cigar she had picked up, and she clamped it between her lips.

"Those are habit-forming," he warned her mildly.

"Only if you light them." *Or taste another person's lips on them.*

He nodded solemnly. "An outlaw prop."

Without invitation he dropped down in the sand beside her.

"I thought you said you weren't hungry," he said, eyeing the chicken.

Good. He understood her refusal had been about him, not about hunger. She shrugged.

"How is it?"

"After Mackay's mother's? Barely edible." She took the unlit cigar from her lips and held it between her fingers, as if she intended to light it at any time.

CHAPTER NINE

"Can I have a piece?"

Matteo's errand was done. Why was he hanging around? Marlee thought.

"Have a piece of chicken at your own risk. But don't feel you have to sit in the sand with me. You've achieved your mission."

She put down the cigar—who was she kidding? She was no outlaw. He was right. It was just a prop. She had no hope—ever—of being the real thing. She dug in the bag he had dropped on her lap and drew out the items one by one.

Sheesh. It was pedicure in a bag. The last item she took out was a bottle of glittering gold nail polish.

"See? Matteo, you've saved the world. Or at least the wedding. Donkey acquisition and pedicure rescue all in one day. You must be exhausted. It will probably affect your golf game. That's a shame."

"You're being sarcastic," he said, his voice low. "I've hurt your feelings."

Marlee did not want to be that transparent!

"Is this part of your intention to be more sensitive? It's completely unnecessary. You haven't hurt my feelings."

Matteo regarded her intently. He said nothing. It felt as if he saw straight through her—right to her soul. It was very discomforting.

"I get it. Entirely. You move in different circles than me. No sense the plain-Jane librarian from Seattle getting romantic notions. Not that I was. But I don't blame you for thinking I was. I mean, who wouldn't? I kissed you. It was an impulse. A bad one. But you're pretty easy on the eyes. You have a jet. You're kind of funny and entertaining. But just for your information, I've had a recent breakup. The last thing I'm looking for—"

He cut off the flow of words—good grief, she was babbling—by laying a gentle finger against her lips.

After all she had just said, how could she possibly be having a temptation to nibble that finger?

She should want to bite it! It was insulting. He was silencing her.

"You thought I didn't want to see you until the rehearsal dinner because I found you a—what did you say—plain Jane? You think I found you unattractive?"

His voice was a low growl that felt like a touch shivering along her spine.

She nodded, which had the unfortunate effect of moving her lips on his finger, creating a sensational feeling.

"Marlee," Matteo said, his voice low and pained, those color-of-the-sea eyes intent on her face, "the exact opposite is true."

She tried to let that sink in, but she couldn't comprehend what he was saying.

"What do you mean," she asked, "the exact opposite is true?"

Matteo looked suddenly uncomfortable.

"It might all be a moot point, anyway," he said. "I don't know if there's going to be a rehearsal dinner."

"What?"

"The lovely bride-to-be is up there throwing a fit at Mike right now."

"About what?"

"Who knows? Gardenias. A delayed champagne delivery. The flower girl's hair. Maybe she wanted Mike to get a pedicure for barefoot pictures in the sand and he missed his appointment. Just like you."

"You're making her sound very unreasonable."

Matteo cast Marlee a look but didn't say anything.

"Okay, she's being a bit of a bridezilla."

"A bit?"

"After what she grew up with, Fiona just wants it all to be so perfect. That's why she has to have control."

"What did she grow up with?"

Marlee felt as if she had to make a choice. On one hand, she didn't want to reveal personal information about her friend. On the other hand, she didn't want Matteo to think Fiona was purely horrible, with no redeeming characteristics.

"Her mom and dad both drank too much. Her house was crazy. Nothing—and I mean nothing—was predictable, except for the fighting and chaos. I think part of the destination wedding decision was because her mom's terrified of flying. Fiona didn't want them here for her big day. She knew they'd wreck everything."

Matteo was silent. "Thank you for telling me that. It puts things in a different light. She's very lucky to have you for a friend. Actually, anyone would be lucky to have you for a friend."

There was something about the look in his eyes that

a woman could fall toward. But Marlee was pretty sure there was a not-so-subtle message in there.

That maybe they could be *friends*.

Friends didn't kiss each other at the end of the day!

She looked at the bottle of nail polish. "I'm going to put it on and go show her. Maybe it'll be a distraction for her. A 'See? Everything is going to be fine' moment."

His lips twitched.

"It's a lot to ask of toenail polish."

"I don't know. It's an interesting color. It looks like it's been mixed with dreams and fairy dust."

He pretended to inspect the bottle. "A little magic mixed in there."

"Here's to magic," she said, and kicked off her sandals and regarded her toes.

"You don't know any more about nail polish than you do about cigars, do you?"

"And you do?"

"Older sisters," he said. "You don't put it on surrounded by sand. I know that much."

"Oh," she said. "Of course!"

"And if you wanted to swim, we should do that first."

We.

"Because I don't think you can get your toes wet for a while after you've painted them."

She noticed the stars winked on in an inky dark sky.

She noticed the air smelled of the sea.

She noticed her breath inside her chest, its simple rise and fall feeling like a celebration of life.

In all its glory, and all its surprises.

You think I don't find you attractive? The exact opposite is true.

It was as good as hearing he'd been dazzled by her kiss.

Still, Matteo was giving her mixed messages. He wanted to be just friends? Or he wanted more?

Maybe it was time for her to make some choices!

And her choice, right now, was just to embrace the moment.

She stood up, peeled off the swimsuit cover-up and let it drift to the sand beside her. She stood there before him in her underwear again, feeling bold.

He had never clarified exactly what he meant by *the exact opposite is true* but Marlee could see the obvious truth in his eyes.

He found her beautiful.

It allowed her to do what she had never done—to see herself as beautiful, too. She liked the way his eyes had darkened to midnight as he took in her moon-painted body.

"You're going to try that, um outfit, again?" he asked, his voice hoarse. "You do like to live dangerously."

"Only recently. Allowing my inner outlaw free rein. I fixed it, anyway. No wardrobe malfunctions tonight."

"More the shame, that," he said.

And then he rose to his feet, and with a shout of laughter, chased her into the water.

Finally, exhausted from playing in the ocean like children, they went and threw themselves on her blanket on the sand. She shivered.

"We should go in," he said. "It's warm here, but it's still chilly at night if you're wet."

We?

What did that mean? She should offer him a nightcap?

"We still have to paint your toenails."

This time she said it out loud, with a lifted eyebrow. *"We?"* She didn't actually think it would be safe to let him touch her feet.

"I know lots about pedicures."

She remembered his lips on her toes last night and shivered.

"I told you, I have sisters."

That took some of the white heat out of her mental meanderings.

"Time to go," he said, getting up. "You're freezing."

Actually, she felt as if she was melting. He waited for her to gather up her things, then shook the sand out of her blanket and put it over her shoulders.

It was a small gesture. It felt so nice.

Inside her cabana, he shooed her into the shower. She debated what to bring in there to change into.

What exactly did one wear when the world's most gorgeous man had offered to help with your pedicure?

She wanted it to be super sexy without giving the appearance she was trying to be sexy. Finally, she chose an oversize pajama top that came to her midthigh. She usually would have worn the top with pajama bottoms. Tonight, she left those off.

She looked at herself in the full-length mirror before she went out into the main room. Her hair was damp and curling. Her face glowed from her day out in the

sun. Her eyes were luminous. She had what some might
have called a come-hither look.

She wondered what she was playing at. What were
they playing at? How was this all going to unfold?

That, she told herself firmly, was the librarian talking.

That was not how outlaws talked to themselves at
all! A proper outlaw didn't think of consequences, or
the future.

A proper outlaw embraced the dangerous thrills of
the moment.

She went out into the main room. Matteo glanced up
at her, then looked quickly back at his phone.

His phone, she thought, disappointed about her
wasted come-hither look. Arthur had always seemed
to find his phone more interesting than her, too.

"You caught me," Matteo said, and flashed the
phone at her.

She burst out laughing.

The screen read: *How to do a pedicure like a pro.*

"You said you'd done this with your sisters."

"Well, a hundred years ago."

"You look much younger than you are," she said,
giving him a wide-eyed look. "How many sisters?"

"Two. Mia and Emma."

"Are you close?"

"Oh, yeah. We run the family business together. I
also have two nieces and two nephews. They're incor-
rigible brats."

"You adore them."

His easy grin gave her the answer.

She liked it that he was close to his sisters and his family.

"Okay, enough chitchat," he said sternly. "Come over here and sit down."

She went and sat at the sofa, while he sat on a stool facing it. Really? A pinch-me moment. The most gorgeous man in the world was at her feet.

"This is serious business," he told her, so seriously that she wanted to laugh. "I don't want to be distracted and chop off your toe. A large, bandaged appendage would wreck the wedding pictures."

"I don't think you could chop off my toe with those," she said, pointing at the clippers. Then she frowned. "You don't think you're going to use those, do you?"

"It's step four: trim and shape toenails."

He took her foot. His hand slid along it as he eyed her toenails. Considering he was only touching her foot, Marlee felt ripples through every cell of her body!

"Just put the nail polish on!"

"Uh-uh. I'm a follow-the-instructions kind of guy."

He did something with his fingertips to her instep that she was pretty sure was not in the instructions.

"That's a long way from my toes," she said, through gritted teeth.

"I know," he said and tilted his head to smile at her.

Marlee wondered how she was going to survive this.

CHAPTER TEN

MATTEO LET HIS hand slide along her instep one more time. Then, with a let's-get-to-work sigh, he picked up the toenail clippers that had come in the kit.

"Give me those," Marlee said. "You are *not* cutting my toenails."

"Wait!" He held them out of her reach when she grabbed for them. "I missed steps. We're nowhere near the part where we argue about toenail cutting."

"Humph."

"Step one," he read, his officiousness coaxing an inward smile out of her, if not an outward one. "Soak your toes and feet. Have you got a basin I can fill?"

"I think the shower and ocean probably looked after that."

"Okay, moving along, then. Step two: get rid of any dead skin."

"That's gross. Let's just skip to the painting the nails part."

"Then we're at step three: remove old polish."

"There is none," she snapped. At this moment, she *hated* it that there was none. It made her feel unglamorous and downright dull.

He had already moved on. "Step four: trimming and shaping your toenails. Now we're at the arguing part."

"They are fine the way they are," Marlee insisted.

He gave her a look, took her foot firmly and inspected it. He was probably deciding they were librarian toenails, nothing elegant about them at all.

"I cut them straight across the top like that because it's recommended to prevent ingrown toenails."

Who said that to a man like him? Sheesh! Worst conversation ever. Still, she shivered at the way her feet looked in his hands, pale against his darker flesh, delicate against his obvious strength.

"Are you still cold?" Matteo asked, glancing up at her.

"No, you're tickling me."

"Oh," he said, pleased. "Ticklish feet. I'll file that away for future reference."

Future?

There was no future, that was what she had to remember about him. They had been thrown together for a few days. After the wedding they would never see each other again.

Which should have given her pause about what was happening between them right now, some exciting and dangerous awareness sizzling in the air between them.

But Marlee was already not who she had been twenty-four hours ago.

Because instead of the fact she would never see him again giving her pause, it felt as if it was giving her license.

Still holding her instep, he studied her toes intently. He leaned very close to them. She could feel his breath tickling them. If he kissed them, as he had done last night, she was pretty sure any hope of a friendship would be lost, and she was going to exercise the liberty that came with never seeing him again.

His mouth on her toes would unleash something in her. She would not be responsible for what happened next. It felt as if a secret side of her was crying to get out, and that side was totally uninhibited.

Shockingly wild. Unabashedly sexy.

He did not kiss her toes, and Marlee was not at all sure if she was disappointed or relieved.

She was aware, too, that she was quite literally leaving it all in his hands.

"I think you're right," he decided. "They're already pretty short. No trim required."

She did something she would not have done twenty-four hours ago. She reached out and touched the silk of his hair with her fingertips.

"What did you mean when you said the exact opposite was true?" she asked him.

Matteo felt her hand in his hair. He glanced up at Marlee.

He was aware he had placed himself in this position, even knowing the dangers inherent to it.

For him, it was delightful that she had no idea how beautiful she was.

In the short time he had known her, he already knew that her beauty not just on the outside of her, but on the inside of her, too.

He had to fight the temptations of her. And he had to let her know why, even if it meant doing what he least liked to do.

Exposing his own fears and insecurities.

It felt as though if ever there was a person he could trust with his deepest secrets, it was her. How could he feel that way?

He barely knew her.

On the other hand, you couldn't spend a day with someone like Marlee and not feel as if you knew her.

He had seen her laugh and fall in love with donkeys and embrace adventures and roll with the punches.

But it was her gentle compassion toward a friend who might not have deserved it that made Matteo feel, not just as if he knew her, but as if he knew her deeply.

To her heart. To her soul.

His trust in her felt extraordinary.

He focused on the array of items that had come from the pedicure kit. Her hand was still tickling his hair.

"Step five," he said, avoiding her question about what he'd really meant, "toe separators. Never mind that we missed the first four steps."

She laughed, low in her throat. It was a sound that could make a man forget he had a history that warned him away from women like this one.

Gently, he inserted the toe separators. Her hand went very still in his hair.

"Step six: base coat." He waggled the bottle at her. "Crucial, apparently."

Carefully, he took out the brush and began to apply a thin layer of the base coat. He began to speak, knowing he had to warn her off, now, before it was too late.

"My mother and my father had a grand passion for each other," Matteo said. He could hear the roughness of pain in the slight hoarseness of his own voice.

"They could not be together enough. They could not keep their hands off each other. The romance never died—the little gifts, the love notes, the exchanged looks, the heat between them. We didn't have a family so much as the two of them, my mother and father, being the sun, and the rest of us orbiting around their light."

He finished the toes of her right foot and moved on to the left. There was a stillness in the room that reminded him of a cathedral.

"And then my mother got sick," Matteo said. "And then she got sicker. And then she died. My father, this man who had been so powerful, and so in control of everything, except his love for her, could not change it. When she died, she took part of his soul with her."

He swallowed hard, capped the base coat, and blew on her toes to dry them. He opened the bottle of gold.

"He never got it back."

Matteo stared at Marlee's toes. Were they blurry? No, of course not! He was a man in control of his emotions.

If she had said anything, he was not sure he could have continued. He dared not look at her. If he saw softness in her eyes, he felt as if it would finish everything he believed about his own strength.

He dabbed the gold onto her nails, took a deep breath and finished what he had to say just as he put the last stroke of the polish on.

"His grief ignored the fact he had children to live for, and it almost destroyed a business that had been in our family four hundred years."

Finally, Matteo got to *the* question.

"I didn't say I didn't want to see you again until the dinner because I don't find you attractive, Marlee.

Maybe you see yourself as a plain-Jane librarian, but I don't. I feel something. Don't you?"

Marlee didn't say anything, and he didn't dare look at her for her answer.

"I feel it," he continued, his voice a ragged whisper, "shivering in the air between us. A terrifying potential. I'm not sure I'm brave enough to know what you could be to me."

He set down her feet abruptly. He looked everywhere but at her.

"I feel foolish saying that." He glanced at his watch. "I've known you all of twenty-four hours. But that's what I wanted you to know. That the exact opposite is true. You may be the most beautiful woman I have ever encountered."

And then finally, Matteo looked at her.

He saw the stillness he had experienced in the room reflected in her face. The greenness of her eyes reminded him of a cool pond on a hot day, a place a man could dive into and find relief from everything that troubled him.

Did he throw himself into such a promise of sanctuary as Marlee offered, or did he flee from it?

What was in the air between them felt as impossible to fight as a tsunami would be if it swept up that beach.

"I've burdened you with my difficulties," he said, and heard the stiffness in his voice. "I'm sorry. I don't usually have jet lag, but I may be suffering from it now. It has—"

Weakened me. Made me less a man.

"—been extraordinarily inappropriate."

With what small remnants of his strength that remained, Matteo made the decision to find higher ground. Without another word, he carefully lined up the things left over from the pedicure kit, got to his feet and walked out of the cabana.

Wiggling her freshly painted toes, Marlee sat there, stunned by the abruptness of Matteo's departure. She felt abandoned. And let down.

Who told someone they might be the most beautiful woman they had ever encountered and then forsook them?

Confusingly, the sting of desertion warred with the incredible gift of Matteo's trust.

"Which he is now sorry he bestowed," she reminded herself sternly. "Jet lag–inspired confidences!"

Besides, she shared his terror of the forces that were drawing them together, didn't she? Though there were much larger forces drawing them apart if she thought about it. Their fears and past experiences formed quite a wedge.

And so did time.

The wedding was on Saturday. She had to see him at the rehearsal dinner tomorrow night, and at the wedding, of course. She could avoid encounters of the truly scary kind. That was what he wanted to do. He was being very sensible.

It would be dumb to put her already battered heart at risk! Matteo had exited in the nick of time, and she would respect that.

The decision for self-preservation made, Marlee got up and, mindful of the fragility of freshly painted nails, tiptoed cautiously into the bathroom. She used the hair dryer to finish drying her toes, then glanced at the clock. It was late, but chances of her going to sleep were nil.

Her family had always taught her the remedy for discomfort was to stop thinking about yourself and do something for someone in need.

Marlee thought that Fiona might be up and in need of comfort. That was why she had done her toenails in the first place, she reminded herself.

She changed out of her pajamas and into that horrible but exceedingly comfy pink sweat suit, then made her way across the darkened resort to Fiona's suite.

As she had suspected, the light was on inside. She knocked lightly on the door. After a long pause, Fiona flung it open.

Her face fell when she saw it was Marlee.

"I hoped you were Mike," she said, glancing over Marlee's shoulder as if she might have hidden Mike somewhere behind her.

"I just came to show you my toenails," Marlee said, hoping to lighten Fiona's mood. She lifted one leg and wiggled her toes.

Fiona bent over and looked at them. "Oh," she said, with an exasperated sigh of long-suffering. "Didn't you get my text?"

Marlee put her leg down. "What?"

"I sent you a picture of what I wanted. I'll show you."

Fiona went and grabbed her phone. "It was bridesmaid photo of the year."

Marlee looked at the picture. Four perfect feet were photographed against a backdrop of powdered sugar sand. Each one's toenails were painted gold, but each had a tiny white flower on it.

"You're supposed to have the flower on your fourth toe. I have one on my big toe, Kathy has one on her second toe, Brenda on her third."

"Well, I'll just have to be plain gold," Marlee said, stung by the criticism.

"You're wrecking everything," Fiona said.

"*I'm* wrecking everything?"

Marlee contemplated catching the next flight home. Three birds with one stone: she wouldn't have to steel herself against meeting Matteo again; she wouldn't have to put up with Fiona; and she wouldn't have to *really* wreck everything by admitting she'd found a donkey instead of a horse.

"I could tell by your face you hate the dress I picked for you. You missed the welcome party by the pool. You missed the pedicures. You're acting like you hate it all."

And here she thought she had been hiding that so well! Marlee was very aware that there was something about having spent the day with Matteo that had brought out this more forthright side of her. She took a deep breath.

"Fiona, I have gone to a great deal of trouble, time and expense to be here for you. I spent the whole day trying to find you, um, an equine. I did miss the pool get-together, and I wasn't here for the spa thing, but I've done my best to give you what you wanted. And instead of being grateful, instead of acting as if you want me here, you're just being self-centered and mean."

How much of having a man at her feet admitting he thought she was beautiful and that he found himself terribly attracted to her had given her the courage to say this?

Fiona's mouth fell open.

"And I *do* hate the dress," Marlee said, while she was getting things off her chest and being courageous. "I'm not wearing it."

"Well, you won't have to," Fiona said, and burst into tears, "because there is not going to be a wedding!"

Marlee took her friend by the elbow and guided her to the couch.

"What's going on, Fiona?" She sank onto the couch beside her.

"Mike said the same things to me as you. Only he wasn't as nice about it. He called me the B-word."

"I'm sorry," Marlee said, and she genuinely was.

"The B-word! My dad used to call my mom that when they were fighting. I screamed at Mike that I wouldn't marry him now if he was the last man on earth.

"How can this be happening to me?" she whimpered. "I knew my parents wouldn't come if I had it here, but it doesn't matter. It's the very same as if they were here. Fighting. Chaos. Name-calling... Marlee, I'm going to end up just like you," she whispered as if that was the worst thing on earth. "Abandoned at the altar."

Marlee considered that for a moment, and the truth unfolded in her like a flag unfurling.

"It was the best thing that ever happened to me."

CHAPTER ELEVEN

IT WAS THE best thing that ever happened to me.

"What?" Fiona said. "You're devastated! You've looked sad for six months."

Either Fiona was actually capable of seeing how others felt, or she was worried about *that* look for the photos. Marlee decided to give her the benefit of the doubt.

"I was sad. But I'm not now."

Marlee could probably pinpoint just about the precise moment when that had happened, and it had been when she had embraced a bolder side, and been drinking rum and contemplating smoking a cigar. The moment when she had met the man who would change it all.

It was as if from that point a new world had opened to her. A world full of wonder.

"You and Arthur were so perfect for each other," Fiona said dejectedly. "When it didn't work, it kind of shook my sense of safety. It made me aware that anything could happen to anybody at any time."

"Why do you say we were perfect for each other?"

"You were just so *stable.* That's what made the breakup so shocking. You were like your mom and dad."

Marlee smiled. "Yes, we were. Arthur actually brought

that up when he called it off. He said we were much too young to be so settled. He used the word *comfy.*"

"Like your mom and dad! That's what I've yearned for my whole life."

"He said we were like two worn recliners in front of the TV set."

Fiona giggled through her tears. "Okay. Maybe that's a little *too* comfy."

"If I had married him," Marlee said softly, arriving at the realization herself for the first time, "I would have missed so much. Boldness. Adventure. Spontaneity."

"Oh! As if *you* are going to embrace those things now!"

"I might surprise you," Marlee said.

"I'm sorry. I didn't mean that to sound as if you're dull and boring. It's just, I rely on you to be the stable one." Fiona sighed. "I've been totally awful, haven't I?"

"Look, I get it. I know what you come from."

"You're the only one here who actually knows. I mean, I've told Mike I didn't have the best family life, and he's seen it for himself when he's met my parents, but I've always controlled everything about him meeting them. Dinner in a nice restaurant with strict timelines. Like, I'd book a show right after, so that they didn't have time to…well, you know, do what they do.

"I've never even had him to their house. It's such an embarrassment to me. Who knows what you'd find this week? A window somebody has thrown something through? A wrecked car in the yard? I wanted this whole wedding to be like the opposite of that. I wanted it to be classy and romantic and beautiful."

"As if you were leaving all that behind."

"Exactly," Fiona said sadly.

"Fiona, you can't leave parts of yourself behind. Believe it or not, some of the things that are best about you come from that."

She contemplated that for a moment. "You think so?"

"You need to go talk to Mike and tell him exactly what you told me just now. You need to let him know why being in control is so important to you. And you need to let him know you believe in the power of love, above all else."

Fiona looked at her hopefully, through wet eyes. "Okay," she said. "Am I a total mess?"

"You are."

"I need to—"

"You need to go to him exactly as you are, Fiona. Exactly."

Fiona stared at her.

"No makeup?" she whispered. "He's never seen me without makeup."

"You wear your makeup to bed?" Marlee asked, astonished.

"Just a little bit."

"Doesn't it end up on the pillowcase?"

"I look horrible without any makeup on."

"I'm sure he doesn't love you because of your makeup."

"I'm not even sure he does love me."

"Go find out. Be brave. Fiona—" she said the next part carefully "—think about what *he* needs. Not what you need."

"Okay," Fiona finally said, as if she was a child who had been given a reprehensible task to fulfill.

Marlee made her way back to her own cabana. She thought she might lie awake for a while but found she was pleasantly exhausted from her day of sunshine and unexpected adventure. She fell asleep thinking about those words.

Be brave.

When her cell phone rang beside her bed, she glanced at her bedside clock. It was one in the morning. She had the crazy hope it was Matteo, even though they had never had a reason to exchange phone numbers.

But it wasn't. It was Fiona.

"The wedding is on!" she cried.

"That's great," Marlee said, sleepy but genuinely happy for her friend.

"Mike hadn't seen me without makeup before and he said I looked *adorbs.*"

"That's true love," Marlee said.

"Isn't it? And my face was all blotchy and tear-stained and he didn't even care."

"That guy is a gem. I've always thought so."

"He thinks the same of you. You were part of what we fought about."

"Me?"

"I was, er, complaining about you missing the warm-up party at the pool and the pedicure, and he said I was being insensitive. He said maybe all this wedding stuff made you sad."

Marlee contemplated that. It made her uncomfortable that she was being talked about, especially in the context of Mike pitying her.

"He seemed very relieved when I told him just now that you decided your wedding cancellation was a good thing. He never liked Arthur for you. He didn't think you should just go for the first guy who paid attention to you."

Again, Marlee did not like the sensation of being talked about, her life and choices dissected. She didn't like it at all that she was seen as some kind of fading wallflower, so pleased at any kind of male attention that her marriage had been seen as an act of desperation instead of love. How much of that was true? She was silent.

"Now that we're on," Fiona said, moving right along, "do you think you could do something about that flower?"

She was confused since she had just been thinking of wallflowers. "What? What flower?"

"The white flower on the fourth toe."

"Um—" Marlee suddenly wasn't sure Fiona had learned anything at all from her wedding nearly not happening.

"I'm not sure painting a white flower on my toe is in my skill set." She was pretty sure it was not in Matteo's, either. Not that she planned to ask him!

"I know you'll figure it out," Fiona said cheerfully. "Thank you for being there for me tonight. Best friend ever!"

And then the phone went dead.

That left Marlee to lie awake, thinking about people pitying her. But her thoughts soon drifted to contemplation of Matteo's abrupt departure last night. She understood why he had gone. He was terrified of love.

He'd made that clear. He had watched it destroy

his father, and he was, understandably, steering away from it.

Lying in the darkness of her room, Marlee thought about the words she had said to Fiona.

Think about what he needs.

She had meant it in the context of Mike, but she found herself thinking about Matteo. He appeared to be the man who had everything, and yet he had revealed a damaged heart to her.

It struck her as sad that a man who had accomplished so much materially had condemned himself to such a lonely existence.

Really, what he had confided in her was that he wasn't going to care about anyone, because caring hurt too much.

Of course he had his sisters, his nieces and nephews, but she wondered how much he held back, even from them.

"You can't fix this," she whispered to herself.

But suddenly she was ashamed that she had made the decision to avoid Matteo, to follow his lead, for self-preservation.

That was not the set of values she had grown up with. Maybe it was even the kind of safe decision that inspired pity for her from people like Mike.

It was two more days.

They didn't have to fall in love.

She shivered as that thought entered her mind.

They just had to believe it was okay to care about each other. It was okay to let their guard down. It was okay to have fun and believe that life had natural checks and balances.

It held sorrow and joy.

It was okay to be curious and open to what happened next. Why not ask him to expand his skill set a little bit?

The next morning, in the safest place on earth, Marlee had absolutely no problem getting his room number out of the front desk clerk. She probably could have gotten the key if she'd asked for it!

Her heart beating unreasonably, she found her way to his room.

Except it wasn't exactly a room. Matteo's villa made her tiny cabana look like a shoebox. She suddenly didn't feel at all as confident that she knew what anybody needed. She had deliberately dressed casually—shorts, sandals, a white shirt—but now she wished she'd given in to the temptation to buy a second sundress from the resort boutique.

Too late for doubts! She took a deep breath.

She knocked on the door. Again, Marlee gave herself the same advice she'd given Fiona.

Be brave.

Think about what he needed, not what she needed.

The door swung open and Matteo stood there.

A towel was wrapped around his waist.

She totally forgot about what he needed, or what she needed.

"Do you open your door like that in Switzerland?" she croaked.

"Like what?"

"With no clothes on."

He glanced down at himself. He looked at her, and a small smile tickled his lips at her discomfort.

"You've seen me in my swim shorts," he said. "I don't think this is any less modest."

"Um…"

"Unless," he said wickedly, "there was a wardrobe malfunction."

She gulped.

He laughed. "What gives me the pleasure this morning?"

A reminder that last night he had been *sorry* about the confidences he had shared with her, sorry he had shown her his poor, bruised heart.

It came back to her why she was here.

To rescue him, the man who had everything, from his self-imposed prison of loneliness.

She waved a bottle of white nail polish at him. "Fiona wants some modification to the design. Can I come in? I have a picture."

He hesitated, and then with a slight bow, he held the door open to her.

Surrender.

Marlee stepped by him and his shower-fresh scent tickled her nostrils. She was aware of the perfect, deep carve of his chest and how utterly and beautifully masculine he was. She remembered the accidental touches of her fingers on his naked skin when they had swum together.

They were alone in his villa. The potential for danger—of the most delicious kind—seemed high.

But then she came to a full stop. Her mouth fell open as her eyes adjusted from the bright light outside to the dimmer interior of the villa.

The ceilings soared. The couches were white leather.

If she sat on one in her white shirt, she would disappear!

The rest of the furniture was rich, subdued and sophisticated. The huge abstract art pieces were gorgeous. The rugs were, no doubt, priceless. A bouquet of island-bright fresh flowers was in a huge vase in the center of a coffee table.

In her cabana, she had gotten a free cigar and a travel-size bottle of rum. The rich and famous got baby-elephant-size bouquets of flowers.

A whole wall was covered in windows that looked out to a pool. A waterfall cascaded off one end of it. Its marble decks were scattered with huge wicker furniture baskets—giant eggs—with bright pillows inside them. Concrete pots held flowering trees and shrubs. There was a bar at the opposite end of the pool from the waterfall.

"Is that a pool?" she asked, though it was obvious it was.

"Yes."

"Just for this unit?" Marlee was aware her voice was slightly strangled.

Matteo wagged a wicked eyebrow at her. "Privacy has its perks."

She glanced down at the towel and blushed. She had assumed he was in the shower, but maybe he'd been in the pool.

In his altogether!

"Why were you going to the ocean to swim that night if you had this at your disposal?" Including, of course, all that privacy!

The danger she had felt a moment ago felt as if it

was diluting, like pouring a glass of red wine into the ocean. He was from a different world than her.

A faster world. A more sophisticated world.

He swam in the nude!

Still, now was not the time to lose courage. She had made it past the first barrier, the front door. The second, if she included him being dressed only in a towel, which a few days ago would have been enough to make her turn tail and run.

"It's a palace," she said. *Who did she think she was?* He was not only from a different world, he was also one of the richest men in that world.

The third barrier appeared to be her own sense of inadequacy, and she was not so certain she could overcome that one.

She had convinced herself he needed rescuing.

It was laughable.

Was it just an excuse to give in to her desire to be with him? There it was—just sharing the same space with him, she became so aware of a deep and all-consuming hunger.

To know him.

To share air with him.

To make him laugh.

To touch him.

To be touched by him.

"What's wrong?" Matteo said, frowning at her.

Marlee reminded herself firmly of the life she had almost had. As comfortable as two old recliners in front of the television set.

She remembered suddenly a part she had not shared with Fiona.

Rump-sprung.

Arthur had called the recliners that he thought represented their future together rump-sprung.

If she wanted a rump-sprung life, she could leave right now. Holding that thought firm, Marlee held her ground.

CHAPTER TWELVE

MATTEO WATCHED MARLEE take in her surroundings. She looked as if she was contemplating bolting.

"Is something wrong?" he asked her, again.

But then she relaxed, and he knew she would stay. He felt inordinately pleased.

He thought about her question. With a pool at his disposal, why had he gone to the ocean to swim that night?

He was not a whimsical man. Not even a little bit.

And yet, it felt as if destiny had drawn him to the ocean, to his path crossing hers, literally.

Last night, after he had opened his heart to her, he had made a decision. No more being weak when he wanted to be strong.

And yet, when he had opened the door to her standing there, clutching that silly bottle of nail polish, something in him had sighed.

With welcome.

And maybe the most dangerous thing of all, hope.

"Nothing's wrong, exactly," she said, looking about, "but it's all just very glamourous, like the set of a movie."

"Is it?" He looked around, seeing it through her

eyes. To him it looked just like a thousand other high-end hotel rooms he had stayed in.

"You don't even know it's out of the ordinary, do you? I mean the bathroom is probably bigger than my whole apartment in Seattle."

"It's not like it's mine," he pointed out.

She didn't look convinced. Her insecurity had a funny effect on him. He wanted to be the one who made her feel secure.

"It's just a rental. I call this decor style 'generic posh.' I mean, look at that painting over there. Would anybody actually hang it in their house?"

"Nobody has a twelve-foot wall in their house!"

"Besides how huge it is, it has no meaning. Big black looping lines."

She cocked her head thoughtfully at it, and he saw, pleased, just a tiny bit of the tension leave her.

"Maybe it's like an inkblot test," she suggested.

"What do you see in it?"

"The LA freeway," she decided, and they both laughed, and Matteo was grateful something eased even further in her. "What about you?"

"Tangled yarn," he decided. "My grandmother used to knit."

He turned back to her and caught a look on her face. Unless he missed his guess, she also knitted. It endeared her to him, and the fact she was embarrassed about it endeared her more.

"I was just having coffee by the pool," he said. "Come join me, and then we'll discuss the latest in bridal demands. Let me guess. It has something to do with photos."

He was satisfied when he coaxed a little laugh from Marlee. "How did you know?"

He lifted a shoulder and led her through to the patio. He settled her at the table and went and got another cup. He poured her a coffee from the carafe on the table, then sank into his chair across from her. She helped herself to cream and sugar and took a sip.

"So good," she said.

The quality of light on Coconut Cay was magnificent. It danced in her hair and lit her eyes.

She was wearing a crisp white shirt today, button-down. She had on a pair of khaki shorts with it.

So good.

How was she making the quintessential tourist outfit look so sexy?

"Are you, um, going to put on some pants?"

"Am I making you uncomfortable?"

"Yes!"

He grinned. "Good."

He deliberately stretched out his legs. She glanced at the length of them, gave him a warning look, then took out her phone and showed him the picture.

"You're kidding, right?" he asked, contemplating the feet in the picture with the tiny flowers painted on the toenails.

"No, I'm afraid not."

"There are people who specialize in painting miniatures. I'm not one of them."

"But you'll try, at least?"

He looked at the picture again. Dangerous to get into this! To be touching her feet, again, the way he had been last night.

When all his barriers had come tumbling down!

So no one was more shocked than he was, to hear himself saying, "Oh, why not? How difficult could it be?"

Actually, it was quite difficult. After they had finished their coffee, Matteo got Marlee settled among the bright, deep cushions of one of those big, egg-shaped wicker things around the pool.

He took her foot in his hand and bent over it, fighting a ridiculous impulse to kiss her instep. Carefully, tongue between his teeth, he took the brush out of the bottle.

"Is your house in Switzerland as palatial as this?" she asked him. "The house of a man who flies around in his own jet?"

"Do you want to know a secret about me?"

Now he was going to tell her *more* secrets? She leaned up from where she was reclining among the pillows and it weakened him in some delightful way that she *did* want to know a secret about him.

It was just to make her comfortable, he told himself.

"I still live in the same room I had as a boy. To be honest, not much has changed about it. The model airplane my father and I made together still hangs from a fishing line in one corner."

She leaned back against the pillows, relaxed.

He was not sure he wanted her quite that relaxed. He thought about running his thumb down the side of her instep that he already knew was so tender, but resisted.

"My house in Zurich is old. Just as our business, it's been in my family for generations. When my father died, neither of my sisters wanted it. Mia said it was haunted, and Emma was worried about her children destroying the antiques. I couldn't bring myself to move into the bedroom my mother and father had shared, so there I am, in my boyhood room.

"I'm planning a complete renovation, eventually, but I haven't gotten to it yet."

It occurred to him that the space called *home* was a low priority to him, linked in some way to the dangers he had revealed to Marlee last night.

The dangers of caring.

"Tell me about your family business," she invited.

Matteo found it so easy to talk to her.

"Family legend has it that it started hundreds of years ago on my mother's side, when my great-great-great-grandmother sold a handmade winter coat. And then another and another. Her name was Rosa, which coincidentally is also the name of Switzerland's highest peak.

"Over many generations, Monte Rosa Alpen Wear became a company that was known for extremely high-quality winter clothing, and a contract to supply an army with wool jackets moved it to the next level. And then it expanded into mountaineering and outdoor supplies and survival equipment.

"By the time my father took it over, the reputation of the company was cemented. But after the death of my mother, he took his hands off the reins. I think that though she stayed in the background, she was the detail person. Maybe even the driving force behind the company. Anyway, after her death, he wasn't watching the quality control. He wasn't interested in trends or how to stay current in an increasingly competitive market.

"My sisters and I watched helplessly as his indifference nearly drove the family business into the ground.

Our four-hundred-year-old reputation was badly tarnished. We were getting reviews and complaints, and many of them said we were overpriced, old-fashioned, and skating on our name.

"I took marketing in university—that's where I met Mike. And by the time I was done, I knew exactly what needed to happen with Monte Rosa. I wanted my sisters involved. It seemed to me it had always been a women-driven company, even when men took the credit. So my sister Emma applied her brilliant design ideas to bring the clothing lines into this century, and Mia took over the quality control for the mountaineering and survival equipment lines. We dropped the *Wear* from the name and surged forward."

Matteo was aware he did not usually talk this much. It was very comfortable to talk to her. That was what he had wanted, wasn't it? Her comfort? But now it felt as if maybe it was too comfortable. The spell he'd tried to weave around her had spun back and caught him.

Because the next words out of his mouth shocked Matteo.

"I sometimes wonder, though I've never admitted it, if saving the family business made me feel as if I could save all that we were before my mother died."

"And did it?" Marlee asked softly.

"Not really," he admitted. "My father died before we began to enjoy the enormous success we have today."

He felt suddenly wildly uncomfortable with his confidences. He renewed his interest in the job at hand.

Matteo dabbed at Marlee's toenail. He frowned. It didn't really look like a flower. He tried to repair it. The brush slipped and a blob of white nail polish nearly obliterated her whole toe. He jumped up, relieved to be away from the intensity, and went in search of something to clean it off.

"I should have thought of this in advance," he muttered, feeling more composed when he came back. He wiped the botched nail polish.

"Toilet paper?" she said, the outlaw dancing in her eyes, and yet there was something right beneath that, too. Compassion. Concern. "I thought this was a classy joint."

He was grateful that she understood his need to move past what he had just said, to keep it light.

The nail polish was a perfect distraction. It had dried ever so slightly and his clumsy attempt to wipe it had left a cloudy smear on her toenail.

"So classy they hid the damned tissue. The nail polish brush is too big. I need something smaller. Aha!"

This was what got him through everything: razor focus, an ability to prioritize. And keep things—especially untidy things like feelings—in compartments.

He went into the suite and came back with a pen. He dipped the tip in the polish. And carefully put a single drop on her toe. Still a blob!

He scowled, wiped it off, dabbed again.

"Quit laughing," he told her sternly, "it makes your toe shake."

"I can't help it. I feel like Cleopatra."

Again, he felt grateful to her for moving on, for keeping it light between them, and shifting the topic away from his confession.

"And to think yesterday you were just an outlaw," Matteo said, in the same vein as her.

"I know. Quite a promotion in one day. Not only am I Cleopatra, but I have a slave."

"Ah," he said. "My queen, your wish is my command."

For a moment, she was very silent. He glanced up at her. His mouth went dry.

"I wish," she said softly, "that you could find what you're looking for."

He stared at her.

"I wish you could have your sense of family back. And safety."

He felt as if what he was looking for—the thing he had been searching for without knowing that he searched—was in her eyes, like a promise.

He looked away from her. He concentrated on the job in front of him. His hand didn't feel steady.

"There," he said, putting her foot away from him, and with it, hopefully, the sense of weakness and wanting that seemed to be enveloping him.

She pulled up her knees and inspected his work. Her suppressed mirth gave way. She gave a shout of laughter.

"I don't get what's so funny," he said gravely.

"It doesn't look like a flower. It looks like an octopus."

He retrieved her toe and studied it. "You might have something there, Queen Cleo. Call Fiona. Change the theme."

"Egyptian?" she suggested.

"Or Down by the Sea."

"Which theme will Henri fit into better?"

"Oh, Henri! Have you told her yet, about Henri?"

"Not yet. The time hasn't seemed right. She's a nervous wreck."

After all the hoops Fiona was making her jump

through, Marlee was still able to think what Fiona was going through?

He was not at all sure he had ever met anyone this big-hearted before.

It was a warning. She was too soft. Too tender.

A person like Marlee would be so easily hurt.

And yet, the impulse to kiss her foot was so great that he sprang to his feet.

"Well," he said, "our work here is done."

Her eyes went very wide.

He felt the sudden breeze on his bare skin.

He looked down, already knowing what he would see. The towel must have caught on the edge of the basket chair. It lay in a white puddle at his feet.

Matteo looked at Marlee, expecting to see her laughing now that the tables were turned and the embarrassing wardrobe malfunction moment was his.

But she was not laughing.

Matteo turned and dove in the pool.

CHAPTER THIRTEEN

MARLEE WATCHED THE faint splash as Matteo dove cleanly into the water and disappeared under its tranquil blue surface. She was unabashedly appreciative of him. He was quite gorgeous with no clothes on. He would make the perfect male specimen to carve in marble.

She found herself continually shocked by the surprises life held after she'd made that decision to be bold, and by the fact a different side of herself was being revealed.

For instance, if she was still the woman she had been when she arrived at Coconut Cay, she would get up now, go inside the villa and give Matteo an opportunity to exit the water and retrieve his towel and his dignity.

Instead, she got up and wandered to the water's edge. She stuck her toe in, just as he resurfaced, treading water. He shook droplets of water from his hair, scowling at her.

"Don't get your feet wet," he ordered her.

"I can if I want."

"You'll spoil the nail polish."

She smiled at him. "As if that's our biggest problem," she said sweetly.

His scowl deepened. "If you could just put my towel where I can reach it and turn your back for a moment, I'd be most grateful."

She leaned over and picked up his towel. She made a grave show of contemplating it thoughtfully. Then she tossed it behind her, well out of his reach.

"Hey! That isn't funny!"

"It is," she said. "Barely."

"Marlee, be reasonable."

"You thought it was hilarious when it happened to me."

"I didn't really."

"Where is all your European sophistication now?" she asked him. Slowly, deliberately, she moved her hand to the top button of her shirt. She flicked it open.

His eyes went wide.

She flicked open the next one.

He licked his lips. "Marlee, just pass me the towel. Before we—you—do something you regret."

"What would I regret?" she egged him on softly.

"Wrecking the nail polish!" he said, and she heard something desperate in his tone.

"It didn't look like a flower, anyway."

"If you'll just be reasonable, I'll try again. I'm sure I can master a flower—"

"I'm all done being reasonable," she interrupted him.

"No, you're not," he insisted.

She laughed. She was not sure she had ever felt her full feminine power quite so delightfully as when she slowly removed her top and let it slide from her hand to the pool deck.

Ever so slowly, she trailed her hand down over her

belly to the button on her shorts. She undid them and stepped out of them.

If she expected sanity to hit her as the sultry tropical air caressed her skin, she was completely wrong.

She didn't feel shy at all. The woman who had run from the ocean trying to hide herself was gone forever. Wallflowers who inspired pity were banished from within herself!

Matteo had done this to her.

He was doing it to her now. The look in his eyes—desperation, hunger, appreciation— emboldened her. She was not who she had been before.

"What are you doing?" he croaked.

"I'm going skinny-dipping."

"No, you're not!"

"But you're doing it."

"By accident!"

"I bet it feels wonderful."

"It doesn't."

"The water right up against your skin, no barriers. I'm curious."

"You've experienced that every single time you've taken a bath."

"I don't think it's the same."

"It is."

She smiled at him, then she reached behind her own back and flicked open the clasp on her bra. It fell away. Nothing awkward about it at all. She stretched up and enjoyed the sensation of sun on her naked skin.

Matteo groaned, an almost animal sound of suffering.

"Imagine that," she said. "I'm twenty-six years old,

and I've never felt the sun on my breasts before. I could get used to it, I think."

"Marlee," he said hoarsely, "you are killing me."

She smiled more deeply at him. "But what a way to go, right?"

She stepped out of her panties and then jumped off the edge of the deck way out into the pool. She felt the water close over her head.

For a split second, she enjoyed the sensation of warm water, silky, against her naked skin. It was just as she had hoped. Utterly freeing. Unbelievably sensual.

But then her feet did not find the bottom of the pool. She had not thought she was going in the deep end. A little too late, she remembered she was not a very good swimmer.

Marlee realized, panic beginning, that she was in way over her head, in every possible way.

Her feet finally found the bottom of the pool. She hated opening her eyes underwater, but she did.

It seemed as if the light was a long way away. She pushed against the floor of the pool and rocketed to the surface. She drew in a single, strangled breath, and managed one distressed yelp. She flapped her arms frantically and struck out for the safety of the side.

But gravity was winning. Panic made her limbs heavy.

And then safety found her.

If it could be called that.

Matteo's arms closed around her, and she twined her arms around his neck.

"Hang on," he said. "I've got you."

Had more beautiful words ever been spoken?

"Relax," he told her, his voice deep and calm and

soothing in her ear. Effortlessly, he moved them to shallower water.

"You can stand now," he said.

But somehow, she could not let go. And somehow, they were not safe.

Probably the farthest thing from it.

She looked up into his face, so familiar to her already. And in some way that was beyond explanation, given the shortness of their acquaintance, beloved.

Maybe that was what happened when someone saved your life.

She traced the wet surface of his face with her fingertips, hungry to know his brow, his eyelids, the straight line of his nose, the cleft of his chin. He moved his head until his lips found her questing fingers.

One by one, as he tasted them, she gloried in the larger sensation of their bodies touching, wet skin slippery as silk connecting them both.

His hand moved to the back of her head, and he drew her face to his. His mouth found her mouth.

There was no tentativeness in either of them. No hesitation.

This kiss had none of the innocence of the kiss she had bestowed on him yesterday after their adventure.

Though it was everything that kiss had hinted it could be. There was savagery and sweetness combined as Marlee was engulfed by sensation.

Every cell in her awakened to Matteo's quest, Matteo's call. Every part of her, from the tips of her toes to the tips of her hair, tingled and sparked. It was as if her desire had been a dying ember at her core and was now flickering to life, after a breath of air had found it.

The breath intensified. A breeze. And the ember

of desire within Marlee flared, glowing red hot. Just when it seemed it could not become any more intense, as if the heat could consume her, Matteo dropped his head to her breast.

That fire within took hold, roared to life.

It felt as if the water should boil around them.

He lifted her easily and carried her from the water. The sensation in the pit of her stomach was deeply primal, as if she was the woman a warrior had come home to. He kicked open the door of the villa with his foot and took her through to the coolness to the master suite, his easy strength stealing her breath.

He laid her on the center of the bed, and she felt herself sinking into the deep comfort of its snowy whiteness.

Matteo stood above her, looking down. He waited, his eyes drinking her in, for a signal from her. She noticed everything: the water droplets on his lashes, the plump line of his bottom lip, the broadness of his shoulders, the deepness of his chest, his ribs marching down his sides to the narrowness of his waist.

The woman she used to be—yesterday, though it felt as if it was a hundred years ago—put up a faint fight.

Think, the old Marlee implored her.

About what? the new Marlee asked.

Consequences. Tomorrow.

But none of that mattered. There was no tomorrow, and the consequence of not following her heart seemed as if it would be the worst one of all.

A form of death.

The kind of nonlife—dull as a rump-sprung recliner in front of a TV—that she had accepted for far too long.

She opened her arms to him.

And everything within Marlee sang.

Live.

And so she lived.

Matteo was an exquisite lover. He wanted her pleasure. He teased. He tantalized. He found each of her ticklish secrets—particularly that delicate instep—and tormented her with them.

And he coaxed her to open a thus unexplored side of herself. She experimented. She indulged. She risked.

Much later, they lay in a tangle of sheets and the glow of utter fulfillment, splashes of sunshine striping them in light filtered green from the thick foliage outside his window.

Then they showered together, learning the textures and secrets of each other's bodies all over again. He shampooed her hair, something in the tenderness of his touch exquisitely possessive.

You belong to me.

And then they dried each other off, kisses following the path of the towel.

And then reality knocked.

Literally.

Someone was hammering on the villa door.

They both froze, silent.

"Hey, Matt," Mike called through the closed door. "What's up? You coming golfing?"

Marlee stifled a giggle. Matteo put a hand on her arm. As if that was necessary. She was hardly going to go throw open the door!

Mike knocked again, and then they heard other male voices join his, jovial. And then they moved on, their voices drifting away.

"Go golfing," Marlee told him, casually, as if it

didn't matter to her one little bit. As if she was suave and sophisticated and did things like this all the time.

Not once in a lifetime.

But she was holding her breath and Matteo was not the least fooled.

"You think I would go golfing after that?" He laughed, and his laughter filled her to the brim.

"Come on," he said, "Let's get dressed. I am not wasting one minute that I could spend with you. What do you want to do?"

She started breathing again.

Be with you. That was it. All of it.

"What I don't want to do," she said carefully, "is risk running into Fiona." She shuddered inwardly at the thought of the grilling that could ensue if the bride saw them together.

"Or Mike," he agreed.

What had happened between them felt raw and real and as if a neon sign was blinking above them announcing their newfound intimacy: *lovers.*

Marlee could not bear the thought of sideways looks, smiles, conjecture, interrogation. For a while longer, she wanted this just to belong to her and Matteo. She wasn't ready to share it with their circle of friends.

Especially her friends.

Who saw her as prim and controlled, always the stable one, always the responsible one. They would be utterly shocked to see her now.

How would she and Matteo get through the rehearsal dinner?

But that was tonight and that seemed a long way away. Only this moment seemed to exist, glittering, sparkling, infused with their newfound awareness of each other.

So much so that it was hard to keep their hands off each other as they made their way to the resort gate, both of them stealing furtive looks about, not ready just yet to have their togetherness spotted. Confronted. *Challenged.*

Outside the gates of the resort, Marlee heaved a huge sigh of relief.

She felt gloriously free. The street—vegetable stands and trinket booths and chickens and cars and children in school uniforms—shone with a spectacular light.

And then she saw the donkey cart, parked at the curb, waiting sleepily for passengers. It felt as if even the universe was on their side, providing a perfect get-away plan for them, two outlaws of love on the run.

CHAPTER FOURTEEN

"Look," Marlee said to Matteo, taking his arm and tugging him toward the ancient and colorful cart, "It's Mackay with Henri and Calamity."

"It's obviously Mackay, but how do you know which donkeys those are? He could have a whole herd of donkeys, for all you know."

"Are you skeptical of my ass expertise?" Marlee asked. She let her hand graze ever so lightly—possessively—over the back of Matteo's shorts.

She relished the unexpected direction of her life: she was teasing her lover on the colorful main street of an exotic island.

"I consider myself something of an expert now, on ass…ets. Having been exposed, so to speak." She leveled him a look and wagged her eyebrows at him.

He rewarded her with his laughter, that rich deep sound that she could live the rest of her life trying to coax from him. Even more precious was the slight blush.

"Right, Mackay? Henri and Calamity?"

"That's right." Mackay tipped his hat to them as if he had been waiting for them to appear. His glance went between them and he grinned, as if he *knew*—

probably from Matteo's blush—that the romance he had predicted for *maybe after lunch* yesterday had unfolded.

To Marlee, his knowing look confirmed the wisdom of them leaving the resort.

"I knew it was Henri immediately because of his cute ears," Marlee told Matteo. "Calamity is sporting a pink feather headdress to let the world know she's a girl."

She went and bestowed each of the donkeys a kiss on their furry, soft noses.

"Miss Marlee. Mr. Matteo. Where can Mackay take you?"

"Where to?" Matteo asked her.

"Anywhere. No plan is a good plan."

Matteo snapped his fingers and turned to Mackay. "We need somebody who can do a pedicure."

"Really?" Marlee said, wiggling her toes and gazing at them. "I kind of like the octopus. It's growing on me."

"It's not faring well after the pool. And the other activities."

It was her turn to blush. And then he was laughing again and her laugher joined his.

"I'm not willing to spoil a perfect day by risking the wrath of Fiona," Matteo decided. "I've already missed the scheduled golf event, so let's make sure we pass pedicure inspection."

Marlee felt a little disappointed. She had hoped for something a bit more romantic.

But then he leaned close to her and said in her ear, "I'm going to watch very closely so I get it just right next time."

Next time.

"I think you got it just right last time," she said huskily.

"I'm talking about the pedicure," he said.

"Oh, *that.*"

And there it was between them: that sizzling connection.

"You know someone, Mackay?" Matteo asked. "Who can paint Marlee's toenails?"

"Yes, yes, my cousin." He regarded them sagely for a moment. "There are all kinds of hunger."

Evidence they were practically telegraphing what had just happened between them.

"But perhaps some food first?"

"Absolutely," Matteo said.

And so they found themselves at the kind of place Marlee would *never* have gone to. It was an off-the-beaten-track establishment that tourists did not find. It was part roadside stand and part house. A picnic area, packed with locals, had been cordoned off on the street and cars steered cheerfully around it. As soon as they sat down, three men appeared on a makeshift stage.

The joyous shouts and sounds of calypso filled the air as Marlee and Matteo fed each other spicy local food off their fingertips.

"I think this may be the most delicious food I've ever eaten," Marlee said with a satisfied sigh when the plates in front of them were empty.

"Or your senses might be heightened," Matteo said in her ear.

Might be?

She hadn't had a single thing to drink beyond water and yet she felt intoxicated. Marlee could feel all of life tingling against her skin. As if she was breathing in the colors and sounds of Coconut Cay until they were part of her.

Her eyes fell on him.

Matteo.

Part of her.

And no matter what happened next, part of her forever.

Not that she was going to spoil one second of this by asking herself what could possibly happen next.

But what happened next was astonishing.

Mackay bowed before her. "Would you dance with me, Miss Marlee?"

She cast a look over his shoulder. A space had been cleared and people were up on the makeshift dance floor.

The music had become even more lively. People clapped and sang along. A spontaneous party had erupted.

"I don't—"

She was about to say she didn't dance. And she particularly didn't dance like *that*.

But that was the old Marlee. The wallflower. The object of people's pity.

The new Marlee was open to all the invitations life threw at her. After just a moment's hesitation, she kicked off her sandals, took Mackay's extended hand and allowed him to lead her out onto the now quite crowded dance area.

The lyrics of the song were unabashedly sexual.

I want you,
I want you moving against me,
I want your heart to beat against mine,
I want you, I want you, I want you.
I want to intertwine.

Marlee stood frozen to the spot. She looked at the people around her. So free. So uninhibited. Celebrating the sensual part of themselves and life.

She closed her eyes. She felt the primal beat of the music stir within her.

She lifted her hands over her head and swayed. Almost of their own accord, her hips did a slow circle. The music caught her and carried her.

Marlee was aware that she felt more fully a woman than she had ever felt in her life. She danced in recognition of her softness. She danced in celebration of her curves. She danced in honor of her rightful place in the cycle of life.

She realized she might be dancing *with* Mackay, but she was dancing *for* Matteo.

Matteo watched Marlee dancing.

She delighted him. From teasing him about asses, to kissing donkeys, to this.

Something in her had been unleashed since they had made love, and all of it was extraordinarily beautiful to watch.

But now, as she danced, he could see the changes in her were remarkable. This was not the same woman who had stood outside in that fluffy dress defiantly contemplating smoking a cigar, as if by doing that she could erase what she so obviously was.

A little shy.

A little uptight.

And yet, even then, he had known something lurked beneath the surface.

And Marlee had unveiled that something for him in the last few hours. She was on fire with life.

It didn't feel as if she was becoming someone else. Not at all. It felt as if she was peeling away layers of reserve, and underneath, with a light that outshone the sun, was the real Marlee.

Everyone seemed to see it. It was as if all the other dancers were orbiting around her brilliant light.

These, he decided, had been the best hours of his entire life.

As he watched her dance, Matteo became aware that something had stolen up on him and come to reside right in the region of his heart.

It had been so long.

Could it possibly be?

Yes.

Happiness.

In its purest and simplest form.

Not the flush of success, not the satisfaction of filling hours with production, not the rush of saving his family business. It was something more intrinsic than that.

The song stopped, and Matteo got to his feet. He was not a dancer. Had two left feet. And yet the dance was within him, calling him, insisting that, like Marlee, he acknowledge the ancient rhythms of life and his part in those rhythms.

And nothing could have stopped him from sharing his just-discovered happiness with Marlee, who was, after all, the source of it all.

Marlee and Matteo danced. They became part of a joyous conga line that stopped traffic and snaked in and out of local yards and stores. They participated in a spirited game of limbo, which, as it turned out, Marlee had a real gift for.

Matteo, not so much.

Finally, they had to acknowledge the time. With Marlee clutching her limbo trophy—a carved coconut—they waved goodbye to all their newfound friends and boarded the donkey cart. Mackay serenaded them as he drove.

Leaning against each other and hands intertwined, they enjoyed the clip-clop of the donkeys' hooves and Mackay's song. He brought them eventually to a tiny salon on a narrow back street, where children were playing with a ball and sticks.

The children stopped and thronged Mackay. Finally managing to put them aside, Mackay took Marlee and Matteo into the shop and introduced them to his cousin, Margaret. Marlee showed her the picture of the painted toenails on her phone, and Margaret indicated it would not be a problem to achieve that result.

"I'll watch." Matteo swept his hand toward Marlee's feet. "I made that mess. Next time I can do better."

Next time.

Tomorrow was the wedding.

And on Sunday they would all begin to go their separate ways. He had an important meeting in Zurich on Monday.

Marlee was watching him, and he could see it in her eyes, too. The questions about next time.

How could there not be a next time?

Margaret was frowning at Marlee's feet. She guided her to a row of rather elaborate-looking chairs, sat her down and slipped her sandals off. She shook her head at Matteo's handiwork and moved Marlee's feet into what seemed to be an ancient, but spotlessly clean, basin. She turned a switch and the basin bubbled to life.

"Oh, it's lovely," Marlee said, leaning back in the chair, relaxing.

"I told you feet soaking was a necessary step," Matteo reminded Marlee.

"Customers only," Margaret said sternly, pointing to a sign. The look on her face clearly said she didn't intend to make an exception.

Instead of leaving, he went and took the spa seat beside Marlee. He kicked off his shoes.

"Okay," he said. "I'll be a customer, too, then."

Margaret, obviously calculating the extra fee, looked quite pleased with this development. She turned on the basin at the foot of his chair and he lowered his feet in. Marlee was right. It was lovely.

Matteo looked around. The shop was very clean, but everything, including Margaret's dress, was faded and worn, and the basin his feet were soaking in was making a whining noise.

What he saw was how poor Margaret was. But it was evident in the set of her chin and shoulders and in the meticulous tidiness of the shop that she was extremely proud.

"I'd like the donkey done, too. Not the girl one."

Margaret's mouth fell open.

So did Marlee's.

"He's to be in the wedding photos," Matteo explained. "It's important we all look our best."

Marlee's mouth closed and she regarded him thoughtfully. It was apparent she could see right through him. To be honest, Matteo wasn't sure that if having someone read you so accurately was a good thing or a bad thing.

Still, Marlee was smiling at him with a look that

could make him want to get up in the morning and decide, every single day, how to be a better man.

Her hand came across the space between the two
chairs and closed over his. When had life ever felt so
right?

Margaret considered him for a moment, trying to
decide if he was a crazy tourist pulling her leg.

"Dead serious," he told her, squeezing Marlee's
hand. She squeezed back, a secret language between
them.

"Expensive," Margaret warned him.

He nodded, and she went to a drawer and began
pulling jars and jars of gold nail polish. At the door
she shouted at the children, handed over the polish and
pointed to the donkey.

"Don't forget the flowers," he called to her. Soon
the sound of children laughing drifted in and filled the
space of the tiny shop.

"I love that sound," Marlee said, settling back in her
chair, a smile tickling the delicious curve of her lips.
"It's better than music."

Matteo considered that. Marlee didn't just love that
sound. She loved children. It felt like a warning trying
to pierce the bubble of happiness around him. What
was he doing, exactly?

CHAPTER FIFTEEN

THE QUESTION BUZZED around Matteo—what was he doing, exactly?—like a bothersome fly intent on ruining a perfect picnic.

"So," he said, carefully, "are you planning on having children someday?"

"Oh, yes," Marlee said. "I've even recently picked names."

Something like panic reared up in him. He'd thought—well, he wasn't sure what he'd thought—but certainly not about naming children!

And then she hooted at the look he could not keep from crossing his face.

"Henri and Calamity," she told him mirthfully.

She was letting him know that it was okay to keep it light. That it was okay not to think about the future.

But was it?

"Do you like it?" she asked. "Calamity for a little girl?"

"That's a terrible name for a child," he told her sternly, and yet it felt as if he could see a little girl—all curls and mischief and green eyes—who could live up to that name.

A shy assistant appeared and began working alongside Margaret, and it was easy to follow Marlee's lead, to dismiss pressing questions, to just be here enjoying the sensations and the novelty of it all.

It was easy to press Mute on the warning bells that wanted to spoil everything.

Matteo and Marlee's feet were removed from the basins and carefully dried. Matteo then watched in fascinated horror as the two women plugged in apparatuses that looked for all the world like miniature circular saws with cement-cutting blades in them.

"What are those?" he asked in an undertone to Marlee.

"I'm not expert on pedicures but I think it's some kind of defoliating device."

"If they pull down welding helmets, we'll run," he said.

"I think we're at step two," Marlee decided. "Remember from last night? Get rid of dead skin."

"Last night you thought it was gross," he reminded her.

"These are professionals," she told him.

"Those look suspiciously like grinders," he said.

"Grinders?" Marlee asked.

"You know. They can grind paint off buildings with them. Destroy concrete. Cut nails in two, that kind of thing."

"Cut toenails in two?"

"Nail nails!"

"Don't worry," Marlee said, "they are not going to grind off your feet."

He wasn't so sure about that. The grinding apparatuses were coaxed to life. He discovered Marlee wasn't the only one with a ticklish instep.

"She's having her wicked way with my foot!" he said to Marlee.

"Is that trepidation I detect in your oh-so-fearless self?" Marlee teased him.

It felt wonderful to be teased by her, to leave the warning bells on silent, to enjoy her hand finding his and tightening on it.

"Be brave," she told him.

And somehow it didn't feel as if her instruction had anything to do with what was happening to his feet.

At all.

Marlee knew the exact moment she recognized the true danger of her fling with Matteo.

And it wasn't when she swam in the ocean with him, or rode behind him on a scooter, or let him paint her toenails. It wasn't when she'd decided to skinny-dip with him. Or when they had made wild, impetuous love together.

All that had deepened the attraction.

Inflamed her infatuation.

But when Matteo asked Margaret to paint the donkey's feet, too, the quiver that had been within her grew to a tremor that felt dangerous, like the pre-earthquake kind.

Because she knew exactly what he was doing.

It was more than apparent to her he was finding a way to be generous that still allowed Margaret her dignity.

Looking at him after he requested a pedicure for Henri, Marlee felt as if she could see him all the way to his soul.

And what she saw was innate kindness.

Decency.

A lovely kind of honor.

But then, because she could see those things, she saw the moment it turned on her.

So, are you planning on having children someday?

As if he could clearly see, despite everything she had become in the last few hours and days, that under all that boldness lurked a traditional girl with traditional dreams of family and forever.

Trapping dreams, if the expression on his face when she said she had already named the children, was any indication.

For once in her life, Marlee didn't want to think about the future. Or forever. She didn't want to complicate things with imagining repercussions or making moral judgments about right or wrong.

She didn't want her world to be predictable or rulebound.

She just wanted to immerse herself in the delightful surprises that were being handed to her, moment after moment.

She would deal with the fallout, the inevitable devastation of the earthquake, later.

And who said there had to be fallout? Couldn't she just have a lovely fling like all the rest of the world was doing?

Of course she could.

An hour later, they were laughing together as they walked gingerly out to the donkey cart. They had been provided with cheap flip-flops and the toe separators were still in.

She had a perfect white flower on the fourth toe-nail of each foot.

He had opted for an octopus.

To the delight of the waiting children, they made a huge fuss over Henri's beautifully painted hooves.

And then, aware they had not left themselves enough time, they urged Mackay to make haste back to the resort.

It was a wild ride as the donkeys clattered through the narrow streets, bouncing Marlee and Matteo into each other and making them hang on for dear life.

At the resort they quickly went their separate ways to get ready for the rehearsal. Thankfully, it wasn't a dress rehearsal!

The yellow sundress had been picked up off her floor, sent to the cleaners, and was now hanging, refreshed, off the shower bar in her bathroom.

Totally wrong, of course, for the rehearsal dinner. It drew too much attention. It was too loud. It was the bride's time to shine.

"That's tomorrow," Marlee told herself and slipped the dress over her head.

She arrived a few minutes late, breathless, and took her place beside Fiona, who threw her—and the dress—a faintly disapproving look.

In response she wagged her newly painted toes and actually earned a nod of approval.

"Love that color on you," Brenda said. It seemed perhaps a defiant reaction to Fiona's look. "You should wear bright colors more often."

"The length is very daring," Kathy chimed in. "I love it! You carry it perfectly. You look hot!"

And she obviously did not mean the melting-from-the-heat kind of hot.

The approval of her friends was really confirmation that Arthur had been right. Somewhere along the way she had become too muted, too comfortable and dull in the way she approached the ultra-predictable life that had made her feel safe, yes, but had also shut down parts of her.

She felt the moment of Matteo's arrival, the air shifting as he joined the wedding party on the beach. She looked everywhere but at him.

How could she look at him without their intimacy being obvious to every single person there?

Especially with the new dress, people might start arriving at conclusions!

Even knowing that, she could not stop herself. She slid a look at him.

He had put on shoes. He was dressed in a light pair of slacks and a shirt so hastily buttoned he had missed the top one.

Her eyes fastened on the part of his chest that she could see.

She remembered her hands on his naked flesh. He glanced at her. Some white-hot memory darkened the turquoise of his eyes to navy blue. They both looked away at exactly the same moment.

The rehearsal was a tense nightmare of trying not to look at him.

Trying not to touch him!

Thankfully, in the wedding party, he was coupled with Kathy, not her. They endlessly practiced gliding down the aisle, to Fiona's instructions.

"Kathy, just a little slower."

"Brenda, hold the flowers up a bit higher."

"Marlee, a little less swish."

Swish. She had become a hot girl in a yellow sundress who swished. She shot Matteo a look.

He was looking deliberately off into the distance. His lips were twitching.

"I think we should practice how we're lining up for the register signing one more time and we'll have it perfect," Fiona decided.

"Forget perfect," Mike said. "I'm famished. Let's eat!"

"But we need to talk about photos. That will happen in between the ceremony and the dinner."

Photos.

Marlee suddenly realized she had not broken it to Fiona yet about a donkey instead of a horse.

"I'm trying to decide if I'll wreck the dress or not. It's a hard decision. Such a nice dress to jump in the ocean with!"

"Decide over dinner," Mike said firmly. "Or maybe don't even decide. You could just be spontaneous."

It felt as if he was speaking to Marlee about the donkey decision, not to Fiona about the photo decisions.

The very idea of being spontaneous seemed to appall Fiona.

No matter what happened next, Marlee thought, she would always be grateful for this: that Matteo had broken her away from her own rigid need for control.

And then, to Fiona's horror, the whole wedding party mutinied and stampeded toward the dinner that had been set up for them at the wedding venue, a private grotto just off the area marked for the beach ceremony.

It was stunningly beautiful, with a waterfall at one

end, the deep greens of thick foliage forming walls of privacy around it. Cables of outdoor lights hung above tables already set up for tomorrow.

As waiters brought out dinner, other staff came and lit tiki torches that illuminated the dining area as well as the dance floor and bar.

Again, they rehearsed. The order of the toasts. The timing. Who would stand where, who would say what, what would make the best photos?

Matteo, appearing neither bored nor as if he had other plans, rose from the table when Fiona finally stopped to catch a breath.

"It's been a long day," he said casually. "And I seem to have jet lag. In the interest of being nice and fresh for the wedding tomorrow, I'm going to head off."

After a suitable amount of time had passed, Marlee also got up.

"I seem to have a tiny headache." This was a bald-faced lie, but not being the woman she had been when she'd arrived at Coconut Cay, Marlee didn't feel even a little bit guilty. "I think, also in the interest of being at my best tomorrow, I'll turn in."

"But we haven't rehearsed cutting the cake yet. Or the first dances."

Once, Marlee would have sat back down.

But not now.

"You can fill me in tomorrow," Marlee said.

Once, Fiona would have argued with her. But now she scanned her face, and must have seen something different there, too.

On the other hand, maybe she thought all the wedding planning was making Marlee sad about her own missed day. Did Mike nudge Fiona?

"All right. But you have to be at my suite really early. There's so much to do."

"I promise I will be." There was so much to do. She had a dress that needed complete altering! But first things first. Marlee set off to find Matteo. His place? Hers? Their beach?

Before she could decide, a hand shot out of the darkened shrubbery and pulled her in. Her surprised cry was silenced by a very familiar hand.

"I thought you'd never leave," he whispered in her ear.

And then he kissed her. Thoroughly. Until she wondered if you could die from kisses. Or, more accurately, from wanting what the kisses promised.

Hand in hand, breathless with anticipation, neither of them acknowledging the end was near, they went to his villa.

And they didn't walk.

They ran.

CHAPTER SIXTEEN

MARLEE WOKE UP in a nest of sparkling white sheets, to the sounds of birds. They were loud as they celebrated the first rays of light that heralded the coming of the new day.

She was beside Matteo, sleeping on her side, one knee up, her hand splayed possessively across his beautiful chest.

It was the wedding day.

And she didn't feel sad at all. There was no longing for her own canceled day. In fact, it seemed like a perfect day to celebrate the glories of love.

She was aware she should feel exhausted. They had barely slept. They had so much to say to each other. It felt as if they needed to squeeze it all into one more day.

He had told her about his carefree days as a young boy, exploring the Alps with his father.

She had told him about her large, traditional family.

And then about Arthur, and the fact that her longing for the traditions of her family was so strong that she might have read qualities into his character that he didn't have, and accepted things in the relationship she should have never accepted.

She had told Matteo about practically being dumped at the altar.

Not as if she was telling him of a terrible tragedy, but as if it was a wonderful story about how something that seemed bad could turn into something good.

"My niece Amey likes gaming," Matteo had said to her. "She told me that in a game as soon as you hit trouble, or more bad guys, you know you're going the right way."

As she looked at his sleeping face now—so extraordinarily handsome, so beautifully familiar to her—Marlee had never been more certain that every single thing she had once judged as bad had just been a way of getting her life on the right path.

Still, as much as she would have liked to linger, taking in his face and the texture of his skin and the gorgeous male aroma of him, she had a great deal to do, and that was before factoring in Fiona's inevitable last-minute errands.

She left Matteo quietly, so as to not wake him. Then, bathed in the first pink stains of dawn, she made her way across the resort to her own cabana.

The morning seemed to shimmer with the same brilliant light that was shining within her.

She took the bridesmaid's dress down from where it was still hanging in the bathroom. She laid it out carefully. And then, using her handy sewing kit, she began to take the dress apart.

Finally done, she put on the dress.

Marlee looked at herself in the full-length mirror behind the bathroom door. She smiled.

* * *

Matteo's first waking thought was that Marlee wasn't there. He could feel her absence deeply, as if something essential was gone from his world.

He buried his nose in her pillow and let her fragrance fill him.

He thought of all the confidences they had exchanged last night. And the other things, too.

He was aware he could not wait to see her again, as if his life would not be complete until the moment he laid eyes on her.

As it turned out, that was at the wedding.

For the first time, as he gathered with Mike and the other members of the groom's party on the beach, he saw the payoff of all of Fiona's persnickety pursuit of perfection.

Because that was exactly what she had achieved. Perfection.

Framed by an arbor arch threaded through with gardenias was perfect white sand and an endless blue sea.

The guests were beginning to arrive and take their seats on the white chairs, a pink silk bow on the back of each.

Mike took his place under the arbor, and just as they had rehearsed—who would have ever thought Matteo would be grateful for that endless rehearsal, but he was—they lined up beside him.

For a panicked moment, Matteo thought he might have been so besotted with Marlee that he'd forgotten the ring. He felt in his pocket and drew in a deep breath. No, there it was.

The notes of a piano filled the air. It wasn't a recording. He noticed the real piano and he had to give kudos to Fiona. The music rising to join the lap of waves and the call of birds could not be more beautiful.

Kathy, the maid of honor, came through a break in the hedge and walked—glided—through the sand and up the aisle between the chairs. He recognized the color of that dress.

Behind her came Brenda, and again, the color triggered his memory of the first time he had seen Marlee.

And then—his mouth dropped, and he quickly slammed it shut—came Marlee.

She was wearing the same dress that he had first met her in. Except that it wasn't the same dress at all.

The neckline had been altered, and the sleeves removed. Every puff and every ruffle had been stripped from it.

It clung to her like mist, and Marlee carried herself like a queen. Matteo was not sure he had ever seen a dress that so perfectly revealed the beauty and the boldness of the person who was wearing it.

Her hair was piled up on top of her head, and her makeup showed off everything about her, the height of those cheekbones, the bow of her mouth, and especially the depth and mystery held in those green eyes.

He felt as if everything faded, except her.

But then the subdued gasp of the crowd made him draw his eyes away from her. Fiona had entered the pathway.

Her dress and veil were extraordinary, but it was the light in her face that kept everyone's gaze on her.

Matteo glanced at Mike.

And felt pure envy for the look on his best friend's face.

Matteo was shocked by what he felt next.

A kind of devastation. *This* was what Marlee deserved. A man prepared to commit to her. A man ready to devote his life to making her dreams come true. A man who wanted a future that held only her.

Last night, lying in the circle of his arms, she had told him who she really was and what she really needed.

Instead, what had Matteo given Marlee?

An affair.

A surrender, not to all the things she deserved, all the things that she had revealed to him last night she longed for—like tradition and family—but to base impulses.

He knew now what he didn't know then. She'd been betrayed by love. And still, she had come to him with hope.

She had never said that. That she *hoped*.

But he knew her now, and he knew she hoped for all the things a woman like her would hope for: a fairy-tale ending. Something with the word *forever* in it.

What he had given her, he thought, shocked, was a place that did not honor her.

Or himself.

Look at how they had been the day they had first made love. Hiding from their friends, as if they had something to be ashamed of.

Marlee arrived at the arbor. She looked at him. A smile, with their every intimacy in it, was directed at him.

Apparently she was not going to hide anymore. The dress said that.

And neither was he.

It was never too late to be a better man, Matteo decided then and there. Or even the best man, just like he was at this wedding.

He could become worthy of all that they had shared.

He could become worthy of this remarkable woman who had trusted him—of all people—with her broken self.

Fiona arrived at the altar and handed off her bouquet. She and Mike joined hands and faced each other.

The ceremony went off as practiced. It was flawless and without a hitch. They kissed to thunderous approval from those gathered to witness the miracle of love.

Her bouquet was handed back to her, and the bride and groom moved off to the side where a white cane desk had been set up on the beach. They signed the register, and then Fiona gathered her bouquet and stood to one side.

As the piano played on, each member of the wedding party took their turn signing the documents.

But then, just as that was finishing, the air was split with an ear-piercing bray.

Down the same path that the bridal party had walked down, came Mackay leading Henri.

The donkey was obviously angry. He was kicking his nicely painted back hooves to the side, nearly hitting the chairs. The guests were diving out of their seats to get out of his way.

Matteo abandoned the wedding party and raced down the aisle to help Mackay. "What's wrong?"

"He's missing Calamity," Mackay told him tightly. "They've never been apart. I couldn't even load him in the trailer without her. Listen."

Matteo cocked his head.

He could hear a smashing sound from the resort parking lot, located right above this entrance to the beach.

"It's Calamity," Mackay said. "In the trailer. By herself. Love-stricken."

Matteo listened to one final smashing sound. And then, not even his strength and Mackay's combined could hold the love-maddened Henri, who broke free of them, turned and stampeded up the aisle, back the way he had come.

But now, Calamity burst in through the hedge.

The donkeys raced toward each other. They skidded to a halt. They rubbed noses. They kicked up their heels, turned and ran down the path through the arbor, which was not wide enough for both of them to be side by side. It toppled. The minister sprang out of the way. The wedding party scattered. Mike threw himself on top of Fiona to protect her from the rampaging donkeys.

CHAPTER SEVENTEEN

HENRI AND CALAMITY cavorted up and down the beach braying loudly and kicking up their heels.

And then, suddenly, they were done.

As if they had created no mischief at all, they clomped back to Mackay, and sending him looks that could be interpreted as faintly apologetic, began to feast on the bridesmaids' bouquets that had been abandoned on the cane registration table.

Mike helped Fiona up out of the sand.

The decision to wreck the dress seemed as if it might have been made for her. It was crushed and had sand ground into it.

It felt as if the whole world had gone still, every single person focused on her.

Matteo, like everyone else, held his breath.

Waiting.

For tears.

For a tantrum.

For the bride to express the inevitable frustration at the moment she had built to for so long being ruined.

Instead, as Fiona stared up at Mike, her expression softened with tenderness. She looked at her new husband with an expression of pure wonder on her face.

"You saved me," she said, brushing at his suit jacket. "You put my life ahead of your own."

"That might be overstating it a bit," Mike said. Matteo could see how his friend's pragmatic nature was the perfect foil for Fiona's more dramatic one.

"What on earth is going on here?" Mike asked, running a hand through his hair. "Donkeys? Seriously?"

They all watched as Henri and Calamity contentedly finished off the bridesmaids' bouquets, flower stems dripping from their mouths.

"Um," Marlee offered, "the one on the right is Henri. He's here for the photos."

"But he's not a horse," Fiona said, a frown creasing her brow. Matteo wondered if perhaps they were going to have their bride meltdown moment, after all.

"Don't tell him," Marlee suggested in a stage whisper, and then, as a distraction, "Look at his hooves!"

Fiona crept a little closer to the donkey and looked.

And then, the best thing of all happened.

She beamed. And then Fiona laughed. Henri noticed her—or more accurately her bouquet—and shuffled over. She held it out to him.

Now the perfect gentleman, Henri bobbed his head and nibbled his acceptance of the bride's offering.

"Best wedding moment *ever*," one of the guests said.

And the beach reverberated with sounds of applause that rivaled the enthusiastic approbation that had been given to the first kiss.

One thing about getting disaster out of the way early, Marlee decided, was that everyone relaxed after that.

The worst had already happened.

Except it wasn't really the worst.

It was just one of those obstacles that showed you that you were probably on the right path.

Marlee thought if she lived to be a hundred she would never forget the look on Fiona's face when she had gazed at her groom after he had thrown his body over her to protect her from perceived harm.

The donkeys also broke the ice as the guests swarmed them, making a fuss and taking pictures. Laughter filled the gathering and everyone was engaged with each other.

Marlee had a feeling the wedding photos—both the spontaneous ones and the official ones—were going to be the best ever. Award-worthy, no doubt.

Or maybe it was just that her own feelings were painting everything around her in shades of joy.

Because something had shifted between her and Matteo, too. How they felt about each other didn't feel as if it should be kept a secret anymore.

It didn't feel as if it *could* be kept a secret anymore.

It was spilling out of them. In the way they looked at each other. In the way they found excuses to touch each other. In the way they laughed together.

By the time the meal was done and the toasts completed and the dancing began, it felt as if they had sent out announcement cards.

Lovers.

Marlee danced with him the way she had danced to the sounds of calypso at the street restaurant.

She came into herself.

He had eyes only for her. He acted as though he were enchanted.

And he was so darned sexy! She could not wait to claim him as her own again tonight. And then, they would talk about the future. What they would do after they left Coconut Cay. How they would work out the challenges and logistics of meeting.

He had a *jet*. That should make everything easier.

The laughter nearly bubbled out of her.

Marlee Copeland was in love with a man with a jet. *Love.*

Despite the party going in full swing around her, everything in her went still. It was way too soon for that. Wasn't it? But she had never felt this way before.

Not ever.

Not even when she'd been planning on marrying another man.

Who had, she reminded herself, walked away from her. If she felt this way about Matteo after just a few days, how was it going to feel when he came to his senses? When the magic they had experienced here was but a distant memory?

This wasn't the real world.

Not one single thing they had experienced here had anything to do with their real lives. He was the man with the jet, the international business tycoon.

She was the unexciting librarian from Seattle.

The thoughts threatened to crush the joy that was bubbling in her.

You didn't go from Arthur Drabeck to Matteo Keller. In the real world a woman like her didn't have a hope with a guy like this. Who did she think she was?

Love? Matteo had never mentioned the word *love*. Why would he? She, hopelessly naive, had fallen for a man who was enjoying a tryst with a willing partner. He knew the rules. He moved in a superfast world that included a jet and topless beaches. A world that she probably couldn't even imagine.

It was she who was breaking the rules by falling for him. By wanting more than he had ever offered.

The devastating fact was, once they stepped out of this bubble, it was over.

But she was not going to be devastated. Not just yet. In the days and weeks ahead, there would be plenty of time for that.

But now, Marlee decided, *this* was her moment. It felt as much like it was her moment as it was Fiona's.

This was the pinnacle of her whole life.

Right now.

This time she would be the one to walk away, before reality set in and Matteo realized the humiliating truth. It had been a fairy tale few days. She had become something she wasn't really. It was inevitable that he would come to realize that.

How much better to leave it like this? On a high note? Everything about them shimmering and untarnished? His memory of her of someone far bolder and more exciting than she really was or could ever hope to be.

She allowed the music back into that moment of utter stillness. She danced, immersed in the intensity of the experience. She knew they were counting down to midnight.

And then, the princess he had made her became an ordinary woman again.

The coach became a pumpkin.

The frills would probably magically reappear on her dress!

But regardless, it would be over. She had to make

certain of that. She had to leave with her dignity intact, not as a woman who had lost her heart.

She danced as she wanted Matteo to remember her. She was uninhibited, sexy, sure of herself.

She danced as a woman who was memorizing every single thing about him. The way his eyes held hers, the curve of his lips, the flop of his hair over his brow, the utter sexiness of the way he moved.

The feeling of bliss, with its counterpoint of loss, was exhilarating and excruciating at the same time.

Be brave, she ordered herself, when the sense of loss would try to overwhelm her. *Just for a little while longer.*

She intended to make the next moments the best of her life. Given what the last few days had held, she was aware that was quite the challenge she had set for herself.

As if the universe understood the momentous occasion of a goodbye, the music slowed and the love song that played was heartbreaking and romantic.

His arms closed around her. He pulled her against himself.

She felt the heat of his body and the beat of his heart. She felt his breath on her hair, and his hand on the small of her back.

She breathed in his scent, hoping to take it in deeply enough that it became part of her, so she could remember it forever.

The music ended.

She reached up and took his lips with her own.

She tasted him as deeply as one human being could taste another. She savored him. She memorized him.

She drew his essence deep into herself, an ember to warm her on the cold days of winter ahead.

A chime rang.

Smiling—the tears would come later—she took a step back from him.

"It's midnight," she said. "And I'm Cinderella. The ball is over."

And then she turned. She forced herself not to run, but to walk away from him slowly, not looking back. Unlike the fairy tale, there was no glass slipper to leave as a clue for him to follow.

Because life was not, after all, anything like the fairy tales.

CHAPTER EIGHTEEN

STUNNED, MATTEO WATCHED as Marlee walked regally past the staff carrying in trays of food for the midnight snack. The darkness of the tropical night folded around her, and she was gone.

What the hell had just happened?

The taste of her was still on his lips, and it felt as if the imprint of her body was seared into his own.

He went to follow her, and then he stopped himself.

Obviously, she was being the sensible one. They needed a cooling-off period. *He* needed a cooling-off period.

Just hours ago, he'd been thinking he'd done it all wrong. That he had dishonored her. That he had needed to do things differently. That he *would* do things differently. What did he think he should do instead? Ask her to marry him?

Insanity.

She'd been right to walk away.

They'd known each other *days.*

But it really bothered him that while he had, apparently, completely lost his mind, she still had good sense about her.

So, no, he was not going to chase her.

Marlee was right. It had been a fairy tale, but she was wrong if she thought she was the one under the spell! This island, from the moment he had walked down that path and found her on it, had put him under an enchantment.

It felt urgent to get away from here, to be restored to the person he had been a few short days ago. Then, maybe he'd be able to do what he did best. What people counted on him to do. What he was famous for, really.

Make a rational decision.

Not be swept along by the powerful currents of attraction and emotion.

Mike appeared in front of him. The look on his face warned Matteo he was not the only one whose magical evening had just come crashing to an end.

"Fiona's just had devastating news," Mike said quietly. "Her mother's had a heart attack. It's serious. Our flight isn't scheduled until late tomorrow afternoon. Even with extenuating circumstances, I'm pretty sure there's only the one flight out every day."

Matteo gave one final look at where Marlee had disappeared, and he drew in a deep breath. There.

Who was he kidding?

He couldn't have resisted the temptation of going to her if she was only steps away from him.

He probably would have ended up *begging.*

The thought was repulsive to him. It was an *attraction.* He was not powerless over it. And he especially wouldn't be powerless over it if he put some distance—physical distance and lots of it—between them.

Selfishly, he realized Fiona and Mike's crisis had just become his perfect escape.

"I'll take you," Matteo said to Mike. "We can use the jet."

Mike tilted his head at him. "You know, I still think of you as my college roommate, that guy who could figure out how to suspend a car from the bottom of a bridge with a budget of zero. I totally forgot there was a jet."

This was what Matteo loved about being with old friends.

His college buddies, in particular, rarely saw the trappings he'd accumulated. Instead, they saw just him.

And oddly, even though she knew of the trappings, it felt as if Marlee had never seen them, either. Just him.

And yet there she was, walking away.

What did that say?

"Thank you," Mike said. "We can be ready right away. We'll just grab passports and essentials. I'll ask the other members of the wedding party to pack up the rest of our stuff and get it home."

As he and Mike gathered a nearly hysterical Fiona and shepherded her toward the plane, Matteo knew it was better this way. Marlee had referenced a fairy tale. They had been on their own cloud, out of touch with reality, for days. Time for the landing, painful as that promised to be.

For one of the world's most respected businessmen, he did not think he had made a rational decision almost since his arrival on this tiny cay.

Except maybe one. This one. To be of service to his friends in their time of need.

Was he being of service? Or was he escaping the enchantment that had held him captive?

In less than an hour, Matteo had tossed his few items into a bag, a flight plan had been filed and they were onboard. Fiona sat in a forward seat. Mike snapped the belt for her. She was still in her wedding gown, covered in a blanket, shivering despite the warmth still seeping through the open cabin door.

"Who doesn't invite their own mother to their wedding?" she whispered. "I was worried she'd wreck it. I deserve this."

Mike made a shushing sound like one might use to comfort a child. "It's lucky she wasn't here. A hotel isn't the best place to have a heart attack."

Fiona seemed to consider it, and it seemed to bring her comfort.

Mike put his arms around her and she sighed into his chest.

But her pain reminded Matteo of the loss of his own mother.

It reminded him, starkly, of the danger of loss always lurking in the corridors, waiting to strike at the most unexpected moments.

As Matteo looked out the window, the lights of Coconut Cay, the safest place on earth, winked off one by one, until the island was lost in a sea of darkness.

He was aware of the irony. It was not, for him, the safest place on earth. The most dangerous thing of all had happened to him here.

The protective layer he had built around his heart had fallen away.

And love had crept past those broken barriers.

Matteo contemplated that word.

Love.

He looked over at the sobbing Fiona and remembered his father.

His father had been one man before the loss of his mother, and another after. His father had fallen on the sword that was hiding in love's cloak.

He couldn't possibly love Marlee, Matteo told himself sternly. They barely knew each other.

And yet that did not feel like the truth, at all.

Which made this quick exit a blessing in disguise. What would knowing her longer do to him?

And then his memory dredged up this: his family picnicking on a wildflower-strewn hillside in the Alps.

His mother was chasing his sisters through the meadow, and shrieks of laughter filled the air.

He and his father were on the picnic blanket, and his father's eyes followed his mother as if he was unable to look away.

People said we were foolish. We got married within weeks of meeting. But you just know.

You just know, Matteo thought, like a fatal flaw that ran through the family. And then he reached for his headphones. To shut out the sounds of Fiona weeping softly.

And the weeping of his own heart as it broke in two.

So, Marlee thought as she packed up Fiona's belongings, she'd been wrong.

Because she had thought the donkey debacle had meant that a wedding disaster had been gotten out of the way early.

Of course, that was based on a thoroughly naive assumption that life was fair.

The truth was that disaster was random. There was no catastrophe roster, where some benign being checked his list and said, *Oh, I see they've already had their run of bad luck. No more for them. Their quota is used up.*

Now Matteo was flying Fiona and Mike home. They

were already gone. Marlee had heard the roar of the jet engine split the quiet of the night.

It meant there were no second chances. Maybe part of her had hoped he would follow her and return the symbolic slipper, after all.

But there were fairy tales, and then there was reality, and reality had returned with a vengeance.

Brenda came into the room. "I just heard from Fiona. Her mother survived the night. I guess it's still touch and go, though."

"I'm glad they got there in time."

"Thanks to your dreamboat."

Marlee shot her a look. Was there just the slightest sarcastic emphasis on *your*? Or were her insecurities making her read things that weren't meant?

And yet, just beneath those insecurities, was there a new strength, too?

Marlee might have been kidding herself about Matteo, but something felt real and true about the woman she had become.

She intended to find out what was true about herself, and those few days with Matteo were what had given her the courage to do that.

To be what she had never been before this time on Coconut Cay.

Brave.

And that was the one ingredient that she had come to know was absolutely required to live a life fully.

Seattle, in November, was probably the dreariest city in the world. Weather roiled up and off the Pacific. The rain fell in ice-cold sheets. Clouds, gray and ominous, shrouded the nearby mountains. After the warmth and colors of Coconut Cay, the November nastiness should have seemed even worse than it normally did.

But the strange thing for Marlee was that it did not seem nasty.

Seattle—maybe her whole life—felt as if she had sleep-walked through it, and now she was wide-awake.

She had expected she might return from her romantic rendezvous on Coconut Cay to find herself more reserved, more fade-into-the-background, more insecure, more rigid in the habits that made her feel safe and secure in the world.

Instead, she was seeing the whole world with different eyes.

Marlee was well aware that she could have felt broken.

But that she didn't.

Some might say she made a choice to be brave instead of broken, but she didn't feel she was making choices so much as acknowledging she was changed in some fundamental way that made her embrace *everything.*

She found herself chatting with neighbors she had ignored in the past. She walked in the rain with no umbrella, loving how it soaked her hair. She said yes to a kayak lesson at a local pool from an expert who had presented at the library.

Fiona's mom, Mary, was released from the hospital, and Marlee dropped by and enjoyed reminiscing with her about the old neighborhood.

Marlee deepened other friendships with women at work and in her book club. And Fiona's rocky relationship with her family—and her close call with her mother—made Marlee appreciate her own family more.

She spent time with her mom and dad, appreciative of the solidness of their relationship, even as she realized the safety of it no longer appealed to her.

She made a full stop at a colorful poster that appeared in the library foyer one morning. It was advertising dance classes, and Marlee pulled off one of the tabs with a phone number on it.

And then she actually called it!

And then she actually signed up for dance classes. And loved them!

She thought missing Matteo would go away. They had only known each other for a few days.

But it didn't. She ached for him: to share these stories with him, to make new stories with him at her side.

One day, she was straightening a closet when the suitcase she had taken to the wedding on Coconut Cay fell off the top rack. After she put it back, she noticed something on the floor.

She picked it up.

It was the cigar. She held it to her nose, then ever so tentatively touched it to her tongue. Had she hoped she would taste Matteo on it?

She did not. Only the sweet, smoky taste of the wine the cigar had been dipped in. She thought of the woman she had been that night, and it was almost like looking at a stranger, and a childlike one, at that.

Had she really believed that sipping rum and toying with a cigar could change everything about you? She tucked the cigar into her bedside table.

As the dreary days of November turned to December, she still wished, every single day, that he would get in touch.

And when he didn't, she celebrated what he had

given her: a verve for life that was like nothing she had ever felt before.

Fiona called and asked her to attend her and Mike's Christmas party.

Marlee's heart nearly stopped.

Would Matteo be there?

Of course he wouldn't! Not even international jet-setters flew to another country just for a Christmas party, did they?

"I know why you're hesitating," Fiona said.

"You do?" Marlee thought of how she had kissed Matteo at midnight and felt her cheeks burn.

But she wasn't sure it was with embarrassment. Maybe passion.

"I was awful," Fiona said. "A horrible person. Mike says he's surprised I have any friends left, and I'm darned lucky he married me. But he's forgiven me, because I have the best excuse ever. Can you guess?"

"Oh! Are you—"

"Yes! Pregnant. A complete surprise! I had no idea. No wonder I was such a wreck. And you were so patient with me. And you found the donkey! I can't wait to show you the photos. I just got them this week. Please come."

Marlee couldn't think of a way to ask if Matteo would be there, so she just accepted the invitation and decided to act as if he would be there even though she knew it was a one-in-a-million chance.

She bought the most gorgeous dress she had ever owned. It was red, in keeping with the holiday spirit, but other than that, there was nothing Christmassy about it.

It was predawn mist, made into fabric. The neckline was daring, and the length was bold. She bought amazing heels to go with it.

She curled her hair and put on makeup. As she looked at herself in the mirror, Marlee was so aware of who she was.

Strong and confident.

And very, very beautiful.

Fiona and Mike were hosting the party at their new condo. It was already packed when Marlee arrived, and it took nearly half an hour to sort through all the people and figure out Matteo was not among them.

Still, all that mingling in search of him had brought her in contact with a lot of people.

After her initial disappointment that Matteo wasn't there, she relaxed. She was shocked by how much men liked her. She was shocked by how good she was at flirting!

And dancing. The lessons had helped her confidence, but she also carried something within herself from that wild street party and the fairy-tale wedding on Coconut Cay. She didn't feel in any way inhibited.

She relished the attention. It egged her on. And she found it so easy to let go, have fun.

"Here she is," Fiona called. "Marlee. Look who I've got on Boom-Boom."

What the heck was Boom-Boom?

Marlee did a whirling turn in the crush of people on the dance floor to find Fiona with her phone pointed at her.

She realized there was something on the screen of the phone. And then she went stock-still as she realized.

Boom-Boom was that new video app.

Matteo.

"Marlee," he said.

He was thousands of miles away. He was talking to her through a screen. His voice felt as if it touched her.

"Matteo."

She was shocked by how he looked. His hair was too long. He looked gaunt. There was something haunted in his eyes when he looked at her.

And hungry.

And yet his tone was cool. "It's good to see you," he said. "I'm sorry. I seem to have a bad—"

And then the picture died.

And so did all the fun she had been having.

CHAPTER NINETEEN

MATTEO STARED AT the blank screen of his phone. Breaking that connection had been the hardest thing he had ever done.

Marlee had been so beautiful. So radiant.

As Fiona moved through the crowds with her phone, he had spotted Marlee well before she knew he was watching. He had seen her dancing. If it was possible, she had come even more into herself than she had on the cay.

Marlee's movements were totally sensual, made even more so by her confidence and her comfort with herself.

Matteo had seen the look on the man's face that she was dancing with.

He was enraptured with her.

And then she had turned, and there had been that moment's hesitation before she knew it was him.

Sometimes a man came face-to-face with his own weakness.

Because the look on her face made him want to beg, just as he had known he would have if he had stayed on Coconut Cay the night of the wedding.

She had been shocked to see him, and then the shock

had melted to a pure welcome, which had made him feel weak.

Be with me.

He was changed since he had come back from Coconut Cay, and not in a good way. Marlee, it seemed obvious, had changed in good ways. She radiated confidence.

He, on the other hand, did not miss the fact his sisters were exchanging worried glances behind his back.

But here was the terrifying truth: if three days with Marlee had made him feel this empty, this bereft for a life without her in it, what would following these feelings do?

Because if he was to give in to the temptation to see what a life with Marlee held, one day, no matter how hard they tried to hold it off, they would say goodbye to each other.

And if he had known her a lifetime, instead of a few days, he would be like his father. It would not be survivable.

And what if he went first? What if he went first and left her to live in a world they had made bright together, and now there was nothing but darkness remaining?

Not, Matteo reminded himself, that Marlee had looked like she was suffering in the world without him in it. Not in the way he was suffering in the world without her.

Still, he'd done the right thing. To shut off the phone. To not feed his hunger to drink her in, to look at her, to let that unexpected glimpse of her feed his spirit.

He was aware he was not as strong as he wanted to be.

Because he went to his computer. He went to the photos that Fiona had just sent him. And he knew another sleepless night lay ahead of him as he drank his fill of the wedding pictures.

The bride and groom interested him only slightly.

It was her, Marlee, that he went to, again and again. One picture in particular made him look at it endlessly, trying unsuccessfully to grasp some secret it held.

"But we haven't looked at the photos yet," Fiona protested when Marlee announced, as soon as she could do so without being too obvious the call with Matteo had upset her, that she had to go.

"Let's do it another time," Marlee said with fake brightness. "There's so much going on here tonight. We have a bit of catching up to do. We haven't had a chance to talk about the baby, even."

"Let me see you to the door."

They stepped outside the noise of the party. Rain pattered on the porch roof.

"Thanks for going to see my mom," Fiona said. "I love that about you. You really care about people."

She *did* really care about people, and the look on Matteo's face was making her feel distressed.

"Did you notice?" Fiona said. "She's sober. And so excited about being a grandmother. She wasn't even mad at me about having a wedding she couldn't come to because she's scared to fly. She said she knew I did it on purpose. That it was the wake-up call that she needed."

"I'm glad for you. Things tend to work out, don't they?"

Did they? She wished she believed that just a little more strongly. After seeing Matteo, she suddenly wasn't that sure.

"I have something for you." Fiona handed Marlee a gift.

It was wrapped but obviously one of the wedding photos. Marlee decided to wait until she got home to open it.

"You look so gorgeous," Fiona said. "I've always known you had that hiding in you."

Not that your choice of dress had been a clue, Marlee thought dryly.

They hugged and promised to get together again soon. And then Marlee went home to her troubled thoughts.

Sitting alone in her living room, she opened Fiona's gift.

She had expected a framed picture of the bride and groom. But instead, it was a picture of herself and Henri. She was nose to nose with the adorable troublemaker, bestowing a kiss.

She radiated light.

A woman in love. And not with a donkey, either.

And Matteo, slightly out of focus, was in the background. But even out of focus, there was a particular look on his face as he watched her.

It was so clear he was a man who cherished her.

The truth was evident in the gaze that rested on her—possessive, protective, utterly entranced.

It was not a look that said—in any way—that she wasn't good enough. And it wasn't a look that suggested that their worlds were stratospheres apart, separated by chasms that could not be crossed.

Matteo looked so beautiful in this picture. As light-filled as she herself looked. Confident. *Sure.*

And yet, tonight he had looked so *awful.*

There was no other way to describe the brief glimpse she had caught of his face before the connection died. She went to bed thinking about it, distressed by it, trying to decipher it.

It could be anything. A bad day on the markets. A poor business decision. Expensive problems with the jet! There were a thousand things that could have been troubling Matteo, and she had no hope of guessing what it was.

But when Marlee woke suddenly, in the middle of the night, she *knew.*

She knew what was troubling Matteo. The look on his face had been the look of a man who had touched a dream he knew he would not ever allow himself to have.

And Marlee was pretty sure that dream was her.

And that every single thing she had done since she got back to Seattle—her embracing of life—had been in preparation for the biggest challenge of all. It was as if she had been in training.

She had to be more confident of herself than she had ever been.

She had to know her strength.

She had to be braver than she had ever been.

She had to rescue Matteo from the lonely life he had set himself up for. With her blankets wrapped around her against the damp chill in her apartment, she went and found her computer.

It occurred to her that the third barrier—her own sense of inadequacy—had already been overcome.

That left only the physical barrier of distance.

It seemed paltry in comparison. She looked up flights to Switzerland. The closer you got to Christmas, the less choice there was and the more expensive they became.

There was one on Monday.

Three days away.

She hadn't gotten that brave. She could not be that spontaneous. She could not just travel halfway around the world because she thought a photo had revealed a secret to her.

She told herself it was crazy. Worse than crazy. Absolute insanity.

She had never been to Zurich.

That's what map apps are for, an inner voice told her with shocking confidence.

She didn't have a clue where he lived.

You know the name of his company, though.

He had an international lifestyle. She didn't even know if he would be there when she arrived.

Could there be anything better than chasing true love around the globe?

Stop it, Marlee told her inner voice. *We have to be practical.*

Fiona and Mike's wedding had already nearly emptied her meager savings account.

Plus, she couldn't just not show up for work. She

wasn't that kind of person. People counted on her to be dependable.

And the days before Christmas were so busy at the library. In fact, on Monday they were having a special guest—a wildlife refuge was going to bring a real live reindeer to story time. How could she not be there to supervise that?

But not one rational thought could stop her.

When the button popped up saying "Purchase seat", she pointed her mouse at it, lined it up, took a deep breath and clicked.

It felt, for all the world, as if she was a warrior who had just let loose an arrow.

She snapped the computer shut and waited for the fear and doubt to set in. She went back to bed. She lay there with her eyes open.

She hoped she could get her money back.

But when morning came, Marlee was shocked to find she was no more interested in getting her money back, no more willing to back down, than she had been when she had clicked on that purchase button.

She didn't really lose her nerve until she was in the back of a cab in a foreign country. In her other life, a reindeer would be entering the library right about now!

Everything she saw reminded Marlee she was not in her own world. The cab driver had greeted her in three languages before settling on English. There was snow on the ground, which was rare in rainy Seattle. To her American eyes, Zurich had a fairy-tale-like atmosphere, with its old castle-like structures, cobbled roads, twisting streets.

She was dropped off in front of a very old building. There was a beautifully carved sign hanging over the street on a wrought iron arm—Monte Rosa Alpen.

So she was in the right place. There was a storefront and offices above it. She went to the display window and looked in.

There was an array of outdoor items: cross-country skis, snowshoes, what might have been a survival stove of some sort.

But what caught her eye was a beautiful, belted, woven jacket.

Oddly, that was what gave her courage. She wasn't a stranger here. She knew about this company. She knew about the great-great-great-grandmother who had started it.

What a courageous woman that long-ago Rosa must have been, striking out in a man's world.

As she opened the door, Marlee felt as if she might be channeling some of that long-ago courage.

The entry to the store was on her left and a narrow staircase went up to the right. She followed it and came to a glass door with the company name emblazoned on it.

What was she going to say?

No doubt some snooty secretary would send her on her way. Matteo probably worked in an impenetrable fortress. He was rich. He was powerful. Even if you had traversed the globe to do it, seeing him wasn't as easy as just waltzing into his office. Was it?

Taking a deep breath, she opened the door and stepped in.

The office space was soothing. The old bricks were

exposed, and there was deep, inviting, leather furniture. There was a striking photo on the wall of the sun rising over a mountain, and Marlee assumed it must be Monte Rosa.

There was a counter and a woman behind it.

She looked up, startled, obviously not expecting anyone so early.

"Yes?" she called.

Marlee found herself frozen. She didn't know what to say. She debated turning and running. Her heart was beating so hard.

He could be anywhere, but Marlee could *feel* it. Matteo was here. Somewhere. Possibly, just feet from her.

The woman's face softened. "You're her," she said softly.

"Wh-who?" Marlee managed to stammer.

"The woman in the photo. I'm Emma."

"His sister. What photo?"

"You know who I am," Emma said approvingly. "He's spoken to you about his family. Go. Second door on the right. Don't knock."

Marlee went down the hallway. She felt as if she was in a dream, floating. She opened the door and stepped inside it. She closed it behind her.

Matteo was behind a desk.

He glanced up.

There were shadows in his face that had not been there before. His hair was too long, and he had not shaved.

Beloved, she thought.

His expression was stunned, and in that moment, Marlee saw everything she needed to see. She saw the reason she had come.

His expression quickly shut down.

"This is a surprise," he said, as if it wasn't a good one.

"Isn't it?"

She came toward the desk, paused in front of it, and then changed course. She scooted behind it. He got up from his chair, backing away from her. He shoved a framed photo facedown first.

"What are you doing here?"

She picked up the photo. She smiled. It was the same one Fiona had given her.

"This really is a good picture," she said.

"It's okay."

"Why do you have it on your desk?"

He was silent.

"Is it because you love me madly?" she asked him softly.

"Don't be ridiculous. We barely know each other."

"Barely," she said. "That reminds me of swimming in your pool."

He actually blushed. He looked flustered.

"Why do you have a picture of someone you *barely* know on your desk, Matteo?"

"I like the composition," he said. "The donkey."

"Uh-huh." That could be insulting, but she was not insulted. The truth felt as if it shimmered in the air between them.

"Do you miss me?" she asked softly.

Silence.

"Do memories of being in each other's arms keep you awake at night?"

Silence.

"Do you dream of my lips on your eyes and your ears, on your chest and your—"

"Stop it!" he said, his voice a croak. "This is all so wrong."

CHAPTER TWENTY

"WRONG?" MARLEE ASKED MATTEO, stunned.

"It's not what you deserve. An affair? You? The world's most decent girl?"

"I was trying out being an outlaw," she reminded him.

"Well, it was a poor fit. It became more than evident that you are not that kind of woman."

"I've realized that. In fact, it seems almost funny that once upon a time I believed a cigar and a sip of rum could change something fundamental about me."

He nodded. "You're decent to the core," he said. "It's obvious."

"Was it when we were swimming in your pool that it became that obvious to you?" Marlee goaded him a bit.

"That was no more who you are than the rum and the cigar."

She smiled. "I disagree. You see, smoking and drinking are just outside things. They could never change what's inside a person. But that day in the pool—"

He interrupted her, obviously not wanting to think about the skinny-dip in his pool!

"I knew," he said firmly, stubbornly, "as soon as I

saw Fiona in her wedding dress how wrong it all was. That's what you deserve. Underneath it all, you're an old-fashioned girl. You deserve forever. Commitment. I thought you had realized it, too. I thought that's why you did your Cinderella exit from the reception."

"No. Some old insecurities reared their ugly heads. They said I was making a fool of myself over you."

Matteo looked stricken. "You weren't," he said, making an effort to wipe the distressed look off his face. "In fact, you looked as if you'd embraced that part of yourself quite nicely when I saw you at Mike and Fiona's Christmas party."

"I think I have embraced lots of parts of myself quite nicely. That's what I'm trying to tell you, Matteo. When I got home, I realized it wasn't about changing myself with silly things like cigars and rum. It wasn't really about changing myself at all. It was about uncovering who I really was, inside, not outside. You gave me the courage to take that journey. To learn how to live."

He was silent.

"Can we talk about forever?" Marlee asked softly. "Since you brought it up?"

"Yes," he said harshly. "Let's talk about it. There's no such thing. Look at the marriage statistics. Abysmal."

He grabbed his phone out of his pocket, tapped away furiously. "Fifty percent end in separation or divorce." He held up the screen so she could see the cold, hard evidence. It felt as if he was holding up a shield.

"That means fifty percent don't," Marlee pointed out mildly. "My parents have been happily married for thirty years. That's my model for being married."

"You're thinking about being married?" he said. "Who said anything about being married?"

"Uh, I think you might have mentioned it."

"Not in the context of *us*," he said. "Like you and me. Married."

"I wasn't suggesting tomorrow. I thought we could have a courtship first. You know, nice and old-fashioned. Exactly what you've decided I deserve."

He was silent. But she thought she saw a faint flicker of hope in his eyes.

"Your parents would have been married forever, too," she said softly. "If your mom had made it."

"Well, she didn't!" he said.

And just like that, they were at the heart of the issue.

"Those few days with you, Matteo, gave me courage I've never had before to embrace life completely. To really live. To find out who I really was, and then to be that. That was your gift to me."

Still, he was silent.

"Do you know why I'm here?"

He shook his head, mute.

"To return that gift to you. To give you the courage to embrace life completely, to really live. To ask you to take the biggest risk of all. To risk loving me, even though there might be pain involved."

"The pain might be yours," he warned her.

Which, he seemed to realize, was not an out-and-out no. He glared at her.

"It might be," she agreed. "You'd like to protect me from that, wouldn't you?"

"I saw what happened to my father."

"Yes, you did. You're not just trying to protect yourself, are you? You're trying to protect me?"

After a long time, he nodded, accepting that he had been unmasked.

"If we can feel this strongly after such a short time," he said, his voice with rough edges to it, "what would it be like to lose each other? After a year? After ten years? After a lifetime?"

"We can't look at all the things that could happen. It would make it impossible to live life, let alone fall in love."

"It's part of what I do," he said stubbornly. "I'm a businessman. I do the cost-benefit analysis. I ferret out all the things that could go wrong."

"And where does choice figure into your calculations, my darling?"

He could have flinched at the use of the endearment. Instead, she watched as he softened toward her.

"Your father made a choice, Matteo, to let his pain break him instead of make him stronger. He made a choice not to see he had three beautiful children carrying the legacy of his and your mother's love into the future."

He was leaning toward her as she crossed what remained of the small distance between them.

She laid her forehead against his forehead and took both his hands in her own. The sensation of his skin against her skin was like a homecoming.

"I think," she said, ever so softly, "a bigger risk than not loving someone because they might die is dying a slow, painful death inside each and every day because you have not loved someone. Be brave, Matteo. We can write our own ending. Say yes."

His voice was a whisper, but it was enough.

"Yes."

She took his lips with her own, with welcome and hunger. At first, he answered, but then he pulled away.

"No," he said. "If we're going to have a happy ending, I must prove to myself I can be a better man—"

"I like the man you are now just fine," she assured him.

But he shook his head, vehement. "I can be everything you deserve. I want to treat you with complete respect and honor."

"I never felt disrespected or dishonored," she said.

"If I can't keep my hands off you, it clouds everything."

"But in the best possible way."

"No," he said. "It's going to be an old-fashioned courtship, worthy of you, or nothing at all."

"If those are your terms, I accept," she said and held out her hand.

When he took it, she pulled him to her and kissed him soundly on the mouth.

Finally, he pulled away from her. "You don't intend to make this easy, do you?"

"Absolutely not," she warned him. And then she took his lips again.

And he answered, and they explored peaks higher than Monte Rosa. Finally, he broke away.

Flustered, he glared at her.

"If you can keep your lips off me for a few minutes—"

"Nearly impossible, but I'll try."

"I can make a plan. For our courtship. How long can you stay?"

"If I combine my Christmas holidays with a few days

of annual leave, I could stay until just after the New Year. But don't make a plan. Let's just be spontaneous."

"That's not a good idea," he decided. "That's what got us into trouble in the first place."

"Outlaws like me love a little trouble," she told him.

"Behave yourself. I'm going to introduce you to my sister."

That night, after being thoroughly wooed over the best dinner she had ever eaten, Marlee was dropped off by Matteo at the hotel room he'd insisted on booking.

His good-night kiss was disappointingly gentlemanly, despite her efforts to tempt him. Now, alone, which was also disappointing, she took in her accommodations.

The room was like a room in a palace. And she felt as if the prince had found her slipper after all.

And there was something quite adorable about him having to try so hard to keep his hands off her!

She called home.

"Um, Mom, I'm in Switzerland."

"What? Where? Have you lost your mind?"

"Maybe. I don't think I'm going to be home for Christmas."

"Not home for Christmas?" In her family this was akin to saying you would be playing a tambourine in an airport with a money collection basket at your feet.

"Mom, I've met someone."

"In Switzerland," her mother said, flatly.

"No, I met him at Fiona's wedding."

"The man from the picture!" her mother said, her whole tone changing entirely.

"What? What picture?"

"Fiona has some posted online on Chatter or whatever that app is called."

"You have the Chatter app?" Marlee asked, astounded.

"You're not the only one full of surprises," her mother said dryly, and then added, with relief in her voice, "That's totally different. You know him. He's friends with Fiona and Mike. You know what your father said when he saw the picture of you and that man and the donkey?"

"No, what did he say?"

"He said, there's the man who is going to marry our daughter."

Was her mother crying? "He did not," Marlee said.

"Do you want to ask him? James, it's Marlee. She's in Switzerland with that man from the picture."

"The news is on. Tell her hello."

That was more like it! Chatty Cathy, indeed.

"He never did like Arthur," her mother confided.

"Did you?"

Her mother hesitated. "I just wanted whatever would make you happy."

In the next few days, it felt as if Marlee discovered an even deeper well of happiness than she had found on Coconut Cay.

Because if there was one thing better than Switzerland at Christmastime, it was being in in Switzerland at Christmastime and being madly in love.

Matteo wanted to show her *everything*. They explored the Christmas markets in Zurich's old town and admired the fifty-foot Christmas tree at the train station. They went to Château de Chillon and Rhine Falls, and they took a dinner cruise on Lake Zurich.

They spent Christmas with his family and Marlee loved his sisters and his brothers-in-law and his two nieces and his two nephews instantly.

And they loved her.

"We've been waiting for you," Mia told her as they did dishes together after Christmas dinner. "I've never seen him so happy. You could not have given us a better gift."

One of the best parts of it all was the wonderful game they were playing, where he tried to resist the temptations she offered him—he still clung to the ridiculous notion that he must now be a perfect gentleman—and she played outlaw to his gentleman by trying to seduce him.

She was winning, and she found it so endearing that he felt guilty about that, as if by finding her totally irresistible he was failing her in some way!

The ten days went by in the blink of an eye.

But then, just as she thought the ball was over, and they were going to have to navigate the lonely days of a long-distance relationship, Matteo granted reprieve.

The day before she was supposed to fly home on the commercial flight she had booked, he informed her he'd cleared his schedule.

"I'm going to fly you home," he said.

She widened her eyes at him. "Does this mean we're going to join the mile-high club?"

She loved it when she did this to him. He was shocked. He sputtered.

"I'm going to meet your family. Have mercy, Marlee."

But she didn't.

Once they arrived, he insisted on staying in a hotel, and even though Marlee felt like that particular horse had already fled the barn, she could tell her father approved mightily of the arrangement.

His approval just made Matteo even more convinced that their courtship should remain unclouded by passion.

And made her more determined to test him at every turn.

It made the most delicious of tensions build between them as they explored her hometown together.

She kissed him madly at the top of the Space Needle, and again in the middle of the crowded Pike Place Market. She didn't work at the Central Library, but she took him to it anyway, because it was the flagship of the Seattle Public Library system and an architectural wonder. It felt particularly naughty dragging him behind the bookcases for an extended kiss!

They spent time at her apartment, but only if she promised to keep her hands off him. So they did ordinary things. Who knew that baking cookies and playing Scrabble and watching movies could make anticipation build to a place that was so painful you just had to give in to it?

It rained and it rained and it rained.

And her life had never felt so light-filled.

The day came when he had to leave. But the light did not go out. In fact, impossibly, beautifully, their relationship intensified.

He sent flowers.

She sent love notes.

They video-chatted deep into the night. He read her

poems. She read him a funny story. They used an app that allowed them to watch movies together.

He sent his jet and they spent a wonderful weekend in Venice. After they'd been apart, his resolve was absurdly easy to overcome. They never even got to ride a gondola! The next time he sent the jet, they went to Paris. She was sure the Eiffel Tower and the Louvre couldn't compare to drinking hot chocolate in bed, anyway.

Saying yes instead of no was really an affirmation that the whole universe seemed to turn its ear to, Matteo had discovered.

Of course, he was saying yes to some activities he had promised himself he would say no to, but no man was perfect, after all. There were temptations no one could be expected to resist, and Marlee made sure he knew that.

He did penance for his weakness by pulling out all the stops in his courtship of Marlee. He made sure every single thing about them falling more and more in love was worthy of the fairy-tale ending.

Now, Matteo had never been so nervous in his life. Marlee didn't even know he was back in Seattle. In what he considered a proper culmination to their romance, he was meeting Marlee's father for lunch. He wished he could be meeting him with a clearer conscience.

And if the meeting with her father went well, he already had a ring, purchased from the best jeweler in Switzerland.

"Mr. Copeland—"

"What? Jimmy."

"Uh…okay, Jim. As you might have noticed, Marlee and I have been spending quite a bit of time together. It's become quite serious. I mean, I've been honorable. Tried to be honorable… What should I order?" he asked, panicking and switching tack.

Mr. Copeland—Jimmy—was looking at him, clearly baffled. "We're in Seattle," he said, as if Matteo needed reminding, and maybe he did. "Seafood is always a good bet."

Matteo stared at the menu. Seafood. Where was he? Speaking of "fish," he wanted to fish in his pocket and have a quick glance at his talking points.

Treated her with honor.

Wooed her.

Old-fashioned respect.

Well, for the most part.

"Spit it out, man," Marlee's father said, not unkindly.

"I love your daughter. I can't even think straight for it anymore. I want your permission to marry her."

Jim Copeland was smiling broadly at him. "It's about time, son. Of course you have my permission. But who asks the dad's permission in this day and age, anyway?"

Matteo could tell he was pleased despite his protest.

And this old-fashioned request felt as if it confirmed what he had been working toward all this time: to be worthy of being not just Marlee's lover—for where was the worth in that?—but worthy of being her husband.

It was pouring rain—did it do anything else here?—an hour later when Matteo knocked on her apartment door.

The look on her face when she opened it said it all.

Surprise became delight.

Delight melted into heat.

She threw herself into his arms.

And he could not wait one minute longer. He slipped the box from his pocket and held it out to her.

"A cigar box?" she asked, puzzled.

"Open it."

She did. Still puzzled, she reached for the cigar. And then she saw what encircled it. The ring flashed bright against the brown paper of the cigar.

"Yes!" she squealed.

"I haven't asked you yet. Stop it. I'm getting down on one knee and—"

"You stop it! Yes, you have asked me. You've asked me a million different ways on a hundred different days."

"Marlee!"

"Okay, okay," she said. She was quivering with excitement.

He sank to one knee and gazed up at her.

"I love you madly," he said. "I cannot picture a life without you in it. You have made me a better man. Braver than I ever imagined I could be. Wide-open to the adventure of life in a way I never was before. I want you to marry me. I want you to be my wife. I want to walk all the rest of my days with you at my side. I cannot imagine a life without you in it."

She reached for his hand. She drew him to his feet. She handed him back the cigar, and he took the ring from it and slid it onto her finger.

She didn't even glance at it. She really didn't care if it was a million-dollar ring from the best jeweler in

Switzerland, or if it was a dime-store ring from the corner confectionery by her apartment.

"Yes," she whispered.

The cigar fell to the floor between them.

EPILOGUE

MATTEO SAT ON the beach alone, his arms wrapped around his knees, his feet dug deep into the sand. He was waiting for the sun to come up, and it was one of the rarest of moments on Coconut Cay. Except for the gentle lap of the waves, it was absolutely quiet.

The beach was not yet transformed. In a few hours, the arbor would be going up, the gardenias woven through it. A piano would be brought down, along with a registry table. There would be chairs—one hundred and fifty of them, at last count—set up on the sand, facing the arbor and the sea.

Matteo sighed.

This was *not* what he and Marlee had planned.

No, they had planned to celebrate their meeting on Coconut Cay with a quiet exchange of vows. They had wanted to ride donkeys down to the private pink sand beach Mackay had shown them over a year ago. They had wanted to say "I do" as a tropical sun set and gilded the entire island in gold.

Then, they had thought they would have one reception in Zurich for his family and friends, and one in Seattle for hers.

The problems had really started when his sisters had caught wind of the plan.

They had been appalled.

Because they thought his and Marlee's wedding plans separated them into two families.

"We're one family now," Emma had informed him sternly.

Never mind the logistics of several thousand miles and an ocean between them. Never mind the logistics of figuring out which of the great-aunts and old friends and second cousins and work colleagues could be asked to make this incredible journey.

Meanwhile, Fiona, high off the success of her own wedding, had started a wedding planning business. Before Matteo and Marlee quite knew what had happened, they were being swept up in Fiona's plans for them.

Fiona was not even slightly slowed down by that adorable baby she now had on her hip most of the time.

Matteo had never considered himself a "baby" guy. In the past, he had found the charm others found in the little creatures quite baffling. When his nieces and nephews had been babies, he had found them to be shockingly boneless little bundles filled with puke and poo. He would do the obligatory uncle-holds-the-baby-and-gets-rid-of-it-as-soon-as-possible.

But that little girl of Fiona's absolutely melted him. She had a smile Matteo was convinced she reserved only for him. He even held her sometimes and was always taken aback by the deep longing he felt when that baby nestled into him.

For the love he shared with Marlee to be made manifest in a child. A little girl or a little boy that he would call Calamity when he teased and chased him or her around wildflower-strewn meadows in the Alps.

Matteo would have thought Marlee would have wanted more say in her own wedding plans, but she laughed at the very suggestion.

"I planned a wedding once," she reminded him. "Devoted myself to it. Every little detail *mattered.* And yet somehow, I was missing what mattered most of all."

How grateful he was that that event had never happened, a reminder to both him and Marlee of silver linings in the clouds of life.

"Planning a wedding was nerve-racking," Marlee continued. "Not to mention time-consuming. Truly? I'm nothing but relieved to have someone else looking after all those endless and pesky details. It leaves me more time to, well, you know."

He did know.

She grinned that wicked outlaw grin that she reserved just for him.

And so now, really, their wedding was completely out of control. The budget was shot, the guest list was bloated, the whole island was bursting at the seams, and the logistics of bringing everything together in just a few hours was mind-blowing.

His wedding, Matteo mused, had a bit of a three-ring-circus feel to it.

Tomorrow, post-wedding, Fiona's mother, once so terrified of flying she had taken a miss on her daughter's own wedding, was going to celebrate one year of sobriety by organizing a skydiving excursion involving a frighteningly decrepit Coconut Cay airplane.

Naturally, the bride, not being the least sensitive of

Matteo's fear of the death of the woman he had chosen to be his life partner, had been first to sign up!

Fiona had egged Marlee on, even suggesting she wear her dress. Ever since Fiona had been nominated for that bride photo of the year for that picture of her feeding her bouquet to Henri, she looked for photo opportunities everywhere.

It seemed to always be in the back of her mind as she organized flower girls and a ring bearer, caterers, florists, donkeys, musicians, special arrangements for Great-Aunt Hetta.

Matteo's wedding: the three-ring circus.

As he thought about it, the birds began to wake. They acted as if it was their job to sing the sun out of the sea, and the quiet air was soon split with a cacophony of sound as each bird tried to outdo the other in welcoming the new day.

Really, Matteo reflected, wasn't this exactly what he'd been missing since his mother died? Family was a three-ring circus: joyous, loud, colorful, a million different things unfolding at all times.

Then, a feather, pure and white—maybe a gift from one of those birds—drifted out of the sky and touched his cheek, feeling for all the world like the gentlest of kisses.

He took the feather and held it. For one stunning, beautiful moment, Matteo knew his mother was with him, and had always been with him, guiding him to this day.

To saying yes to love.

To realizing it was the one thing worth risking everything for.

He knew, of course, that he and Marlee were not promised a life without challenges. Hardships. Losses.

Just as he knew this was the message from his mother: that it was the power of love that sustained the human spirit, even through unfathomable sorrow.

In the face of it all, love was the only real power.

That sense was confirmed a few hours later, as he was standing under the arbor. He was wearing a simple white linen shirt and dark slacks, and he was barefoot. Mike was at his side. Waiting.

They came first: family, his giggling nieces tossing flower petals, his nephews solemnly leading Henri and Calamity. The donkeys had bright pink hooves and each carried a ring on the matching pink pillow on their backs.

His nephews, Matteo noticed with enjoyment, had looks of pure terror on their faces, not from the donkeys or from the responsibility they'd been entrusted with, but undoubtedly from the fear of incurring Fiona's wrath if they blew this.

And here came Fiona, now in a hideous dress that she and Marlee had shrieked with laughter over as they chose it.

"My mother isn't the only one who knows how to make amends," Fiona had declared, admiring herself and twirling in the fluffy dress in the glorious shades of a three-day-old bruise.

And then, Matteo's whole world stopped as Marlee appeared.

Her mother was on one side of her and her father on the other, not so much giving their daughter to him as joining them all together in that ancient circle of love that was family.

He was only peripherally aware of her parents.

All he could see was her.

Marlee.

She was not wearing a wedding gown. She had put her foot down with Fiona over that.

"In the heat?" she had said. "Forget it."

And he was so glad she had *forgotten* it. She came toward him in a white sheath that was exactly like her. Simple, unpretentious, natural. The dress sang of the summer that Marlee carried within her, even on the rainiest of days.

The most unnatural thing about her would be her toenails, which he had snuck into her room last night to painstakingly paint bright pink, to match Henri's and Calamity's. She had something Henri didn't have, though. There was an octopus on the fourth toe of each of her feet.

Marlee's smile put the sun to shame.

The look in her eyes as she gazed at him filled him to the top.

In Marlee's unfaltering stride, he could see everything that she had become, loving and being loved, unveiling her innate beauty layer by gorgeous layer.

And he could see his whole future walking toward him.

And it was brilliant.

* * * * *

COMING SOON!

We really hope you enjoyed reading this book. If you're looking for more romance, be sure to head to the shops when new books are available on

Thursday 7th July

To see which titles are coming soon, please visit

millsandboon.co.uk/nextmonth

MILLS & BOON ®

Coming next month

HIS MAJESTY'S FORBIDDEN FLING
Susan Meier

Jozef handed Rowan's two cards to her. "You're fired."

She settled into the chair. "No. Theoretically, you didn't hire me so you can't fire me. Plus, we have work to do. I'm thrilled that you decided to come out in public for this performance—"

"For my sons."

She inclined her head, causing her pretty curls to shuffle. "It's a good start, but you need to say something to the press when you leave. Just say, 'the opera was lovely,' while you're racing down the stairs before your security team escorts you into your private elevator that will take you to your limo in the parking facility on the ground floor."

"No."

Her delicate eyebrows rose. "No?"

He didn't want to make a scene by standing and pointing at the curtain and ordering her to leave. God knew how many camera lenses from cell phones were pointed at him right now.

He tried the easy way, smiling and saying, "I didn't hire you. I don't want you. I don't need you. I'm not going to do what you say."

She laughed.

Her impertinence infuriated him, but he suddenly noticed that her shiny auburn hair cascaded down her naked back. The color set off her creamy skin, so smooth and white that it probably never saw the sun. It also accented her green eyes.

He blinked, taken aback by the fact that he even noticed her looks. Worse, his heart rate had accelerated, and his pulse had scrambled.

He'd been married for over two decades before his wife passed five years ago, and he'd never felt this overwhelming desire to stare at a woman. He'd never been sucked in by a woman's beauty. And he wouldn't be now. If his sons or the castle staff thought it was funny to throw a beautiful woman at him to see if he turned into a wimp who would melt at her feet and do what she wanted, they were crazy.

He was a king.

Kings did not melt.

They did what the hell they wanted.

Continue reading
HIS MAJESTY'S FORBIDDEN FLING
Susan Meier

Available next month
www.millsandboon.co.uk

Copyright © 2022 Susan Meier